When the G

M J Lee has worked as a university researcher in history, a social worker with Vietnamese refugees, and as the creative director of an advertising agency. He has spent 25 years of his life working outside the north of England, in London, Hong Kong, Taipei, Singapore, Bangkok and Shanghai.

Also by M J Lee

DI Ridpath Crime Thriller

Where the Truth Lies
Where the Dead Fall
Where the Silence Calls
Where the Innocent Die
When the Past Kills
When the Evil Waits
When the Guilty Cry

M J LEE
WHEN
THE
GUILTY
CRY

CANELOCRIME

First published in the United Kingdom in 2021 by

Canelo
31 Helen Road
Oxford OX2 0DF
United Kingdom

A CIP catalogue record for this book is available from the British Library.

Print ISBN 978 1 80032 567 8
Ebook ISBN 978 1 80032 566 1

Printed and bound in Great Britain by Clays Ltd, Elcograf S.p.A.

1

THE INQUEST

Chapter 1

Ridpath was worried.

He stared out across the Coroner's Court, watching everyone take their place. But for some reason, a vague sense of disquiet seemed to permeate his body. He couldn't put his finger on it; a feeling of unease seemed to be lodged deep in his bones.

He coughed twice into his handkerchief.

Was it the myeloma returning?

He didn't think so. There were none of the usual symptoms: no weakness, no weight loss, no feeling of nausea.

Just a strong sense that something, somewhere was wrong.

The inquest was about to start and he had no idea where it would lead. Perhaps that was what worried him; being out of control, events happening around him when he could do nothing to alter or stop them.

For a second, a darkness descended on him and he closed his eyes.

Get it together, Ridpath. Focus.

He had already helped Mr Ryder to his seat at the desk facing the coroner. The man's wife wasn't there, of course, she was in no condition to make it.

To his right, socially distanced, Greater Manchester Police were represented by their legal counsel, as was Manchester City Council. Both parties were involved, not to ensure the truth would be revealed, but to make certain no blame would be attached to the actions of either organisation.

The other witnesses had arrived in dribs and drabs. Sergeant Dowell, wearing his best uniform, with freshly polished shoes and brushed-back grey hair. He scowled at Ridpath as he walked past him to take his seat close to the witness box. Doreen Hawkins, the charity worker, sat behind him, draped in a one-piece kaftan and encircled by a cloud of expensive perfume. Rose Anstey, Jane's friend, was sitting next to her, following the requisite separation for indoor social distancing. She didn't make small talk with the woman next to her; instead, she stared straight ahead as if wishing she were somewhere completely different.

A tall man entered. Ridpath hadn't seen him before. He glanced at the witness list. Was this the teacher, Mr Roscoe, or was it somebody else? Before he could check the man's identity, two social workers rushed past. He recognised them from previous hearings. Both of them had a harassed air, as if the world and its problems sat heavy and unsolvable on their shoulders. Following them, his bald head freshly shaven, Detective Chief Inspector Turnbull ambled by. He glanced briefly at Ridpath, nodded once, and took his seat, ready to be called.

The press gallery was occupied too. Three reporters sat with their notebooks open and ready, the recent publicity surrounding the case fuelling the public's desire to discover more.

In the public gallery, the Covid regulations were being implemented to the letter. Despite the social distancing, every available seat was taken and occupied. Jenny Oldfield, the office manager, had even added a few more close to the door, to cater for the inevitable latecomers, stragglers and busybodies who would attempt to wheedle their way into the inquest.

As Jenny banged the gavel on her table, the door at the back of the court opened and Mrs Challinor entered.

Ridpath moved to take his place standing by the door. Still the feeling of disquiet lingered like a bad smell in a bouquet of fresh flowers. Would he have to take part in this drama after all? He hoped not.

The buzz around the court ceased and Mrs Challinor began speaking.

'This inquest is now open regarding the disappearance of Jane Ryder in 2009 and the application from the family for a presumption of death certificate from the Coroner's Service. The inquest has been called by the terms of the Coroners Act 1988, section fifteen and the Presumption of Death Act 2013, both of which allow for such a certificate to be issued if there is no possibility the person involved, in this case, Jane Ryder, is still alive.' She paused for a moment, looking around the court. 'We will hear evidence from witnesses to help us decide if Jane Ryder can indeed be presumed dead.'

Mr Ryder, sitting in front of her, sighed audibly, his shoulders hunched, and he rocked back and forth.

'Throughout these proceedings, the Covid guidelines established by the chief coroner will apply, including the giving of evidence in person and externally by witnesses. The family is represented by Mr James Ryder, parent of the missing girl. Greater Manchester Police is represented by Mr Jonathan Spielman, while Mrs Jennifer Harris represents Manchester City Council.'

On hearing their names, the legal representatives rose slightly and bowed the heads.

'A reminder for everyone. This is an inquest, not a court of law. Our job... my job... is to discover the truth, not to apportion blame or to discover who may, or may not, have abducted or murdered Jane Ryder.'

Another audible sigh from Mr Ryder.

Mrs Challinor carried on. 'We have one focus and one focus only. It is simply to ascertain to the best of our abilities whether this young girl, sixteen as she was in 2009, is still alive.'

At the back of the court in the public gallery, somebody had risen from their chair. From where he was standing, Ridpath couldn't see who it was.

Mrs Challinor raised her head and stared at the person. 'Can I help you?' she asked.

Ridpath craned his neck forward, looking for the person who had stood up, hearing a short response.

'No, but I think I can help you.'

SEVEN DAYS EARLIER

THE INVESTIGATION

MONDAY/TUESDAY

Chapter 2

'Are you sure you've brought all the equipment from the van?'

'Just get on with it, Ian, it's bloody cold.'

'Batteries charged, infrared camera ready, Kira?'

The woman nodded her head, eyes glancing upwards in disapproval.

Behind his head the dark shadows of an old Victorian house loomed, its slate roof glistening in the light of the full moon. In the distance, a dog fox barked his ownership of this abandoned land, receiving no answer from any rival. Nearby, a mouse scurried through the once manicured lawns, now overgrown and forgotten, while the wind rustled through the spring leaves of an old oak tree planted years before, when the house was first built.

The man coughed twice, clearing his throat, bringing his mike up to his mouth.

'Rolling,' said the woman. A red light blinked brightly on top of her camera.

'Welcome to another episode of *Ghost Hunters UK*. My name is Ian Rodgers. It's just after midnight and we're in Manchester, outside an abandoned children's home, Daisy House, a pretty name for a place where dark deeds were done.'

The man whispered rather than announced, his voice adding to the drama.

'From the 1950s, this place was used to house orphans and children abandoned by their families. It was closed in 2006. Visitors to the home have reported strange sounds of children crying. Others have heard the sound of laughter. One even reported hearing a children's nursery rhyme whispered in her ear by a young voice.'

He took a deep, dramatic pause. 'Tonight, we're going inside with the latest scientific equipment to check out the reports. Because we are… *Ghost Hunters UK*.'

The man stepped aside and the woman holding the camera rushed forward, tilting left and right, getting angles on the broken windows, graffiti-splattered walls, the sharp edges of mould-covered stone, finishing with shots of the full moon stabbed by the stark blackness of the tall chimney.

The sound recordist, a chubby, bearded man, switched off his digital recorder. 'Cue eerie music, title cards and promo clips. You forgot to ask them to subscribe to the YouTube channel, Ian.'

'Shit, you want me to do it again?'

'Nah, it's too bloody late and too cold and you'll only balls it up again. We can VO it at the end.'

'Thanks for the vote of confidence. You try working in these conditions. Look at this.' Ian Rodgers breathed out, revealing a fog of cold air coming from his mouth. 'Even in bloody spring it's freezing.'

'Brilliant, could you do it again inside?' said the camerawoman. 'Be great for atmosphere.'

'You got the shots, Kira?' The female producer, who so far had remained silent, chivvied people along.

The camerawoman nodded.

'Right, grab the gear and let's get moving. We have three more hours of filming to finish tonight. This is a thirty-minute segment, so we need lots of stuff.'

'You're sure we have permission to film, Pamela?'

'For a paranormal investigator, you are such a wuss, Ian. I did the recce inside this morning, we'll be OK. Let's get moving.' She picked up a steel case and moved towards the door of the old house, pushing it open with her foot. It swivelled open halfway, with the hinge on the bottom half coming away from the jamb. 'We'll film you entering on the way out, so you can do some nice dramatic irony pieces to camera, Ian, once we know what happens inside. Oh, and people, be careful in here…'

'What? There may be ghosts?' joked the sound recordist.

'Don't be stupid, it's the local junkies, they sometimes use this place as a shooting gallery. Don't pick up any needles and watch where you tread.'

'Now she tells us.'

The producer switched on her torch and they followed her through the half-open door, their feet rustling against the dried leaves that littered the hall. 'The old kitchen is straight ahead. We'll start in there filming the setup, before going into the dining room. Afterwards, it's upstairs to the former dormitories to shoot the final scenes.'

Ian Rodgers shivered. 'I don't know about you, but this place gives me the creeps.'

On the monitor, his eyes had a glassy, opaque stare, the lens of each eye like an opal glistening in the dark walls of a cave. The film had a green tinge to it from shooting in low light, which gave it a veneer of authenticity.

'Every place we shoot gives you the creeps, Ian,' replied the producer, 'it's what makes you so believable. Over two hundred and fifty thousand viewers now and counting…'

'Does that mean I get a raise on the next job…?'

'In your dreams.'

They walked slowly forward, the producer pushing open another door to reveal the kitchen. 'We'll set the lights up here, Kira.'

An old table stood in the centre, with two bent and battered institutional chairs lying next to it at an angle, as if the people sitting there had just risen from their supper.

'Ian, you'll do the first piece to camera, giving the history of the place and the rumours about it. You know the script?'

He nodded. 'What I don't know, I'll ad-lib.'

Once again, the producer rolled her eyes. 'Try to stick to the script, Ian.'

Behind her, Kira bustled around setting up a soft light directed at one corner of the room. 'Pam, you want the look we created in the pub in Knutsford last week?'

'Yeah, same again. *Blair Witch Project* meets *Bambi.*'

'No problem. We're set.' The woman hoisted the camera onto her shoulder.

'Ian?'

'Ready, when you are.'

'Right. Rolling...'

'We're now inside the children's home. Listen...' He paused, his eyes flashing left and right. 'Do you hear anything? The sound of a child sobbing, perhaps? This place used to be the home of a wealthy merchant, then it was a temporary hospital for wounded soldiers during the Second World War. In the 1950s, it became a home for orphans. It was supposed to be a place of safety and refuge for these children. Instead, it became a house of horror...'

'Cut. Great, Ian, and thanks for sticking to the script. Kira, move round and shoot him from the right and below. You continue speaking the intro, Ian.'

The camerawoman moved round, squatting down with the camera pointing upwards. On the monitor, the shot had a green glow with no other colours visible.

'Ready, Kira?'

'Rolling,' said the bearded soundman.

'Action,' whispered the producer.

'A house of horror. Because here children were abused, physically, emotionally and sexually, by the same adults who were supposed to protect them, their pain increased and multiplied by the betrayal of their hopes and dreams. It is this pain that we believe remains in this place, giving rise to the sightings of ghosts and the audible echoes of past trauma.' His eyes widened and his head swivelled round. 'What's that noise?' he shouted, his voice rising in fear.

'Cut, cut. Ian, what are you doing? You're not supposed to do that until we're upstairs in the dormitory. If you do it now, there will be no build-up of tension through the sequence.'

'But... but... I heard a noise. Didn't you hear it?'

The producer shook her head, looking around at the others. 'Didn't hear anything, Ian.'

'It came from over there.'

He pointed to a door in the far corner.

'It was probably a mouse.'

'Great, so now we're going to die of rabies.'

'You can't get rabies from mice. You get salmonella, leptospirosis and tularemia,' said the bearded soundman.

'Thanks for putting my mind at ease. I'll sleep comfortably tonight. I'm sure I heard a noise coming from over there.'

The producer scratched her head. 'Can we continue? Or we won't get done tonight.' She checked the script.

Ian took two deep breaths, trying to calm himself. 'Can we check it out anyway, for my peace of mind?'

'Listen, this is entertainment, not real. We shoot these things for the punters because it gives them cheap thrills. In the two years doing it have we ever seen a ghost?'

Ian shook his head and blinked twice, begging. 'Please?'

For the third time the producer rolled her eyes. 'If it keeps you happy, but I checked it this morning.' She stomped over to the door and wrenched it open. The camerawoman followed her, the red light blinking on top of the camera.

'See, it's only a corridor leading to our next location. We may as well go there now.'

'Only if you go first.'

'You are such a wuss, Ian.'

The soundman made the noise of a chicken and flapped his arms.

'It's all right for you. Didn't you hear anything?'

'Not a sausage, mate, and this picks up everything.' He pointed to his boom mike.

'Come on.' The producer was standing at the now open door. They followed her down a short, dark passage with a dogleg turn after four metres. At the end, a heavy wooden door blocked the passage.

'You're going to go in there, Ian, and speak the next part of the script. We'll give you a hand-held camera to film yourself.

Remember to keep the lens pointed at your face. We'll watch the take on a monitor out here.'

'What?'

'You're going to film yourself as you say the script.'

'Why doesn't Kira film me?'

'That would be difficult with the door closed, the space is too small for two people.'

'Door closed?'

'How's sound, Dan?'

'I'm attaching a wireless mike. Should be fine.'

The soundman was fiddling with the presenter's collar.

'You want me to go in there alone?'

'Won't be long, Ian. Say the lines and come straight out. It's gonna look great and set the atmosphere.'

The presenter nodded doubtfully.

'Here's the camera, keep it pointed at your face.' The producer gently pushed him into the room. 'You know the script, Ian?'

He nodded.

She closed the door.

From the inside, the room was six feet square with a glimmer of moonlight seeping through the iron-barred window set up high on the left-hand side. Lime-washed plaster walls came halfway down where they joined to white-painted wooden panels.

'Ready?' the producer asked.

He shivered, looking around the walls of his cell. 'I don't like it in here, Pam, let me out, please.'

'Just say the lines and you can come out.'

He heard the sound of a metal bolt being slotted home.

'Why are you bolting the door?'

'For atmosphere.' The producer's voice was muffled. Ian could have sworn he heard the sound of laughter from outside. Was it the crew? Or something else?

'Stay calm,' he said to himself, 'it's just a room like any other.'

The presenter switched on the camera, his hands shaking as the green light on top illuminated the room, throwing the shadows into sharp relief. He glanced over his shoulder before pointing it at his face. 'I'm in one of the rooms on the ground floor.' He panned around the small room, focusing on the walls and the barred window. 'It was in this room, only six feet square, where the children who broke the rules were locked for hours on end, screaming to be released.' A long pause was written in the script. 'But their cries went unheard and unanswered.'

He focused on the door. The white paint was covered in long, thin scratches.

'Right, I'm done. Let me out,' he shouted at the closed door.

No answer from the film crew.

'You can let me out now, guys.'

Still no answer.

'Hey, the joke's gone far enough. Let me out.'

He banged twice on the door with his free hand.

'Pam? Kira? Dan? Are you there? Let me out.'

He kicked the door with his foot, again and again. He could feel the sick taste of panic rising up in his throat. He kicked the door again. 'Let me out.'

The room was closing in on him. It felt so small and terrible and cold. 'Let me out,' he screamed, kicking wildly at the door and the wooden panels surrounding him, hearing one splinter and break as his foot crashed through it.

The noise was followed by the sound of the bolt being pulled back and the producer's voice. 'Coming in now, Ian.'

Light flooded through the open door. The producer stood there. 'The film of you panicking was great, but you didn't need to kick in the wooden panels.'

But Ian wasn't listening to her. He was staring through the gap in the wall he had made with his foot. 'There's something inside here. It looks like a bag of some sort.'

She pushed him out of the way and reached into the opening, pulling out a faded green and red striped backpack.

'You told us not touch anything,' said Ian. 'It could have been left here by a junkie.'

She carried it out into the corridor and walked back towards the lights in the kitchen, followed by the rest of the crew. She placed the backpack in the centre of the table. 'Can you swing the light over here, Dan?'

The soundman put down his machine and moved the light so it shone directly at the backpack. On the wall, a large black shadow loomed large.

'You're not going to open it, are you?'

'Of course we are, Ian. Could be something important.'

Pulling the toggle holding the zip, she peered into the backpack. There was something inside. *What was it?* She pulled the opening wider.

'Careful, there might be rats nesting. Or worse.'

She ignored the presenter. 'Can you bring the light closer, Dan?'

The producer peered inside. There was something hard and white. Slowly, the shape coalesced in her head. She jumped backwards. 'Jesus Christ,' she shouted.

'What is it?'

'I think it's a hand. A human hand.'

Chapter 3

Two people were already waiting behind police tape when John Schofield arrived. A constable held the log sheet for him to sign in. 'Sorry I'm late, it's Monday.'

A shadow loomed over him. 'Actually, it's Tuesday morning, 3.10 a.m. to be precise…'

'You're right, Hannah. Good to see you again, we'll have to stop meeting like this.'

The crime scene manager smiled. 'Fat chance in Manchester these days.' She was already wearing a full protective suit.

A small, rotund man stepped forward. 'Good morning, sir. DS Dave Connor, local CID.' He stuck his hand out and then retracted it, stepping backwards to maintain distance, remembering that lockdown protocols still existed. 'Sorry, force of habit.'

The sky was still dark, the house looking even more sinister reflected in the flashing blue lights of the police cars. Off to one side the film crew were hanging around impatiently, stamping their feet, arms wrapped around their bodies to keep out the chill and damp of a Manchester morning.

'What have you got for me?' asked Schofield, his high-pitched voice almost boyish rather than that of an experienced pathologist.

'A film crew found a backpack with what they think is a human hand inside.' Dave Connor pointed towards the four members of the film crew, now whispering to each other. One of them began filming with a phone. 'They called 999 and we responded. I looked inside the backpack and called you and Hannah.'

'You didn't touch anything else?'

The detective shook his head. 'Of course not.'

'No body?'

'None we can see, Dr Schofield,' replied the crime scene manager.

'Are you sure this isn't a prank, or a publicity stunt?'

Hannah shrugged her shoulders. 'No, but they were adamant there was a human hand inside the backpack—'

'And if there is, you have to call me out.' He shook his head. 'Have you checked it yourself?'

'Not yet, waiting for you.'

'And the other CSIs are on their way?'

'Me first, I'll call the others out after you've checked out the backpack and confirmed the hand is human and not some plaster model.'

'Right, give me a second while I put on my gear and you can show me where it is.'

Five minutes later, Schofield returned in a full Tyvek bodysuit complete with mask and eye protectors, carrying his medical examiner's bag. 'You can't be too cautious when dealing with human remains.'

'Yes, sir,' said Connor dubiously.

While the detective sergeant stayed outside, Hannah Palmer and the pathologist stepped carefully though the open door, avoiding the detritus on the floor and, using stepping tiles, edged along the hall to the kitchen.

'What was this place?'

'According to the film crew, it was a children's home, but it closed in 2006.'

The backpack was sitting on the table, exactly where the producer had left it.

'Is that it?'

'It is, Doctor.'

'And nobody has touched it?'

'Only the person who found it. A Ms Pamela Best, the producer of the film.'

'What were they doing here late on a Monday night?'

'They're paranormal investigators.'

Both Schofield's eyebrows and voice rose. 'What?'

'Apparently it's all the rage on the internet. Film crews visit old houses looking for ghosts. My son watches them.'

Schofield grunted. 'OK, let's take a look at what we've got. I hope this isn't some stunt pulled by the film crew.'

'If it is, they'll be spending the rest of the week down the nick, charged with wasting police time.'

'Isn't that a hanging offence?'

'Should be.'

They both stared at the backpack. The only light was provided by the arc lamp left behind by the film crew. Schofield took out a lamp attached to a headband from his examiner's bag, putting around it around his head so the bulb looked like a giant third eye in the centre of his forehead.

He switched it on and the light immediately illuminated the faded green canvas of the backpack, a large white label sticking out from one side with the word CLAK in bright red letters.

Hannah followed suit, pointing her luminescent white-light torch at the dark opening. The top of the backpack looked like the mouth of a giant toad, the inside dark and forbidding.

Schofield reached into his doctor's bag and took out a pair of stainless steel forceps. 'You'd better have an evidence bag ready in case there is something inside.' Cautiously, he peered into the top.

There was something there.

In the light from his headband, it looked greenish white and slightly scaly with a hard, discoloured yellow top.

He widened the opening in the top of the bag with the forceps, the light revealing something longer with a hard dirty yellow nail at the end and a green tinge to the cuticle.

'Is it human?' asked Hannah.

'Looks like it,' he answered.

He sniffed the air. No smell of putrefaction. Strange.

He reached in with the forceps and pulled. The hand gave a little, then stuck fast.

'Damn.' He widened the opening in the bag. He could see the whole hand now. Quite large, short fingered with a masculine heaviness, the hand of a middle-aged man, perhaps.

He reached in again with the forceps, gripping the hand on either side of the palm and pulling. 'Got you.'

He held the hand up to the light from his lamp. 'A human hand severed from the arm though the scaphoid and lunate bones, all metacarpals and phalanges intact, it would seem.' He examined it carefully. 'A right hand, from the position of the thumb.'

Hannah held open the evidence bag and he dropped the hand into it.

She took it off to one side, sealed it and wrote her name, time and location on the cover. When the CSIs arrived, she would catalogue it, assigning the correct number.

'When you've finished, can you send it on to my lab? And make sure it's placed in some ice. I don't want it to decay any further.'

'No problem, Doctor. This is a crime scene, then?'

He pointed to the hand. 'Well, it's human, separated from the arm through the wrist. I could see saw marks on the bone.'

'Where's the rest of the body?'

Schofield looked around the old house. 'Your guess is as good as mine.'

He was about to call for Dave Connor to come in when it occurred to him to re-check the interior of the backpack. He looked inside, noticing a zipped-up internal pocket.

'Hang on, there may be something here.'

With his gloved hand, he reached in and pulled the zipper across. It moved smoothly, as if it had been recently opened.

Hannah Palmer moved closer to him, directing her light inside the new opening.

Another hand.

More decayed this time, as if it had been in the bag for longer, the flesh sloughing off to reveal the gleaming whiteness of a finger bone beneath.

Schofield reached in with the forceps and grasped it firmly, pulling it out to hold under the torch light.

'Is this the left hand?'

Schofield thought for a moment, stared intently at the hand and then shook his head. 'This is another right hand. And from its smallness and the length of the fingers, I would say a female.'

'Jesus,' said Hannah.

'No, this one is female.'

'I meant—'

'I know what you meant, and I would prefer it if you didn't take the Lord's name in vain.'

Hannah Palmer ignored the admonishment and held open another evidence bag. Schofield dropped the smaller hand into it.

As she wrote on the outside of the evidence bag, he peered into the backpack once more.

'You'd better get me one more of those.'

'What?'

'There's another. It's a right hand too.'

'Jesus,' whispered the crime scene manager under her breath.

It was going to be a long night.

Chapter 4

Mornings were always the most difficult for Ridpath. It was when he missed the elegant chaos of his wife the most.

The continual drinking of endless cups of the strongest black coffee to kick-start her brain. The perpetual loss of this textbook or that piece of marking as she packed her briefcase before school. The constant indecision over which clothes to wear or not wear, as if the ten-year-olds she taught were fashion critics from *Vogue*. The last-minute search for lip gloss, or eyeliner, or blusher, or any other cosmetic enhancement to help a female teacher create a mask to hide from her class.

It was in the mornings he missed Polly the most.

Nowadays, he only had to shout upstairs three times before his daughter dragged herself out of the wasteland she called a bedroom.

'Eve, it's time to get up.'

'Eve, you're going to be late.'

'Eve, if you don't get up right this minute, I'm coming upstairs and turfing you out of bed.'

'Eve—'

'There's no need to shout so loudly, Dad, you'll wake the neighbours. Remember, Mr Dawes is on nights at the Park Hospital this week.'

They had moved into the new house a month ago. It was closer to Eve's new school and after nearly a year in a serviced apartment, he was happy to have a place of his own. Luckily, Eve had come to live with him before the second lockdown, or was it the third? He couldn't imagine not being with her over December or the New Year.

They had spent the time together during the pandemic in their own little bubble, Eve skyping her friends and grandparents, and as the daughter of a key worker, still attending school.

He still went into the coroner's office, of course, and Greater Manchester Police, but figured out more and more ways of working from home. He knew for others it had been a difficult time, but for him, he had been strangely happy. It was a time to be with his daughter, watch her grow up, become the spitting image of his deceased wife in looks and in character.

Selling the old house had been relatively easy – it was close to good schools and the quasi-bohemian delights of Chorlton. Neither of them could live there again after what had happened to Polly just over a year ago.

She still haunted Ridpath's dreams at night, though. The ring of the doorbell. Her shout of, 'I'll get it.' Mrs Seagram at the door. Two loud bangs and Polly was lying in the hallway, her blood staining the carpet and the acrid smell of cordite in the air. The life slowly dimming in her eyes as the blood flowed from her chest.

Ridpath breathed in deeply three times, concentrating on his safe place, high on the hills in the Peak District, wind blowing through his hair, as the memories flooded in of that terrible day.

'Earth to Dad, come in, Dad. What's for breakfast?'

He shook his head. 'Boiled eggs with toast soldiers. Orange juice on the side.'

'Great, I'm starving.' Eve stumbled past him, into the kitchen.

It was either feast or famine at the moment with Eve. She either didn't want to eat or was perpetually hungry. Like all parents, he worried about eating disorders and teenage girls, but he couldn't see her obsessing about her weight or vanishing into the toilet after meals. Instead, she seemed to have no interest in food. For her, it was only fuel that gave her the energy to exist, not a pleasure to be enjoyed. With one exception: sushi. For some obscure reason, she loved the Japanese raw fish and rice. Perhaps it was another taste she had inherited from her mother.

He followed her into the kitchen and sat down opposite, sipping his black coffee. 'What's on today?'

'Double Maths, History and then PE. God, I hate PE. I think the teacher has been to a special school for sadists. She seems to spend most of her life working out how to embarrass all the girls. The other day, Maisie Watson's bra strap broke and her boobs were all over the place when she was running. Like two jellies in a sack.'

'Too much information, Eve.'

Despite the lockdown, Eve had started at her new school as planned last September. She had seemed to handle the experience well, making new friends and settling in comfortably, according to her teachers. She still went once a month to see the child psychologist, more because Ridpath forced her to rather than out of any desire to go herself. He too reported that she was coping with her mother's death, and was able to explain and understand her grief.

Sometimes Ridpath worried she handled it too well. As if she were too adept at putting the emotions she didn't want to deal with into a little box deep inside herself and closing the lid.

'Earth to Dad again. You seem to be a bit dreamy this morning. Worried about something?' She spoke to him through mouthfuls of egg and toast.

'Not really.'

'What's your day like?'

'Meeting, then another meeting followed by, guess what? Another meeting.'

'Sounds fun.'

'Yeah. The usual WIP at the coroner's office, followed by an update on the latest Covid stats around the country, and afterwards a meeting at Police HQ.'

'You coming to pick me up this afternoon?'

'Can you take the bus home?'

'No problem, but…'

'But what?'

'Remember Maisie Watson?'

'Her of the two jellies in a sack?'

'The one and only. Well, she's invited me and two other girls to her house to work on our science project after school. We're doing human lungs.'

'I'll need her address and her mum's number.'

'Dad—'

'That's our deal, Eve. And I want you back by six thirty at the latest.'

'But—'

'No buts, agreed or not?'

Eve rolled her eyes. 'OK, the others will have to go home by then anyway.'

'Good, you can text me the details later. I don't want to have to ring Maisie's mother…'

'I'd never live it down if you did. My name would be mud, I'd have no rep in the school. I'd be the girl with the deranged dad. A laughing stock. It's bad enough you're a copper.'

Ridpath frowned. 'What do you mean?'

She paused, dipping her toast soldier into the liquid yolk of her egg. 'Don't take this the wrong way, but my friends don't like the police very much.'

'So even twelve-year-old girls don't like us. And I thought it was just criminals.'

'Can I be honest?'

'Always.'

'I tell them you work for the coroner.'

'But you know I'm a detective who's just seconded to the coroner's office?'

She nodded.

'I'm a detective inspector with MIT?'

She nodded again.

He thought for a moment about whether to push this or not. Was she ashamed of him for being a policeman? He glanced at the clock. 'Shit, is that the time? Come on, young lady, or you'll be late.'

'You're not supposed to swear, Dad.'

'And you're not supposed to be late. Get a move on.'

Eve stood up and drained the glass of orange juice, taking a soldier of toast with her to eat in the car.

Outside in the hallway, she was slipping into her school jacket, gripping the toast between her teeth. Already the sleeves were too short for her arms. He would have to buy another one soon.

At the door, she stopped, her hand on the latch. 'You're not upset about what I said, are you, Dad?'

'I could never be upset about anything you tell me, Eve.'

She thought for a moment. 'What if I said I was going to be back home after midnight?'

Ridpath frowned. 'That would be an entirely different matter. Six thirty, OK?'

'OK, Mr Grumpy. Love you, Dad.'

'Love you too, Miss Ridpath.'

As they walked to the car, his phone rang. 'Ridpath.'

'Hi there, this is Sophia. We've had a call from the police, they'd like you to attend an incident in Northenden. Apparently, three human hands have been found in an old house.'

'What about the work-in-progress?'

'We'll postpone it till you get here.'

'OK, text me the address.' He ended the call.

'Who was it, Dad?'

'Nothing, looks like my working week has started early.'

'Welcome to Tuesdays, Dad.'

Chapter 5

'Mr and Mrs Ryder are outside, Coroner.'

'Thank you, Jenny, please show them in.'

A few seconds later, two old people stood in the entrance to Mrs Challinor's office.

'Please come in.' She stood up and placed another chair six feet in front of her desk. The husband, dressed in an old-fashioned Mackintosh, helped his more frail wife to sit down first, before taking off his mask and sitting next to her.

Mrs Challinor took the file from the left-hand side of her desk and began speaking. 'Good morning, it's great to see you both again. I have some good news; the Secretary of State for Justice has approved your request for an inquest into your daughter's disappearance and, if it can be shown she hasn't been seen for the last eleven years, I will be able to issue a presumption of death certificate which has the same legal standing as a normal death certificate.'

The couple looked at each other and the man touched the back of his wife's wrinkled hand.

'Could you explain the certificate again, so we understand it?'

'A presumption of death occurs when a person is legally declared dead despite the absence of direct proof of the person's death, such as the finding of remains or a body. Such a declaration is typically made when a person has been missing for an extended period and in the absence of any evidence the person is still alive.'

'Our daughter, Jane, disappeared in June 2009, and nobody has seen her since.'

'That's why the Secretary of State has approved the inquest. Only about ten of these cases come to light each year.'

'After all these years...' The wife spoke for the first time, but didn't finish her sentence. It was as if she was heavily drugged or sedated.

'I am so sorry for your loss.'

'Jane was such a sweet girl...'

The husband patted the back of his wife's hand again. 'With this certificate we can wind up our daughter's affairs?'

'It's exactly the same as a death certificate.'

'You see, she has insurance, and she's the beneficiary in our will. We don't have long left so we need to sort this all out before we go.'

'If you don't mind me asking, why did you wait so long? You could have applied to the High Court after seven years.'

The wife dropped her head. It was the husband who answered in a low voice. 'We always thought she would come back.' A long pause. 'She didn't tell us she was going, and we're sure Jane would have let us know if she wanted to leave. But we haven't heard from her at all, not a letter or a phone call in all these years.' There was another long pause and his voice became stronger. 'Last year, during lockdown, when there was just Margaret and myself in the house, we missed her so much.'

There was a long pause. Mrs Challinor was about to explain the inquest procedure but the husband began talking again.

'Then something happened which helped us decide we had to do something. Jane is never coming back to us, we know now.'

Mrs Challinor wanted to reach across the desk and hug this man, but she didn't. Instead she asked, 'What happened?'

The man glanced across at his wife and she nodded, almost imperceptibly. 'Marjorie has cancer, Mrs Challinor. A particularly virulent form of leukaemia, according to the doctors. We don't know how long she has left.'

'I am so sorry, Mrs Ryder, if I'd have known, I would have come to your home with this information.'

'We don't like to make a fuss, Mrs Challinor. And it's good to get out of the house, we were locked up for so long.'

'Is there anything I can do?'

'You can a make the inquest happen as quickly as you can.'

The wife spoke, her voice quiet and weak. 'What will happen during the inquest?'

'According to the Presumption of Death Act of 2013, the inquest strives to bring any suspicious circumstances to light. I will call on the police and any witnesses who saw your daughter on the day of her disappearance to give evidence. The most important question I will ask is if senior officers believe your daughter is no longer alive.'

'And then you will declare she is dead?'

Mrs Challinor nodded. 'And I can issue the certificate.'

'Immediately?'

Mrs Challinor frowned. 'As soon as I can.'

'When will the inquest be held?'

'It's just a question of finding a time in the calendar. Usually, these types of inquests take less than a day.' Mrs Challinor pressed a button on her intercom. 'Jenny, can you come in, please?'

A minute later the door opened and Jenny entered the room in a waft of Chanel No. 19.

'This is my office manager, Jenny Oldfield. How quickly can we arrange a presumption of death inquest?'

'Is a jury involved?'

Mrs Challinor shook her head. 'A jury won't be necessary.'

Jenny consulted her diary. 'You are in court all this week and next week...' She turned the page. 'You have the Curran inquest on Thursday and Friday.'

'So we could do Monday or Tuesday?'

'We have to give the witnesses notice of the inquest. The very earliest is next Monday, but it is a rush, Coroner, we don't know if they will be available and Mr Ridpath will need to interview them beforehand. I would advise a later date would be better.'

'OK,' Mrs Challinor said doubtfully, 'we need to move quickly on this one. Give me the earliest possible date, Jenny.'

'I'll get on it, Coroner.'

She started to leave.

'And Jenny, can you get Ridpath to call me? I need to see him as soon as possible.'

'He's at the incident in Northenden, but he'll be back for the work-in-progress.'

Mrs Challinor glanced across at the Ryders sitting quietly opposite her. 'We need to get moving on this as soon as possible. I'll speak to him after our meeting.'

Chapter 6

Ridpath arrived at the house in Northenden just as some of the CSIs were packing up to go. He'd already signed the register before being allowed to enter the cordoned area around the crime scene. 'Hi, Hannah, long time no see.'

'Hiya, Ridpath, this one of your cases?'

He had worked with Hannah before on a few investigations. She was an excellent crime scene manager; meticulous, thorough and, best of all for a detective, quick. Haloed by her Tyvek suit with its mask and cap, her face looked tired and careworn.

'The coroner asked me to look into it. Who's the SIO?'

'Dave Connor, but his boss is lurking around somewhere too.'

He remembered Dave Connor from his time in MIT. A good detective, dogged and determined, but not the sharpest tool in the shed.

'The boss is helping, is he?' Ridpath formed quotation marks with his fingers.

'Like a brewer at an AA meeting.'

Ridpath laughed. '*That* helpful. Give me the lowdown.'

'Three hands from three different people, found in a backpack on Monday night or Tuesday morning by a film crew. It was hidden in a room at the back of the house in a wooden compartment, We searched the rest of the house but found nothing of interest except some graffiti and a few needles and burnt spoons.'

'From the local druggies?'

'Probably. Apparently, the house has been unused since it closed in 2006 and has gradually fallen into disrepair.'

'Have the hands been there long?'

'I dunno, Ridpath, you'll have to ask the pathologist, Dr Schofield. But they weren't skeletal, they still had flesh on them. The woman who found the backpack said she didn't notice it in the morning when she did the recce.'

'Right. Did you find the rest of the bodies?'

'No bodies anywhere in the house, nor any signs of blood or violence. A herd of uniforms from Stretford are just assembling to perform a search through the grounds now it's light enough. I think the hands were cut off somewhere else, placed in a bag and then transported here.'

'Why?'

She smiled. 'I just collect the evidence, Ridpath, I don't try to interpret it. Your job, remember?' Tiredness was making Hannah a little snappy. 'Speak of the devil...'

A small rotund detective was approaching them, his hands in his pockets. 'Ridpath, good to see you again.' He looked around and surprise crossed his face. 'Where's the rest of the MIT mob?'

'Dunno, Dave, I'm here from the coroner's office.'

The little man's eyes screwed up. 'That's right, you were transferred across there a couple of years ago. I remember hearing about it.'

'Seconded, Dave, not transferred.'

'That's what they all say. Anyway, my boss, Chief Inspector Holloway, is not going to be a happy bunny. He thought he was getting the full support of MIT, not one man from the coroner's office. No disrespect meant, Ridpath.'

'None taken, Dave. When does the search of the grounds start?'

'As soon as we can get all the plods and CSOs organised. A couple of years from now, at this rate.'

'Right...'

'I presume you are from MIT?'

The man who spoke was wearing a chief inspector's uniform and walked as though a broom handle had been inserted painfully into one of his orifices. His shoes and buttons were polished and shiny, glistening in the early sun of what looked like a beautiful Manchester day.

'Detective Inspector Thomas Ridpath, sir, from the coroner's office.'

'Where's the rest of your unit?'

'I am the unit, sir. I'm the coroner's officer for East Manchester.'

'What? MIT was supposed to send me help. I was promised full support.'

'I know nothing about more people. The coroner has asked me to attend as the representative of her office as this could be a possible murder. I am seconded from MIT to her, but I haven't heard anything from them.'

'This just isn't good enough. I have two CID self-isolating after positive Covid tests, another on a series of burglaries and one more following a fraud. Dave Connor is the only senior man who is free.' He glanced disdainfully at the round detective as if to say 'this is what I have to work with'.

Ridpath stayed silent. Then his phone rang loudly.

Holloway frowned as Ridpath reached into his pocket to check the caller ID. Jenny Oldfield.

'I'm sorry if I'm disturbing you,' sniffed Holloway.

'Sorry, sir,' said Ridpath, declining the call.

'This is most unsatisfactory. I'm getting on to the ACC and Claire Trent. It's unsupportable.'

He turned and walked away, bringing out his mobile phone.

'Hello, nice to have you here, welcome to the investigation.' Ridpath mimicked the chief inspector's voice.

'He's not great at welcomes, is Holloway. Not great at anything, actually,' whispered Dave Connor.

'Right, I'm off to check in the evidence bags back at the lab. Who are you going to appoint as pathologist, Ridpath?' Hannah Palmer picked up her evidence tray.

'You're sure this is a crime scene, Dave?'

'Three human hands in a backpack? We have to look into it, Ridpath.'

'And the medical examiner was John Schofield?'

Both Hannah Palmer and Dave Connor nodded.

'I'll call him and let him know he's to proceed with the post-mortem.'

'I already had a phone call from him. We're booked in at five p.m.,' said Hannah.

'He's moving quickly.'

'You know what he's like. Told me he was looking forward to this one.'

'Only he could look forward to a post-mortem. Before you go, Hannah, could I take a quick shufti at the backpack?'

'Sure, Ridpath.' She pulled out the clear bag from the evidence tray.

Inside, Ridpath could see a small green backpack, with white and red stripes. It was conventional in design, with a big 'CLAK' logo in red on the side. It was covered in a fine white powder. 'Any fingerprints?'

'None we could find. But we've just done a quick check. We'll go through it properly under lab conditions.'

'When can I get a report, Hannah?' asked Dave Connor.

'I'm knackered, Dave.'

'But you know the first week is key to cases like this. Once it gets stuck, it will just go on the back burner.'

'As soon as I can.'

'As soon as I can, when? Tomorrow?'

'Don't push. I'll try my best.'

'But—'

Ridpath stopped Dave Connor from speaking by putting his hand on his wrist. 'Thanks, Hannah, you're a star. Whenever you can will be great.'

She picked up her evidence tray and walked slowly back to the CSI van, tiredness evident in every step.

'Is that how you butter up the CSIs, Ridpath? "You're a star"?'

'A word of advice, Dave. The sooner you get some forensics to work with the better, and you don't get the reports by nagging tired CSIs. Otherwise this investigation is going to be quickly dumped over to the cold-case unit.'

'I know, I know, but I've been here since two a.m. My brain isn't working.'

'You've no support?'

'You heard Holloway, we're short-staffed.' He looked down at his feet. 'I could do with some help, Ridpath, I haven't done one of these investigations for a long time. The most we usually deal with is vandalism or burglary. And Holloway's on my back...'

Ridpath went to put his arm around his colleague's shoulders, then remembered the bloody Covid restrictions and stopped, simply saying, 'You're made from tough Salford stuff, Dave, you can handle it. Now, do you want to walk me through the scene so I can help with some pointers?'

'You're a star, Ridpath.'

'That's my line, remember?'

Chapter 7

'This place was built in 1886 by Liverpool firm Owen and Livingstone for the cotton merchant Elijah Cartwright. He'd made his fortune selling Lancashire calico to the Indian market, buying opium there for China and then bringing back tea to England. Clever man, was Mr Cartwright. He called it Daisy House, after his eldest daughter.'

Ridpath raised his eyebrows. 'Sounds like you ate an encyclopaedia for lunch, Dave.'

'Googled it when I was waiting for the CSIs to complete their work. You know how slow they can be sometimes. It's like watching sloths on downers.'

As they entered the hallway of the house, they were joined by a young detective whom Dave Connor didn't bother to introduce. In the cold light of day, the house looked more derelict than threatening. Flock patterned wallpaper peeled from the walls and a dark, mahogany staircase led upwards to the next floor. Lighter patches on the walls revealed where pictures had once hung.

'Anyway, the place was used as a convalescent home for injured soldiers during the Second World War and then bought by Manchester Council in 1949, turned into a children's home in 1952 and finally closed in 2006. Before you ask, Ridpath, it was one of the places investigated by Operation Pharaoh in 2012.'

'The police investigation into child abuse?'

'The one and only. Jimmy Savile was a regular visitor.'

'He certainly got around.'

'Particularly when kids were involved.'

They walked into the kitchen on the stepping tiles, past the last CSI finally leaving the house.

'All clear, Fred?' asked Dave Connor.

'We're done. Glad to get out of this place. Gives me the willies.'

'Get Hannah to call me the minute she gets anything.'

'Will do. Hiya, Ridpath, sorry about the missus, by the way.'

Images of Polly flashed into Ridpath's mind. Quick reminders of how much he loved and missed her. 'Thanks, Fred, it's kind of you.'

The CSI looked slightly embarrassed and edged out of the kitchen, carrying his bag of tricks.

Dave Connor pointed to a door at the back of the kitchen. 'There's a room at the end of a corridor behind the door. The backpack was found in there.' They put on their latex gloves and walked through the door and down the corridor. 'Apparently one of the film crew was filming in here and somehow managed to kick in one of the wooden panels.' Dave Connor pointed to the now empty space in the wall. 'The backpack was inside.'

'Hidden, or in open view?' asked Ridpath.

'Hidden in a secret compartment,' answered the young detective. He stuck out his elbow in the new manner of shaking hands. 'I'm Detective Constable Oliver Davis.'

'He's new,' sniffed Dave Connor.

'Morning, DC Davis,' answered Ridpath, ignoring the proffered elbow.

The young detective pointed to the wood. 'Apparently, the panel could be removed. The backpack was hidden in an alcove behind it.'

'Interesting. Could it have been there long?'

'What do you mean?' asked Dave Connor.

'Could it have been there when the house was a children's home?'

'So more than fifteen years old?'

Ridpath nodded, examining the small, empty compartment where the backpack was hidden.

'Maybe. But these are adult hands, according to the doctor, not from kids.'

Ridpath stood up, looking all around him. Light fought its way through the small barred window high on the left-hand wall. He closed the door, instantly feeling a cold shiver dance its way down his spine. The walls seems to move closer, collapsing in on him, He quickly opened it up again. 'Have you noticed the scratch marks on the back of the door, Dave?' he said, his voice quivering slightly.

'One of the CSIs pointed those out. Said they were quite old, from the amount of dirt in them. We took some samples anyway.'

Ridpath looked outside. In addition to the lock there were two bolts: one at the top and another at the bottom. 'Where's the key?'

'I dunno, the door wasn't locked.'

'What was this place anyway?'

The young DC spoke again. He'd obviously spent time with the crime scene manager, learning on the job. 'We're not sure. Hannah thought it was for storing food. It's off the kitchen, so it should be a larder.'

'But why are the windows barred and the door reinforced?'

'To prevent the mice getting in?' said Dave Connor. 'I don't know, Ridpath. The place closed fifteen years ago.'

'You need to talk to somebody who worked here then.'

'You mean somebody who wasn't locked up?'

'What?'

'One of the wardens was charged after Operation Pharaoh. Harold Davidson. He got eleven years.'

'Still inside?'

Dave Connor shrugged his shoulders. 'Probably not, you know what it's like, could be out by now.'

'You need to find out.'

'I'll see if I can find the time. Holloway is on my back for a full report, plus I need to keep the case file up to date.'

'Can't somebody else do it?'

Dave Connor looked dramatically around him. 'I don't see anybody else, do you?'

Oliver Davis's face showed no emotion at the comment from his boss, he seemed used to it.

Ridpath sighed. 'You also need to check up on the backpack. Who made it? When was it made? Where was it sold and who sold it? And you need to organise the uniforms for a local canvas. See if anybody noticed anything unusual.'

'Oliver and the uniforms are doing it after they search the grounds… when they get their act together.' He stared pointedly at the younger officer.

Oliver answered. 'I'm on it, Ridpath, Sergeant Mac and his men are nearly ready.'

'You've already interviewed the film crew?'

Dave Connor nodded. 'Yeah, nothing from them. The producer did a recce on Monday morning but didn't see anything. The others only turned up for filming late on Monday night. I checked out their YouTube channel. It's the usual scary stuff. I'll type up the interviews back at the station.'

Ridpath's phone rang. It was Jenny Oldfield again. 'Ridpath.'

'Hi there, it's Jenny. The coroner would like to see you.'

'I'll be in soon, we're nearly finished here. What's so urgent?'

'I think you'll have to ask her, not me.'

'You have to go?' asked Dave Connor.

Ridpath nodded. 'I'm needed for some reason. Can you send me pictures of the backpack, and the case file numbers? And can you also send me the witness statements from the film crew when they are ready? I'll take a look at them when I'm free and see if there is anything else I can come up with to help.'

'You're a star, Ridpath,' said Dave Connor with a smirk.

'One more task, check if there have been any reports of missing hands recently. Perhaps some medical students have been messing around stealing stuff from anatomy departments or from funeral parlours. Could be someone's weird idea of fun.'

'I'll check, but this is too strange even for medical students.'

'I'll call you later, Dave, if I get anything. Let's meet later at the mortuary.'

'You're going?'

'Somebody from the coroner's office has to be there.'

Dave Connor looked down at his feet, suddenly finding a speck of dirt on his scuffed shoes. 'I don't know if I can make it, Ridpath.'

'What?'

'I'll send Oliver.'

'You should be there, Dave.'

'I hate post-mortems, give me the willies, they're like a butcher's shop. Oliver can watch the ghoul and listen to his squeaky voice.'

The young DC smiled innocently.

'Have you ever been to a post-mortem before?' asked Ridpath.

He shook his head.

'Bring the Vicks.'

Chapter 8

'You wanted to see me, Claire?' Detective Chief Inspector Turnbull's bulk filled the doorway.

Claire Trent looked up from her spreadsheets. 'Come in, Paul. Take a seat. Won't be a minute. The acting chief constable wants them before the end of today. Stats time. Unless I finish these numbers, we won't have a bloody department.'

'That bad?'

'Worse.'

Turnbull took his seat in front of his boss, Detective Superintendent Claire Trent, as she peered into the long list of percentages and case numbers. Officially, she ran the Major Investigation Team, but if he had his way, it wouldn't be for long. 'Still, trying to tweak the stats, boss, rather you than me.'

'Just a minute.' Her pen poised over the printout and then scored a deep line though one of the items. She placed the pen down and sat back in her chair. 'How's morale at the moment?'

Turnbull shrugged his shoulders. 'As good as can be expected. Being put in special measures by the Inspectorate of Constabulary was a kick in the teeth for the team. Most of them had worked their guts out only to be told everything they were doing was shit.'

'Not exactly true, Paul. We had reporting issues, a failure of the systems, it was not the work of the force.'

'People don't see it that way, boss.'

'It's your job to convince them. Just because the chief constable took a hit and retired, doesn't mean we're out the woods.'

'On a nice, sweet pension. Any news of a replacement?'

She nodded her head. 'Somebody from Yorkshire, apparently, but I don't know anything about him except he has a reputation for sorting out failing organisations.'

'Bringing in a new brush to sweep the place clean?'

'Something like that. Above our pay grade, Paul.' She leant forward, placing her elbows on the table. 'Our job is to keep going, locking up the bad guys and working cases. Understood?'

'Understood.'

'How are we right now?'

Turnbull sighed. 'Stretched very thin, boss. The Liverpool gang shooting is taking up a lot of resource. The Rochdale murder, the county lines investigation with Cheshire, and the ongoing drugs investigation with South Yorkshire. Not to mention a spate of Post Office robberies in Levenshulme and Fallowfield. Plus we've had intelligence the Salford and Cheetham Hill mobs are about to kick off again.'

'The last thing we need right now, another gang war.'

'We could do with some more warm bodies, boss.'

'Not going to happen, Paul. We make do with what we have at the moment. Budgets have to be balanced.'

'We're burning through a lot of overtime…'

It was Claire Trent's turn to sigh. 'You have to do more with less, Paul.'

'The only thing you do with less is less, boss.'

'I'm afraid I have to give you something else.' She slid a file across his desk. 'A film crew discovered a backpack when they were filming.'

'I heard about it. Thought it was con, paranormal investigators looking for free publicity.'

She ignored him. 'Three human hands were discovered inside the backpack. We don't know how long they have been there.'

He picked up the file and flicked through it. 'Just the hands, no other body parts?'

She nodded. 'The CSI team has finished its work and the full post-mortem results will come in soon.'

'DNA?'

'Sent off to the lab. But they are backed up, results could take a while.'

'Fingerprints?'

'Sent off. But—'

'I bet they are backed up too...'

'Got it in one. We'll get the results when we get them.'

'Can't the local CID handle it?'

'They don't have the resource.'

'Neither do we.'

'Could be a big case, could be nothing. A few medical students having a joke.' Claire Trent stared across the table. 'I've already promised the assistant chief constable we're going to help the local plod.'

Turnbull didn't look up from the file. Suddenly his eyes narrowed. 'Has this already been reported to the coroner?'

'I presume so.'

'And they will be holding an inquest?'

'Probably. What are you thinking, Paul?'

'Why don't we give it to Ridpath? He's going to be looking into it for the coroner anyway, and we still pay for him. He's not doing anything for us right now.'

Claire Trent thought for a moment without answering.

'It's a win–win for us, boss.'

'Could be a conflict of interest.'

'I'm sure we could work out something. If it turns out to be something, we can put more resource on it later.'

The detective superintendent sat back in her chair, chewing the end of her pencil. 'I'll have a chat with Mrs Challinor.'

'And you'll tell Ridpath after this afternoon's meeting?'

She nodded and stared at Turnbull as he stood up. 'Why are you giving Ridpath a case, Paul? I thought you and him didn't see eye to eye?'

'At the moment, we have no other choice, our resources are so stretched. Plus it sounds like the sort of investigation Ridpath is good at.'

'And keeps him out of your hair?'

Turnbull ran his fingers along his newly shaven bald head. 'You could say something like that.' He turned to go, stopping as he reached the door. 'You did say the hands could have been in the backpack for a long time?'

'The CSIs weren't sure how long. We should know more after the post-mortem.'

'Doesn't that make it a cold case? If Ridpath doesn't find anything, we could move it quietly across to Holburt and his team, especially if it links to an old murder.'

'And off our stats?'

'Win–win–win, boss.'

Chapter 9

Ridpath walked into the coroner's office to find Sophia, his assistant, waiting for him at his desk. 'You're here, I was about to call you.'

'Am I?' He pretended to check his arms and body. 'So I am, and here was I thinking I was in Barbados lying on a beach holding a long, cool cocktail with a paper umbrella sticking out of the top.'

'Nah, you're in sunny Stockfield and we're about to look at East Manchester deaths for the last week. Here's your drink.' She passed him a latte. 'Starbucks aren't doing paper umbrellas today. How was Northenden?'

'Same as ever; cold, windy, beside the Mersey and now with the addition of three human hands in a backpack.'

'At least they're not in a curry. Here's the WIP list.' Sophia passed him the photocopied sheets; it ran to three pages.

He glanced down at it. 'One hundred and fifty-five deaths over last week...'

'About normal for this time of year, despite Covid. I've highlighted the ones I think the coroner will want to talk about. And here's the updated calendar from Jenny. There's an inquest on Wednesday and Thursday in Court One with Mrs Challinor presiding, and another on Friday in Court Two with Helen Moore in charge.'

'Anything else I need to know?'

'Nothing at the moment. Our side is all under control.'

Sophia had joined the office in 2019 straight from university and since then, she had made herself indispensable to Ridpath. He knew his strength wasn't in the bureaucracy of any large organisation. Even in the police he had found the endless form filling, ass covering, memo-sending and general paper-shuffling to be tedious in the extreme. Sophia handled it all five times more quickly than he did and with ten times more grace.

'Shall we go through?'

'I don't know what I'd do without you, Sophia.'

She smiled over her shoulder at him. 'Ain't that the truth.'

All the others were already in the meeting room as they entered. Mrs Challinor was sat in her usual place at the head of the table. She looked up from her notepad as they entered. 'Ah, Ridpath and Sophia, as you're here, we'll get started.'

Beside her, Jenny Oldfield, the office manager, was dressed in bright purple with matching eyeshadow, her vibrant colour choice standing out against the wood panelling of the room and the corporate black and white clothes of all the others.

On Mrs Challinor's right sat Helen Moore, the area coroner. She had only been at East Manchester for a year, having to deal with the worst of the pandemic and all it entailed, as well as handling her other work. For some reason, Ridpath had kept her at arm's length. He didn't know why, she was certainly competent at her job, but there was something about her that left him cold.

As he sat down at the table, Ridpath nodded to David Smail, the part-time coroner from Derbyshire. The whole Coroner's Service in England and Wales operated a strange system of coroners from different districts working part-time in other areas. Ridpath had once asked Mrs Challinor why, and had received her usual blunt answer.

'Money. It's cheaper to do this than hire a full complement of coroners and, as the system is funded by local councils and not central government, the number of part-time coroners has increased as the funding has decreased.'

It was one of the things he loved about working for this woman. She called a spade a spade. It wasn't a metal implement for moving dirt. Corporate speak, most of it American, had taken over the police in the last few years, introduced by the myriad consultants who'd been hired and fired to tell coppers how to police a city.

Ten-thousand-foot view. Org charts. Actionable. Face time. Headcount. Change agent. Back burner. Bang for your buck. Behind the eight ball. Skillset. Best practice. Timeframe. Core competency. Due diligence. Value-added. Level the playing field. Low-hanging fruit. Micromanage. Pushback. Ballpark. Stakeholder. Take away. Zero-sum game.

He hated all of their catchphrases with a passion. Luckily, with Mrs Challinor, he heard the truth in plain English and that was good enough for him.

'Jenny, why don't you lead us through the work-in-progress?' The coroner opened the meeting.

'Thank you, Mrs Challinor. We have experienced a hundred and fifty-five deaths this week. The first death the coroner wants to discuss is Mark Deane from Fallowfield, number 3657/21DE.'

Ridpath looked down and found the name already highlighted by Sophia.

'This man died in a house fire on last Tuesday afternoon. He was seventy-five years old and lived alone. There seem to be no suspicious circumstances, but we're still waiting on the pathologist, police and fire examiner's reports—'

'Once we receive them I'll see if it's necessary to hold an inquest,' Mrs Challinor cut in. 'Ridpath and Sophia, did you follow up?'

'I went to the scene last Wednesday, Mrs Challinor. From my discussions with the fire inspector, there seems to be no suspicious activity. He thought the man was smoking and fell asleep, the cigarette dropping onto the sofa and starting the fire. I have asked Mr Schofield to perform a post-mortem. You should wait until you receive the official reports before deciding whether an inquest is necessary.'

Mrs Challinor nodded.

Jenny continued. 'The next case is Fiona Olugwe, case number 3876/21OL...'

The rest of the meeting examined the cases Sophia had highlighted. No action was advised on two of them, with the remaining four considered for public inquests after further investigation. Ridpath was instructed to open communications with each family and advise them of the possibility of a coroner's inquiry.

'Finally, the calendar for this week.' Jenny opened her laptop while Ridpath looked at his printout. 'There is an inquest into the death of Mrs Ivy Siddall. We've pencilled in two days for this, on Wednesday and Thursday.'

Mrs Challinor took over from the office manager. 'Mrs Siddall was a woman living alone with a history of addiction to prescription drugs and alcohol. The police and ambulance services were called after a neighbour knocked on the door, getting no answer. She was inside, lying on the floor, and had been dead for four days. The pathologist has ascribed death to a myocardial infarction, a heart attack, in layman's terms.'

'Why are you holding an inquest, Coroner?' asked Helen Moore.

'Because, as ever, our job is to be an advocate for the dead to safeguard the living. Let us not forget that as we go about our work. We only deal with five questions in an inquest. Who the deceased was. How, when and where they died. And finally, how such deaths may be prevented from recurring. This woman had spent time in hospital and in rehab to deal with her alcoholism. She was well known to social workers and the hospital follow-up team, but she seems to have slipped through the cracks in the system. Her last social worker visit was...' Mrs Challinor checked her notes '...four months before her death. There won't be a jury involved, but I would like to see if her death was in any way preventable. Were there any systemic issues leading to this woman being left alone for four months, despite having numerous health, drug and alcohol issues?'

'I presume you've already written to the relevant NHS trust and local authority?' asked David Smail.

'Of course. Are they going to be represented, Jenny?'

'A Mrs Ivory Sennett QC for the NHS trust and a Jennifer Quigley for the local authority, Mrs Challinor.'

'Good. Anything else, Jenny?'

'On Friday, Helen will hold an inquest into the death of Mr Jordan Harrison, who died while cleaning out a septic tank on Holdern Farm in Carrington.'

The area coroner coughed. 'There are serious health and safety breeches in this case. Mr Harrison was ordered to clean out the tank without the use of any safety gear or breathing equipment.'

'Are you ready to proceed with the inquest, Helen?'

'I am, Coroner.'

'Good, we're done. Have a good week, people. Ridpath, could you stay behind, I'd like a chat.'

Chapter 10

After everybody left and the door was shut, Ridpath was expecting the usual small talk from Mrs Challinor. Instead, she said, 'You have let me down, Ridpath.'

What? What had he done now? 'I don't understand, Coroner, we're up to date with all the paperwork and everything is running smoothly.'

'Not the job. You had a check-up appointment at Christies last week, which you missed. Apparently, this is the second one you haven't attended.'

'I didn't know they informed you.'

'After Polly died, you put me down as your next of kin, remember? The hospital rang me this morning to advise me you haven't attended.'

Ridpath had been diagnosed with myeloma in 2017 in the middle of a major investigation for MIT. Chemo, isolation, a whole pharmacy of pills, the sterile coldness of hospital and nine months off work until he was finally pronounced cancer-free. It was one of the reasons he had been temporarily transferred to the coroner's office, a supposedly less stressful assignment than being a member of the Major Investigation Team. Three years later, he was still here and loving the freedom of being a detective without the bureaucracy of the police.

'They shouldn't have contacted you,' he finally answered.

'Let's not focus on what they did, but on what you didn't do. Why haven't you been to the clinic?' As ever, Mrs Challinor went straight to the heart of the matter. 'And don't say you were too busy. Or you couldn't go. Or the dog ate your homework.'

'It's been three years since I was declared in remission. It seems a waste of time. Plus, in the middle of a pandemic, it didn't seem fair to bother the doctors, they have so many other patients to deal with.'

She turned over a page and Ridpath could see she was reading his personnel file.

She shook her head. 'No, it's not here.'

'What's not there?'

She stabbed her finger on the page. 'Your medical degree. I've looked and looked but I can't see it. And you don't seem to have done any postgraduate work in oncology, nor delivered any papers at international medical conferences.'

Ridpath smiled. 'Point taken, Mrs Challinor.'

She closed his file. 'I hope I don't have to do this again, Ridpath. You are responsible for your health, nobody else. If the specialists didn't want to see you, I'm sure they would have made it very clear.' She ran her fingers through her nest of grey curls. 'Now, can we return to work, there's something I'd like you to look into for me. But first, how was Northenden?'

'Three human hands in a backpack hidden in a secret compartment at the back of an old children's home.'

'Have they been there long?'

Ridpath shrugged his shoulder. 'I don't know at the moment. The post-mortem is later this afternoon. I'm sure Dr Schofield will tell me more.'

'I've asked Jenny to open a file and we'll schedule a preliminary inquest, postponing it until the police have completed their investigation. Who's the SIO?'

'Local CID, Dave Connor.'

Mrs Challinor picked up a note off her desk. 'Do you know why Claire Trent is calling me?'

'Haven't a clue, Coroner. I can ask her at the MIT meeting, if you want.'

'Don't worry, I'll call her back. There's one more concern.' She placed the note back on her desk and formed a steeple with her fingers as if she was praying. 'As you know, I was approached two months ago by an elderly couple, Mr and Mrs Ryder, who wanted me to grant a presumption of death certificate for their daughter.'

'Sorry, I know nothing about this, Coroner.'

'No matter. The Secretary of State for Justice has granted me permission to hold an inquest on Jane Ryder, who went missing over eleven years ago on the weekend of June 12, 2009. The information we have is in the file.' She pushed a pink file across the desk.

'And nobody has seen her since?'

'Correct.'

'What do you want me to do?'

'It should be a fairly straightforward procedure. Look into the case. Have there been any sightings of the woman, or any evidence she may be still alive? If there's nothing, discover who the policemen involved in the missing person report were and ensure they attend the inquest to give evidence. If they are of the opinion Jane is missing and probably dead, I will be able to grant the certificate.'

'They may have already retired.'

'You'll need to find them. Plus any witnesses who last saw her.'

'The information will be in the police files. I'll have to meet the Ryders to get as much background as I can on Jane.'

'Get Sophia to arrange a time.' The coroner looked down at the desk, running her fingers through her tight grey curls once more. 'There is one issue you should be aware of.'

Ridpath looked at her dubiously, waiting for the sting in the tail.

'The inquest has to be as soon as possible. It could be as early as next week.'

'What?'

The coroner held her hands up. 'I know it's short notice, but there is a reason.'

Ridpath stayed silent.

'Mrs Ryder has inoperable cancer. Leukaemia. We don't know how long she has left and the family would like closure before she dies. Jane was an only daughter.'

The mention of cancer threw Ridpath back to his own dark days. At least he was in remission now, unlike Mrs Ryder. He'd never heard the doctor pronounce the dreaded words, 'You only have a few months left to live.' He'd imagined them many times during his treatment, but he'd never heard them.

'I don't know if I can do it in such a short time, Coroner. Establishing there is no evidence of her still being alive and going back through the old files takes time. The case is over eleven years old.'

'Unfortunately, it needs to be done as soon as possible, Ridpath. A woman is dying and we do not know how long she has left to live. The sooner we complete the inquest the better.'

'It's just—'

'Just what?'

'It might take longer than a week.'

'Do the best you can.' She tapped her fingers on her desk impatiently. 'Listen, Ridpath, I understand I share your time with MIT, but it's a matter of priorities. The Ryder case is important to the coroner's office; you need to give it your full attention.'

'Of course, Mrs Challinor, I'll work it out. I have the post-mortem on the hands to go to this afternoon. I'll let you know Dr Schofield's report.'

'Our job in the coroner's office is to support those impacted by the death of a loved one. Can you imagine the hurt and grief of not knowing what happened to your only daughter for over eleven years? They need closure, and we need to give it to them. Understood?'

'Understood, Coroner.' Ridpath stood up. 'Is that all?'

'I think so. How's Eve?'

'Good. Twelve going on twenty-seven. They seem to grow up so quickly these days.'

The coroner glanced at a picture on her desk of her daughter and grandchild. 'Hang on to them for as long as you can, Ridpath.'

'I'll remember, Mrs Challinor.' He turned to go.

'And Ridpath…'

He turned back.

'Remember to re-book your appointment at the hospital, won't you?'

Chapter 11

'Hi, Ridpath, I bought you another latte, thought you might need one.' Sophia pointed to the drink next to his laptop.

'Perfect, I'll drink it in the car on my way to Police HQ. A couple of things before I go. Can you ring the Ryders and arrange an interview for tomorrow morning at their home, around nine thirty?'

'The family involved in the presumption of death inquest next week?'

'An inquest has already been scheduled?'

'Nothing confirmed on the timetable, but Jenny gave me a heads-up. I'll ring them now. Do you want me to be there?'

Ridpath thought for a moment. 'It would be good idea, there might be follow-up.'

'No problem.'

'Can you also check the usual areas for Jane Ryder. She went missing in 2009. The basic information from the parents is in this file.'

Sophia glanced through it. 'Not much here.'

'That's why we're meeting the Ryders tomorrow, but you may as well get started this afternoon. Check electoral rolls, driving licences at the DVLA, and the registrar of births, marriages and deaths.'

'She may have changed her name.'

'Do the preliminary search on her original name. We're looking for any documentary evidence she may be still alive. I'll ask Chrissy at Police HQ to check HOLMES 2 and police reports. You won't be able to get access to those.'

'No problem. We're up to date on our work so I can do it this afternoon. I'll send you anything I have this evening.'

'Great.' He checked his watch. Still ten minutes before he had to leave for Police HQ and afterwards for the morgue. Luckily, Eve was at her friend's today so he didn't have to pick her up. But he still wanted to be home before 6.30 when she returned. He would hate for her to arrive home to an empty house.

He sipped his latte, feeling the milk with a hint of bitter coffee warm his throat. 'How's things?'

'You mean how's my mother?'

He smiled.

'Same as ever. Still trying to marry me off. Actually, she introduced me to somebody interesting for a change, an A&E doctor. According to her, right faith, right job, right income, GSOH and all that bullshit.'

'Sounds like a lonely-hearts ad.'

'My mum's been reading them. But I liked him. Committed to his work and has no time to meet anyone.'

'Bit like you.'

'Says the man who has just given me more work.'

'Yeah, sorry.'

'No worries, it keeps me out of trouble. The mother may even have come round to accepting I work here. Apparently one of her friends was impressed I worked in the coroner's office.'

'At least somebody knows what we do.'

'So, I'm feeling pretty good at the moment. You? How's Eve?'

'Twelve years old and twice as opinionated.'

'She's a teenage girl, what do you expect? All mouth and legs.'

'Speaking from experience?'

'Yeah. Katy Perry, Lorde and Ariana were my saviours.'

'Who?'

'You're showing your age, Ridpath.'

'There was no good music after Northern Soul and Bowie.'

Sophia shook her head. 'You'll be wearing flares and glitter in your hair next.'

'The new uniform for coppers, don't you know. Add a rubber truncheon and fluffy handcuffs and we're ready for work.'

Sophia glanced at the clock. 'You'd better leave now if you want to get to Police HQ by three.'

'Shit, where does the time go to?'

'Soon it will be 2525—'

'That's Zager and Evans.'

'Not Bowie?'

'No, he was Major Tom. Commencing countdown, engines on.'

Her eyes rolled. 'Back to the drawing board.'

'I'm off.'

'Say hello to Eve for me.'

He waved goodbye, and then stopped at the door. 'It's good to have you here, Sophia.'

'It's good to be here, Ridpath. Now go, otherwise you'll be late.'

Chapter 12

Ridpath grabbed a sausage sandwich from the canteen and went up to the MIT floor. He tried to avoid the place these days, except for the weekly meetings. Each time he went, there were fewer and fewer people he knew. Turnbull was gradually replacing all the detectives with his new hires. And the DCI had made it pretty obvious Ridpath was persona non grata, one of the old mob, not one of the new blue-eyed boys.

Emily Parkinson was still there, though. She was far too valuable to Turnbull to get the chop or be re-assigned.

'Hi, Em, how's it going?'

She looked up from her computer. 'Hiya, Ridpath. Same shit, different day.'

'That good?'

'Claire Trent has me collating statistics to show how cost effective the department's recent investigations have been. It's all part of the PMA programme.'

'PMA?'

'Protect my arse. They are all jockeying for position while waiting for the new chief to come aboard. I don't catch criminals any more, I catch numbers.'

'While the cat's away, the mice will play.'

'Why are you here?'

'The weekly meeting was moved forward to this afternoon.'

'Nobody told me.'

'Are you on Turnbull's shit list again?'

'When was I ever on his good list? Speak of the devil.'

DCI Paul Turnbull was staring across at them as he walked from his office to the meeting room.

'You'd better go, Ridpath, leave me in the happy embrace of my numbers.'

'See you later, Em.' He stopped, looking across at another empty desk. 'Where's Chrissy?'

'She was here earlier, probably waiting for you in the meeting room.'

Ridpath nodded and strode over to the open door. The other detectives were already seated behind the desks, with Turnbull and Claire Trent vying for position at the head of the table. He sat down in the nearest empty chair, placing his sandwich in front of him and taking out his notebook.

'Right, let's get started. We're going to have a short briefing today because Claire has another meeting with the acting chief this afternoon. Where are we on the South Yorkshire drugs case, Peter?'

Peter Swift, one of Turnbull's new hires, opened his notebook. 'In a good position, boss, we've had surveillance on Mrs Docherty since the beginning of the month. On Friday, she met Marcus Holden in a motorway services on the M62.'

'The Moss Side supplier?' asked one of the detectives, Ridpath didn't know his name.

'The one and same. We think they are arranging to work together.'

'Manchester supplying South Yorkshire with heroin and crack?' asked Claire Trent.

'And in return we get free bags of coal and a set of knives and forks,' joked Turnbull.

Claire Trent didn't smile. 'What are the next steps, Peter?'

'We're still keeping them both under surveillance and we're up on their phones. Both South Yorkshire and ourselves want to catch them when they make the deal.'

'What? We think they are going to be stupid enough to pass cash and drugs to each other at a meet?' asked Claire Trent.

'That's about it,' said Peter. 'And, yes, we think it will be soon.'

'Anything from the National Crime Agency?'

'Nothing, boss.'

'Watch the hours on this, Peter. Your overtime is going through the roof.'

'We've got them on twenty-four-hour surveillance, boss. Nothing I can do about the overtime.'

'I said watch you hours, am I clear? Use South Yorks resources as much as you can.' The detective superintendent spoke sharply, making certain all the detectives understood her priorities.

The rest of the meeting continued on in the same way. It was obvious to Ridpath the team was stretched, with too few people chasing too many jobs in too short a time.

'Ridpath. Earth to Ridpath...'

He zoned back into the meeting. Had Turnbull been taking lessons from his daughter?

'Yes, sir.'

'Your report.'

'All is running smoothly at the coroner's office. Only a hundred and fifty-five deaths in Manchester last week, with three being ascribed to Covid. In total, one thousand and thirty-six people have died from the disease in the city. Of the recent deaths, I'm following up on six of them, but there's nothing overtly suspicious I need to report. I also have one missing person case from eleven years ago. The family has asked the coroner to hold a presumption of death inquest.'

'Why?'

'No communication or sightings for over eleven years. Perhaps they are seeking closure.'

'Or they're trying to claim on insurance,' snarled Turnbull.

Ridpath ignored him. 'In the absence of a body, the coroner needs to seek the home secretary's permission to hold an inquest and grant a presumption of death certificate. So I'll need your help going through the police files, Chrissy.'

The civilian researcher was wearing a new Manchester City scarf proclaiming them League Champions 2021 even though the league hadn't officially finished playing yet.

'No problem, Ridpath.'

'Chrissy is busy at the moment,' said Turnbull.

'She can still find the time to help Ridpath, Paul. We need to work with the coroner at the moment.' Claire Trent stared at her chief inspector.

Turnbull stayed silent.

'Right, that's sorted. Anybody with anything else? Worries? Concerns? Information?'

The detectives collectively shook their heads.

'Good.' She took a deep breath. 'I know it's difficult at the moment. We're understaffed, under resourced and under pressure. Going into special measures was the worst that could have happened at the present time. But do understand the action by the Inspectorate of Constabulary had nothing to do with your work or that of your teams. It was a systemic failure, not a failure of police work. Understand?'

Another collective nod.

'Be careful out there. Ridpath, you can stay behind.'

Chapter 13

When the rest of the detectives and civilian researchers had filed slowly out, Turnbull gestured for Ridpath to move closer. 'We have a new job for you.'

'A new job?'

'You've heard about the discovery of three hands on Monday night?'

'I've already been to the crime scene as the coroner's officer.'

'Good, you already understand the case.'

'What do you want me to do?'

Claire Trent leant forward. 'You job is to assist the local CID in any way you can.'

'Assist?'

'The SIO is DS Dave Connor. Do you know him?'

'I used to work with him in MIT when Charlie Whitworth was in charge. He's a good copper, is Dave.' He paused and scratched his nose as his two bosses watched him. 'But why me? Emily... DS Parkinson could handle it just as well.'

'She's working for me on something,' said Claire Trent firmly.

'And there could be a conflict of interest. As a coroner's officer, I am supposed to be independent of police investigations.'

Turnbull snorted. 'Do you want the case or not?'

Claire Trent laid her hand on his arm to calm him. 'I've discussed the possible conflict with Mrs Challinor. She believes it can be negated if your assistant—'

'Sophia Rahman.'

'—handles the case from the coroner's side, leaving you to aid the local CID.'

A light bulb went off in Ridpath's head. 'You two have already decided everything, haven't you?'

'Of course, I needed Mrs Challinor to understand why your services were necessary to help the local CID. She wants you to prioritise the presumption of death inquiry but has accepted you need to work with local CID on the hands case.'

'And in return, she gets Chrissy's help checking up on our missing person, Jane Ryder.'

Turnbull raised his eyebrows and glanced across at his boss.

'Got it in one, Ridpath. Mrs Challinor and I both agree such an arrangement could be mutually beneficial.'

He shrugged his shoulders. 'So this is a done deal?'

'Trussed up like a turkey waiting for Christmas,' said Turnbull, smirking.

'What about other resources from MIT to help Dave Connor?'

'The rest of the squad is tied up on live cases. You're it, I'm afraid.' Turnbull opened his arms as if to say sorry, but Ridpath could see in his eyes he wasn't.

'We also think you're the right person for the job,' added Claire Trent quickly. 'We want to see a result on this case, Ridpath, don't let it drag on.'

'I'm a detective inspector, how can I report to a detective sergeant?'

'You're not reporting to him, Ridpath, you're assisting the local CID on behalf of MIT. It's their case, not ours, but I've been asked to help them and I've promised the ACC I would.'

'Could DS Parkinson and Chrissy Wright help me if I need it?'

'No, they are busy with our live cases.' Turnbull ran his fingers across his bald scalp as if combing through hair. 'Listen, we have too much work and too few people. You're still on our books, so we've nominated you to help the local CID. Think of it as playing for another team on loan. And besides, this case will probably lead nowhere. My bet is a couple of medical students have been messing around in anatomy classes, nicking body parts to scare their girlfriends.'

Ridpath realised he had no choice in this, it had already been decided for him. 'Right, when do I start?'

Before Turnbull could answer there came a knock on the door. It opened and Peter Swift stood in the doorway. 'Boss, the acting chief is ready for the meeting now. And DCI Turnbull, I've brought the car round for our trip to South Yorkshire.'

'Right, Peter, I'll be out in minute.'

Claire Trent packed up her folders. 'I have to go. Good luck, Ridpath.'

'Am I going to need it?'

'Old cases are always difficult.'

'You're telling me.'

Before she left, Claire Trent turned back to Turnbull. 'I'll let you know how this meeting goes later, Paul.'

'Keep fighting, boss.'

'I intend to. Nobody is going to mess with my patch.'

She strode out, leaving the door open.

'One last question.'

'What is it, Ridpath?' sighed Turnbull as he stood up.

'Has anybody told Dave Connor yet?'

'We thought we'd leave it to you, Ridpath.'

Chapter 14

Ridpath stood downwind of Emily Parkinson, inhaling as much second-hand smoke as he could. He'd given up smoking for almost a year now as Eve hated the smell on his clothes and his breath. But Ridpath still enjoyed the vicarious pleasure of standing next to Emily as she puffed away.

They were outside Police HQ in the reserved area for smokers around the back. A large ashtray was in front of Ridpath, filled to the brim with sad fag ends. It was joke in the building that the quality of the air-conditioning was so bad the only way to get some fresh air was to go out for a smoke.

He'd already briefed Chrissy on Jane Ryder. 'I'm afraid I've got some work for you. And if Turnbull gives you trouble, it's been approved by Claire Trent.'

'Great, anything to get off bloody stats.'

'I'm looking for missing person files.'

'No worries, Ridpath, have you done a misper check before?'

'Did the course in training years ago, but that's about it.'

'Give me the name and I'll go through the databases for you. When did she disappear?'

'Her name was Jane Ryder and she was last seen on June 12, 2009.'

'How old was she?'

'Just sixteen. Had her birthday a week before, according to the file.'

Chrissy made a smacking sound with her lips. 'Did the parents report it to the police?'

'I think so. I'm meeting them tomorrow morning to get more details.'

'Somebody will have gone round to the house if she was only sixteen.'

'Even though she's no longer a child?'

'As ever, the law is a bit vague. Once a young person reaches sixteen they can leave home or their parents can ask them to move out. However, parents are responsible for their children's well-being until they turn eighteen. Police would follow the usual procedure for a sixteen-year-old.'

'Which is?'

Chrissy adjusted the scarf around her neck. 'Conducting a search of the house and outbuildings, obtaining two pictures, fingerprints, DNA and any other items of interest, with the parents' permission. The investigating copper would look for diaries or notes. Finally, they'll fill in a Form 737 and place all the information on OPUS.'

'The old operating system. Can we still access it?'

'I can. There'll also be a risk report, and they may have contacted a missing person search manager. Depending on the risk assessment, there will be a list of actions taken on OPUS and the report will be sent to the Missing From Home Unit for follow-up. The officer will also seek permission to place the child's details on the Missing Children website.'

'There doesn't seem to have been much follow-up.'

'She was probably evaluated as not high risk; a runaway rather than somebody who'd been taken.'

'You know a lot about this.'

'Spent my first five years at the MFH unit. Know it like I know City's players.'

'Will the form show who was the responding officer?'

She nodded. 'Plus all the other coppers involved, the SIO and the missing person's manager.'

'Great, I need to find witnesses for the inquest.'

Chrissy was silent for a moment, chewing the end if her pencil. 'Given her age, she may be on two other nation-wide databases: the Vulnerable Persons database and Missing Persons

DNA database, plus the Missing Kids website. Want me to check them out for you?'

'It's for the coroner, so I don't want you to go to too much trouble, Chrissy. Point me in the right direction and I'll do the work myself.'

'No worries, anything rather than looking at more bloody stats. I'll send you the info as soon as I have it.'

'Thanks, Chrissy.'

Of course, Emily Parkinson had collared him as soon as he'd finished with Chrissy, making the universal sign of the invisible cigarette to the mouth, which actually meant she wanted to chat.

He inhaled another satisfying cloud of secondary smoke.

'I hear you've been put on the Northenden case.'

'News travels fast. I was only told myself five minutes ago.'

'Nothing is secret on the floor, you should know.' She paused for a moment, taking another long drag. 'Need any help?'

'You know I'd love to have you on the case, but apparently, I'm to "assist" the local CID in their investigation.' He formed quotation marks with his fingers. 'You desperate to get out of HQ?'

'Nah, desperate to get off the computer. And so is Chrissy.'

'What are you doing?'

'Comparing crime-solving statistics from all forty-four police districts of England and Wales.'

'You must be up to your eyes in numbers.'

'I dream bloody numbers.' Another drag on the cigarette, followed by a furtive lowering of the voice. 'If you need any help on your case, let me know. I mean it, Ridpath.'

'I did suggest it to our lords and masters, Em, but they were keen for you to carry on doing what you're doing.'

'Justifying our existence.'

'MIT needs justification?'

She assumed the voice of a police spokesperson. '"In the modern world of policing, each and every resource must be examined and quantified to justify its allocation in the fight against crime and the protection of the public." I know the bullshit off by heart now.' Another long drag on her cigarette. 'I'll even come in on my days off if you want, and so would Chrissy.'

'You must be desperate.'

'You don't know the half of it. I'd kill to work on a case again.'

'There's an idea for you.'

'It would be one way of getting out of HQ and away from the stats. Are you going to be the SIO?'

'Nah, like I said, just assisting. The SIO is Dave Connor.'

'Who's he?'

'A good copper, old school, like Charlie Whitworth.'

'Must be close to retirement. Why'd he leave MIT?'

'Wanted an easier life and more regular hours. After John Gorman retired, he was seen as part of the problem, not part of the solution. You know how it is.'

'The new brush sweeps clean. Now, Turnbull is doing exactly the same.'

'How you getting on with him?'

'Badly, he's doing his best to force me out, but I'm hanging in there by the skin of my teeth.'

'You're too valuable to MIT, Em, he won't let you go.'

'You should tell him.'

Ridpath checked his watch. 'Time to leave.'

'Where are you going?'

'Off to see Dr Schofield.'

'I love the smell of the mortuary in the late afternoon. Enjoy yourself.'

'It's a post-mortem, not a party.'

'Funny, I'd give my left arm to spend an afternoon with the bodies in the mortuary right now. Better than wasting time with the corpses in there.' She gestured back towards Police HQ.

'Don't let them get to you, Em. I'd better be off.'

Emily Parkinson waved goodbye, the cigarette still clapped between her fingers. 'Knock yourself out, Ridpath, and call me if you need anything.'

'Will do, Em. Take care of yourself.'

Chapter 15

They were already in the hills above Glossop on the quaintly named Snake Pass to Sheffield before Turnbull spoke to his driver.

'Can't stand the Peak District, it's only rocks and gorse and endless bloody moors. Why do people bother coming here?'

Peter Swift looked in his rear-view mirror. 'It's to get away from the city to somewhere more open, boss.'

'Waste of bloody time, if you ask me. And have you ever been up here on a weekend? You meet more people than you do in the centre of Manchester. I was on secondment in Buxton once, hated every bloody second of it. Tramping the moors, searching for lost walkers, finding the occasional body in a gully. If they wanted to kill themselves, why not do it quietly at home?'

Peter Swift recognised that no answer was needed or wanted.

'Now I have to deal with the idiots in South Yorkshire. Couldn't find a brain cell between the lot of them.'

Outside in the wooded valley leading to Ladybower Reservoir, spring was kicking the trees into life and the birds were singing joyfully. Inside the car, silence had descended once more, until Peter Swift plucked up the courage to speak.

'Gaffer?'

'What is it?'

'I thought we didn't like Ridpath. Why are we giving him a case?'

Turnbull sucked in air between his teeth. 'You have to understand, it's not personal between myself and Ridpath.' He chuckled and a wry smile crossed his lips. 'At least, it not *too* personal. For me he represents the old school of policing, based on hunches and intuitions, copper's nose and all that malarkey. We should have junked people like him years ago. Modern policing is all about following systems, integrated operations and the best-case management of investigations. It's the only way we can consistently achieve success. No time for bloody hunches.'

'I think I get it, boss, but—'

'Peter, if you're going to advance your career in the police,' Turnbull interrupted, 'you have to understand that only one thing is important. Not degrees or diligence or even street smarts, just one thing.'

Dutifully, Swift asked the question. 'What's that, gaffer?'

'Success, Peter, success. And the wonderful thing is, you don't even have to do the work yourself, you only have to be associated with it. Someone once said, success has a thousand handmaidens and failure has none. This is more than true of the police. Everybody remembers our successes, nobody is ever associated with our failures.'

'What's it got to do with Ridpath, boss?'

'Well, a little dicky bird in the lab told me at lunchtime that the hands are too degraded to get fingerprints and there may even be a problem with DNA.'

'But if he can't identify the hands—'

'And no body is found...'

'A case with body parts is going nowhere.'

'Oh, it's going somewhere, Peter. Straight down on his record as a failure and, afterwards, to the Cold Case Unit where it will sit along with all the other failures of GMP, unloved and unwanted.'

Silence descended again, before Peter Swift once more summoned up the courage to ask: 'But what happens if Ridpath solves the case, has a success?'

'Unlikely.' A long pause as Turnbull stroked his bald head as one would a good-luck charm. 'But if he did, who was the one who recommended he be assigned to the job?'

'You, gaffer?' Swift said tentatively.

'Me. And I'll make sure everybody knows, too. Plus, if he somehow manages to find a lead, I'll be back on the case as quick as a Manchester stripper whips off her clothes on a cold December night, leading the team to victory with Ridpath consigned to the knacker's yard.' A long pause. 'What's the one thing that matters in your career, Peter?'

'Success. Or being associated with it.'

'Here endeth the first lesson of policing, Peter. Remember this and you will go far.'

'All the way to Sheffield, gaffer?'

'We all have to do some penance, Peter, even the most successful coppers.'

Chapter 16

The smell of the mortuary was worse than Ridpath remembered. A white, sterile, inhuman smell, a deadly combination of disinfectant, formaldehyde and immense human sadness. As it always did when he entered the place, a shiver kicked down his spine. For a fleeting moment, Ridpath was tempted to turn tail and do a runner down Oxford Road, getting himself and his nose as far away from there as possible.

Luckily, Oliver Davis was waiting for him in the lobby.

'Did you bring the Vicks?'

Sheepishly, the young detective produced a family-sized jar from his pocket.

'Couldn't you get anything smaller?'

'It was all they had in the shop.'

'Put a splodge beneath your nose. It'll keep most of the smell out.'

'What about you?'

'I'm used to it,' he said with bravado. He dabbed his finger in the open jar anyway and smeared a splodge over his top lip.

At that moment, a swing door opened and Dr Schofield appeared, dressed in his usual fetching outfit of bloodied apron, face mask and hairnet. 'Come on through, Ridpath, we've already finished so we can give you the topline right away. You'd better get kitted out first though.'

'We?'

'I asked a colleague from Liverpool for help on this one. Dr O'Casey is a forensic anthropologist, human skeletal remains are her speciality.'

Ridpath thought for a moment of the person who spent their life examining decaying body parts. He imagined some wizened old academic crouched over a skeleton; amongst her students she would, no doubt, have the nickname Bones.

He followed the doctor into a changing room, Oliver Davis close behind.

Schofield indicated the row of fresh PPE garments folded on a shelf. 'Find your size. I'll be on Table Three. Do get a move on though, I have a reservation for dinner at El Gato Negro for seven and I'd like to go home and change into something warm as we're sitting outside.'

When the doctor had gone, Davis whispered. 'How does he do it? Cuts up bodies all day and then goes out to eat in the evening.'

'He once told me his favourite meal was liver and onions.'

'With a glass of chianti on the side?'

'Don't take too long getting changed, I want to get back too,' answered Ridpath, zipping up his PPE.

Two minutes later, they entered the post-mortem room. Six stainless steel tables were arrayed along one wall. Above them, adjustable lights hovered, waiting to be switched on. The soft hum of an air conditioner was the only noise to disturb the two corpses lying on the tables.

Dr Schofield was waiting for them at Table 3. Standing next to him was a young woman with the clearest blue eyes Ridpath had ever seen.

'This is Dr O'Casey.'

'Hi there, you must be the detectives on the case.' She had a pure Dublin accent, as warm as the Liffey on a summer's afternoon. 'Interesting job here, not much to work with though.'

Ridpath dragged himself away from the eyes and down to a line of three hands laid out in a row on a plastic mat in the centre of the stainless steel table.

'This is DI Ridpath.' Schofield pointed to the detective. 'And the other is...?'

'DC Davis,' added the young detective. He reached forward to shake Dr O'Casey's hand, realised she was holding a sharp scalpel and hurriedly recoiled.

'You said you've already finished.'

'Well, we've done as much as we can until the results come back from the lab, anyway,' answered Schofield in his high voice. 'Shall we begin?'

Ridpath adjusted his mask. The smell of disinfectant with a top note of putrefaction was particularly strong today. Perhaps he should have borrowed more of Davis's Vicks. He had bought enough to carry him through twenty years of post-mortems.

'As you can see, we have in front of us three human hands. All three are right hands and have been rather crudely severed at the wrist, and the amputations were carried out post-mortem.'

Davis wrote feverishly in his notebook. 'So they come from three different bodies?' he asked.

The anthropologist's eyebrows rose and Dr Schofield glanced across at Ridpath. 'Well, unless there is a new human species with two right hands, that would appear to be the case.'

The young detective coughed. 'Sorry, it's my first post-mortem, bit nervous.'

'Let me make this clear,' Ridpath interrupted, 'the three hands came from people who were already dead?'

'That's correct,' Dr Schofield grunted in reply and continued speaking. 'Both Dr O'Casey and I believe we have a female hand and two male hands.'

'How do you know?'

'From observation, one can see two of the hands are bigger than the third, with a heavier bone and finger structure. Work by Abdul Hagag and Soheir Mohamed in Egypt attempted to determine sex by hand dimensions and index finger length ratio. Using their indexes, I determined two of the hands were male and one female. There were also a couple of other giveaways.' Dr O'Casey turned over one of the hands. 'Under the microscope I could see traces of scarlet nail polish along the cuticle.' A slight smile towards Davis. 'Not unknown, but not common amongst men. The slender length of these fingers would suggest this is a woman. The other two hands are rougher in look and appearance. There is an absence of care about the cuticles and nails, particularly this one.' She turned it over. 'And please notice the calluses at the base of the fingers. This person did heavy manual work at one time in their life. Now, none of this is conclusive, but, taking all factors into account, I'm happy with my conclusion on the sex of the hands.'

'What age do you think they are?'

'The age of human hands is more difficult to ascertain, except in children under the age of eighteen. It would be easier if we had more to work with; the pubic symphysis is one of the most reliable areas of the skeleton for adult age estimation. Other methods include changes in the morphology of the auricular surface and the sternal rib end. But as we do not have the complete skeleton, only the hands…'

This last sentence was delivered with a tone suggesting the lack of more bones to examine was the detectives' fault.

'…one needs to use one's experience to come to any conclusion. Please remember, any estimation of the age of an adult hand is not an exact science, but mere guesswork.'

Dr O'Casey walked across to a computer, the sound of her heels echoing on the sterile floor. Despite the entrancing blue eyes and the Dublin accent, Ridpath felt she had all the warmth of a white walker from *Game of Thrones*.

'We took a plain posterior–anterior X-ray of each hand and wrist. As you may or may not know, the pattern of ossification in the hand and wrist bones proceeds in a fairly predictable manner up until the age of eighteen, when the elongation of the bones is complete. We can compare the level of maturation of hand and wrist bones with normal age levels using the GR Atlas.'

She pressed a key and an X-ray of one of the hands appeared on the screen.

'The female hand still shows growth plates between the carpals, indicating this belonged to a young girl aged between sixteen and seventeen years old. But remember, skeletal age and chronological age can be different.'

'She's young,' said Oliver Davis.

'She *was* very young,' corrected Dr O'Casey. 'The other two hands are more difficult to age. The larger male hand has indications of rheumatoid arthritis, here and here. There is also evidence of past trauma in this fracture of the index finger.'

'Did this fracture happen at the time of death?' asked Ridpath.

'Definitely not. It is well healed. My estimate would be at least five or six years, and probably longer, before death. I would estimate this hand belonged to a male aged between fifty and sixty. But absent of more of the skeleton, I couldn't swear to it in court.'

She paused for a second to see if there were any other questions. When there weren't, she pressed a key on the computer and a third X-ray appeared. 'The second male hand displays little or no arthritis and has no fractures or distinguishing marks. Again, estimation is difficult, but I would say it was younger, between thirty and forty years old.'

Ridpath nodded. 'Thank you. So we're looking for a girl and two older males, one who has arthritis and has had a fractured index finger in the past?'

'Correct, DI Ridpath.' There was a slight tone of surprise in Dr O'Casey's voice. 'An accurate summary.'

He turned to the pathologist. 'You said the hands were severed at the wrist, Dr Schofield. How were they cut from the body?'

'I'll defer to my colleague again, if I may. Filomena, can you take them through it?' He nodded his head towards Dr O'Casey.

'In addition to X-rays we used PMCT to analyse the hands—'

'PMCT?' asked Davis.

'Post-mortem computed tomography. In the simplest of terms, a CT scan can reveal anatomic details of internal organs that cannot be seen in conventional X-rays. The tomograms, or slices, can be created as thin as one millimetre and seen as 3D images, like this.' She pressed another key and a blue image of a human hand appeared on screen. 'We can revolve the image and take measurements across each plane.'

'Wow,' said Davis.

'It is rather amazing, isn't it?' For the first time, Dr O'Casey displayed something approaching humanity, but quickly recovered. 'As you can now see, we are looking at a section through the scaphoid where it was severed from the hand and the bones of the radius. You see the residual cross-section striation?'

She pointed to the screen, but Ridpath could only see it was a little less blue than the surrounding area.

'If I zoom in, we will be able to get a closer view.'

She tickled a few keys and the image became bigger. 'See, there are saw marks in the bone. We measured the gap between the teeth and concluded the bone was severed using a superfine hacksaw, similar to this.' A picture of a small hacksaw appeared on the screen. 'Unfortunately, this a common or garden tool, available at any B&Q or hardware store. It has thirty to thirty-two dents or teeth per inch and, in this case, the teeth were set in a zigzag or wave pattern.'

'Did the perp have any medical knowledge?' asked Ridpath.

'I don't think so. See here.' She pointed to the hand on the screen again. 'Hesitation cut marks. This perpetrator attempted to start at least twice before going through with the amputation. The work was done with little skill – this person was not a surgeon, more of a butcher.'

'You think that was his profession?' asked Davis.

Dr O'Casey eyebrows raised again. 'It was a figure of speech, Detective. I was merely pointing out the hands were severed roughly and without finesse.'

'Oh, I see.' He scribbled in his notebook.

'Shall I continue, Ridpath?'

'Be my guest, Doctor.'

'As I was saying, the hands have been severed from the arm roughly. This act was performed approximately twenty-four hours after the time of death for the male hands and forty-eight hours for the female one.'

Davis was about to ask another question, received a withering look from the forensic anthropologist and wisely decided to continue taking notes.

'I have ascertained this through the level of putrefaction of the hand. As you may well remember, there are five stages of decay for any body; initial breakdown, bloating, active decay, advanced decay and dry remains.'

She pressed another key and a drawing of a hand appeared. 'This is a visual representation of the appearance of the stages of decay, with each finger drawn as one of the stages.' She pointed to the index finger, which was labelled 'bloating'. 'During initial breakdown, muscular tissues become rigid and the blood pools into the lower extremities. As the bacteria in the intestines devour the intestinal walls, cells lose their structural integrity and cellular enzymes are released. Microbes also start breaking down carbohydrates, proteins, and lipids. Most of this breakdown occurs inside the body and is not visible from the outside. At the end of this stage, blowflies and flesh flies arrive to lay eggs.'

Dr O'Casey stopped speaking for a second. In the silence, the only sounds were the scratching of Davis's pen across the paper and the constant hum of the air conditioning.

'This cellular breakdown causes the greenish tinge along the edges of the fingernails and cuticles, as well as the pasty, almost cream alabaster colour of the skin.' She pointed to the nails and the skin tone of the hands lying on the stainless steel table. 'Now, the speed of decomposition depends on several factors: surrounding temperature, whether the body is buried or exposed to air or water, and the number of bacteria present. Looking at these male hands, the process of bloating has begun, but it isn't at an advanced stage. The skin hasn't started to slip or split. And there are fly eggs present but they haven't yet hatched into maggots...'

'Meaning?'

'Meaning, the hand was probably kept in a sealed area rather than in the open air. A sealed area where flies still managed to enter. There is more skin slippage on the female hand, plus the fly eggs are more advanced in development. I thus conclude this hand was severed later, around forty-eight hours after death. But please don't quote me, it is an approximation based on the available science. Without knowing where the hands were severed and kept, it will remain an approximation.'

'I don't understand, Doctor. If these hands were severed, wouldn't they have continued to decay, even away from the body?'

'Well spotted, Ridpath, it's the first thing I noticed,' said Schofield.

'I don't understand. How come they haven't decayed after separation from the body?'

'Somebody actively intervened to prevent decay.' Dr Schofield removed his mask and bent close to one of the hands. 'I used the old sniff test, and it's definitely there.'

'What is?'

'The strong scent of formaldehyde, probably formalin.'

'What?'

'Smell for yourself?'

'I'll pass, Doctor.'

Schofield indicated for Davis to come forward. He immediately shook his head and resumed taking notes.

'Please yourself. Somebody has embalmed these hands.'

'What?' exclaimed Davis.

The doctor repeated himself, emphasising each separate word. 'Somebody… has… embalmed… these… hands.'

Chapter 17

'How have these hands have been preserved?' asked Ridpath frowning.

'Probably by placing them in a sealed jar with the embalming fluid. Think of a museum or a lab keeping a specimen.'

For a second, Ridpath remembered what Turnbull has said about medical students. Was this a university prank by somebody with a perverse sense of humour? 'Somebody placed these hands in jars?'

'That's what I said, Ridpath. It means they have been preserved as they were when they were severed from the arm. I've sent some samples to the lab for testing. We should know the composition of the embalming liquid soon.'

'How does that help?' asked Ridpath.

'Each company produces embalming fluids with different levels of formaldehyde, glutaraldehyde, phenol and methanol,' Dr O'Casey interrupted. It was almost as if the two pathologists were competing with each other to provide information.

'Interestingly, the EU voted to restrict the use of formaldehyde by funeral directors for embalming in 2018, but there was a delay in the introduction of the legislation to allow them to find alternatives until 2023. As we have now left the EU, nobody has a clue whether this legislation will ever be introduced.'

'Why was it banned?'

'Strictly speaking, it wasn't banned,' said Schofield, 'its use was restricted because studies had shown prolonged exposure was linked to nasopharyngeal cancer.'

'It causes cancer and you asked me to smell it,' said Oliver Davis.

'A single exposure is not likely to cause any harm, Detective.'

'Unlikely?'

Ridpath brought them back on track. 'If we know the composition, we can find out where the embalming fluid came from?'

'Correct, Ridpath. There are also different levels of saturation of the embalming liquid in each hand. The two male ones seem to have far less than the female hand.'

'Does that suggest the person who severed the hands was an undertaker, mortuary attendant or maybe a scientist?'

'Not necessarily. These days many people have access to embalming fluid, all the components can be bought on the internet.'

'My dad buys embalming fluid,' said Davis.

All the other people in the morgue stared at him.

'What? He stuffs animals. It's his hobby.'

'I would keep that quiet in the station, if I were you, DC Davis. Anything else, Doctor?'

'A couple of things. Because of the use of embalming fluid, I have no way of knowing when these hands were severed.' Dr O'Casey spoke again.

'So they could be two, twenty, or two hundred years old?'

'Probably not the latter,' said O'Casey.

'Why?'

She tapped the computer keyboard again, bringing up the X-ray of the male hand. 'See the white circles on the proximal phalange on the index finger.'

'Sorry, where?'

She held up her own hand to show him. The fingers, despite being sheathed in a glove, were long and surprisingly elegant. 'Here. They indicate a plate was placed to help support what must have been a bad fracture. The plate was later removed, however. Looking at the hand, the scar is small, with flap surgery by a plastic surgeon used to give the hand a near normal appearance, indicating for me that the surgery was performed in the last twenty years or so, certainly no later.'

'From roughly the year 2000 onwards?'

'Correct. I don't think it would have been done earlier. Probably in the last ten years or so.'

'So our older man had surgery recently. Interesting. What about DNA and fingerprints?'

'Until a few years ago, it was difficult to extract DNA from embalmed specimens. Its recovery is often severely compromised by the presence of formalin. But can you imagine the research possibilities if scientists could extract DNA from mummies or from embalmed specimens held in old laboratories?'

'They could investigate ancient diseases and evaluate how DNA has changed or been modified.'

The doctor stared at him. 'You surprise me, Ridpath.'

'My daughter has been doing DNA in biology. I have to keep up.'

'Congratulations to your daughter. Anyway, new techniques have been developed using a three-step enzymatic digestion protocol. This procedure can then be integrated into traditional phenol and chloroform extraction, a modified manual DNA IQ or automated DNA IQ/Te-Shake-based extraction in order to recover DNA for downstream applications.'

'What? Could you repeat that?' asked Davis.

'It means we can get the DNA,' answered Ridpath.

'Maybe.'

'There's a "but", is there?'

'In science, there's always a "but", DI Ridpath.' A slight pause. 'But brain, heart or liver tissue have generally been used. We can obtain DNA from bones or bone marrow, but I don't know if the embalming process has deteriorated the quality of these bones.'

'How will you know?'

'By trying to extract DNA. I've already rung the lab and warned them of the issue. At the moment, they are frantically ringing up their pals at the University of Manchester to check the process. A couple of years ago they extracted DNA from two mummies that were thought to be brothers. They found they had the same mother but different fathers.'

'So it is possible?'

'It *might* be possible.'

'And what about fingerprints?'

'We've already taken them...'

'There's another "but", isn't there?'

'Fingerprints decay on corpses; skin slips and shrinks. And what most people don't know is fingerprints themselves change slightly as people age. In this case, we would normally use thanatopractical fingerprinting.'

'What?'

'Fluid is extracted from other parts of a body's remains and used to restore tenseness and volume to the fingers in order to plump them for printing.'

'But we don't have other parts of the body.'

'Precisely. We hope the embalming process has prevented the decay so we can get prints, or we could use silicone putty to obtain a casting capturing the detail of the ridges.'

'Again, we won't know until the lab reports back?'

'Right. One final matter. We have taken scrapings from beneath the fingernails on all three hands. We've sent them to the lab, but again...'

'Not my favourite word, "but"...' said Ridpath.

Dr O'Casey ignored him. '*But*, again, if the hands have been in embalming fluid, any material we discover may have been compromised.'

Dr Schofield checked his watch. 'There's nothing else from us, Ridpath. From now on, it's a waiting game, until we get the tests back. We'll send our topline report tomorrow, following up with the lab reports as and when they come in.'

'Can you ring me as soon as you find out anything?'

'No problem.'

'One last question. Do we know how these people died?'

'Without the bodies, it's difficult to tell. Toxicology might help, but I doubt it. There's only so much science can do, Ridpath. I'm afraid the rest is up to you now.'

'Isn't it always?'

Dr Schofield stopped for a moment. 'One more thought has occurred to me.'

'What's that?'

'If the hands were all severed using the same type of hacksaw, it suggests—'

'The same killer in each case,' interrupted Ridpath. 'Doctor, I think we are thinking along the same lines. Are we looking for a serial killer?'

Chapter 18

'You want one?'

Ridpath's hand hovered over the open pack of Trebor mints. He hated these things, but anything to rid his mouth and sinuses of the taste and smell of the mortuary.

They were standing outside on the street after the post-mortem, the sun thinking about going down over Manchester and the rush-hour traffic honking with impatience.

'Right, Oliver, you need to let Dave Connor know what happened in there.'

'Will do.'

'We have a couple of leads you need to follow up. I want you to check with local hospitals, universities, funeral homes and labs. See if any human hands have gone missing recently. The fact that they were placed in embalming liquid suggests they may have been stolen, perhaps as a prank.'

'Right, sir. It could be a lot of places to check.'

'Nonetheless, it needs to be done. We can't launch a major police investigation if these hands have been sitting in some university lab and have been stolen by somebody with a bizarre sense of humour. We won't know until you check. And it's Ridpath, not sir, not Tom, not boss. Just Ridpath.'

'Yes, sir… I mean Ridpath.'

'Second, ring up Hannah and find out how she's getting on with the backpack. It's our one piece of tangible evidence. Hopefully it will have a nice juicy fingerprint somewhere, but I wouldn't hold my breath.'

'Will do.'

'Follow up also on the DNA and fingerprint analysis of the hands. We need to work out who these people were.'

Davis stopped scribbling for a moment. 'If we have three hands, it must mean there are three bodies out there somewhere?'

'Good question. Check up on reports of body parts found in the last twenty years using HOLMES 2. Particularly any bodies missing hands. And, finally, we need to know who underwent hand surgery in the last twenty years. Start with the Greater Manchester area first.'

'Right.' He sighed loudly. 'It's a lot for me to do, Ridpath.'

'And Dave Connor isn't much help?'

'I'm not criticising Dave, but he's a bit slow. Half his time seems to be spent handling Chief Inspector Holloway.'

'It's the way of the world, Oliver. You need to do the running around.'

'What are you going to do, Ridpath?'

'A couple of things. I want to know more about the place the hands were discovered—'

'Daisy House, the children's home?'

'I want to know why it was referenced in Operation Pharaoh.'

'Right,'

'Plus I have a misper to look into for the coroner.'

'Misper?'

'Missing person. What are they teaching you in the academy these days, Oliver?'

'Not a lot, according to Chief Inspector Holloway.'

'Ignore him. There's always idiots like him in the force, continually finding fault with others because it's easier than helping them. Let's meet up at Stretford nick tomorrow at eleven a.m. to check progress? I have to meet a family in the morning.'

Davis glanced down Oxford Road. 'Fancy a pint? I'm sure there's a pub round here.'

'Sorry, I can't. The daughter is waiting for me at home. You married?'

'Nah, got a steady girlfriend though. A PC in Wythenshawe.'

'At least she understands the life.'

'But trying to co-ordinate shifts is a bastard.'

'Right, I'd better be off, otherwise I'll suffer the wrath of a twelve-year-old. Frankly, I'd rather have my nadgers strangled in vice.'

'See you tomorrow.'

'Do as much as you can before we meet. If necessary, I'll go back to Claire Trent and ask for more resource.'

'The head of MIT?'

'The one and only.'

'Bit of a dragon lady. Gave a speech at the academy about policing in the modern world. Scared the shit out of all of us. Apparently computers are going to be more important than coppers in the future.'

'Don't you believe it. Somebody has to actually take down the villains and I've yet to see a laptop chase after and collar a thug running away through a Salford housing estate.'

Davis looked at the list he had written down in his notebook and frowned. 'Holloway also wants a report on the post mortem on his desk at nine a.m. too.'

'Welcome to the world of coppering, Oliver. Nobody said it was going to be easy.'

'Nobody said it was going to be this hard either.'

Ridpath patted him on the shoulder. 'See you at eleven tomorrow. Do what you can before then.'

Oliver Davis nodded. 'One more thing. What you said to the pathologist about this being a serial killer. Were you serious?'

Ridpath shook his head. 'I don't know, Oliver, I just don't know. Maybe it's something worse.'

'What's worse than a serial killer?'

'Two serial killers. But then again, it could be a medical student with an incredibly warped sense of humour.'

'How will we know?'

'We do the work, Oliver. We just do the work.'

Chapter 19

Patricia Patterson slumped down in the armchair, kicking off her shoes.

'Tired, love?'

'Knackered. Do you know what it's like dealing with the council? First, they haven't any money to do anything. Second, what money they did have has been spent during the pandemic. And third, people don't stop getting old and disabled just because some bloody virus decides it wants to screw around with the world.'

Her partner, Cherie Morgan, passed her a well-filled glass of white wine.

'Exactly what I needed.' She took a large swallow. 'And I had another fight with the DWP. You know the bastards have stopped Isobel Lloyd's benefits because she missed an appointment? The poor woman can't walk to the end of the road, yet they expect her to hop on a bus and travel five miles into the centre of town for an interview. I made them reconsider the decision and I'll take the bastards to the tribunal if they don't reinstate her benefits immediately. Bastards.'

Cherie sat down next to her. 'Keep fighting, Pat.'

'I will, but it's so bloody draining. What's for tea?'

'Lamb curry. I used the leftovers from the weekend.'

'Smells great. Kids with their dad?'

Cherie nodded. 'It's their week with him. I hope he woke them up in time for school.'

'You missing them already?'

'Yeah, but it's what we agreed. He's not a bad father, just a shit husband. It means we have a week to ourselves for a change. What do you fancy doing?'

'Anything, as long as it's far away from the council and the DWP.'

'How about going to Holcombe Top in Ramsbottom? We haven't been out for ages. We'd have to sit outside, but anything to get out of the bloody house.'

'Yeah, lovely, you want to make a reservation?'

As Pat finished speaking her phone buzzed with a new message.

Cherie sighed. 'That bloody phone. One day, I'll chuck it down the toilet where it belongs. Anyway, I'll get the curry, you relax.' She rose and walked to the kitchen.

Pat glanced at the message.

We need to meet.

The social worker's face went an ashen white.

'Who is it?' Cherie shouted from the kitchen.

'Nowt, just work.'

Pat glanced at the text again.

We need to meet.

She'd been expecting this message for a long time.

Chapter 20

Ridpath stared at his computer, the words blurring. He read the Ryder files and the search history Sophia had sent him. There were no documents relating to Jane Ryder after 2009.

He had been at it since nine o'clock, ever since Eve had gone to bed.

She'd come back exactly on time at 6.30, carrying her heavy school bag and complaining about her friends. 'You know they just don't get it. Blackpink is so much cooler than BTS, but they prefer the boys.'

'I seem to remember you liked BTS too.'

'That was years ago, Dad, when I was still a kid.'

He stood up, stretched and climbed the stairs to check her light was off. He opened the door a couple of inches, peering round to see her fast asleep, the night light gently illuminating her features.

He always loved watching his daughter sleep, her face peaceful and calm, her arms wrapped around a rabbit her mother had given her after she was born.

At her back lay a stuffed dog he'd bought her for Christmas. A tough time for both of them, when Polly's absence was felt the most. He did his best to inject some joy, dressing up as Santa Claus on Christmas morning and cooking what almost resembled a Christmas lunch complete with overcooked sprouts, dry turkey, burnt roast potatoes and oily gravy. Desert was much better. He could hardly go wrong with microwaved mince tarts and custard from Marks and Sparks.

For Christmas he gave her three new BTS posters, a voucher for H&M, a new pair of cool trainers (at least he thought they were cool), the latest album from Blackpink and another shopping voucher for Claire's. He knew the vouchers were pretty weak, but at least she could get something she really wanted.

She'd done her best to be excited, getting him a new Christmas jumper and a Montblanc pen for his notebook with money she had saved from her allowance. After lunch and the Queen's Speech, they had played Monopoly as they always did on Christmas Day, but the third player was missing.

Polly.

Her absence a massive gap in both their lives.

It was on Boxing Day that Eve spoke to him, her face dark and brooding.

'Dad, you know what I'm most afraid of?'

'Spiders? Heights? Homework?' he joked, trying to lighten the mood.

'I'm most afraid of forgetting Mum. What she looked like, what she smelt like and even what it felt like to hug her.'

So that morning, they had created a memory box together using an old vanity case. She chose what she put inside: her mum's lucky green jumper she always wore when Ofsted inspected the school. A bottle of her perfume, half used and still redolent of Polly. A bright red lipstick, the end shaped by Polly's lips. Her whistle from school when she prowled around the playground, watching over her charges. A drawing Eve had made of her mum when she was five – a child's drawing, but the likenesses still there. And, finally, a picture of all three of them, taken when they had visited London in the year before Polly's death.

'It's like she'll be with us forever now,' said Eve, placing the box next to her bed, 'it's the best Christmas present ever, Dad.'

Afterwards, both of them decided to visit her grave at Stretford Cemetery. In front of the headstone, Eve arranged the flowers, and without any sense of embarrassment, told her mum of the time they had both had since she had died. Of the lockdowns and Covid and living with her grandparents and the new house and her new school.

Her mum didn't reply, but Ridpath knew she was listening.

Somewhere.

Afterwards, he had taken Eve to stay with her grandparents for the New Year and he was left alone.

Not really alone, though. He still had his memories to keep him warm at night when the temperature dropped and frost rimed the garden.

It was all he had left now.

Memories.

He shook his head, closed the door and went back downstairs to his waiting computer.

He opened the history of Daisy House he had found on a blog. Dave Connor had most of the details correct, from its construction to its final closure as a children's home in 2006. He'd correlated this information with the details of Operation Pharaoh. The police operation had been clinical in its examination of Daisy House, indicating the place had witnessed widespread abuse with physical, mental and sexual torture of the young inmates. Jimmy Saville had been a regular visitor, even shooting one of his *Jim'll Fix It* programmes there. A predator lurking amongst the most vulnerable in society.

Some of the children had received compensation, up to £15,000, from Manchester Council, but nothing could compensate for a childhood lost. Many had gone straight from the children's home to a life of crime. Others had become dependent on drink or drugs, using narcotics to forget the anger of the past. Yet more had simply bottled up their abuse, hiding it deep within their souls like an incubus ready and waiting to hatch.

He remembered a quote he had read somewhere: 'Every childhood lasts a lifetime.' Such simple words, but with such a profound meaning. Would Eve's childhood trauma affect her in later years?

He would do whatever it took to make sure it didn't.

The clock above the mantle chimed. It was midnight already, where had the time gone? He shivered, the room was getting cold. He'd set the central heating timer to go off at eleven p.m.; no sense in wasting money heating an empty room.

He switched off his laptop. It was time to climb the stairs to bed. For a nanosecond, he thought about pouring a glass of Macallan to help him sleep, but decided against it. The brain had to be clear for tomorrow's meeting with the Ryders.

In the middle of the room, he stopped and listened to the joists creaking as if a ghost walked across the ceiling. However, his rational mind knew it was only them cooling and contracting.

His rational mind also told him he was going to spend another night alone.

That was harder to bear, much harder.

WEDNESDAY

Chapter 21

The following morning, Ridpath dropped Eve off at school and continued on to the Ryders' home.

Sophia was waiting for him outside the semi-detached house in Sale; classic English 1930s suburbia complete with carefully tended gardens beginning to show the signs of spring

'I checked with the DVLA, the electoral register and the registrar of births, marriages and deaths and there is no record of any Jane Ryder applying for a driving licence, registering for an election or getting married, giving birth or dying. Not a sausage. It's as if she never existed, Ridpath.'

'Great, Sophia. I still haven't received any misper files from Chrissy. I'll follow up with her when I'm at HQ later.'

'Misper?'

'Sorry, police jargon. Missing person. But let's not use it with these people. OK?'

'Right.'

He opened the wooden gate and walked up the drive,knocking on the door. It was immediately answered by a grey haired, dapper man wearing a cardigan complete with a moss-green knitted tie. The house was warm, as if the central heating was set for winter rather than spring.

'Is it Mr Ridpath from the coroner's office?'

Ridpath flashed his ID. 'And this is one of our officers, Sophia Rahman.'

'The wife is waiting in the parlour for you.'

Such an old-fashioned word, 'parlour', but it perfectly described the room kept for best by the old couple. The wallpaper had the dominant tone of brown, a cupboard filled with china cups and knick-knacks stood in one corner, and a flock of china ducks soared above an old-fashioned tiled fireplace. Inside, a seventies gas fire added to the heat.

An old woman sat in the corner, surrounded by balls of knitting, a cat lying across her lap.

'The wife won't get up. Her knees, you know.'

Ridpath smiled. 'Good morning, Mrs Ryder.'

'Are you the man from the council?'

'Maureen, this is Mr Ridpath from the coroner's office. He's here about Jane.'

'Have they found her?'

'Not yet.'

The woman smiled and went back to her knitting.

'She hasn't been right since Jane left. And now the drugs for the cancer, well, they don't make her feel well.'

'I understand completely, Mr Ryder.'

'Do you want to sit down, Mr Ridpath and Miss Rahman? I'll make us some tea.'

'Don't bother on my account, Mr Ryder.'

'It's no bother, it's time for morning tea anyway.'

He vanished, leaving Ridpath and Sophia alone with the woman and the clack, clack, clack of her knitting needles. The detective sat down on the couch, joined by Sophia. He pulled out his notebook and, as he did so, noticed a framed picture on a side table of a young girl, nearly a woman, wearing school uniform and jumping in the air with joy.

'That's Jane on the day she finished her GCSEs.' She continued knitting as she spoke, the ends of the needles whirring in a blur of pink and white wool. 'I'm making a jumper for her when she gets back. She always suffers when the weather gets cold. Well, children do, don't they?'

'They do.'

'Do you have children, Mr...?'

'Ridpath. I have a daughter, aged twelve.'

'It must be nice to have a daughter. You know, I used to think—'

She stopped speaking as her husband re-entered the room carrying a tray of tea things. 'We only have Eccles cakes, garibaldi biscuits and a few Hobnobs, I'm afraid. We haven't been shopping this week. Friday is shopping day.'

'Don't worry.' Ridpath smiled. 'You had me at Eccles cakes.'

Mr Ryder poured the tea, passing china cups to Ridpath and Sophia, placing a thick, currant-filled round of flaky pastry on a small plate for each person.

Through mouthfuls of crumbs, Ridpath asked, 'Tell me about your daughter's disappearance.'

'It was a Friday, June 12, 2009. I remember the date as if it was yesterday. She'd asked us if she could go to a festival with her two friends from school...'

'Which festival was it?'

'I don't know. Some music festival, I think. She loved her music, did Jane, a pair of headphones always clamped to her ears when she was studying. She'd done so well in her exams so we promised a little treat and she asked us to pay for the ticket. I remember it cost fifty-five quid, not cheap, I'll tell you.'

All this time, his wife was knitting away furiously, not reacting to his words.

'Shouldn't she have been at school?'

'She'd just finished her exams.' He paused for a moment, swallowing slowly. 'The results came through after she disappeared. We found out afterwards, she got three A* and the rest As and Bs. She was a clever girl, Jane.'

'Which school did she go to?' Sophia asked.

'Sale School. She did well there, loved it.'

Ridpath nodded. 'What time did she leave on the morning she disappeared?'

'Around ten a.m.' For the first time, he began to show signs of emotion, his voice beginning to break. 'I said goodbye to her, told her to be careful, and we never saw her again.'

For a second, the wife stopped knitting and then carried on even faster, if that was possible.

'And her friends, did they call round for her?'

He shook his head. 'She said she was meeting them outside. Of course, when she didn't return by Monday, we went round to their houses, but they hadn't gone to the festival at all.'

Ridpath frowned. 'Why did you wait until Monday?'

'She'd told us she was going to camp there and come back on Sunday evening. We were worried, but thought she might have missed a bus or something.'

'She didn't ring you?'

Mr Ryder shook his head. 'She didn't take her phone, said it wouldn't work at the festival.' A long pause. 'We haven't heard a word from her since the day she left.'

Ridpath made a note in his book. 'The friends? Do you remember their names?'

'Rose Gray and Andrea Briggs. Rose was a lovely girl, Jane's best friend. Andrea was about two years younger.' Mr Ryder laughed as he remembered. 'She always looked up to Jane, followed her around like a sick puppy. They're both probably married now.'

'Don't worry, we can find them even if they've changed their names after marriage.'

There was a long pause as Mr Ryder stared out into mid-air. 'You know what was the worst, Mr Ridpath?'

The detective stayed silent.

'I used to see them out on the street in their school uniforms afterwards. I watched them grow older, even saw them with their first boyfriends. My daughter, my Jane, never had that. She never had that joy.'

Tears filled his eyes. Once again, his wife stopped knitting, looked at him for second and carried on without saying a word.

'So she didn't return from the festival and you reported her as a missing person to the police.'

He nodded. 'We went to her friends first and rang the police station on Monday afternoon.'

'If you don't mind me asking again, as I want to understand, why did you wait so long before reporting it?'

Mr Ryder glanced across at his wife and sighed loudly, looking down at the cup of tea in his hands. 'She'd spent weekends away before.'

Ridpath put down his empty plate. Sophia was scribbling notes in her pad.

The old man continued speaking, not looking at either of the coroner's officers. 'Twice before. But she always came home on Sunday evening. It was when she wasn't back by noon on Monday that we became worried.'

'You say she disappeared before?'

'Only for a couple of days each time. We thought it was just the way girls were at the time. Life has changed since myself and Maureen first married.'

'She was still underage. Did she tell you where she had been?'

'Didn't say anything. Of course, we asked her, but she didn't want to talk about it, said she'd been with her friends.'

'Girls these days are different, aren't they?' Mrs Ryder interrupted the interview without stopping knitting. 'Too much freedom, if you ask me. I blame the television. We didn't like Jane watching TV.'

A catch in Mr Ryder's voice. 'Perhaps I should have chastised her more, told her it mustn't happen again, but she was doing so well at school and I loved her so much...'

His voice trailed off.

Ridpath waited a few seconds before asking, 'So you made a police report?'

'The sergeant at the station was very nice. He asked me to fill in a form and I did. He said she'd probably met somebody at the festival and would come back soon. But she never did. She never did.'

'What else did you do?'

'Well, I rang them again that evening and the police came round the next day. A constable this time.'

'Do you remember his name?'

Mr Ryder looked confused, as if trying to remember. 'It escapes me. I filled in more forms and he checked out her room.

They returned a couple of times, but said they had heard nothing from her. Neither had we, not even a postcard. We know she would have sent us a postcard if she could. Just to let us know she was OK.'

'You received nothing? No communication at all?'

He shook his head. 'I even put up posters around here and in the park, but nothing came of it. I can show you Jane's room, if you like. We kept it exactly how she left it. One day she would come back...' Again his voice broke.

'I'd like to see it, if I may. Sophia, you stay here with Mrs Ryder.'

'Will do, Ridpath.'

Mr Ryder stood up. 'We'll be back in a moment, Maureen,' he said to his wife. She didn't look up.

They climbed the steep stairs slowly, Mr Ryder gripping the bannister.

'It's this way.' He pushed open the door. Inside the room there was the essence of teenage girl. Girls Aloud, Duffy and Chris Martin posters on the walls, a small dressing table with a few creams from Boots, a hairbrush and inexpensive make-up next to a square jewellery box. A single bed was pushed up against a wall and there was another table with books on it and a notepad open to a page with a pen resting on top.

'Like I said, we kept it exactly as she left it.'

'Do you mind if I take a look?'

Mr Ryder stepped back to allow Ridpath to enter. He put on a pair of plastic gloves and opened the box. Inside were a few items of costume jewellery, nothing expensive. He checked through the drawers, the usual teenager stuff. Socks, knickers, bras and T-shirts all separated neatly into different piles. He checked underneath and at the back. 'Do you know if she kept a diary?'

'I don't know. Maybe, but I never found one. I searched this place with the police after she disappeared, hoping to find a clue to where she'd gone, but didn't find anything, no diary.'

'Speaking from experience, the room looks a bit tidy for a teenage girl.'

'My wife may have tidied it up. She wanted it to be perfect for when Jane returned.'

Ridpath checked under the bed and beneath the pillows. Nothing.

He flicked through the books on her desk: *Romeo and Juliet*, *Wuthering Heights*, *Far From the Madding Crowd*, *To Kill a Mockingbird*. Each had been annotated in a small, crabbed hand. The English texts for her exams for the year, probably.

The wardrobe still had all her clothes hanging inside. Fabrics from a different time and era. 'Do you remember what she was wearing on the day she disappeared?'

'We gave a description to the police. A red and white striped top and a pair of jeans with trainers.'

Ridpath nodded, taking one last look at the girl's bedroom. He noticed a picture on the wall. Eve didn't know he knew, but behind a picture in her room was where she kept her secrets; a love note written in crayon from a boy in her primary class, a badge and a ticket from a visit to the Beatles Museum in Liverpool, a dried flower from a day in the park. All things that mattered to Eve and nobody else.

He stepped forward and unhooked the picture, turning it around. The backing paper was peeling away on one side. He pulled it further and checked inside.

Nothing but a small corner of paper. Had there been something there before, and it was removed? 'Did you take anything from the room?'

Mr Ryder looked down at his feet and mumbled an answer. 'I don't think so.'

Ridpath placed the picture back on the hook, talking one last look round the room. 'I think I've seen enough, Mr Ryder, thank you for your time.'

'My wife, Mr Ridpath, she's not right at the moment. It's the drugs she's taking for her cancer.'

'I was told she has a form of leukaemia.'

'It's aggressive, according to the doctors. She doesn't have long, so they are only managing the pain.'

'That's why you asked the coroner to grant a presumption of death certificate?'

'She wants everything sorted before she goes. The insurance, the house, our wills. My wife was a teacher, she was always organised.'

'I understand Mr Ryder. It's why I'm here.'

'What will you do next?'

'I'll check the police Missing Persons file and then I'll meet the police involved in your case. We have to arrange for them to testify at the inquest into your daughter's disappearance.'

'When will that be?'

'It's up to the coroner, but soon, I'm sure. We have to affirm your daughter—' he paused for a second, searching for the words '—is no longer with us. After the coroner has heard the evidence, she will decide if a presumption of death certificate can be issued.'

He nodded once. 'It's time to get it over and done with. My wife needs peace of mind before she dies.'

They went back down the stairs and into the parlour. Ridpath spotted the picture on the table and asked, 'Could I borrow this?'

'Please return it, though, it's all we have left of her. A picture. Not much, is it?'

'It's time to go, Sophia.'

His assistant stood up, placing her empty cup on the table. 'Goodbye, Mrs Ryder.'

The woman didn't look up from her knitting.

As Ridpath was leaving, he thought of one more question. 'Forgive me for asking, but you are both in your seventies, correct?'

'My wife is seventy-four and I'm seventy-one. I was her toy boy.'

'It seems quite old to have a child of Jane's age.'

'Jane came to us late in our lives, Mr Ridpath. She was our present from God.'

Chapter 22

On the way to their respective cars, Ridpath asked immediately, 'Did Mrs Ryder say anything when he were upstairs?'

'Not a lot, she carried on knitting, but…'

'But what?'

'Did you feel something wasn't right about the house? I dunno, but it felt more like a prison than a family home.'

'Interesting. I wonder if Jane Ryder felt the same way too?'

'And Mrs Ryder, well, she's a bit strange, Ridpath, like she's not really there. I mean, my mum's weird, but Mrs Ryder makes her look like Josephine Normal.'

'She's on drugs and, let me tell you from experience, nobody is normal when they're on those things.'

'I guess you're right. It's just…'

They reached Ridpath's car. 'Right, Sophia. We have to follow up.'

'What do you need me to do?'

He passed the picture he had been given across to his assistant. 'First, make copies of this. We need to put a face to the missing girl, particularly when we're interviewing people.'

'You said "we" – does it mean you need me to come along too?'

'As much as you can. Officially, I'm assisting you this time. Seems to be the story of my life at the moment.'

'I quite like the idea of having you as my assistant. Does that mean you get the coffees from now on?'

'Don't bet on it. Second, which festival did she go to?'

'Mrs Ryder couldn't remember. But it should be easy to google.'

'Problem is, we don't even know if she went to the festival, or was ever planning to go. It may only have been a ruse to escape her parents.'

'I know the feeling. I bet her school friends used to cover for her. That's what mine did.'

'You ran away?'

'No, but I wanted to meet people without my parents knowing. Paula and I had a mutual support society. If parents rang up, we were always meeting soon.'

'Did it work?'

'Yeah. Particularly as Paula was seen by my parents as a goody-two-shoes girly swot and I was seen by her parents as a quiet, subservient Muslim girl. If only they had known the truth about both of us...'

'Seems like Jane may have had the same scam going on. Her friends were called Rose Gray and Andrea Briggs. It was only after Jane disappeared that they admitted they didn't go to the festival together.'

'Obvs.'

'Can you find out where they are and check their stories? We'll decide later if we need them to testify at the inquest.'

'They could be anywhere, Ridpath. It's been nearly twelve years.'

'I know, but I'm sure you can find them.'

'OK, any last address?'

'I'll message you later. It may be in the misper files.'

'Right. Anything else?'

'Can you follow up with her school too?'

'OK, will do.'

'See if any teachers remember her. I'd like to know about her state of mind around that time. Any problems the teachers noticed? Unhappiness? Academic problems? Friends?'

'Mr Ryder said she'd just finished her GCSEs,' Sophia reminded Ridpath.

'Was it a factor? Mr Ryder said she passed with good grades. She will have sat all of the papers, but the results wouldn't have come out until the end of August. Find out if the teachers thought she had done well.'

'Teachers never know the truth. She will have talked to her friends Rose Gray and Andrea Briggs though. It's all we ever talked about. What grades we were going to get? What questions did or didn't come up? How to answer each particular topic?'

'Stressful?'

'Through the roof. I was a wreck. My mum started cooking chicken soup for me to drink as I studied. Even today, the smell of chicken soup brings back nightmares.'

'You did OK, though?'

'But thousands didn't. You should have seen some girls on the day the results came out. It was as if their lives had been wrecked by one stupid piece of paper.'

'Might be an angle worth following up. She was an only child, perhaps the parents put too much pressure on her and she did a runner?'

'But if that happened, why did she never go back?'

'There, Sophia, is the sixty-four-thousand-dollar question. Why did she never go back? What happened to her?'

'What's your hunch, Ridpath?'

'No hunches.' He stared into mid-air. 'But she was a young, pretty sixteen-year-old on her own, as far as we know, maybe at a festival or maybe on the streets, perhaps in a vulnerable state...'

'Perfect prey for any predator.'

A long silence.

'When I get the misper files from Chrissy, I'll send you them. We're going to have to put something together for the coroner well before next week.'

'But that's only a few days away?'

'I didn't set the timing, Sophia. You'd better get working.'

'Mrs Challinor said you were working another case for MIT.'

He nodded. 'It's not straightforward either.'

'Let me know if you need any help.'

He smiled. 'You have enough to be working on.'

'Anything to stay away from the house at the moment.'

'The mother?'

'She wants to introduce me to a friend of a friend's son. Problem is, he doesn't speak much English and my Urdu is probably as good as yours, Ridpath.'

'Love always finds a way.'

'Don't take the piss, Ridpath, it's what my mum says.'

He picked up his briefcase. 'Call me tonight.' He made the sign of a mobile phone against his face. As he did so, his real mobile phone rang. It was Dave Connor.

'Hi Ridpath, Hannah rang me. She wants us to go to the lab, she's found something.'

Chapter 23

'You not going in?'

Patricia Patterson was lounging around the kitchen, nursing a cup of coffee.

'Nah, thought I'd give it a miss. Can't handle the idiots any more.'

Cherie sat down beside her. 'You know we need the money. What with me furloughed, your job is the only thing keeping our heads above water.'

Pat leant forward and gently kissed her partner on the lips. 'Don't worry, I know I'm the only one keeping you in PG Tips.'

'And sausage rolls, don't forget them.'

'How can anybody forget sausage rolls?' She sat back, playing with the handle of her coffee mug. 'It's just… sometimes it's hard to keep going. Keep banging your head against the brick wall, knowing the same shit is going to keep floating to the surface. Nothing ever gets done. I feel like I'm sticking plasters over the wounds rather than ever fixing anything.'

'You've only just realised?'

She shook her head. 'I've known it for a long time. But sometimes, the ugly truth rises up and decides to kick my head in.'

Her partner began washing the breakfast plates. 'Why don't you call in sick and I'll make us some chicken soup? I'll even nip down to Greggs for a few sausage rolls.'

Pat smiled as an idea flashed into her mind. 'Why don't we move somewhere new, get away from all this?'

'Where would we go?'

'I don't know. Ireland, or the north of Scotland. Anywhere to get away.'

'And what about the kids? Danny has his exams next year, you know he wants to go on to sixth-form college, and Holly is more settled than she's ever been. And there's all the Covid bollocks.'

'I know. Only a thought, a dream.'

Pat's mobile phone rang. She sat there for a long while.

'Aren't you going to answer it? Could be important.'

Slowly, Pat pressed the answer key.

A voice on the other end. 'We need to talk.'

Pat stood up and strode out of the kitchen, up the stairs to her private office, closing the door behind her.

'You said you would never call me.'

'I lied. Something has come up, we need to meet.'

'I can't, I have to go to work.'

'Call in sick.'

'I can't.'

'You must, don't make me tell them.'

Pat's shoulders collapsed. She slumped down in the chair in front of her desk.

'Where?'

'Somewhere quiet, Davyhulme Millenium car park overlooking the Ship Canal. Do you know it?'

'Yeah. When?'

'Let's say eleven.'

'This will be the last time?'

'I promise.'

Pat clicked off the call. She wished she'd never become involved with them. She covered her eyes with her hands and began to sob quietly.

Chapter 24

Ridpath waved goodbye to Sophia and slipped behind the wheel. 'What did she say, Dave?'

'Not a lot. Just said she wanted to show us something at her lab.'

'Where is it?'

'In Manchester Science Park, close to Oxford Road.'

'I know it. I can be there in thirty minutes, I'm in Sale now.'

'Can you pick me up from Stretford nick on the way?'

'So I'm a bloody taxi driver, am I?'

'You've been promoted, Ridpath. I'll wait outside on Talbot Road for you. Holloway is still on the warpath, pissed Claire Trent refuses to release more resource to him.'

'He's right, Dave. We need more warm bodies. I'm meeting with her at noon to go over the case, I'll see if we can get some help. Did DC Davis tell you about the post-mortem last night?'

'Mr Goody-two-shoes presented a typed report to myself and Holloway at nine a.m. Holloway was as happy as a Bury black pudding on a bacon roll. That lad will go far if he can keep it up. I'll give you a copy of his notes when you pick me up. But I have some bad news.'

'Go on.'

'Holloway has taken him off the case temporarily to look into a series of burglaries in Urmston.'

'You're joking.'

'I wish I was. We'll get him back tomorrow.'

Ridpath shook his head. No wonder Holloway was desperate for more resource. 'Anything from the canvas of the local area?'

'Nothing except the usual rumours and gossip. Apparently, it's haunted by the ghost of a young boy who died there.'

'Is that why the film crew went?'

'Probably. Bloodsuckers, all of them. Anyway, other than a few complaints to the council about druggies using it, nobody saw anything.'

'Shame. And the film crew?'

'They've all signed statements. We checked up on them. None of them have records, all clean as whistle, except one is banned from driving for DUI.'

'Which one?'

'The presenter, Ian Rodgers, caught pissed as a newt driving on the A6.'

'He's obviously one for the spirits.'

'Boom, boom. See you in ten minutes.'

The phone clicked off and Ridpath went through his messages. One from Mrs Challinor.

How were the family?

He typed using one index finger.

In the office this afternoon. Will update you.

He always envied his daughter, whose texting was a blur of fingers and sometimes toes.

The next message was from Claire Trent.

Don't be late for the noon meeting.

He was about to text back saying the more time he spent texting the later he would be, but decided it would not be a good idea. Better to be on time.

The last text was from Eve.

Love you Dad

Followed by three emojis: a dancing heart, a smiley face and an ape picking its nose. He checked the time. Seconds after he had dropped her off at school this morning.

He texted back.

Love you too, Eve.

He was hopeless at emojis so he just added a small smiley face as it was the easiest to do. She wouldn't see the text till after school, but at least it would be waiting for her.

He checked the time on his phone. Time to pick up Dave Connor.

He needed twenty more hours in each day.

Chapter 25

Patricia Patterson drove along the M60, exiting opposite the Trafford Centre at Junction 10 towards Urmston. She hadn't come this way for a long time, at least two years, avoiding the area like the plague.

She stopped at the lights and remembered to switch off her phone. The council had installed a safety app on it to track her when she was off-site. The last thing she wanted today was stupid questions from those idiots about her whereabouts.

The lights turned green and she took a right along Davyhulme Road, past Trafford General and the golf course. A long time ago she had spent happy days there, nicking golf balls and selling them back to the members.

Now she resented the existence of a golf course in the middle of a built-up area when it should have been a public park, open to all.

Sod 'em.

Her bottom lip curled over the top. How was she going to handle this meeting?

Play dumb?

No, be yourself, be aggressive. The bastards have had enough from you over the years, they can't give you any more grief. She'd done what they asked, again and again and again.

No more.

She had Cherie and the kids to think of now. She hated lying to Cherie, telling her she was going to work and instead coming to this meeting, but she had to sort it out, get it over and done with.

For the first time in her life she felt vaguely happy with a partner. Not in a Mary Poppins sort of way, but she looked forward to going home in the evening, being with Cherie.

Home. Now there was a word she didn't use often.

She turned right into the Millennium car park.

Another car was already there. They were waiting for her. The rest of the spaces were empty.

It was quiet. Too quiet.

Two people got out and walked towards her car.

'Hiya, Pat, long time no see.'

'What do you want?'

'Don't be like that.'

'I told you never to call me at home. I don't want to worry Cherie.'

'Always thinking of others. Let's go for a walk, shall we?'

'No, just tell me what you want, let's get it over and done with. I can piss off home and you can piss off to your little rats' nest.'

'That's not a pleasant way to talk about the place you lived for five years, is it?'

'You call that living?'

'It's what we do. At least step out of the car so I don't have to bend down to speak to you all the time. My back is killing me.'

Patricia opened the driver-side door and started to climb out of the car.

She didn't see the needle as it was jabbed into the top of her arm, but she felt the pain almost immediately.

A pair of arms encircled her neck, pulling her upright.

She tried to push away, kicking backwards with her shoes against shins, striking hard and hearing a sharp scream of pain.

But another pair of arms was pushing her back across the top of the car. She felt a hand thrust into her neck. Her arms were weak; she could hardly lift them up to strike her attacker's face.

'Shhh, sleep now, Pat, you know you want to sleep. Shhhhhhh.'

The warm blackness engulfed her mind, her bones became jelly and she slumped down with her back resting against the car.

'Still got fight left in her,' said one of the attackers.

'Pat always did. Shame she lost her anger at the world and what it did to her.'

Chapter 26

The forensics lab was in a modern office block close to Manchester University. Hannah greeted them both at the door and ushered them through to the secure facility.

The green striped backpack Ridpath had last seen at the children's home was sitting on a lightbox table in the middle of the room. Around it, technicians worked, staring through microscopes, adjusting sampling slides, standing over centrifuges spinning loudly.

'Right, we've had a look at the backpack and we've come up with a few points of interest. Firstly, the pack itself is pretty distinctive – luckily it's not one of your common or garden ones like Jansport, used by millions of kids.'

'I've never seen one like it,' said Ridpath.

'It's because only six hundred were produced. As the large logo says, it was manufactured as a limited edition by CLAK in 2009. The factory is in Leicester and they are still operating today.' She passed the contact details to Ridpath. 'I'll leave it to your team to follow up.'

'Team?' sneered Dave Connor. 'You're looking at it.' He pointed at Ridpath and himself.

'Shall I continue?'

'Please, Hannah, give us some good news.'

'Good news coming up. There was nothing in the main pocket of the bag, but in one of the side pockets, hidden behind the plastic lining, we found this.' From beneath the table, she produced a picture of a small stub with a frayed end stained brown. The scale next to the object showed it was just less than one centimetre in length.

'What is it?' asked Dave Connor.

'It's the end of a joint. A roach.'

The crime scene manager smiled. 'Right first time, Ridpath. It's a rolled-up piece of paper, I'd say 110gsm. We tested it for DNA and then we opened it up.' She produced another picture, again with a scale. It was a piece of orange paper four centimetres long and less than one centimetre wide. 'It seems to have been torn from a flyer of some sort.'

Ridpath could make out the beginnings of printed words at the side, but they were very faded. 'It looks like an M, then an F, the rest is too faded to see. There seems to be drawing of some kind at the bottom.'

'We have one of our forensic document investigators on it at the moment to see if we can find the source material. I'll get back to you as soon as I can.'

'How are you going to be able to see anything?' asked Dave Connor.

'We'll use the VSC.'

'What's one of those when it's at home?'

'Using different wavelengths of light, a video spectral comparator can reveal writing or printing which has faded over time. We process and enhance the result to appear far darker and, hopefully, more legible.'

'When will you know?'

'As soon as Mike has finished the work.'

'But when?'

'When he's finished,' Hannah emphasised.

'Did you find anything else?' interrupted Ridpath before the crime scene manager totally lost the plot with Dave Connor.

'Nothing, it was clean as a whistle.'

'Any fingerprints on the backpack?'

'None. Whoever placed it in the larder was wearing gloves, or was careful enough not to leave any trace of themselves.'

Ridpath thought of a question. 'Any DNA on the roach?'

'Great minds think alike, Ridpath. We're trying to process it, but we're not hopeful of a result.'

'Why?' asked Dave Connor.

Hannah sighed loudly, as if she had explained this a thousand times to a thousand different detectives. 'There are four steps in DNA processing: extraction, quantitation, amplification and capillary electrophoresis. We've done this first, which is extraction. The lab technicians are now seeing if the DNA has been contaminated and if enough can be extracted to provide a viable result.'

'Contaminated?'

'It's sat in the bottom of backpack on the end of a roach for countless years; mould, damp, heat or any of a hundred other environmental factors may have degraded the DNA.'

'Right.' Dave Connor scratched his head. 'When will we know?'

'A couple of days.'

'What about the DNA and the fingerprints from the hands?'

'A different set of problems. They were immersed in an embalming liquid with the following chemical composition.' She checked her notes. 'Twenty-two per cent formaldehyde, forty-three per cent methanol and eight per cent glutaraldehyde. The rest is water and fragrant oils.'

'And this helps us how?' asked Dave Connor.

'Different manufacturers use differing quantities of chemicals in their embalming liquids. We should be able to find out who made the stuff our hands were swimming in.'

Dave Connor frowned. 'Right, all gobbledygook to me.'

Hannah continued. 'And because they were immersed in an embalming liquid; we're having to use a special technique to extract the DNA.'

'Special technique?'

'Formaldehyde causes DNA damage, chemical modifications and degradation, thereby reducing the quantity and quality of DNA available for downstream genetic analyses. However, DNA can be obtained from embalmed nail samples using the QIAamp FFPE, quantified using the QuantiFilerTrio and genotyped using the GlobalFiler®PCR Amplification. Do you really want me to spend the next hour explaining to you the details of these processes?'

'No, thanks.' Both Ridpath and Connor spoke at the same time.

'Suffice to say, we may be able to get DNA from the nails even though they were embalmed.'

'Great, when can we have the results?' asked Dave Connor.

'It takes time. We also have the nail scrapings from the post-mortem to handle, plus the fingerprints from the hands. Do you know how difficult it is to identify people when all you have are the hands?'

'I know, but we're up against the clock too.'

'A couple of days, maybe earlier, I should have something.'

'You're a star, Hannah.'

'But I'm not promising, Ridpath, so don't try to butter me up.'

'No, but you're the best, Hannah. I'm sure you'll get us the results as soon as you can.'

'You're such a bullshitter, Ridpath, but I'll do my best. Now, if you have no other questions, get out of here and let me do my job.'

Chapter 27

'It's a bugger, Ridpath.'

'I know, Dave.'

'I mean, how are we supposed to deal with a case when the only clues we have are three embalmed hands and an old backpack?'

They were walking out of the Science Park building and crossing Lloyd Street to get to Ridpath's car. 'It's going to be difficult, Dave, but I'm meeting Claire Trent in half an hour and I'm going to try to get more resource for us.'

'We could do with some help. I've got Holloway breathing down my neck on costs and asking when are we going to get a result. At the same time, he takes away my DC for a day to work on a bloody burglary.' He shook his head.

'Nothing we can do yet, Dave. The real work will start once we get DNA and fingerprints back from the lab. At least we'll know whose hands they were.'

'They might not be on NDNAD.'

'If they are not on the National DNA database, we try others, like the Vulnerable Persons or Missing Persons DNA database.'

'What if they are foreigners?'

'I don't know, Dave. After Brexit we don't have access to SIS or PRUM any more.'

'What are they?'

'Haven't you been keeping up, Dave?'

'I'm two years off retirement, Ridpath, give me a break. I need this case like I need a new arsehole.'

'They are EU police reporting and DNA sharing schemes. We don't have access any more.'

'So if any of the hands used to belong to a foreigner, there's nothing we can do?'

'We have to go through "channels".' Ridpath made two marks with his fingers. What used to take a couple of days could now take a couple of months. 'Let's hope we don't need to check.'

They were passing the Ducie Arms. The early drinkers were already sitting outside in the spring sunshine enjoying a pint.

Dave Connor licked his lips. 'Fancy a quick one?'

'And walk in to see the boss reeking of beer?'

'It was an idea, Ridpath, no need to go all Salvation Army on me.'

'Listen, Dave, unless I can get us more resource, we are going to be stuffed on this investigation. I gave a list of things for Oliver Davis to do. Any progress on checking with local hospitals, universities, funeral homes and labs? We need to know if any human hands have gone missing recently.'

'I haven't heard anything other than his report on the post-mortem. Do you want me to ring him? He's somewhere in the dark heart of Urmston at the moment.'

'What about finding reports of bodies without hands using HOLMES?'

The detective shook his head again. 'I know nothing.' Dave Connor did a passable impression of Manuel from *Fawlty Towers*.

'Jesus, Dave, you're supposed to know what's going on in the investigation. You're the SIO.'

'Sorry.' He stopped for a moment. 'There's too much to do and too little time to do it. Do you get there feeling everybody is watching, waiting for us to fail? Or is it just me being paranoid?'

'No, it's not you being paranoid, I feel we're being set up, too.'

'We need more help, Ridpath.'

Ridpath sighed. 'I'll see if I can get it when I meet Claire Trent. In the meantime, start ringing around the local hospitals, universities and funeral parlours. OK? The first thing we have to do is check this isn't some enormous schoolboy prank.'

'OK. Will do.'

'I'll ask Chrissy to check HOLMES for us. See if any bodies have been found without hands anywhere in England or if other hands have been discovered. It's the best we can do until the DNA and fingerprints come through. I'll follow up myself on the backpack. Oliver can check on hand operations in the last twenty years.'

Dave Connor didn't answer, staring at a man sitting outside reading an early edition of the *Manchester Evening News*. 'Shit,' he said loudly, pointing to the newspaper headline.

Ridpath looked across. In big, black letters, the headline shouted:

THREE HUMAN HANDS FOUND IN MANCHESTER HOUSE

Chapter 28

'The shit has truly hit the fan, Ridpath.' She threw the newspaper down on the table in front of him. The large black headline stared out from the white paper.

He was sitting in front of Claire Trent. Turnbull was standing on his left, hands in his pockets.

'I've already had the acting chief constable on the phone, plus Chief Inspector Holloway spent an hour last night bellowing in my ear about our lack of support. He's not a fan of yours, Ridpath, how have you managed to piss him off so quickly?'

'It's what he's good at...' said Turnbull, smirking in Ridpath's direction.

'And this morning I've had Mrs Challinor on the phone telling me you are busy with an urgent job for her. Where were you this morning?'

'Interviewing the family of a girl who disappeared eleven years ago.'

'Not working our case?' Turnbull's smirk turned into a glare.

'Afterwards, I went to the see the crime scene manager with Dave Connor. Our case is complicated.'

'Why?' asked Claire Trent.

'The hands were embalmed—'

'Embalmed? Like at an undertakers? Who would do that?'

'Whoever removed the hands with a hacksaw in the first place.' Ridpath took a deep breath. 'Look, boss, we need more resource if we are going to get anywhere near cracking this.'

'We're already too stretched as it is, Ridpath. We have nobody extra to spare.'

Ridpath ignored Turnbull, speaking directly to Claire Trent. 'You know what distresses me most, boss?'

'Tell us, Ridpath,' said Turnbull.

The detective ignored him again. 'We keep referring to these objects as "hands". The truth is they are people. Three people who have been murdered and their limbs amputated. Possibly by a serial killer, or killers.'

'We don't know they were murdered.'

'The hands were removed about twenty-four hours after death and placed in a jar of embalming liquid. They once belonged to people, fathers or sons, mothers or daughters. We have a duty to investigate and find out who these people were and who removed their hands.'

Claire Trent stared into mid-air, past Ridpath's head.

'You have a right nerve coming in here and telling us about "duty".' Turnbull's face was turning bright red. 'It's your *duty* to solve this case.'

Ridpath ignored him. 'Boss, we need to find out who these people were.'

She nodded. 'Right, who do you want, Ridpath?'

'What?' shouted Turnbull.

'I only need Emily Parkinson and Chrissy Wright, boss, we work well together and with Dave Connor, I think we can crack it.'

Turnbull slammed the flat of his hand down on the desk. 'You can't have them, Ridpath, I need them for MIT's work.'

'Last time I looked I was in charge of MIT, Paul, and I will decide the allocation of resources. Emily and Chrissy are yours, Ridpath, for this case and this case only. You have them until Monday. If you haven't made any progress, we'll put this on the back burner and transfer it to the Cold Case Unit.'

'What? You're giving him resource we don't have?'

'I'm re-allocating resource working for me on my projects, Paul, it shouldn't affect your workload in any way.'

'But—'

She leant forward. 'Ridpath, I'd get working straight away, if I were you. You only have until Monday.'

Chapter 29

'Emily and Chrissy, could you join me in the situation room?'

Both women rose from their workstations and hurried over to join Ridpath.

'What is it?' asked Emily Parkinson.

He closed the door. 'We're on again, ladies.'

Emily rubbed her hands. 'Brilliant. What's the case?'

'The three hands found in a backpack in Daisy House Children's Home.'

'No more stats?'

'No more stats, Chrissy.'

She brought her hands together as if in prayer, looking up to the ceiling.

'But there is a problem.'

'I knew there was a catch.'

'We only have till Monday.'

'Well, we'd better get started.' Emily opened her pad. 'Brief away.'

Ridpath took them through the details of the case so far, including the evidence from the pathologist and the crime scene manager. 'So what do you think?'

Emily spoke first. 'Not a lot to go on, is there? Three hands found in an old house. We've no idea how long they've been there, or if they were all placed in the backpack at the same time.'

'Are we sure this isn't a publicity stunt by the film people? The *Evening News* has gone big on the story. Interviewing the producer and the announcer. They could have purchased the hands from a bent undertaker or from an anatomy lab.'

'That's Turnbull's theory. It would certainly fit with the hands being embalmed. But Dave Connor has interviewed the film crew and has cleared them. All their stories match and he felt they were genuinely surprised at the discovery.'

'So we're treating this as real? The murder of at least three people?'

'Until we find evidence to the contrary.'

They both nodded.

'For me, we have four questions to answer.' He took up a pen and began writing on the whiteboard. 'How did the hands get in the backpack? What are the identities of the victims? Where are the rest of the bodies? Why place them in Daisy House Children's Home? And finally, who killed these people? Before you say anything, I know it's five questions. Next steps? Chrissy?'

The civilian researcher adjusted her City scarf. 'Well, the obvious place to start is with HOLMES. The programme should tell us if any bodies with hands missing or a similar MO have been found in England.'

'I asked Dave Connor to do that, but you would be far quicker. Can you go back to at least 2000 on the first pass?'

'Why 2000?'

'Wouldn't 2006 be better? Surely somebody would have noticed the backpack as they closed and emptied the home?' Emily Parkinson prodded the air with her pencil.

'The forensic anthropologist thought one of the hands had been operated on after 2000, so let's use it as our starting point. We can refine it later when we get more information.'

'No problem. It seems logical.'

'I'll let Dave Connor know Chrissy is working on this. He'll be relieved to know he has one less job to do.'

'What about the backpack? Who's checking up on it?' asked Emily.

'It's supposed to be me, but I haven't had time. Can you do the job? Get the details from Hannah Palmer.'

Emily scribbled a note to herself. 'Also, I'd like to relook at the film crew. See if any of them have a record.'

'Dave Connor has their statements. He seems to think they were kosher.'

'Doesn't hurt to check. I'll also look at the door-to-door responses. It's a quiet area, people could have seen somebody strange loitering around.'

'Dave has the sheets too.'

She paused for a moment. 'Is there a possible link to Daisy House?'

'I've checked the Operation Pharaoh investigation. The place was a hellhole for kids in the eighties and nineties.' Ridpath wrote the words 'Daisy House' followed by a question mark on the board.

'I could find the staff roster, it's sure to be in the operational files of the investigation,' said Chrissy.

'What about the kids who went there?' asked Emily.

'The information is with Manchester Social Services. We'll need a court order to get it, data protection laws are a bastard.'

Ridpath held his hands up. 'Let's not go there yet, I don't want us to be swamped with information at this stage. Thousands of kids attended Daisy House, finding and contacting them all will be a nightmare.'

'You're right, Ridpath.'

'We have more than enough to keep us going until we get the DNA and fingerprint results back.'

'When are they coming in?'

'Hannah says two days, but I'll push for them earlier.'

'We need them, Ridpath.'

'Don't I know it. Until then, I'll get Dave Connor to set up a situation room in Stretford nick—'

'We don't have to come here?'

'Nah, for the next few days, we're on secondment to Stretford.'

'Brilliant, shame it's so close to Old Trafford though.'

'Don't worry, Chrissy, you won't catch anything… much,' laughed Emily.

'Right, let's get going. We have until Monday to sort it all out. Chrissy, can I have a word – did you find the files on my misper, Jane Ryder?'

Chrissy patted a sheaf of printouts in front of her. 'Got them here, Ridpath, what there is.'

Emily stood up. 'I'll get on with this stuff. I hope this isn't a hoax with the hands stolen from some university or lab.'

'Dave Connor is checking if there are any reports of break-ins or losses of human tissue anywhere. We should know soon.'

'Right. Next meeting?'

'Tomorrow at eight.' Ridpath remembered he had to drive Eve to school. 'No, make it nine a.m. at Stretford.'

'Right.' She turned to go and stopped. 'Monday – it's not a lot of time, Ridpath.'

Ridpath ran his fingers through his rapidly thinning hair. 'Don't I know it, but it's all we have.'

Chapter 30

'Tell me what you have, Chrissy.'

'Sorry it took so long, Ridpath, I kept being pulled away by Turnbull. There's not as much as there should be. This is the original missing person report with the Form 737, compiled by the investigating officer…' She opened the file and checked the name at the bottom. 'A Colin Dowell. I don't know him, but he was based in Sale at the time. His inspector was Ron Roper. I knew him, loved his forms did Ronnie, bit of a stickler for stuff in triplicate.'

'One of those?'

'A classic jobsworth. He retired and died not long after. Happens to a lot of coppers. Heart attack, I think it was. The original form is here but there's none of the search materials that should be enclosed.'

'Like?'

'Like diaries, notes or any follow-up. And the toothbrush is missing, even though according to the form Dowell took it for DNA.'

'Missing?'

'Not here. It should be with the file.'

'Why's it not there?'

'Lots of reasons. Separated and thrown away. Lost, or simply never put back together with the original file after testing. The case was in 2009.'

'But you said Roper was a stickler for bureaucracy.'

'That's what's so surprising. I'll carry on looking, though, and see what I can find. Also, there are no follow-up documents.'

'Please explain.'

'Normally, there would be meetings with the missing person's manager, contacts with social workers, visits to the family to update them, interviews with witnesses, all the usual stuff in an investigation. But there's nothing here. Zilch. Nada. Not a sausage.'

'Is that strange?'

'There should be something, she was only sixteen.'

'But we have the names of all the police involved?'

She patted the file. 'They are in the original form, plus the name of the missing person's manager, Doreen Hawkins.'

'You sound like you know her?'

'A person I avoid like the plague, as does everybody else who ever worked with her. Did well for herself though. Now running a kids' charity in Salford, appears regularly on *Granada Reports* pontificating on the issues of the day. Made a career out of missing kids, has our Doreen.'

He took the file. 'Right, I'll go through this when I get a second.'

'And I'll follow up on those missing files.'

Ridpath started to leave but turned back. 'Weren't there some other websites she could have appeared on?'

'Yeah, I checked those too, and that's where it gets weirder. Even though she was only sixteen, she wasn't on the Vulnerable Persons database or the Missing Persons DNA database or the Missing Kids website. No mention of a Jane Ryder on any of them.'

'Is that unusual?'

Chrissy nodded. 'At her age, the information should have been flagged on one of them. I'll check again, as I may have missed it, but I don't think so. It's like she vanished into thin air.'

'It's getting stranger and stranger, Chrissy.'

Chapter 31

'Hi Sophia, is the coroner in?'

Ridpath had driven back to the coroner's office after briefing Emily and Chrissy, picking up a Gregg's sausage roll on the way. The flakes still stuck to his jacket like pastry dandruff.

'Afternoon, Ridpath. She's in her office, preparing for the inquest, I think.'

'Let me update her, then we need to have chat regarding the Ryder case. I need you to do some follow-up.'

'Great, I'm sick of doing Covid forms for the chief coroner in London. I spend more time sending stuff to him than I do actually doing work.'

Ridpath knocked on the coroner's door. The meat of the sausage roll was nestling uneasily somewhere between his sternum and his belly button, lying there like a dyspeptic octogenarian.

'Come.'

He walked in to find the coroner hunched over her casework. She looked up slowly and took off her glasses. 'Ridpath, just the man I wanted to see. How did the meeting with the Ryders go this morning?'

'Fine, Mrs Challinor. Understandably, they are still hurting over the disappearance of their daughter, but seem to have come to terms with the fact she is no longer alive. Chrissy has obtained the old Missing Persons files from 2009. I'll go through them later. There seem to be some anomalies, but at least we know who the investigating officer and the missing person's manager were.'

'Great, and you'll follow up with both of them?'

'Of course. You're still planning to hold the inquest asap?'

'I am, Ridpath. After waiting nearly twelve years, I don't want them to wait any longer. Given Mrs Ryder's illness, the sooner we hold the inquest the better.'

'I agree, but there may be a problem getting the witnesses to the court.'

'Problem?'

'Availability, enough notice. I know at least one of the policemen involved has since died.'

'And what about the witnesses to her disappearance?'

'There don't seem to be any.'

'No friends?'

'None were with her. The parents did say she was supposed to be going to a festival with two friends, a Rose Gray and an Andrea Briggs, but it was a lie. They didn't meet her.'

'So you think she went with somebody else?'

'We don't even know if she went to the festival. She told her parents she was going, but we have no proof she ever arrived.' He put the picture given to him by Mr Ryder on the desk between them. 'According to the parents, this was the last picture of her before she went missing.'

The picture of a pretty girl with long blonde hair and a beguiling smile lay between them.

Mrs Challinor stared at it for a long time. 'What do you think happened to her?'

'I don't know, Mrs Challinor. Young girls vanish all the time. They want their freedom. Or they meet a man. Or they just want to get away from home. Perhaps the home life wasn't as rosy as the Ryders have painted it. Girls go missing all the time.'

'That's shocking, Ridpath.'

'Most return eventually.'

'But some never do, like Jane Ryder?'

'Exactly. Go on any of the missing person websites. It's like a novel of sad stories and even sadder pictures. I checked with the National Crime Agency Missing Persons Unit. There were three hundred and twenty thousand missing person incidents in 2019, about thirty-seven being reported to the police every hour.'

Mrs Challinor sighed and slumped down over her desk. 'So many?'

'Most people were found, or returned later of their own accord, but some didn't. I checked – there are still four hundred and twenty-six cases outstanding from 2019, never mind all the other years.'

'What are the next steps?'

'Sophia will contact Jane's school and friends, while I work the police side.'

'Ideally I'd like the policemen involved and the last people to have seen her to give evidence at the inquest.'

Ridpath stood up. 'I'll arrange it, Coroner. And thank you for calling Claire Trent. I now have more help on the Daisy House case.'

'Can you manage both, Ridpath? If you can't, let me know and I'll talk to her again.'

'With Sophia's help and the new resources, I think I can manage, Coroner.'

'What about Eve?'

'I'm going to speak to a neighbour this evening. Her daughter goes to the same school. I'm sure they can do homework together until I get home.'

'Sounds like a plan, Ridpath.'

He turned to leave.

'And one more matter – have you contacted the hospital yet?'

'Not yet, but I'm on it.'

'Contact them, Ridpath. You're far too valuable to me and the coroner's office to get ill again.'

'I'm on it, Mrs Challinor,' he said, opening the door to leave. 'I'll try to slot it in next week.'

Her voice dropped a register. '"Try" is not an option, Ridpath. Make it happen.'

Chapter 32

'Right, Sophia. Did you manage to follow up from this morning?'

'Here are the copies of Jane's photo.' She passed across a small pile of colour copies. 'Pretty girl, wasn't she? So full of life and energy.'

Ridpath picked up the top copy. 'The more I look at this photo, the less I understand why she went missing. There seems to be no real reason, other than something bad happened to her. Or perhaps we're not seeing the full picture, just looking at the surface; a young, pretty girl with her whole life in front of her.'

There was a moment's silence between them, before he asked, 'Anything from the school?'

'I rang them. Luckily, the school secretary had worked there since the dark ages. She remembered the disappearance of Jane, caused a big stir in the school, she told me. Her form teacher is long gone, but the present day deputy head, a Mr Roscoe, taught her history. I'm interviewing him tomorrow at eight thirty before school starts. Want to come?'

'No, you handle it. I'm up to my eyes in stuff. Make sure he understands we may call him for the inquest.'

'Will do. It's all a bit of rush, isn't it?'

'Anything else?'

'I think so.'

'Go on…'

'Jane Ryder said she was going to a festival. I thought it might have been Glastonbury, since it's such a rite of passage for her age group.'

'But…'

'Glastonbury didn't start until June 24 in 2009. There were three music festivals taking place on the weekend she disappeared. One was the Download Festival at Donington Park between Derby and Leicester. A real headbangers' convention this one, featuring Whitesnake, Mötley Crüe and a host of other heavy metal bands.'

'Not a bad line-up.'

She grimaced and continued speaking. 'Another was on the Isle of Wight, with The Prodigy, Neil Young, Stereophonics and Simple Minds. Much more my cup of camomile tea.'

'Seems a long way to travel.'

'That's what I thought. The third was in Manchester at Platt Fields, the Mad Ferret Festival, set up by a bunch of students. It later became Parklife.'

Ridpath's eyes tightened. 'I think I know the festival. I may have even worked there.'

His mind went back to one of his first jobs as a probationary constable. It was the summer Polly was pregnant with Eve, and he was working all the overtime he could get to save up for the birth.

Had he worked in Platt Fields?

A festival kept coming back to him in flashes, like clips from a film. Hot sun shining in a cloudless sky. Him in his shirtsleeves and helmet. A briefing from a sergeant at the station. Vaguely remembered words; low key, be friendly, don't arrest unless trouble, safeguarding not a police role, ignore drug taking unless evidence of dealing. Loud music played off-key and an endless, hot summer day, watching all the students having a great time.

He'd gone in the van with Sergeant Mungovan.

'Got your sunscreen?'

'No, Sergeant.'

'You're gonna need it. Here, borrow mine.'

Walking from the van to the positions on the outskirts of the park, just inside the festival's hastily erected fence. The whistling of 'Colonel Bogey' by the students as the coppers marched along bringing a smile to his face.

The music, loud and boring, or soft and melancholic. He would have preferred to have listened to Bowie or danced to Northern Soul, but there was none. It was student music with all its lack of melody or harmony. Only The Streets were at all interesting, Mike Skinner prowling the stage like a young Bowie.

He'd earned a nice bit of overtime. He'd even volunteered for the next day, though it was his time off.

He never worked another festival afterwards, already being fast-tracked as detective material while Eve grew older and Polly went on to train as a teacher. Somehow, he missed out on the whole festival experience, never going to Parklife or even to Glastonbury.

Days he missed that he would never see again.

'Didn't Jane Ryder's parents say she was going to be away for the weekend, returning on Sunday evening?' said Sophia, interrupting his memories.

'Yeah, so she could have gone to any of them.'

'I'll call and check if the names Mad Ferret, Donington or the Isle of Wight ring a bell.'

'I don't think they will. The father seemed distracted and the mother, well, her drugs…' Ridpath didn't finish the sentence. 'The less we disturb the family these days, the better.'

'OK, I'll follow up on the festivals, see if I can find out more.' She checked her watch. 'Weren't you supposed to be picking up Eve?'

'Not until five p.m., for once I'm not rushing around. She has the school computing club today. They are coding some game or other. You know she helps me when I can't work out stuff on the computer. It's a bit embarrassing, if I'm honest.'

'She can come round to my place if she wants, give my mum lessons.'

'A new business for me: hiring my daughter out as a computer consultant. Not a bad idea.' As he spoke, his mobile phone rang. It was Dave Connor.

'Hi Ridpath, Hannah rang me. We have a hit on the DNA of one of the hands.'

Chapter 33

Dave Connor was waiting for him at Stretford Police Station. He had already set up a situation room with pictures of the hands and the backpack pasted to the walls and boards. Just looking at it reminded Ridpath of how little they knew.

On a video screen in front of them, Hannah Palmer had started talking. 'These are the topline results. I've hassled the lab to rush them out. They are performing another test on the DNA to make sure these are correct – you can't be too careful when it's been contaminated by embalming fluid.'

'Just give us the results, Hannah, enough with the excuses.' Dave Connor was tapping the table impatiently.

'It's important you understand, Dave. These are preliminary.'

'OK. OK, I get it.'

Ridpath tapped his arm lightly. 'You have a hit on the DNA, Hannah?'

'We have, Ridpath. So far two of the hands have given us nothing. We haven't been able to extract enough undamaged DNA to make a successful analysis. We're trying again as I speak.'

'Great, but you've been able to extract DNA from one of the hands?'

'Correct, and even better, I checked it against the NCNAD, the National DNA database. We had a hit to a Joseph Rowlands, aged fifty-two when he disappeared.'

Ridpath frowned. 'Disappeared?'

'He was reported missing in 2018.'

'What?'

Hannah was reading from a report. 'His last known address was 14 Styal Road, Moston.'

'Who reported him missing?'

Hannah scanned the file. 'It doesn't say on this. But I'm sure he has a missing person file.'

'Any other information?'

'None, but I'm wondering why he was on the database in the first place? We must have collected his DNA for some reason.'

'Great work, Hannah. Can you send across the results?'

'Will do, Ridpath.'

'When do you think you'll get the others?' asked Dave Connor.

'I don't know, Dave. It's like asking how long is a piece of string.'

'A rough estimate.'

'Six feet, give or take a few inches.'

'Ha bloody ha.'

'You asked for it. A rough estimate is when I get them, Dave, you'll get them.'

The detective was about to push again, but Ridpath stopped him. 'Thanks, Hannah. What about the fingerprints?'

'Should come in tomorrow with a bit of luck, we're stretched and it's proving difficult to obtain good samples.'

'OK. Anything on the backpack or the paper in the joint?'

'Nothing so far. I'll call you if anything comes up. Look, Ridpath, I'm working as hard and as fast as I can.'

'I know, Hannah, sorry, we're under immense pressure to get a result here. Please keep going, OK?'

'Will do. You'll be the first to hear if we get anything.'

'What about me? Am I just chopped liver around here?'

Ridpath clicked off the Zoom link before Hannah heard Dave Connor's outburst. 'She's doing her best, Dave, we have to be patient.'

'Tell it to Holloway.'

'If you want, I will, but pissing off the people who can help us is not a smart move.'

The detective stayed silent.

'At least we now have a place to start. Can you check up on this Joseph Rowlands? Find out everything you can, visit the address and see if anybody has a picture of him? Plus see if he had a hand operation. It'll confirm the DNA result is correct if he did. I'll ring Chrissy and get her to check the Missing Persons database. She seems to be doing a lot of that at the moment.'

'Right, Ridpath. I haven't started checking HOLMES yet.'

'Don't worry, Chrissy is doing it. Emily Parkinson is going over the house to house and the TV crew interviews, as well as checking the backpack.'

'Thank God or Claire Trent, whichever is more powerful. Having more people on board will help.'

'We only have them until Monday, so we need to get working. Let's meet here tomorrow morning at nine a.m. and consolidate. We'll make this the base moving forward.'

'Sounds like an idea.'

'How is Holloway?'

'Like a caged lion. I told him about the extra resources and his response was, "Is that all? A DS and a civilian researcher?" He's not a happy camper.'

'Is he giving you Oliver back?'

Connor nodded. 'Tomorrow morning, I'll get him to come to the briefing. He's keen anyway.' The detective scratched his head. 'I've been meaning to ask, Ridpath…'

'What, Dave?'

'Holloway's put me in charge, but you are the ranking detective, and you have SIO experience…'

'So you want me to take charge but not let him know?'

'Exactly. At the moment, I have only two years to go before I can put my slippers on. I will have done my thirty years, Ridpath, I need this sort of case like I need a hole in the head. Don't get me wrong, I'm happy to do the legwork, but my days of running investigations are a long way behind me.'

Ridpath thought for a moment. 'It would be good for you to go out in a blaze of glory, Dave.'

'My problem is, I think I'm going to go out in a blaze of failure. I can't do it any more, Ridpath.'

'OK, I'll take it on, but on one condition.'

The detective looked at him warily.

'When we find who did it, you announce it to the press.'

'When we find him? Or if we find him?'

'Oh, we'll find him, Dave, I'm certain we will. It's just whether we can do it before Monday.'

Chapter 34

'You're late again, Dad.'

Eve was sitting on the wall outside her school, backpack at her feet.

'Sorry, love, you know what it's like when I'm in the middle of an investigation.'

She opened the car door and slid into the front seat. 'It's not good enough, Dad.'

For a second, her voice sounded exactly like her mother's. Polly's face flashed into his mind and he quickly dismissed it. Now was not the time to dwell on the past. 'I know, that's why I've asked our neighbour, Mrs Dunwoody, to pick you up tomorrow when she comes for her own daughter. You can do your homework together in her house until I get home.'

'But Jessica's one of the mean girls. Why can't I do my homework with Maisie instead?'

He pulled away from the kerb. 'Because Maisie's mum can't pick you up. It won't be for long, just till next week. I can still take you to school every morning.'

'OK,' she said grumpily, crossing her arms and pouting.

Ridpath knew OK meant it wasn't OK. 'It'll only be for a couple of days.'

'A couple of days of hell.'

Ridpath smiled as he drove along. A troupe of opera singers couldn't match Eve for drama. 'I thought you liked Jessica?'

'We were friends until she started hanging out with Rachel's squad. They're *sooooooo* plastic.'

Plastic was the worst put-down in Eve's eyes, standing for everything she despised.

'It won't be for long,' he repeated weakly.

'A day with Jessica is like a year in hell.'

'That good, huh,' he said trying not to smile. Teen angst. Was he as bad at her age? Probably even worse. 'What would you like for tea?' He changed the subject. 'How about sushi? I could drive to the shop in Chorlton and pick some up.'

This was an out and out bribe. Sushi was her favourite food. When he was kid, his had been Holland's meat and potato pie and chips. How the world had changed.

She brightened for a second, and then remembered she was supposed to be sulking. 'OK, I'd like some sake—'

'You're too young to drink.'

'Dad, sake is salmon sushi. And some ebi and some California rolls.'

It was all Greek to him, even though it was Japanese. He would just go into the shop with her while she chose, making sure they wore their masks; he always kept a pack in his car.

'What are you going to have?'

'I guess some spicy chicken.' It was about the only the dish he could eat on the menu. Unless he nipped down to the chippie opposite the baths. 'Or I could have a bit of haddock and chips, with a side order of mushy peas.'

'But they don't do...' She stopped as she realised what he meant. 'Dad, one day you're gonna have to expand your food horizons away from chips. Try some healthy eating.'

'It's a vegetable, isn't it? One of my five a day.'

She was about to launch into a long diatribe on the heavy starch and carbohydrate content of the humble potato when she saw he was teasing her. 'Dad, you're making fun of me.' She slapped his arm.

'Only a little.'

She laughed, and then her face became stern. 'But seriously, you have to eat more healthily. I've noticed you've been putting on weight recently.' She stared obviously at the roll of stomach lying over his belt.

After losing a lot of weight after Polly died, he gradually started to eat again, sandwiches and chips being the major component of his new diet. He'd been meaning to lose the spare tyre for a while. Perhaps it was time.

'And did you arrange your check-up at Christies?'

It was the second time he'd been reminded. 'I'm doing it.'

'Do you want me to do it for you?'

God, she did sound exactly like Polly.

'No, I'll do it first thing tomorrow.'

'I'll remind you.'

'No need.'

'No problem,' she said, smiling.

Now he was being teased. 'I promise I'll do it.'

She held out her finger with pinky and thumb extended. He did the same and they touched and twisted. It was some sort of teenage confirmation of a promise.

They parked up in Chorlton, bought her sushi and his fish and chips and went home.

He decided to wait until after he'd finished eating before reading the missing person report for Jane Ryder. Instead, they both sat with their food, watching television as they ate. He used his fingers, twisting crispy bits of salt-and-vinegar-soaked batter off the fish, followed by two or three crunchy, fat chips. Eve picked up her sushi with her chopsticks, dipping it casually into a mixture of wasabi and soy sauce before nibbling on it daintily.

They both enjoyed *Pointless* and *Eggheads*. It had been so long since he'd been to a quiz night. Another pastime fallen by the wayside in the last year.

'Dad, you know what I'd like to do on Sunday?'

'Fly to the moon?'

'*Daaaaddd*.'

'Give me a clue.'

'I'd like to visit Mum's grave, if we could. I've lots to tell her.'

'OK, and afterwards, I'll take you to your grandparents for lunch, they want to see you.'

'Do I have to?'

'I promised. Deal?'

'Deal.'

After they'd finished eating, Eve went upstairs to do her homework while Ridpath was left alone with the television. He thought about opening a bottle of wine and decided against it, knowing once he started drinking he wouldn't stop till the whole bottle was finished.

At that moment, the email on his laptop pinged.

Work was calling. He could put it off no longer.

Chapter 35

The text message from Chrissy was as succinct as ever:

> Have you looked at the misper file yet?

He typed back:

> Not yet, about to do it. Can you find another misper file for me? DNA on one of the hands in the backpack has come back with a match to a Joseph Rowlands, who disappeared in 2018 from 14 Styal Road, Moston. Can you also check the PNC to see why his DNA is on file? Ta muchly.

He didn't have to wait long for her response:

> OK, will do. Still looking for the other missing files and correspondence. Not here, very strange. See you tomorrow.

He was about to type, 'don't work too late' but didn't. Unfortunately, with the little time they had, everyone had to work late. Instead he just wrote, *Thanks, Chrissy*, feeling immensely guilty as he did so.

At least the wheels were now set in motion and, knowing Chrissy, they would have the information tomorrow morning.

He opened the missing person file for Jane Ryder. At the top of the report the old OPUS logo with its handcuffs dangling from the 'O' stood out. This was the police computer system copied from Northumbria, which he knew well. It was an old system but at least it had worked, not like the new screw-up, iOPS, introduced in 2019.

The next page detailed the precise procedures for dealing with a missing person. Ridpath read them through carefully.

ROUTE MAP TO AID MISSING PERSON INVESTIGATIONS. DO NOT FORGET THIS MISSING PERSON REPORT MAY BE THE FIRST INDICATION OF A SERIOUS CRIME OR CRITICAL INCIDENT

1. Obtain permission to search address thoroughly and legally; do not leave it to family or friends to search.
2. Ensure the informant signs the 'Search Authorised By' section on page 2 of the report.
3. Make an initial risk assessment from the evidence available.
4. Seize (for future investigation) items of the misper's property such as diaries, computers, letters, notes and sources of fingerprints and DNA. This is in accordance with the revised ACPO guidance on missing persons.
5. Obtain two original photographs of the missing person.
6. Complete thoroughly the Missing Person Report Form 737.
7. Notify the duty CID officer if there are any reasons for concern.
8. Consider seeking the advice of a missing person search manager – this can save time and help prevent resources being incorrectly allocated.

On return to the station:

1. Ensure your supervisor reviews the risk assessment (page 3) against the risk definition.
2. Email pages 1–4 of this report to GMPCRU

3. If the website consent form is completed (page 5), have it signed by the duty inspector.

4. Remove pages 5–6 of this report and send them via the internal mail to the Force MFH Section, LPIB, SVPU including one of the photographs obtained earlier.

5. Retain the second photo for section use.

6. Check if missing person is known the Domestic Violence Unit.

7. Update supervision and action logs to ensure all are aware of the case progress.

The checklist made clear the procedures to be followed by the person completing the form. Ridpath was surprised at the use of the word 'misper' but, as this was an internal police document, it was excusable.

He turned the page to read the list of 'Golden Hour' tasks to be completed by the investigating officer. Golden Hour was the time immediately after any incident, the most productive in any investigation, when people's memories were freshest and the correct investigative wheels had to be set in motion.

He turned the page again to find the completed form, checking the signatures at the end first. The investigating officer was a PC Colin Dowell and the duty inspector was Ronald Roper.

He thought Mr and Mrs Ryder had said a sergeant came to see them. Perhaps the station sent a PC first, following up afterwards.

He checked the rest of the form. It was the one thing he didn't miss about being a police officer: the interminable bureaucracy. He understood why it was all necessary, but the man hours used on completing these forms made every officer's life miserable. In this case, the form was completed on a computer, probably back at the station.

MISSING PERSON REPORT FORM 737.

SECTION ONE: PERSONAL DETAILS AND DISAPPEARANCE CIRCUMSTANCES.

W1 British Female, JANE RYDER, aged sixteen last birthday, reported missing, last seen morning of 12.06.09. Report made 15.06.09 by her parents, MR JAMES RYDER AND MRS MAUREEN RYDER. She was going to a music festival and was due to return the following evening before ten p.m. Parents checked with friend, ROSE GRAY, but friend did not go with her to festival. Other friends not aware of her present whereabouts.

Complete all boxes

Ethnic Origin Codes/Ethnic Appearance: (Codes on reverse)

1 White European XX

SECTION TWO: SEARCH AUTHORITY

This should be signed by the informant to authorise searches of buildings and grounds

Signed by: James Ryder

SECTION THREE: RISK ASSESSMENT & RISK ASSESSMENT CONFIRMATION

The Initial Investigating Officer (IIO) is to complete the risk assessment on page 3 and sign it.

CLASSIFICATION OF RISK AND RESPONSE (ACPO Manual of Guidance 2005 – Para 3.5)

High: There is an immediate risk and definite grounds for believing the missing person is at risk through their own vulnerability or mental state, or there are grounds for believing the public is at risk through the missing person's mental state. Such cases should lead to the appointment of a senior investigating officer (SIO). There should be a press/media strategy and/or close contact with outside agencies.

Medium: The risk posed is likely to place the missing person in danger, or they are a threat to themselves or others. This category requires an active and measured response by police and other agencies in order to trace the missing person and support the person reporting.

Low: There is no apparent risk of danger to either the missing person or the general public.

After Consultation with DOREEN HAWKINS, the missing person's manager for this case, JANE RYDER was assessed as a MEDIUM RISK.

SECTION FOUR: MISSING PERSON REPORT

RESTRICTED – when completed

Surname/family name: RYDER
Fore/given name: JANE
MP Reference No.: 2309/2012/MFH
Div/Area: TRAFFORD
Website consent signed: YES
OIC/IIO name: COLIN DOWELL (PC 2354)
Missing From Home category:
Runaway XX
Missing from care: NO
Out of area placement: NO
DNA source available: YES
If YES – give details: TOOTHBRUSH
DNA source current location: MFH FILE
Blood group: O
Dental chart available: NO
Dental chart sent to MFH sect: NO
Mobile phone no available: NO
Photo available: YES
Photo sent to MFH sect: YES
Part 2 – Misper's personal details and disappearance circumstances
Age: 16 YEARS OLD. 20 APRIL 1993
Ethnicity: WI
Hair style: LONG, BLONDE, SHOULDER-LENGTH HAIR

Glasses: NO
NI no: NONE
Sex: FEMALE
Religion: CHRISTIAN
Last seen on JUNE 12, 2009
Transgender: NO
Build: SLIGHT
Disability: NONE
Eye colour: BLUE
Nationality: BRITISH
Sexuality:
Mental Impairment: NONE
Place of birth: MANCHESTER
Marital status: SINGLE
Relationship of informant to misper: FATHER
SURNAME: RYDER
Forename: JAMES
Date of Birth: 14.08.1943
Information: FEMALE FRIEND – ROSE GRAY. 24 Earlington Road, Sale.

There it was: the address of the friend. He'd send it on to Sophia after he finished reading the report. He continued with the details taken by PC Dowell.

Details of clothing and jewellery believed to be worn or in misper's possession: RED AND WHITE STRIPED COTTON SHIRT, BLUE JEANS, NIKE SNEAKERS, SKULLS HEAD RING ON INDEX FINGER. BACKPACK WITH SPARE JACKET AND CLOTHES, DESCRIPTION UNKNOWN.

Last seen location: HOME. 10 A.M. 12.06.2009
Last seen by: PARENTS
Who are they missing with? ALONE (SUPPOSED TO BE WITH FRIEND, ROSE GRAY)
Reason for disappearance: NONE

Venue searched by: PC COLIN DOWELL

Known mental health issues: NONE

Previous history of wandering: YES

Address previously found: NONE. RETURNED HOME AFTER TWO DAYS

Garden/garage/outbuildings searched? YES

Local parks/fields/school grounds/vehicle searched? NO

Search authorised by: JAMES RYDER (FATHER)

1. Suspected victim of murder or abduction? NO
2. History of attempted suicide or self-harm? NO
3. Suffers from depression? NO
4. Subject of abuse/bullying or history of abuse? NO
5. Subject's behaviour has changed to cause others concern? NONE NOTICED
6. Subject has changed appearance recently? NO
7. Subject has recently joined new groups/sects? UNKNOWN
8. Subject has displayed grievances against state/society? NO
9. Subject has travelled abroad often or for significant periods of time? NO
10. Subject has recently associated with groups who have radical or extremist views, or has joined new religious/faith groups or sects? UNKNOWN
11. Out of character? HAS PREVIOUSLY RUN AWAY
12. Previously reported missing? YES
13. Work pressures/worries? RECENTLY FINISHED EXAMS
14. Known medical condition causing concern? NONE
15. In possession of required medication? NONE NEEDED
16. Drug or alcohol dependent? NO
17. Access to money? NO
18. Danger to others? NO
19. Familiar with area believed to be frequenting? UNKNOWN
20. Known hazards/dangers within search area? NO
21. Access to vehicles? NO
22. Passport taken? NO

32. Child abuse marker? NONE

24. Domestic violence marker? NO

25. On Child Protection Register? NO

26. Otherwise known to Social Services? YES

Care Worker completing report:

Police officer completing risk assessment: COLIN DOWELL (PC 2354)

Police supervisor confirming risk: RON ROPER (INSPECTOR 478)

Supervising Officer's Risk Assessment: MEDIUM

SECTION FIVE

Name of person with parental responsibility: JAMES RYDER

Name of officer witnessing: COLIN DOWELL

Rank: PC 2354

Ridpath stared at the file. Questions stormed into his head. Why was a sixteen-year-old girl only seen as a medium risk? Why had she run away before? The parents had played it down, merely saying she had spent a weekend away. What follow-up to the report was completed?

And the final one, the most important, which leapt out at him from his screen.

Why was she known to Social Services?

Chapter 36

They stood over Patricia Patterson as she was sleeping in the cell. Both women were dressed simply in work overalls. The cell itself was four bare whitewashed walls with no windows. A single light above the door illuminated the scene.

The taller of the two knelt down and touched the sleeping woman's face. 'How long will she be out?'

'Your guess is as good as mine. Depends how much she ate this morning and her constitution.'

'Has it been decided yet?'

'Not yet. We're waiting for his answer.'

The woman stroked Patricia's hair. 'A shame, I liked her.'

'She left us. We can't allow it to happen again.'

The taller woman stood up. 'Shame though.'

'Make sure there's somebody outside her door at all times, but there is to be no contact. Not until it has been decided.'

'I'll take the first shift myself.'

'We have cameras and sound?'

The tall woman pointed to the light. 'I tested them myself this morning before we brought her here.'

'And her car?'

'Left in a busy garden centre. It won't be found for a while.'

'Good. Do not enter, whatever happens, is that understood?'

The tall woman nodded.

'There is to be no communication with her, that is the instruction.'

They both left the cell, ensuring the door was locked and the bolts were in place. From the outside, the woman checked the camera and then turned out the light, plunging the cell into blackness.

On the rough mattress, Patricia Patterson slept on, her eyes flickering from side to side as she dreamt her drug-troubled dreams.

Chapter 37

Ridpath read through the Jane Ryder file again, writing down the questions in his notebook as they occurred to him.

Which festival did she go to?

Who had she gone with or met there? Obviously not Rose Gray or Andrea Briggs.

What had happened?

Where had she gone afterwards, and who had taken her?

A ping on his computer brought him back to the present. He checked his mail, finding a message.

> Tried to track down the backpack. Not having a lot of luck. CLAK is a skateboard brand popular in the early 2000s. Will check retailers tmrw. regards Emily.

There were four attachments: pictures of the backpack from different angles and a close-up of the logo.

'Cool backpack, Dad, where did you get it?'

Ridpath jumped; he hadn't heard Eve come in the room. She leant over his shoulder, looking at the screen.

'I've not seen a CLAK like that before. Is it one of the limited editions?'

He pointed at the screen. 'You know this brand?'

'Yeah, it's cool. A lot of kids at school have this backpack. Mum refused to buy it for me, said it was too expensive. So I got this Jansport instead.' She pointed to the backpack sitting on the couch with her school books peeping out of the open top. 'She let me decorate it with some mint patches though. I love the anime characters from *Demon Slayer*, and the Manchester Bee.'

'You wanted to buy a backpack like this?'

'Yeaaahhh.' She lengthened the answer into a long sound like a rolling Derbyshire dale.

'Where would you buy it?'

'Only one place in Manchester. You and Mum used to take me. You dropped us off and went off to do your stuff.'

He frowned. 'Afflecks? The old department store now full of trendy shops?'

'Right first time, and only you would use a word like trendy, Dad. Remember, you hated climbing the stairs the one time you went with us and kept complaining about how expensive it all was.'

'Sounds like me.'

'Mum loved it though. She used to get her scarves there.'

Ridpath remembered Polly's multi-coloured scarves. They had been a running joke between the two of them for a long time, bright purple being her favourite colour. 'Where would you go to buy this backpack?'

'Only one place, and it's been there for years. Bagsy on the second floor. I don't remember you ever going that far upstairs with us.'

'Didn't I stop at the weird cafe? They didn't have any bacon butties.'

'Not surprising, since it served vegan food.'

'You should have seen their faces when I asked.'

'One of your dad moments, Dad.'

'You sure it's the only place you can get this brand?'

'Is United a football team? Does the earth circle the sun? Are BTS the bestselling music artists in 2020?'

'I guess that's a yes.'

'Correct. You know, you could make a pretty good detective with a little training.'

'Right, smart arse, brush your teeth and off to bed.'

She kissed him on the forehead. 'Can I have scrambled eggs on toast for breakfast tomorrow, like you used to make…?'

She didn't finish the sentence. Like you used to make when Mum was alive, was what she meant. He smiled. 'Of course, one Dad's special scrambled eggs tomorrow morning. You have to get up in time to eat them.'

'I will, promise.' She held out her hand with the thumb and pinky pointing forward. It was that strange teenage ritual again.

'You're supposed to do the same.'

'Right.' She touched the ends of her fingers and then twisted. 'It's a promise now.'

'Words aren't good enough?'

'Not any more.'

He heard her pad across the room and up the stairs. He was left staring at the backpack on the screen.

Emily would have to visit Afflecks tomorrow.

THURSDAY

Chapter 38

They were all waiting for him when he arrived at the incident room in Stretford station the following morning.

'Morning, Ridpath.'

Chrissy smiled warmly. Emily grunted a greeting, while Oliver Davis handed him a coffee, bought from the drive-thru Costa at White City, before sitting down next to Dave Connor.

'Sorry I'm late. The daughter...' His voice trailed off and he shrugged his shoulders.

'Trouble waking up in the morning?' asked Chrissy.

Ridpath nodded.

'Use dynamite under the bed, that's what I did. Worked every time.'

'Sometimes I wonder whether you are joking, Chrissy.'

'I'm not,' she said with a straight face.

Ridpath noticed there was more information on the boards now, not just a few pictures. 'Let's get started, shall we? You go first, Chrissy, give us some more dynamite. You were checking up on the staff at the children's home. Find anything?'

'I've only done the workers with direct contact to the children, not the ancillary staff yet.'

'And?'

'Four were found guilty of child molestation in 2013, after the Operation Pharaoh investigation. By that time, one had even been promoted to be the deputy head of Children's Services for Manchester City Council...'

'Unbelievable...' muttered Emily.

'I spoke to one of the coppers who worked the case. He said more were involved but they couldn't prove it. Files were sent to CPS and they decided not to proceed. I'll go through them, there should be a list of employees somewhere, it'll save us applying for a court order from Manchester.'

'Anything on HOLMES 2, Chrissy? You were checking for similar cases, and if any bodies had been found without hands.'

'Nothing so far. I've sent a query through to the National Police Agency but I didn't get any hits on HOLMES.'

'So what happened to the bodies?'

They all shook their heads.

'Write it on the board, please, Oliver.'

It always fell to the most junior officer, or the one with the neatest writing, to put the questions that needed answering on a whiteboard at the side of the incident room.

'Great, Chrissy, keep pushing on HOLMES and find the list of employees, including ancillary workers. And you, Emily, how did you get on?'

'Not great, I'm afraid. I did full background checks on the film crew and, with the exception of the usual speeding tickets and one DUI, they all seem kosher. Their statements add up and they were all together during the filming.'

'Who decided to film at Daisy House?'

Emily checked her notes. 'It was a production decision five weeks ago. They film the series quickly.'

'They've been talking to the press.'

'Looking for free publicity, I think.'

'Right, anything on the house to house?'

'I went over it again. Oliver did a good job. One old biddy thinks she saw somebody wandering around a week ago, but couldn't give a description or an age.'

'Not very useful.'

'No. As for the backpack itself, I rang the manufacturers in Leicester. The lady was extremely helpful. This particular model was produced in 2009 as a limited edition, only six hundred made.

They were popular with skateboarders, selling out as soon as they went on release. Apparently, three were sent to Manchester.'

'My daughter spotted something last night as I was looking at the backpack—'

'The one who sleeps late?' asked Chrissy.

Ridpath nodded. 'She said this backpack is only available at one place in Manchester. It's called Bagsy in Afflecks.'

'I know it. On the second floor, I used to get stuff there.' Emily wrote a note in her book.

'Great, can you check it out? See if they remember the backpack. Even better if they remember who they sold it to.'

'Could be difficult after nearly twelve years.'

'Have a go anyway, we might get lucky. Oliver, have you anything?'

'I checked the hospitals, university anatomy departments and funeral directors in a forty-mile radius to see if any body parts had been stolen recently. Nothing. They were all a bit miffed with my questions, citing the laws regarding the protection of human tissue. Apparently, these were strengthened in 2004. Didn't teach us that at college. They were all scared shitless I was accusing them of breaking the law.' He laughed to himself. 'I also checked police reports and there are none with embalmed body parts being stolen.'

'Great, well done, Oliver. Your work rules out a prank or joke played by some students.'

'Thank God,' said Dave Connor.

Ridpath ignored him and carried on. 'Right, your turn, Dave. Yesterday, Hannah Palmer had a hit on the DNA of one of the hands. It came up as a Joseph Rowlands, aged fifty-two, of Moston. What did you find?'

The detective walked over to a picture of a dour man with short, cropped hair and close-set eyes. 'This is Joseph Rowlands. He came up on the DNA database because he was convicted of child molestation in 2013 and sentenced to two years in prison. He was placed on the Sexual Offenders Register and released in late 2014. I checked his old address yesterday and the one he gave to the register. Nobody had heard of him. There were no further arrests in Manchester.'

'Nothing on the Police National Computer?'

Dave shook his head. 'Nothing. And the last address on the Sexual Offenders Register was after he was released. In 2015 he was living in Moston. I also checked with Walton Gaol where he did his time. Apparently he was badly assaulted in prison in early 2014. His hand was broken and he went for surgery at the Royal in Liverpool. The plate was removed in 2015.'

'So we have confirmed the identity is Joseph Rowlands?'

Oliver Davis was sticking a summary of the case notes under Rowlands's picture.

'We have,' replied Dave Connor.

'He vanished, until yesterday when we discovered his DNA. No reports of him missing?'

'There was a report filed in 2018 that Chrissy dug up. It's been emailed to you. I also checked the case files from his arrest in 2013.'

'And?'

'Guess what?'

'I hate guessing games, Dave, just tell me what you found out.'

'Joseph Rowlands was employed from 1995 until 2006 as head gardener at Daisy House Children's Home.'

Chapter 39

'What?' shouted Emily Parkinson.

'Joseph Rowlands worked at Daisy House for eleven years.'

'Is that our link?' Ridpath marched over to the picture and tapped it. 'We need to find out more about this man. I'm becoming increasingly convinced that finding the hands in a backpack at Daisy House was no coincidence. Dave, you stay on Rowlands. Discover what happened to him after he was released from prison.'

'Will do.'

'And, Chrissy, find out about all the people who worked at Daisy House, there's a link there, I feel it in my water.'

'What do you want me to do?' asked Oliver

'You help Dave, he's not as quick on his feet as he used to be.'

The older detective smiled. 'I'm built for comfort not speed these days. But I can still beat you in a race to the pub, Ridpath.'

The door to the incident room opened and Inspector Holloway barged in. 'Connor and Ridpath, see me in my office, now. I want a full update from both of you.'

The door remained open as Holloway walked away down the corridor.

They all stared at each other.

'His Master's Voice,' said Dave.

'We have a nightmare amount of work and only a short time to get it done,' said Ridpath. 'Work quickly, but even better, work smartly. I guess he wants us to see him now, Dave.'

'After you, Ridpath.'

Slowly, they both followed the chief inspector down the long corridor to his office.

'This feels like going to the headmaster when I was at school, worrying I was going to get the cane.'

'They don't use corporal punishment in schools any more, Dave.'

'More's the pity.'

The chief inspector was waiting for them. 'Sit down, you two.' He pointed to the two seats in front of his desk. When Dave Connor and Ridpath had made themselves uncomfortable, he continued speaking. 'Bring me up to date. The acting chief constable is up my arse looking for a result and he wants it quickly.'

Ridpath was tempted to check under the table to see if the acting chief constable was there, but felt it wouldn't have gone well with Holloway. Instead he glanced across at Dave Connor. Even though Ridpath was, to all intents and purposes, now running the investigation, he knew enough about GMP politics to understand that Dave had to take the lead on this. After all, it was his manor and his boss.

The detective understood immediately. 'We discovered the identity of one of the victims—'

'One of the hands?'

'Yes, sir, one of the victims,' Connor repeated, making sure his boss understood they were talking about people here. 'His name is... was,' Connor corrected himself, 'Joseph Rowlands, and he was reported missing in 2018. We're actively looking at his record and checking out his last known address, relatives, friends and acquaintances.'

'Record?'

'He was a convicted sex offender, sir, served sixteen months of a two-year sentence in Walton.'

'Shit, just what I need, a bloody paedo...'

Dave Connor ignored him. 'We also have a lead on the back-pack the hands were found in. We should be able to get more by this afternoon.'

'Nothing on the other two hands?'

'One is a male and the other a female, but both had been embalmed, so the DNA may have been compromised. Hannah Palmer and the lab are trying their best to obtain usable DNA.'

'What about fingerprints? You've got bloody hands, haven't you?'

'There wasn't any blood on the hands, sir.'

'Don't take the piss, Dave. Any matches on IDENT 1?'

'They're still trying to get good samples, sir, so no matches on the fingerprint database so far.'

'Push them to work harder, Dave.'

'They are doing their best, sir.'

A grunt greeted this statement. Holloway thought for a moment. 'Is his lot helping?'

It was as if Ridpath wasn't there.

'Most definitely, sir. DI Ridpath and his team have been indispensable.'

Another grunt.

'Listen, Dave, I want this wrapped up quickly and off our books. I see you've logged it as three different cases?'

'Three different victims, sir, plus there may be more.'

'More?'

'We may not have found the others, sir. They may be kept in a different place. Plus we haven't found the bodies yet. We don't know what happened to them.'

'Don't tell me there could be more, Dave, it's not what I want to hear.'

'It's a possibility... *sir*.' Ridpath spoke for the first time.

Holloway eyed him with disdain, before turning back to Connor. 'Keep your investigation to what you've already found, Dave, don't go hunting for more. Understand?'

'Understood, sir, but—'

'No buts, Dave, just clear these three... victims as quickly as you can, preferably before Monday. We have the divisional meetings next week and I want these off my books. I want to report a win to the acting chief constable and if it's not possible, I want to move this investigation over to the Cold Case Unit. The hands are at least ten years old, correct?'

'That's probably not true, sir, Joseph Rowlands didn't vanish until 2018.'

Holloway stared at Ridpath. 'Right, over three years old. Good enough for me.'

He opened up a file on his desk covered in numbers. 'Well, I won't hold you back from your work.'

Both Ridpath and Connor understood they had been dismissed. They stood up and walked towards the door.

'Make sure you clear it by Monday, Dave,' Holloway said without looking up from his file.

Chapter 40

'Rather you than me, Dave.'

Ridpath was walking to his car accompanied by the rotund detective.

'Yap. Yap. Yap. Sometimes I feel like one of those bloody Pekinese lap dogs. I stand there yapping and nobody is taking a blind bit of notice.'

Opposite, Lancashire Cricket were playing a match of the Country Championship season to an empty ground, a situation no different from their usual levels of attendance.

'Having Holloway as a boss. He seems like a real pain…'

'At least I know where I stand with him.'

'Up against a wall?'

'Being pissed on from a great height.'

They both laughed.

'We've known some numpties in our time, Ridpath.' Dave Connor went quiet for a moment. 'I miss the old days with Charlie Whitworth, when the only job was to find the bad guys and get the evidence to put them away for a long, long time. Now, it's become all so… political.'

'I think it always was, Dave, remember the miners' strike? It's just more obvious these days, there's no longer a pretence that we aren't involved in politics. Our job hasn't changed though; we still need to find out who did it and why, and put them behind bars. Let our bosses play their games, Dave.'

Connor expelled more smoke. 'What's it like working for the coroner?'

'A breath of fresh air. There's only one focus; to represent the dead in the land of the living. Mrs Challinor never forgets what her job is.'

'I wish it were true of our lot. But you heard him, Ridpath, we have to wrap this up quickly.'

'We have two good leads to work on. I'll call Emily and Chrissy to let them know we need to get together this evening rather than tomorrow morning.' Luckily, Eve was going to be picked up by Mrs Dunwoody and he didn't need to go to her school. 'Let's meet at five in the situation room. The others can join by Zoom if necessary.'

Dave Connor thought for a moment. 'I thought it over last night. I've decided I've had enough, Ridpath.'

'I though you said you had two more years to go.'

'I've done twenty-eight years now and it's enough. Time to work on the garden the missus keeps nagging me to fix, and she's always wanted a new conservatory. This case will be my last.'

'Sorry to hear that, Dave, you're one of the old school.'

'The last of the dinosaurs, huh? Fred Flintstone going around with his big club?'

'You know that's not what I meant.'

'I know, but that's what it feels like. Being a dinosaur in a world I don't really understand any more.'

'Let's go out with a bang not a whimper, Dave. Leave them asking for more.'

For the first time, the detective smiled. 'My thoughts exactly, Ridpath, it would be good to shove Holloway's nose in it.'

'You going to visit Rowlands's old address?'

'Yeah, time to see what I can dig up. Where are you going?'

'Off to see an old mate of mine. An undertaker.'

'Only you could be friends with an undertaker.' Dave Connor scratched his nose, looking up at Ridpath. 'Let's show them what some real old-fashioned coppering can do, before they put us out to pasture. What do you say?'

'Couldn't agree more, Dave, but let's still use DNA, OK? Sometimes this modern stuff helps.'

Chapter 41

'Morning, Padraig, how's tricks?'

The undertaker was in his back room dusting the head of the mannequin lying in an open coffin. As Ridpath tapped him on the shoulder, he jumped into the air.

'Jesus, Mr Ridpath, don't go sneaking up on a man, not in a funeral parlour. You'll be after sending me to an early grave. I didn't hear you come in and now my heart's beating faster than a horse at the Curragh.'

Despite living and working in Manchester for the last twenty years, he still retained his Irish accent.

'What can I do you for? I hope this isn't a business visit? With the corona and all, I've been too busy to take a breath.'

'No, I need to pick your brains, Padraig.'

'Thank God, I thought you were here to pick my pocket. Now didn't I have your bloody boss, the bald-headed fella—'

'DCI Turnbull.'

'Him as well. He was in here looking for donations to the Benevolent Fund last week. An ugly-looking man, hands that scraped the floor, if you know what I mean.'

'How much money did you give him?'

'Money? I never give those fellas money. Sure, I offered him the free use of a coffin when the need arose. He wasn't a happy man when he left, but you have to have some craic with the eejits, don't ye.'

'Don't cross him, Padraig.'

'Ach, I've buried far better than him. Now, how can I help you?'

'We've discovered some hands in a backpack. They were embalmed.'

'I read about it in the papers and one of your young Johnnies rang me to ask if the hands were mine. As if they were. I wouldn't last long in this profession if I didn't look after my clients.'

'The lab have given me the chemical composition of the embalming fluid.'

'And you want me to tell you where it came from?'

'You're a sharp man, Padraig.'

'I wasn't born yesterday, Mr Ridpath. Let me check online for you.' He walked across to the laptop on his desk. 'What's the chemical composition?'

Ridpath read from his notes. 'Twenty-two per cent formaldehyde, forty-three per cent methanol and eight per cent glutaraldehyde.'

'I can tell you straight away with the level of formaldehyde, this embalming fluid was used for preservation, not presentation.'

'What's the difference?'

'Lots. As funeral directors, we're looking to make the client as natural as possible, so we use our machines to inject the fluid into the arteries in a closed circulatory system. Afterwards, some embalmers drain the fluid and others, like me, leave it in the client. I think it gives a better, more natural look.'

'So what happens when you are simply preserving the… object?'

'You inject it in multiple sites to saturate the tissues. Generally used by researchers or medical professionals. It's the old organs in jars from movies like *Frankenstein*. These days I don't even use formaldehyde, too dangerous, there's lots of new embalming fluids without formaldehyde. Ah, here it is. Twenty-two per cent formaldehyde, forty-three per cent methanol and eight per cent glutaraldehyde. Your embalming fluid is American, they're always a little behind the times. A company in Virginia, sells mainly online.' He frowned. 'That's strange.'

'What?'

'They closed down a long time ago.'

'When?'

He scanned the web page. 'It says here they ceased trading in 2009.'

Chapter 42

Patricia Patterson was shivering when she woke up.

It wasn't from the cold, if anything the room was quite warm, even though she was only wearing shirtsleeves. It was pitch dark and Bible black. So dark she couldn't see her hands even though she knew they were lying only three inches away from her face.

What time was it? How long has she slept?

A paralysing fear gripped her body, making even the slightest movement impossible. She tried to lift her head and immediately let it fall back heavily against the rough mattress.

She knew where she was and it scared her.

Were they going to do to her what they had done to the others?

She began to scream.

Again and again and again.

She didn't want to die.

Not like the others.

Chapter 43

'Hi, Sophia, what have you got for me?' After finishing with Padraig Daly, Ridpath had driven straight back to the coroner's office.

'I went through the missing person file you sent me for Jane Ryder.'

'And? What do you think?'

'It's a bit weak, isn't it? No follow-up with the friend, Rose Gray, and I noticed there was a referral to Social Services, but again, no report. Are you sure you sent me everything?'

'It's all there is in the file. I forgot to ask Chrissy if she'd found more documents when I saw her this morning, but I'm sure she would have told me if she'd dug them up.'

Sophia checked her notes. 'I googled Rose Gray. Of course, there were over two and a half million results.'

'Not helpful.'

'Not at all. So I checked the missing person file and her address was give as 24 Earlington Road, Sale. I cross-checked the name on the electoral register for 2009 and found a family with the surname Gray living at the address. It was a Mr and Mrs Alfred Gray.'

'Great, Sophia, we need to go round there.'

'I already checked it out, Ridpath.'

'I thought you might. And?'

'And… they aren't living there anymore.'

'Not surprising, it was nearly twelve years ago. Well done, at least we know she existed. Why didn't the police check with her? The parents certainly did.'

'I'm not finished yet. I guessed Rose may have married in the meantime and perhaps changed her last name. So I went to the registrar of marriages and found three Rose Grays had married in England in the period between 2009 and 2020.'

'You're going to tell me you found her, aren't you?'

'I rang all three possibilities and found the girl we were looking for living in…'

'Manchester?'

'Right first time. One of the new developments on Palatine Road. She's now known as Rose Anstey and she works for ITV at Salford Quays. I've arranged for you to see her tomorrow during her lunch break. I hope it was the right time for you?'

'Perfect.'

'There's more. I went to see Mr Roscoe, Jane's old teacher, this morning at the school. He basically said she was the perfect student: bright, attentive, hard working and punctual. She was expected to go straight into the sixth form, studying History and English. He seemed genuinely devastated she disappeared.'

'Did you check up on him?'

'Of course. The school secretary had nothing but praise, said he doted on his pupils. Perhaps a little too much.'

'Interesting, worth following up. It wouldn't be the first time a teacher had a relationship with a young female pupil.'

'I can ask around.'

'Do it. You asked him to make himself available for the inquest?'

'He wasn't too chuffed, neither was the school secretary. They were complaining about having to arrange a substitute teacher.'

'It's a hard life,' said Ridpath, without any sympathy. 'How about the other friend, Andrea Briggs? She's not mentioned in the misper report.'

'Perhaps the police didn't talk to her? Anyway, nothing so far. Couldn't find any Briggs listed in the electoral register and I forgot to ask the school.'

'No worries, keep looking. Have I ever told you, you're a bloody marvel, Sophia.'

'No.'

'Well, you are.'

An awkward silence stretched between the two of them for a second before Ridpath pointed over his shoulder. 'I'd better be off. Time to see a copper about a missing girl.'

'Take care, Ridpath.'

'Will do, but it'll be easier to take the car.' He blushed. 'Sorry, one of my daughter's jokes.'

'The old ones are still the best.'

Chapter 44

Emily left the car up in the multi-storey car park off Tib Street and crossed Oldham Road to Afflecks.

She remembered her old stomping ground so well. Every couple of months, she would hop on the train with her mum from Preston to Manchester early on a Saturday morning. It was a day out for the girls, away from their dad, away from everything.

One of their first stops was Afflecks, to pick up some new clothes and accessories to impress the other girls at her school. Lunch was always in Yang Sing and afterwards they wandered around Primark, Market Street and the Arndale, checking out the shop windows and trying on as many outfits as they could.

Lovely days, a time she would remember for the rest of her life.

She stood outside the old building for a moment, looking up at the yellow and pink painted sandstone. It had been spruced up a bit since she used to come here. In fact, the whole area had been tarted up and rebranded as the Northern Quarter. Gone were the dingy old pubs and textile importers and exporters, replaced by fashionably distressed cafes serving artisan espressos and homemade biscotti, sleek bars with a range of obscure cocktails, and incredibly expensive restaurants where the cute and trendy could waste their hard-earned money looking cool and collected.

Afflecks was still the same though. Next to the entrance, the painted wall still held the delicious description of what waited inside: *Afflecks. The eclectic arcade of the geekily hip and the lovingly handmade and the skilfully pierced lip, not to mention our treasures and trinkets and tokens, so come in, dear friend, we're unique and we're open.*

She smiled to herself and walked through the entrance beneath a riot of fading Christmas decorations. Inside, it still looked the same. Sure, the names above the shops may have changed, but the atmosphere was still there; more a market than a shopping mall, selling everything and anything for the young boy or girl on a visit to the big city.

She remembered she had her first piercing here. Only her left ear, the nose was to come much later. After an age of gentle and not so gentle persuasion, her mum had finally agreed. Thirteen-year-old Emily had climbed the stairs to the shop on the third floor, sat down in the chair and waited in expectation for the sharp pain of a piercing. Instead there was a slight click, a dab of rough-smelling alcohol and the words, 'That'll be six ninety-nine, love.'

Touching her ear, she could feel the slight indentation of the piercing. She didn't wear earrings on the job, though, they weren't safe. What if some nutter grabbed hold of one and ripped it away during a struggle?

She given up a lot to be a police officer. Perhaps she should have listened to her parents and stayed as a management trainee. But she knew she would have hated every second. She loved her job, despite the Turnbulls of the world and the long hours and the shifts and the bloody sexism that still ran through the police like letters in a stick of Blackpool rock, even though they swore it didn't.

She was a bloody good copper and now was the time to prove it.

She climbed the stairs, past the posters and stickers on the walls, past the fashion shops, the nail bars, the emo stores, the anime cafe, a display cupboard of skull merchandise, a tarot reader, a shop selling old cassettes and all the rest.

It was like she'd been transported back to being a fourteen-year-old girl who'd found her own private heaven. Bagsy was still on the second floor, close to a record shop, a crystal henge and the store's resident poet.

Inside and outside, the shop was festooned with backpacks and bags; checkered, skate, cute and cool, emo, goth, skulls and punk designs looked down on Emily. She even recognised a skull backpack she had bought for school, only to be told it was 'inappropriate'.

Luckily, before she could buy it again, the manager appeared. 'Can I help?'

'I'm DS Emily Parkinson, I rang earlier.' She flashed her warrant card.

'About the CLAK backpack?'

'That's it. You still sell them?'

'One of our popular skater brands. Not as big as when Avril Lavigne was singing, but still going strong.'

'Did you sell them in 2009?'

'A long way back. I'm pretty sure we did.'

'And you worked here when they did?'

'Since it opened in 2004, love. This is my life.' She pointed to all the bags and backpacks on the wall.

Emily pumped her fist. Sometimes the god of detectives smiled down on her. 'You're the owner?'

'I am, love. Opened it years ago and the only time we ever closed was last year.'

'Can you remember this backpack?'

Emily showed her the picture taken by Hannah Palmer at the lab.

'Sorry, we've sold so many over the years.'

Emily frowned. It looked like a wasted journey. 2009 was too long ago.

'But we've still got some of the inventory ledgers from back then – you can take a look if you want. I'm afraid I write everything down, a bit old school. I don't trust computers, never did.'

Emily smiled. It looked like she would be spending a lot longer here than she thought. Hopefully she would resist the temptation of the backpacks. 'Thanks, that would be great,' she finally answered, following the woman into the storeroom.

Chapter 45

After Ridpath left, Sophia thought about going out for another coffee, but realised she'd already drunk two that day. If she went for a third, she would be up all night staring at the walls, trying to make sheep jump over stupid fences, or even worse, wasting her time on Twitter reading the latest gossip.

'Time to do some work,' she said out loud.

The office was quiet.

The coroner's door was closed as she was preparing for her inquest. Helen Moore was somewhere in Derbyshire being a locum coroner, while Jenny was in the courtroom making sure the Covid protocols were being followed to the letter.

Ridpath's absence only emphasised the emptiness. Somehow, he filled it whenever he was there. Sophia hadn't seen him much recently. Yesterday at the Ryders was the longest she'd spent with him in the last week. He always seemed to be rushing here and there, never really spending long enough in any one place to get anything finished. She was beginning to worry about him. A diet of soggy sandwiches, pasties and coffee was not good for his health.

'Not your job to worry about me,' she said, mimicking his voice. 'Just do the bloody work.' She mock-saluted. 'Yes, sir, Mr Ridpath.'

She wrote out a to-do list.

1. Ring school re Andrea Briggs

2. Check up on the teacher

3. Festivals. Which one did Jane Ryder go to?

Picking up the phone, she dialled the number for the school secretary.

'Hi there, this is Sophia Rahman from the coroner's office again. Sorry to bother you, but I wonder if you could tell me about one of the pupils who attended school at the same time as Jane Ryder. Her name was Andrea Briggs.'

'I'm sorry, I don't remember anybody of that name. Hang on, here's Mr Roscoe, perhaps he'll know her.'

A male voice came on the line. 'You're asking about an Andrea Briggs?'

'That's right.'

'I vaguely remember her. Tall for her age, left school when she was sixteen. Younger than Jane Ryder though.'

'Younger? They were supposed to be friends.'

'At least a couple of years younger. I can't remember if they spent time together though. If I'm honest, I can't remember much about Andrea Briggs, she was a quiet girl.'

Sophia glanced at the second item on her list. She decided to take the plunge and ask her question. 'Do you get close to the pupils, Mr Roscoe?'

'Some of them. It can't be helped. It's easier working with some rather than others.'

'Do you find getting close to the female pupils can lead to problems?'

The voice changed. Sophia could detect a note of wariness. 'What are you insinuating, Miss Rahman?'

She laughed to put him at ease. 'Nothing at all, Mr Roscoe. I just remember when I was at school we always had crushes on the teachers.'

'I don't know what kind of school you went to, Miss Rahman, but I can assure you nothing of that sort ever happens in any establishment where I work. Now, if you'll excuse me, I have a class to teach.'

The line went dead.

'Well, that went well. Defensive much?' she said to the phone.

She wrote a quick note to herself to investigate further, but how do you find out about a teacher? She tried the ratemyteacher site, but there was nothing on it about Mr Roscoe. A google of the school's name simply revealed it was well regarded in the community and it had a Good rating from Ofsted, with a particular commendation for the school's management.

Perhaps another visit to the school might be necessary to get the info she needed direct from the horse's mouth or, in this case, direct from the pupils. She'd check with Ridpath first though, just in case that wasn't the right way to go about the job.

She glanced down at the last item on her list. Festivals. The obvious place to start was with the nearest event: Mad Ferret in Platt Fields. What a great name. She had once asked to go to Glastonbury for the weekend but her mum had been firm.

'Good Muslim girls don't go out on their own, and they certainly don't go to music festivals with half-naked men and women dancing. What if you were seen? I'd never hold my head high in the community again.'

She had been tempted to say that if she were seen, it would mean somebody else had gone too. But she kept her mouth shut. Sometimes it was better to beat a strategic retreat rather than face the forces of Mum head-on.

Later, she had found ways to get around her mother's rules. There were always ways.

She googled the Mad Ferret Festival. 2009 was one of the last years before it changed into Parklife, moved to Heaton Park and became massive, attracting over 160,000 people from all over the world. In 2009, though, it was still small and frequented mainly by students. A couple of laid-back days in Platt Fields rather than a crowded extravaganza.

Glancing down the responses, she noticed one interesting hit: a picture in the *Evening News* of a forest of heads and in the background a stage with a band playing. The photograph was taken by a man called Gary Trueman.

She googled his name and had twenty-seven major hits, mostly on photography websites. But one stood out. It was captioned 'Mad Ferret 2009', and was stored on the Wayback site. She clicked it, stared at the landing page for twenty seconds and whispered, 'Shit.'

Chapter 46

Ridpath showed his warrant card to the copper on duty at Longsight Police Station. 'DI Ridpath, here to see Sergeant Dowell.'

The copper waved him in and he parked in the only remaining visitor's bay.

Longsight was one of those places where streets and streets of Victorian back-to-back housing had been knocked down in the 1970s in the race for regeneration.

Unfortunately the government cuts had come in and for a long while the place had been a wasteland of fly tipping, ugly advertising hoardings and brick-strewn, half-abandoned building sites. The regeneration had finally occurred and acres of brick houses had been built, each as ugly as the one next to it.

In the middle of this morass of modernisation, the police had knocked down a beautiful old Victorian school and replaced it with this monstrosity. Longsight Police Station. From the outside, it looked like a Travelodge designed by Dr Frankenstein.

The inside was not much better, with stained walls, sticky carpets and a sour smell oozing from the walls.

Ridpath met Colin Dowell in one of the interview rooms before the man went on duty. The young police constable of the missing person form had been replaced by a dour, moon-faced sergeant, fond of a Holland's pie or three. He was still buttoning up his uniform over an expansive stomach when he entered the interview room.

'DI Ridpath. I'm duty sergeant today and Terry will go apeshit if I'm late.'

'This won't take long, Colin. As I told you over the phone, I'm seconded to the coroner's office. In 2009, you took a statement from the parents of a missing girl, Jane Ryder.'

'I did?'

'You don't remember?'

The man shrugged his broad shoulders. '2009? I was a PC then, attached to Sale station, I think.'

Ridpath passed across the missing person file. 'Is this your signature on the bottom?'

Dowell glanced at it. 'That's me.' He read through the document. 'I remember now, this was the runaway with the weird mother who kept knitting all the time.'

'Runaway?'

'Yeah, she'd gone off to some music festival and didn't come back. Must have met some guy or other. With a mum like hers, I wasn't surprised she did a runner.'

'Is that why you put her down as a medium risk even though she was sixteen at the time?'

'Because of the age, I was going to put it down as high risk, but I talked to the boss—'

'Ron Roper?'

'That's right. Sad about him. Retired and two years later collapsed from a heart attack on the golf course.'

Ridpath ignored the last remark. 'What did he decide?'

'We consulted with the missing person's manager and the social worker and decided to make her a medium risk.'

'What was the name of the social worker?'

Dowell shrugged his shoulders. 'Who remembers social workers?'

'Why not make Jane Ryder high risk?'

'It was twelve years ago, Ridpath, I can't remember.'

'Have a think.'

Dowell sucked in air between his teeth, making a whistling noise. 'She had a history of running away, and the manager spoke to Social Services. The girl was known to them, I think. I also chatted to her best friend—'

'Rose Gray?'

'I can't remember the name. She said there was a possible boyfriend who the parents didn't like. So we put two and two together and—'

'Came up with five.'

'What's all this about, DI Ridpath? Why is the coroner looking into it after all this time?'

'The parents have asked for a presumption of death certificate, so I've been told to investigate. The inquest could be as soon as next week. You'll be called to give evidence.'

'I'm off next week.'

Ridpath smiled. 'Not any more. I'll get our office manager to send you a note to make yourself available.'

'And if I don't?'

'You'll be subpoenaed and arrested if you fail to appear. Not a good career move, Colin.'

The sergeant remained quiet, but Ridpath could see his face gradually becoming redder and redder, a blood vessel pulsing on his temple.

'Who was the missing person's co-ordinator?'

'A woman, Doreen Hawkins. A civilian officer with the Missing From Home lot. I'll leave the missing person report with you to help refresh your memory before I go.' Ridpath stood up. 'One last thing. You said you interviewed Rose Gray, but there's no contact report in the file.'

Colin Dowell shrugged his shoulders. 'Of course I reported the interview. But you know what our filing system is like. I'm surprised you've found this form.'

'What about her friend, Andrea Briggs?'

The sergeant shook his head. 'Never heard of her.'

'See you next week, Colin.'

'Do I have to, DI Ridpath, can't somebody else do it?'

'Sorry, with Inspector Roper no longer available, you're it, I'm afraid.'

The sergeant shook his head. 'First time off in six months. Me and the missus were planning on going to Wales.'

'Come to Stockfield instead. Not as pretty, but the bacon butties are better.'

'Ho bloody ho.' Then a look of recognition came into Dowell's eyes. 'Ridpath, I remember you. Wasn't your missus killed by some nutter? Shot down in her hallway?'

Ridpath nodded slowly.

'OK, let me think about this Jane Ryder woman, see if I can remember anything.' He stood up and stuck out his hand.

Ridpath hated sympathy, he never knew what to say. The words always came out wrong, or sounded clichéd. So he just took Colin Dowell's hand saying, 'Thanks, anything you remember could help.'

Chapter 47

In the car park, Ridpath put Bowie on the car's stereo, listening intently to the opening bars of 'Aladdin Sane'. As the piano chords struck home, he was transported to dancing with Polly in their living room, being watched by Eve, a half-chewed rusk in her mouth.

Immediately, tears stung his eyes as he thought about the unfairness of it all. They should have grown old together; him balding as she greyed, enjoying the long walks and holidays they had planned. Instead, her body was lying in a graveyard, cold and silent.

He beat the steering wheel with his hands in frustration.

Pull yourself together, Ridpath, this is not helping.

He concentrated on going to his safe place on the mountain above the reservoir, feeling the wind through his hair. A sense of peace washed over him.

She was gone and wasn't coming back; he couldn't change the past. All he could do was look to the future, ensuring Eve had the best childhood she could.

He shouldn't play Bowie any more, it brought back too many memories. It was funny the way music transported you to a time and a place so easily. As if memories were embedded in the chords, woven through the melody and knitted into the chorus.

He put the radio on instead. An announcer on Radio Manchester was talking about the latest easing of lockdown, the stupidity of the owners of football clubs, and the cricket scores at Lancashire.

Polly was dead, but life carried on.

He forced himself to think about the case. The two investigations were operating and he was running to catch up with both of them. Could he presume Jane Ryder was dead? Nobody had heard from her since that fateful June morning when she had left for a festival to meet somebody. Had she been murdered? Had she simply vanished? Why had she not contacted her parents? And where were the reports, the ones Colin Dowell said he had filed?

Perhaps it was time to advise the coroner to postpone the inquest for a few more weeks. There were too many unknowns at the moment.

And what about the other case? The hands in the backpack. It didn't seem to have advanced much either. True, they knew one of the victims now, but what about the other two? And what happened to the rest of the bodies? Why were the hands placed in the old children's home? And why were only hands taken? Where they trophies for some killer, or did they have some deeper meaning?

Again, it felt like he was swimming through treacle. Two investigations going nowhere fast and him paddling like a demented poodle desperately trying to stay afloat.

Luckily, he didn't have to pick up Eve tonight. The neighbour would do it for him.

Sitting there in the car park of the ugliest police station in Manchester, Ridpath remembered something he had forgotten to do in all the rushing around, something he had promised Eve.

It was time to get it done.

'Christies Hospital, appointment booking service, Dora here, how can I help?'

After he'd booked the check-up, he relaxed for ten seconds before his phone rang.

'Ridpath, it's Sophia.' He could hear the excitement in his assistant's voice. 'You need to come back here right away, I've got something to show you.'

Chapter 48

When Ridpath walked back into the coroner's office, Sophia was already waiting for him, sitting on the edge of the desk, her whole body charged with excitement.

'I checked up on the festivals. The Mad Ferret was held at Platt Fields Park in Manchester on June 12 and 13, 2009.'

'You told me already. It was the same dates as the Isle of Wight Festival and Download at Donington Park.'

'Now we know Jane left on Friday morning and was due back on Sunday evening as she had her last week at school.'

'That's what Mr Ryder told me.'

'It seems too far to travel all the way to the Isle of Wight, doesn't it? So for me that left Donington Park and Platt Fields, with the latter being the most likely.'

'I'm with you…'

'I checked on the Wayback Machine.'

'What the hell's that?'

'It's a website archiving old web pages no longer in use. I found some pages for the 2009 Mad Ferret Festival. Guess how much it cost for a ticket?'

Ridpath smiled. 'It wouldn't happen to be fifty-five quid, would it?'

'Right first time. And there's more. The website also has pictures taken on the first day of that year's festival. I was scanning through them and saw this.' She tapped her laptop and a picture came up. A blonde girl with her back to camera was dancing in the middle of the park with her arms raised. In the background, an out-of-focus band played on the stage.

Ridpath moved closer, squinting his eyes. 'Is that who I think it is?' he said tentatively.

'The hair looks right, doesn't it? And the clothes match the description given by Jane's parents; a red and white striped T-shirt and jeans.'

'But those clothes were pretty common for the period, especially at festivals.'

'So I hunted through the rest of the pictures. There are fifty-eight, in total but most are of the band and the stage.'

'Damn...'

'Except two.' She tapped the laptop again and another picture came up. This time, the picture was taken from the stage looking back into the crowd. 'See the girl here. She's sitting on somebody's shoulders.' Sophia zoomed in and the picture began to break up. 'But we can see her face, and it matches Jane Ryder.'

Ridpath stared at the screen. 'It certainly looks like her. Who's she with?'

'I can't make out his face. The man in front is shielding him.'

'I'll ask the photo specialists at the lab, see what they can do.'

'Hang on, there's one more.' Another picture appeared on the screen. 'Here we see her from the side. The photographer, Gary Trueman, must have liked her. She's talking to a man but he has his back to us and we can't see his face.'

Ridpath leant in closer. 'What's that at her feet?'

Sophia moved closer. 'It looks like her backpack.'

'Or his?'

'Didn't the parents say she had taken a backpack with her?'

Ridpath moved even closer. 'But what they didn't say was that it looks like the same backpack in which we found three human hands. Get on to the photographer, see if he has any other shots of the festival he didn't put on the website.'

'Will do.'

'Is the coroner in?'

'I think so.'

'I need to see her, now.'

Chapter 49

Ridpath knocked on the door and entered without waiting for the usual invitation.

'Ah, just the man I want to see.' The coroner was packing her notes and files into a briefcase.

'I need to talk to you, Mrs Challinor, something has come up.'

As Ridpath was closing the door, Mrs Challinor asked. 'How is the Ryder investigation?'

'That's what I came to talk about.'

'I'm afraid you'll have to make it brief. It's my grandson's birthday today, and I've promised to dress up as his favourite character—'

'Which is?'

'Don't laugh. The Wicked Witch of the West. For some obscure reason, he's obsessed with *The Wizard of Oz*. He's even made his own Tin Man costume.'

'Kids. Can't beat 'em, may as well join 'em.'

'My philosophy exactly. And during lockdown we were lucky enough to be bubbled together.' She stopped for a moment and smiled. 'I can't believe I said "bubbled". What strange times we live in. Anyway, for the first time in years, my daughter and I actually talked about life, the universe and everything.' She laughed to herself. 'Of course, we concluded the answer probably was forty-two. Have there been developments in your investigation of Jane Ryder?'

'A lot.'

'A lot good, or a lot bad?'

'Both.'

She sat back down. 'Tell me all, Ridpath.'

'I checked her missing person report and met the copper who interviewed the parents back in 2009. It seems little was done to follow up on her case, despite her only being sixteen when she disappeared.'

'Why?'

He frowned. 'It's difficult to say. She was classified as medium risk because, apparently, she'd run away before—'

'The parents never mentioned anything to me.'

'And she was known to Social Services, but there are no attached interviews with any social workers. In fact, the only document in the file is the missing person report.'

'Is that common?'

'For a girl of her age, probably not. The reports may have been misfiled or gone missing. The policeman involved, Sergeant Dowell, told me he did interview the friend and talked to the social worker, but doesn't remember her name.'

Mrs Challinor glanced at the family picture on her desk. 'This may show police negligence at the time, but does it impact a finding of a presumption of death? Nobody has heard from her since 2009. Has she appeared on any passport applications, driving licence records, been arrested or even applied for a bank account?'

'We couldn't find any records of her doing any of those things. However, we did find these.' He passed across copies of the photographs of Jane Ryder at the festival. 'They are from the 2009 Mad Ferret Festival. She told her parents she was going with a friend to this festival, but it was a lie. I believe she met somebody else there.'

Mrs Challinor stared at them. 'Is this her?'

'We think so.'

'Pretty girl.'

'It's obvious she either knew this man or met him at the festival.' He pointed at the man standing next to Jane Ryder. 'But even more important is this.' His finger moved down to the backpack at her feet. 'Exactly the same backpack was discovered at Daisy House Children's Home. Inside were three embalmed human hands.'

The coroner looked more closely. 'How can you be sure it's the same backpack?'

'We can't. But we know only three were sold in the Manchester area. It's a limited edition, manufactured by a skateboard company.'

Mrs Challinor put the photographs down. 'So what are you saying, Ridpath?'

Ridpath pulled down his bottom lip. 'I think the two investigations are linked, Mrs Challinor. I don't know how yet, but they are. You may need to postpone the inquest.'

'I can't do it, Ridpath.'

'But, Mrs Challinor, one of the hands we discovered in the backpack was a young girl's. The pathologist thought she was around seventeen years old. What if the hand was Jane Ryder's?'

'It would prove conclusively she was dead.'

'But if the cases are linked, this now becomes a murder inquiry, and Coroner's Rules state all inquests should be postponed until the police have completed their enquiries.'

A small smile played on Mrs Challinor's lips. 'The training has been effective, Ridpath. You are now able to quote my own rules back at me. But you make the presumption that the backpack belonged to Jane Ryder and her embalmed hand is inside. If these are both true, then I can issue a presumption of death.'

'And if they are not true?'

'In the absence of any evidence to the contrary, her total lack of documentation for the last eleven years and the lack of any communication for the same period means I can still issue a certificate.'

'Despite there being no body?'

'Despite the lack of a body.'

Ridpath sighed loudly. 'But, Coroner, I just need more time and I can give you the proof of her death.'

Mrs Challinor ran her fingers through her grey curls. 'What if we proceed with the inquest next week, calling the parents, the friends and the police to give evidence? You can introduce the backpack and request more time to follow up. I will then postpone the inquest. But at least we will have begun the process and there will be no need to waste time instituting a full inquest later on. When you have finished your enquiries, as quickly as you possibly can, I can simply call a short inquest to grant the certificate. What do you think?'

Ridpath knew Mrs Challinor was trying her best to give him more time and still accommodate the needs of the family.

'It's the best I can do. This family needs closure and to put their financial affairs in order before Mrs Ryder dies.'

Ridpath finally nodded. 'We still have a few more days. Perhaps we can solve it in that time.'

'But you don't think so, Ridpath?'

'For some reason, I have a feeling this is only the beginning.'

The phone rang on the coroner's desk. 'Just a minute.' She picked it up and began listening. 'OK, I understand. It does change everything. Thank you for the call.'

She put the phone back on its cradle. 'That was Mr Ryder. His wife has now been taken to St Jude's Hospice in Cheadle Heath. The doctors have decided she doesn't have long to live and she needs end-of-life care.' A long pause as Mrs Challinor made up her mind. 'We have to go ahead with the inquest next week, Ridpath, whatever happens.'

Chapter 50

The traffic must have been light. Either that or he drove fast. Ridpath tried to remember how he had arrived at Stretford nick, but the details of the journey eluded him. He remembered getting in the car outside the Coroner's Court and working out the journey, heading towards Stretford up the A6, past the O2 Apollo and onto the Mancunian Way.

Since then, it had all been a bit of a blur. He must have been on autopilot, his body driving the car but his mind thinking about the two cases he had to solve quickly. They both seemed to be linked, but how to pull it all together?

He locked the car and strode up the steps and through the lobby. The sergeant in charge merely nodded as he passed. They had become used to the arrival of the detective inspector from MIT now.

The others were waiting for him in the situation room.

'Right, we're all here,' said Dave Connor, rubbing his hands together. 'Chrissy sent me a message. She's still at HQ but she'll join us on Zoom when we're ready.'

Ridpath opened up his laptop and connected to the Zoom meeting. Emily sat there quietly, a coffee from the canteen in front of her. Oliver Davis was poised in front of the whiteboard, marker pen in hand. Dave Connor tapped the desk nervously while waiting for the link to connect.

'I've had Holloway in my ear all afternoon, Ridpath, he's hassling for a result,' he whispered.

'He made it clear this morning, Dave, but you know what we have to do.'

'But he doesn't. His background is traffic.'

Ridpath's eyes rolled. 'OK, you want me to handle him?'

'No, I'll do it.'

'Hiya.'

A bright voice and even brighter face appeared on the screen.

'Hiya, Chrissy, I hope you have some good news for us.'

'I do, Ridpath, and some bad news.'

'Go on.'

'I've tracked down the list of people who worked at Daisy House from 1986 until it closed in 2006. There are thirty-two names on it, including ancillary workers, residential social workers, managers and admin and even gardeners. Joseph Rowlands's name is on the list.'

'Great, Chrissy, so what's the problem?'

'Well, it only includes full-time staff. It doesn't include any volunteers or part-time staff.'

'Why is it a problem?' asked Dave Connor.

'Well, it doesn't include names like Jimmy Savile, who we know visited the home in 1996 and 1998.'

'Because he was only volunteering?'

'Correct, Ridpath.'

'Still, it's a start. Can you look into those names and find out where they are now?'

'Will do, Ridpath.'

'And how did you get on with Jane Ryder's missing documents?'

'You want me to do that now, or after this meeting?'

'Now, please. I'll explain why later.'

'I still haven't found them, but I have a good idea of where they might be. I'm heading there later, after I've been through the 2013 Operation Pharaoh files. Too much to do and too little time, Ridpath.'

'Don't I know it. Emily, how did you get on?'

The detective took out her notes from her new backpack, covered in a skull motif. 'Bagsy did sell the CLAK backpack.

It was part of a limited edition produced in early June 2009. According to their inventory ledger, the shop only received three pieces and all of them sold out in one day. The owner remembers it clearly. She tried to get more stock, but the factory said there wasn't any.'

'Who bought them?'

'I don't know. I went through her sales records, but the ones for 2009 weren't there. She thought she threw them out a while ago when she cleared old paper from her office.'

'A dead end?'

'Not quite. She remembers selling them all on one day. June 1, 2009, the day they arrived. She seems to think they were all bought with a credit card.'

'Great, we can check with the company for receipts for the day.'

'Already on it, Ridpath. They are going to get back to me.'

'See if you can push them, Emily. Dave, how did you get on?'

'I tracked Joseph Rowlands's movements after he came out of prison in 2014. He returned to Manchester, reporting on the Sexual Offenders Register as he was supposed to, but disappeared after the operation to remove the plate in his hand in 2015. We don't know what happened to him or where he went until he turns up in 2016 in Wolverhampton—'

'We found him through DVLA. He applied for a HGV licence, working for a haulier in the West Midlands,' interrupted Oliver Davis.

'Are we sure it's the same man?'

'Positive. I sent a mugshot of him from his 2013 arrest and the haulier confirmed it was Rowlands. He worked there until early 2017—'

'They remembered him?'

'Yeah, said he was a good, conscientious worker, always on time, but he didn't mix much. A bit of a loner. Then he vanishes again until the missing person report on him in 2018. He was living in Moston and working for Oldham Council.'

'What happened between 2017 and 2018?'

'We're still looking at it.'

'Keep going, but good work, Dave and Oliver.'

'Anything from Hannah?'

'Nothing more. I'll give her a call, but I'm sure she would've let us know if they'd pulled more DNA.'

'Of course. Now, I said I would explain why I want Chrissy to follow up on the coroner's misper, Jane Ryder.' He placed the photographs Sophia had found on the desk. 'Come and look at these. Chrissy, I'll send you copies later.'

'Right-oh, Ridpath.'

The others stood up and rushed across to the desk. It was Oliver Davis who spotted it first. 'The backpack. It's the same as the one we found in the house.'

'These photos were taken at the Mad Ferret Festival in 2009. A girl, Jane Ryder, this girl—' he pointed at one of the images '—disappeared there and vanished completely. No contact with her parents, no phone calls to friends, nothing. And there is no documentation on her after 2009. The backpack in the photo matches the one with the hands. Was it hers? We have to prove the link.'

'I'm on it, Ridpath,' said Emily.

'Plus who was this man standing with her?'

'But—'

'What is it, Dave?'

'If this is her backpack, one of the hands we discovered belonged to a teenager. You said this girl—'

'Jane Ryder.'

'Was sixteen when she disappeared.'

'Exactly, Dave. Is our female hand Jane Ryder? If it is, we need to find this man as soon as possible.' Ridpath prodded the photograph with his index finger. 'He could be our killer.'

Chapter 51

The drug had finally worn off.

Her head was woozy but at least she could now sit upright with her back against the wooden wall.

Ten feet above her head, a neon strip light was now on, illuminating the stark whiteness of the walls of her cell.

Were they watching her?

She checked the walls and the door for hidden cameras, but there didn't seem to be any. They were probably watching though.

They always watched. It was what they enjoyed.

She tried to swallow but couldn't. Her throat was hoarse and sore from screaming. What a waste of time and energy. They were never going to respond.

Not yet.

A raging thirst ravaged her body. She needed to drink, and soon, otherwise she was going to die in this white room.

Perhaps they were listening?

'I'm extremely thirsty. I need water, I feel like I'm dying,' she said out loud, hearing a slight echo off the walls. 'I'm extremely thirsty,' she repeated.

No response.

Was she going to die here?

Not yet. Not until they were ready.

The door opened and a hand slid a tray into the room with a jug of water and a sandwich. Before she could move, the hand withdrew and the door was slammed shut.

They were listening.

She wasn't going to die.

Not yet.

Chapter 52

Emily glanced around the situation room. She loved times like this.

Dave Connor and Oliver Davis were arguing over how to enter the IDENT 1 database. Chrissy was working through the Operation Pharaoh files. A pile of pizza boxes lay empty on another table alongside used and battered cups from Costa.

Emily had finished updating the case report, including her own investigations into the backpack.

Ridpath wasn't there, but Emily knew he was working at home after picking up Eve, going over the files one more time to see if they had missed a possible lead.

The case was moving forward, probably not as fast as Ridpath wanted, but still they were making progress, and quickly.

Emily wondered what she would be like as a mother. The prospect was extremely unlikely at the moment; the job left little time for socialising and she had decided a long time ago that the last place she would look for a potential mate would be the available police gene pool.

The whole idea of dating and marrying somebody from the job appalled her. The usual joke of giving the baby a truncheon rather than a rattle appalled her even more.

She shook her head and grimaced. She was only twenty-eight, there was plenty of time for babies later. For now, she wanted to concentrate on her career.

Perhaps tomorrow she would approach Chief Inspector Holloway. The gossip in the canteen whispered he was desperate to find detectives for his team. Her days at MIT seemed to be numbered; Turnbull had made it pretty obvious her face didn't fit. If she was going to be promoted, she would have to spend some time working in one of the divisions anyway. At least Stretford wasn't far from where she lived. Imagine if she was placed somewhere a long way away, like Oldham; the commute would kill her.

Chrissy punched the air. 'Yes.'

Had Manchester City scored?

'I think I've found the misper files for Jane Ryder. Now I have to traipse down there and trawl through them. They've not been digitised. Bugger.'

Chrissy lowered her head close to the laptop once more, unaware she had been talking to herself. Dave Connor and Oliver Davis were still arguing about IDENT 1.

A slice of pizza was staring at Emily, peeping out from beneath the box lid. She checked a thin sliver of tummy hanging over the waistband of her trousers.

Sod it, she'd go to the gym when the case finished.

She loved times like this, working a case. There was no other feeling like it.

Chapter 53

Ridpath went over the missing person reports again, checking to see if he had overlooked anything. On his right, the pictures of Jane Ryder at the music festival were leaning against a glass of Macallan.

What had happened to her?

He picked up the whisky, the golden liquid swirling around like molten honey, and swallowed, feeling the bite on the back of his tongue.

Eve was in bed, the TV was off and silence reigned supreme. He'd picked his daughter up from the neighbours at 7.30 p.m.

'Hi, Dad, you're late again.'

'Sorry.' He put his arm around his daughter's shoulders. She was getting taller. 'Has Eve been any trouble, Mrs Dunwoody?'

'Please call me Angela. None at all. It's always a delight to have Eve over.'

'Hello, I'm standing here. Please talk about me behind my back or not at all.'

They both laughed.

Angela pushed a strand of hair off her face and behind her ear. 'I'm just sitting down to spag bol and a glass of wine. If you've nothing better to do, perhaps you'd like to join me.'

Ridpath shook his head. 'Sorry, I'd love to, but I have some work to follow up after I put Eve to bed. Another day, maybe.'

'I'd like that.'

'If you two are done arranging your date, perhaps I can go home. It was gym today and I need a bath.'

'Can you pick Eve up again tomorrow?'

'No problem.'

'I'll come for her at the same time. I'll call if I'm going to be late.'

'OK, see you.'

'Bye, Jessica. I think we have maths homework tomorrow.'

'Great, Eve, can you show me what trinomial equations are?'

'Don't worry, they're easy.'

'Trinomial equations, piece of cake, Jessica,' said Ridpath, hoping nobody would ask him to explain.

'Sure, Dad, last time I looked you had trouble with long division.'

'I'll have you know, daughter, I have O-level maths. I don't know how, but I managed to scrape a pass.'

'There was probably a question on trinomial equations. Anyway, bye, Jessica, bye, Mrs Dunwoody. Thanks for the spag bol.'

They walked back to the house.

'You've already eaten?'

'Yeah, but Mum's spag bol was ten times better than Mrs Dunwoody's.'

'Your mum's was legendary. As was her duck a la banana.'

Eve's hand snaked into his. He loved it when she did this. It was like she was three all over again and they were walking along a crowded street.

'Be careful, Dad, I think she's trying to get into your Y-fronts.'

'Eve, how can you say that? Mrs Dunwoody is a wonderful person who picks you up from school when your dad is too busy.'

'Only an observation. Methinks the man doth protest too much.'

'It was a lady, and it's from *Hamlet*.'

Eve went silent for a moment. 'I wouldn't mind, you know.'

'Wouldn't mind what?'

'If you hooked up again. I mean, you're still a catch and you're still young, well young-ish. Maisie Wells thinks you're a bit of a hunk.'

He stopped and turned towards her. 'Look, Eve, promise you won't talk like this any more. I loved your mum, and the thought of getting involved with somebody else, it's... impossible.'

'Ok, Dad, just letting you know.'

He pulled out his key and opened the door. 'You go run your bath and I'll make you a nice hot cup of cocoa.'

Replaying the conversation in his head, he couldn't imagine talking with his mum in the same way after his dad had died. But kids were different these days. More open and more questioning, but still naive in so many ways.

He picked up the Macallan, hearing the ice rattle against the side of the glass, before taking a small sip. Its sweet bitterness nibbled at his throat, dragging him back to the present.

They had finally started to make some progress on the case today, but there were still so many questions that still needed answering. He felt constantly rushed and out of control, like the *Titanic* steaming across an icy sea, the passengers dancing the night away, not knowing what lay ahead.

He hoped and prayed there wasn't a bloody enormous iceberg waiting out there for him.

The questions flooded into his brain. How did Jane Ryder's backpack end up hidden in Daisy House Children's Home?

Was the female hand hers?

And what linked her to Joseph Rowlands, if there was any link at all?

He wasn't happy continuing with the inquest, but he could understand Mrs Challinor's reasons. At least now she would allow him to request a postponement until he had investigated the case properly.

He took another sip of Macallan.

He remembered what Charlie Whitworth had taught him on his first day on the job.

'All our jobs are about people, Ridpath, their hopes and dreams, their petty jealousies and hidden desires, their love and their hatred. It's always about people, not victims, perps or suspects. People, like you and me.'

The hands in the backpack weren't objects. They were three people who had lost their lives, and their killer had removed the hands with a hacksaw.

Was it the man in the photo?

He didn't know, but he wouldn't stop until he found out.

FRIDAY

Chapter 54

The detectives gradually stumbled into the situation room at Stretford nick. All had worked late into the night, returning at nine a.m. for this meeting.

Dave Connor had bought coffees for everybody. At least, Dave had paid for them, but it was Oliver Davis who'd had to stop off at Costa to pick them up.

Behind them, Oliver had marked up the boards, adding the latest information on the backpack, pictures of Jane Ryder and the festival.

Ridpath strode to the front. 'Hannah's decided to join us for this briefing. I hope you have some good news for us.'

The crime scene manager was looking as tired as everybody else. 'I think so, Ridpath, two pieces of good news.'

'I also asked Sophia to join. She works with me for the coroner.'

Sophia waved hello to the rest of the team. She was the only one who looked completely rested.

'Away you go, Hannah.'

'First off, we have a hit on the other male hand from the fingerprints late last night. It belongs to a Gerald Duffy. That's spelt D-U-F-F-Y. He's in the IDENT 1 database for a DUI back in 2006.'

Oliver wrote the name on the board.

'Dave, can you follow this lead? Find out who this Gerald Duffy was, when he disappeared, where he last lived. You know the drill.'

'Will do, Ridpath.'

'What's the other piece of news, Hannah?'

'Well, we put the roach we found in the backpack through the VSC and it came up trumps.' She showed a printout of the unfolded rectangle of paper. The letters, which had been invisible before, were now solid black.

'And it turned out to be a corner of a ticket for the Mad Ferret Festival of 2009.'

Hannah Palmer laughed. 'How'd you guess?'

'Not a guess, Hannah.' He stood up, walked over to the boards and pointed out Jane Ryder's pictures from the festival. 'As you know, we've been trying to trace this missing person from 2009 for the coroner. Last night, we had a breakthrough when Sophia found these pictures of her at the festival. Did the photographer get back to you, Sophia?'

'He thinks he has other photos in his archive somewhere. He has to dig them out.'

'Call him and put a rocket under his arse. This is important. Send any through as soon as you get them.'

'Will do.'

Ridpath pointed to one of the pictures. 'The backpack here is similar to the one found at Daisy House.'

'You think the female hand could be this girl?'

'It's a distinct possibility, Hannah. Dr O'Casey, the forensic anthropologist, gave an age range of sixteen to seventeen. She was sixteen when she went missing. There should have been DNA in the misper file taken when she disappeared, but guess what?'

'It's gone missing too.'

'Right first time.'

'If you can find it, we can try to compare her DNA with our hand and see if we get a match.'

'That's what I was hoping you would say, Hannah.'

'It still might be difficult, Ridpath, the lab thinks her hand was immersed in the embalming fluid for the longest time.'

'Chrissy, did you find the files yesterday?'

'Not yet, after this meeting I'm off to trawl through the old MFH cases. I think it may have been misfiled there.'

'I'm interviewing the missing person's manager later. She may know what happened.'

'Knowing Doreen Hawkins, I wouldn't bank on it, Ridpath,' muttered Chrissy.

'Emily, how did you get on with the backpack?'

'As I said yesterday, three were sold in Manchester on June 1, 2009. Two people paid with credit cards, a Miss Wendy Taylor and a Mrs Hilary Swindon. I contacted them. Both remember buying the bag and Miss Taylor still has hers. Mrs Swindon said her bag was stolen two years ago when she was on holiday.'

'It could be the one,' said Oliver.

'Except it was stolen in Greece, and she said her daughter had resprayed it bright blue.'

'It leaves only one left. Sophia?'

'I checked with Mr and Mrs Ryder earlier this morning. I showed him the picture and Mr Ryder remembered it well. He told me he gave his daughter the money to buy the backpack in 2009 as a present for finishing her exams.'

Ridpath stared at the pictures on the whiteboard. 'Looks like we have our link. But how did it get into Daisy House nearly twelve years later?'

Oliver Davis wrote the question on the whiteboard in neat block letters.

'Dave, anything else on Joseph Rowlands?'

'We managed to pick him up back in Manchester in 2017. He didn't report to the Sexual Offenders Register though. He was working as a gardener again, this time for Oldham Council. He seems to have kept his nose clean, no police reports or problems. Again, his workmates say he was a good worker, always on time and kept himself to himself. He was reported missing on June 10, 2018 by his partner. Apparently he went to work one morning and never came back. No note, no explanation, nothing. She reported him to the police two days later. Here's the misper report Chrissy gave me.' Dave handed over two sheets of paper. 'I talked to the copper involved. They thought he'd had enough of the relationship and walked out. The copper didn't know he was on the Sexual Offenders Register.'

'So no follow-up?'

'No. He was put down as low risk. His partner had three kids from a previous relationship—'

'Shit,' Emily said loudly.

'I asked the partner as subtly as I could how Rowlands had behaved around them and she told me he had been a great step-father, taking them to the beach and on camping trips.'

'Without her?'

'Apparently.'

'Shit,' repeated Emily.

'Did you inform her that we may have found him?'

'I did. She still misses him.'

'Dave, how old are the kids now?'

'Fifteen, twelve and eight. A boy is the youngest, still at primary school.'

'You'd better notify Children's Services at the council. They'll need to follow up.'

'Do I have to?'

'We must, Dave, can't let it go. Once we know of the slightest possibility of an offence, we need to report it.'

'Even though nothing may have happened.'

'Not for us to decide, Dave, children may have been at risk.'

'OK, but the woman still misses Joseph Rowlands – this will devastate her.'

'It has to be done.' Ridpath turned to the civilian researcher. 'Chrissy, how did you get on with finding the staff from Daisy House?'

'Without applying for a court order for the information from Manchester Council, here are the names collected by the Pharaoh investigation. Thirty-two in total.'

'So just those investigated, not all the people who worked there?' asked Dave Connor.

'That's correct.'

'How many of these people were submitted to CPS for possible prosecution?' Oliver asked.

Chrissy checked her notes. 'Good question. Seven people, of which only four were actually put on trial.' She produced a short list of names and job titles, which Oliver stuck to a new board.

Harold Davidson – Social Worker

Eliot Sandberg – Social Worker

David Wallace – Care Assistant

Joseph Rowlands – Head Gardener

'All of them were charged with a variety of sexual offences against children, receiving between two and six years, and all were placed on the Sexual Offenders Register.'

'The kids, of course, received life sentences.'

This was spoken with bitterness by Emily. Ridpath glanced across at her, surprised at the reaction.

Chrissy carried on. 'Davidson committed suicide shortly after the verdict. Sandberg was shanked in the showers in prison. He died three days later, but his attacker was never caught.'

'Exactly what he deserved.' Emily spoke again without looking up from her notes.

'Nobody deserves to die, Emily, particularly not when they are in prison.'

'Listen, Ridpath, these men committed offences against children, some as young as six years old, whilst they were supposed to be caring for them. We give them a little pat on the head and stick them inside for a few years. The whole case disgusts me.'

Ridpath didn't answer. 'Carry on, Chrissy.'

'David Wallace died in 2016, apparently from a heart attack.'

'That leaves Rowlands, who vanished in 2018 and whose hand has now turned up in our backpack. What about the other three who weren't charged by CPS?'

'Here's the list of names.' She passed out a sheet for everyone.

Robert Dunphy – Care Assistant

Patricia Patterson – Social Worker

Peter Clarke – Odd Job Man

'I haven't checked on their whereabouts yet. My next job.'

'Have you looked at the Sexual Offenders Register?' asked Emily.

'Not yet. You're wondering if any of them went on to offend again?'

Emily nodded.

'I'll do it as soon as this meeting ends.'

'And one of them is a woman. What offence did she commit?' The surprise registered in Emily's voice.

'I'll dig out the files sent to CPS.'

Before Emily could ask another question, Ridpath began to sum up. 'Right, we have a new lead, Gerald Duffy. Dave, we need to find out who he is as quickly as possible.'

'Right, Ridpath.'

'Last night I asked myself a few questions. The first: what links Joseph Rowlands, Jane Ryder and now Gerald Duffy? Is it Daisy House? Or is it something else, something we missed?'

'Like what, Ridpath?' asked Chrissy.

'Like, were they all at the festival in 2009? Or were they all the members of some gang? Find the connection and I think we'll finally be able to understand what the hell is going on.'

He paused for a moment, looking out at the small team assembled in front of him. Could they do this? Usually MIT would have a pool of twenty detectives to chase down leads on any case. Here he had only four people. Five, if he included himself. Was it enough?

It had to be enough.

He carried on. 'Second: how did their hands end up in a backpack owned by Jane Ryder in Daisy House? Third: what happened to the bodies? Why haven't the bodies been discovered?' He stopped, remembering Chrissy was supposed to be checking with HOLMES. 'Still nothing, Chrissy?'

She shook her head. 'Not a sausage. It's like the bodies vanished into thin air. I cross-checked with discovered bodies on the NCA Missing Persons website. And still nothing.'

Ridpath made a clicking noise with his tongue. 'Fourth: why collect and amputate the hands? Is this person collecting trophies? Or do the hands have some other meaning, some hidden meaning?'

'Or is it something more personal?' Emily whispered as if speaking to herself. 'Is this a form of revenge, removing the object that hurt them?'

The room went quiet before Dave Connor gave a short laugh. 'Bit too deep for me, Emily. Perhaps he's just handy with a hacksaw?'

Nobody laughed at Dave's joke.

Ridpath continued to sum up. 'Last question. Who placed the hands in the backpack? In other words, who is our killer?'

'That's the sixty-four-thousand-dollar question, Ridpath.'

'The problem is, Chrissy, at the moment, I don't have a bloody clue what the answer is. Is everybody clear what they have to do?'

Emily put her hand up. 'What about me?'

'You're coming with me to see the missing person's manager in the Jane Ryder case, Em, and afterwards we're meeting Jayne Ryder's best friend, Rose Anstey, in Salford Quays.'

'Ridpath, why are we looking for the coroner's missing person? Surely we should be trying to find out more about the hands in the backpack?' asked Dave Connor.

Ridpath stared at him. 'Because I'm becoming more and more convinced the answers to our questions are connected to the disappearance of Jane Ryder. I don't know how yet. Or why. But they are connected, I feel it in my bones.'

Chapter 55

They were both sitting in Ridpath's car. He hadn't turned over the engine.

'Are we going to meet this woman or not?'

Ridpath paused, tapping the steering wheel, before deciding to ask the question that had been troubling him. 'Did you mean what you said in the briefing?'

Emily Parkinson frowned. 'What?'

'About Eliot Sandberg deserving to die in prison.'

'Yeah, every word of it.'

Ridpath stayed silent, waiting for an explanation.

'Don't give me the silent treatment.'

'Our job is to catch criminals, not hope they die, Emily.'

'But they assaulted young children in their care. For God's sake, these people were supposed to look after those kids.' Her eyes began to moisten. She looked down at her hands and began to interweave her fingers as they lay on her lap. Finally, she sighed loudly and spoke in a quiet, restrained voice. 'Remember when we first started working together? I told you my dad was a draughtsmen at BAE in Preston and my mum was a nursery nurse.'

'I remember. You also studied English Lit at Manchester.'

She laughed. 'What a waste of time.' She looked down at her hands again. 'I didn't tell you the complete truth. I always thought of Ted and Irene as my mum and dad, but they weren't my biological parents. I was adopted when I was eight from a council children's home.'

'I'm so sorry, Emily, I didn't know.'

'It's not so bad. I had a great childhood, and they were wonderful parents, Ted and Irene, I couldn't have asked for better.'

'When did you go into care?'

'I think I was two, or so they tell me. I don't know. I have vague memories of being pulled away from my birth mum and crying myself to sleep in an empty bed surrounded by all these other kids.'

'Do you still remember your time at the home?'

She nodded. 'It wasn't great. Please understand, I wasn't abused or anything. The home I lived in was actually pretty nice. There weren't many kids and I got on with all of them. The place itself had a big garden, swings, an orchard where we picked fruit and the people tried their best.'

'But…?'

'But it wasn't a home.' She paused again. 'You know, until I went to live with Ted and Irene, I'd never been hugged. The first time Irene wrapped her arms around me I didn't know what to do, I froze and stood there. And school was the worst. All the other kids and the teachers knew we came from the children's home.'

'So you were picked on?'

'I swore I was never going to be bullied again.' She laughed. 'Perhaps that's why Turnbull hates me. I look at him and don't see another copper but one of the bullies at school.'

'What happened to your birth mum?'

Emily Parkinson swallowed. 'I found out much later, she died not long after I was taken away from her. She was an alcoholic, had been for a long time apparently.'

'Em.' Ridpath put his hand on her arm.

She wiped her face. 'I feel so silly telling you all this. It's all in the past, happened a long, long time ago. And now we have a case to work and not a lot of time to do it.'

'Do you still want to be on the team? I can ask for someone else, if it's too much for you.'

'No, no, I want to work this.'

'Are you sure? Can you handle this? We need people to be distanced, not emotionally involved, Em. To work the case, collecting evidence, and understand what actually happened.'

She stared at him. 'I can't believe I'm hearing this from you. When have you ever been distanced from any case you ever worked?'

He smiled. 'Touché. But I never allow my feelings to influence the way I work the case or the results I expect.' His voice changed tone. 'If you can't remove your feelings about children's homes from the case, DS Parkinson, you need to remove yourself. Do I make myself clear? Right now, the case is all that matters; finding the truth about who placed those hands in the backpack.'

'Understood, Ridpath. But we're never going to find the truth in a car park outside Stretford nick. I suggest we go and see our witness.'

He turned the engine over. 'Let's go back to work.'

Chapter 56

Doreen Hawkins was a big woman, both in stature and in presence.

Her secretary had sprayed Ridpath and Emily's hands twice before they were allowed to enter the great woman's presence.

'She's frightened of germs, washes her hands at least ten times a day. You don't know what it's been like during the pandemic.'

'Difficult?' asked Emily.

'Bloody impossible, but I need the job.' She knocked tentatively on the door. 'The police to see you, Ms Hawkins.'

'Ask them to wait.'

The secretary raised her eyes skyward. From inside came the sound of papers being shuffled and chairs moved. 'Come,' came the imperious order.

The secretary ushered them into the great woman's presence. She was dismissed with a nonchalant wave of the hand.

Doreen Hawkins filled her office. Literally. But there was a nimbleness, a subtlety about her movements that belied her size, as if an athlete were trapped in the wrong body.

The office in question was the Kool Kidz Klubz, a children's charity that helped support kids in need throughout Manchester and Salford.

'Mrs Hawkins, I'd like to ask you a few questions, if I may?'

'It's Ms Hawkins, and what's this about? I don't have much time. In exactly ten minutes, I have a meeting with the lord lieutenant of Lancashire, Baron Shuttleworth. We may be extending our services into the county.'

Barons? He thought they went out with the Magna Carta? If the name was supposed to cow Ridpath, it failed miserably.

'My name is DI Ridpath and this is DS Emily Parkinson. We're looking into the disappearance of a young woman, Jane Ryder, in 2009.'

'Actually, your name is Ridpath and your rank is detective inspector. Let us be precise, Detective. I dislike imprecision of language amongst my staff and I won't tolerate it from anybody else.'

'I'm sure you will tell Baron Shuttleworth exactly the same when you meet him.'

'Which is in exactly nine minutes, so I would let me know what you want.'

Ridpath took a deep breath. He wasn't going to be rushed or intimidated by this woman. 'We believe you were working as missing person's manager for GMP in 2009?'

'I was employed in that capacity from 2000 to 2015, when I took early retirement.'

'Do you recognise this missing person report?'

Ridpath passed across the file. Doreen Hawkins glanced at it and saw her name, tapping the paper. 'That's me. Must have been one of mine.'

'Could you tell us about this case?'

Doreen Hawkins laughed. It sounded like the bark of a deer. 'You must be joking.'

'I'm deadly serious, Ms Hawkins.'

'Do you know how many people are reported missing each year?'

'Yes, but I am sure you are going to tell me anyway.'

Without taking a breath, she rattled off the statistics. 'Somebody is reported as missing from home every ninety seconds. The latest figures for 2019 show there were one hundred and seventy-six thousand people reported missing in the UK. In Manchester alone there were over thirteen thousand reports of missing people.'

'It's a lot.'

'But that's not all. Of the hundred and seventy-six thousand, approximately seventy-five thousand were children. In

Manchester, the figure was slightly less than five thousand children. These figures are probably under-reported. The truth is we haven't a clue how many people or children vanish in the UK. At Kool Kidz Klubz, we work to target at-risk children, persuading them not to run away or, if they do, helping them to return home.'

'I'm sure you are doing wonderful work, Ms Hawkins, but I have a specific investigation I am looking into. Jane Ryder, who disappeared on June 12, 2009. This is a photograph of her. Do you remember her case?'

Ridpath slid across the photo from the files. This time Doreen Hawkins picked it up and stared at it.

'Sorry, I don't remember her. It's nearly twelve years ago, and as I said, close to five thousand of these pictures used to cross my desk each year when I worked for GMP.'

'Could you read the report, see if it jogs your memory?'

Mrs Hawkins sighed, glanced at the clock and picked up the report, reading it properly. 'Sorry, still nothing.'

'Why was this girl only classified as medium risk when she was just sixteen years old?'

The woman frowned. 'That is strange. Normally, she would be high risk, particularly if she came from a stable family background. There are four reasons why children go missing, DI Ridpath.' She began counting them off on her ring-laden fingers. 'First, conflict, abuse, neglect or simply problems at home. Second, they have been trafficked for sexual or physical exploitation. Third, they have spent time in care. Or, lastly, they have untreated mental health issues.'

Ridpath glanced across at Emily. She had been quiet throughout the interview. Finally she asked, 'Which was it in Jane Ryder's case?'

Ms Hawkins picked up the file and read it through again. 'A couple of things are coming back to me. I remember the copper on this case being worried about the girl, wanting to make her high risk. That would mean more resource and effort would be put in to finding her. But the social worker was adamant the girl was in no trouble and wanted her to be placed in the low-risk category. She seemed to think there were problems at home and the girl had run off to live with her boyfriend. As she was over the age of consent, we agreed to put her in the medium-risk category.'

'Social worker? There's no social worker named in the report.'

Doreen Hawkins leafed through the papers. 'There should be more documentation. I would have minuted any discussions and follow-up on the case.'

'Nothing in the files.'

'It doesn't surprise me. Even when I left, the police computer systems were totally inadequate for what they needed to do.'

'Can you remember the name of the social worker?'

Ms Hawkins thought for a long while. 'Sorry, no name comes to me. I dealt with so many during my time with the police.'

Ridpath glanced at Emily and nodded. 'OK, thank you for your time, Ms Hawkins. If you remember anything else, please call me at any time.' He passed over his card.

She stared at it. 'You work for the coroner. I thought you said you were a DI?'

'I am. I'm seconded to work with the coroner. We are investigating a presumption of death on behalf of the parents. Do you think Jane Ryder has died?'

'Has anybody heard anything since she disappeared?'

'Nothing. No communication with her parents or anybody else, as far as we are aware.'

'About two per cent of children are never found, DI Ridpath. It's safe to say they are dead, either through an accident, a drug overdose or murder.'

'Thank you once again, Ms Hawkins.' Ridpath stood up and went to shake the woman's hand, before turning it into a touching of elbows.

At the door, he turned back. 'One more question, a thought, really. Why would Jane Ryder have had a social worker?'

'I would have thought the answer was obvious, DI Ridpath.'

'Not to me.'

'From memory and looking at her form, it is obvious she had been in care. The Ryders were probably her adopted family.'

Chapter 57

Outside on the street, Ridpath stood around as Emily fumbled for one of her cigarettes.

'What happened here, Em? Did Jane Ryder simply fall through the cracks in the system?'

She shook her head. 'I don't think so. There seems to be more going on. Didn't her parents tell you she was adopted?'

He thought back to the first interview. 'The father kept calling her his daughter. No hint of any adoption. The mother seems to be on some powerful drugs for her cancer, the father did most of the talking.'

'It is strange they didn't mention it.' She lit the cigarette, nervously taking a long drag.

'When did your parents tell you?'

'I always knew, so they didn't have to tell me. Perhaps the same was true of your Jane Ryder.'

'But your parents told other people you were adopted.'

Emily shook her head. 'To them, I was their daughter and that was everything. I mean, it wasn't a secret, but we certainly didn't talk about it, and I never mentioned it at school.'

'Colin Dowell, the copper who did the interview back in 2009, didn't know she was adopted either. I don't think they told him.'

'But Ms Hawkins, the missing person's manager, did?'

'She was in touch with the social worker. Perhaps it's how she found out?'

'Why was the social worker so keen to put a sixteen-year-old girl who disappeared into a low-risk category? Did she know something we don't?'

'Perhaps she knew about the boyfriend?'

'But if Jane Ryder simply ran off with a boyfriend because everything wasn't as hunky dory at home as you were told, why didn't she get in touch later? A letter. A phone call. Or just a Christmas card, letting her adoptive parents know she was OK. Wouldn't she have at least communicated in some way? I would have done, in her position.' Emily Parkinson stopped talking.

'What are you thinking?' asked Ridpath.

'Not if she hated them. Not if she hated them so much she never wanted to see them again. Not if...'

'Go on.'

'She wanted to punish them so much, and the harshest punishment was silence...'

Ridpath's phone rang. He checked the screen; it was Chrissy. He put her on speakerphone so Emily could hear.

'Hi there, what have you got for me?'

'I've found the files on Jane Ryder. There were duplicates in the MFH, with a lot more follow-up and interviews than in the documents we have.'

'Great, Chrissy, can you scan them in and send to me?'

'Will do.'

Ridpath thought for a moment. 'Do you have them now?'

'I'm at MFH, they're in front of me.'

'Are the DNA samples taken by Colin Dowell still there?'

'There's an evidence bag. Let me check it. Yep, it's a toothbrush.'

'Great, Chrissy. Can you send it to Hannah at the lab and ask her to compare a sample with DNA from the female hand?'

'But I thought we were unable to obtain DNA?'

'Perhaps not enough for identification, but enough to compare with an existing sample.'

'OK, I see what you're doing. Does the sample from the toothbrush match DNA from the hand? You know it probably won't stand up in court, Ridpath.'

'But it would stand up in an inquest for a presumption of death. At least it might give us an ID.'

'Sending it as soon as we finish this phone call.'

'Can you also take a quick look and give me the name of the social worker involved? There should be a minuted meeting with the missing person's manager, Doreen Hawkins.'

'Just a sec.'

Ridpath heard the turning of pages as Chrissy mumbled a few words to herself. 'Here it is. The social worker was a... Patricia Patterson.'

'What?'

'It says here Patricia Patterson. Doreen Hawkins had a telephone call with her on June 20, 2009.'

There was silence for a second before Emily spoke. 'Hang on, wasn't that the name of one of the social workers not charged by CPS after Operation Pharaoh?'

'Chrissy, we need the files submitted to CPS as soon as possible. Obviously the investigating officers thought there was enough evidence to charge Patricia Patterson, but CPS disagreed. Why?'

'Probably insufficient evidence to gain a conviction in their opinion, Ridpath.'

'We need to know, Chrissy.'

'Next job, Ridpath.'

He switched off the phone.

'What is it?' asked Emily.

'Something's not right with this case. There seem to be lies, more lies and even more untruths. But I know one thing is true...'

'What?'

'Daisy House Children's Home seems to be at the heart of everything.'

Chapter 58

A cold, dread wind swept down the Manchester Ship Canal from the Irish Sea and draped itself over the new developments and television studios of Salford Quays.

Once, not so long ago, this area had resounded to the whirr of cranes, the shouts of stevedores and the foghorns of ships as bags of grain, pallets of steel and boxes of consumer goods had come from all over the world, bypassing the port of Liverpool and sailing straight into the heart of Manchester.

These days, the traffic was in the opposite direction as programmes shot, produced and developed in the studios lining the old docks were transmitted out to the world.

Ridpath didn't like the area much, always finding it cold and grey and sterile. For a place full of creative people, it was a remarkably uncreative environment. A factory manufacturing a product, rather than a place to nurture ideas.

He'd arranged to meet Rose Anstey in a cafe at the bottom of the Quayside Centre. She worked at ITV and only had a short lunch break.

'You must be Rose Anstey?' Ridpath stood up.

'Right first time. How did you recognise me?'

He pointed to the badge hanging round her neck with the words ITV and ROSE ANSTEY written in block letters. 'I wouldn't be much of a detective if I couldn't work it out.'

She laughed and sat down.

'This is my colleague, DS Emily Parkinson. We're investigating the disappearance of Jane Ryder in 2009.'

Rose Anstey made a moue with her mouth. 'I'm impressed. I thought by now the police would have stopped looking for Jane. Top marks for persistence.'

'You haven't heard from her since she disappeared?'

Rose shook her head. 'Nothing. I mean, we were best mates back then. I would've thought she'd send me something. A text or an email.'

'But nothing…'

'Not a word. It's like she vanished into thin air. Kudos to you lot for still looking for her though.'

'Actually, her parents have asked for a presumption of death certificate to be issued, that's why we are re-investigating her disappearance.' Ridpath decided not to mention the backpack or its connection to his case.

'Oh?'

'I wonder if you could take us through that time. Anything, even the smallest detail, could help us.'

'The truth?'

'The truth.'

'Jane and I were best friends. Had been since we both started high school at eleven. We sort of hit it off straight away.'

'So you knew each other's secrets?' asked Emily.

Rose smiled. 'We told each other everything. A proper little cabal of two misfits we were.'

'What do you mean?'

'Well, neither of us was too happy at home. Jane had been through a tough time in care…'

'You knew she was in care?'

'She didn't talk about it a lot, only to me, but it wasn't a happy time for her. Her mum had given her up when she was five years old, drug problems, I think. She'd been first fostered and then adopted by the Ryders when she was nine years old.'

'You said there were problems at home for her?'

'The Ryders were old and set in their ways. I think they wanted the perfect daughter, and Jane didn't live up to their expectations. The dad was OK, but the mum… well the mum was… difficult. Jane didn't talk much about it, but I had the feeling it was all too much for her.'

'She'd run away before?'

'Before 2009? Yes, twice before. Once with me. We travelled as far as Stoke before we were caught and brought back. We both had this crazy idea we were going to meet Robbie Williams. We thought it would be easy to find him in a place like Stoke. We found out later he was living in Los Angeles, shows you how naive we were.'

'How old were you?'

'We were both thirteen. Young, innocent and stupid.'

'What happened when you were caught?'

'We were both brought back. I was grounded and had to see some social worker or other. It was tougher for Jane though. She was adopted and still being monitored by Social Services.'

'But she ran away again.'

'When she was fifteen.'

'You didn't go with her?'

'Not that time. I realised it was all a bit futile and decided to keep my head down and pretend.' She stared off into the distance for a second. 'I was good at pretending, Jane wasn't.'

'She was brought back again?'

'A lorry driver picked her up on the M6 services, she was heading to London, but as soon as she told him her age, he dropped her off at the side of the road. The police found her walking along the hard shoulder trying to hitch a lift.'

'Where was she going?'

'She had this daft plan to go to London and work there. She wanted to be an actress and thought the bright lights of the big city would give her "life experience".' Rose formed quote marks with her fingers. 'Instead, she discovered the bright lights of the big motorway. She was different after she came back.'

'How?'

'More wary and closed. She said she'd met someone. Didn't tell me who. But he'd helped her to see stuff differently.'

'That was all?'

'Like I said, she was more closed after she came back. She didn't talk much about what had happened.'

'And June 12, the day of the festival, you were supposed to go with her?'

She shook her head and laughed. 'No, it was just a story for our parents. I'd met this boy, Billy Drury. I was supposed to go camping with him on the weekend and Jane was meeting her friend at the festival, so we covered for each other, said we were going together.'

'You never found out who her friend was?'

'She wouldn't say. I came back on the Sunday night and Jane's parents rang my mum on Monday asking where she was.' Again, she seemed to vanish back into her memories. 'It all came out. I was forced to admit we hadn't been at the festival together.'

'You told this to the police?'

Rose nodded. 'A social worker rang me and I told her most of it.'

'Most?'

'I didn't go into all the details about the person she was supposed to be meeting. I thought she was going to come back and didn't want to get her into trouble. I had enough shit from my parents.'

'What about Andrea, Jane's other friend?'

'The hanger-on? She used to follow her around everywhere, puppy-dog eyes staring up at Jane. I didn't like her much myself. Don't know what happened to her afterwards, we weren't close.'

'Was she supposed to go to the festival too?'

'No, that was the point. Jane wanted to go alone, we were supposed to give an alibi. I don't know what Andrea did. Perhaps she did go to the festival, wouldn't put it past her.'

'One more question.' Ridpath stopped taking notes and looked her straight in the eye. 'Did Jane have a backpack?'

Rose smiled. 'Her dad, I mean, Mr Ryder had given her some money for doing well in her exams. Dead chuffed she was with it. Showing it off around the school. A limited-edition something or other, can't remember the brand. She bought it at Afflecks though, I remember because I was with her.'

'What colour was it?'

Rose's forehead lined as she tried to think. 'A sort of green with red stripes. CLAT or CLAK was the brand, something like that. Sorry, can't remember, it's such a long time ago.'

'No worries, you've been great so far. OK, any questions, Emily?'

The detective shook her head.

'Anything else you'd like to say? Something you've thought about but wasn't important at the time?'

Rose thought for a long time. 'There was one thing that troubled me. Might be nothing though.'

'What was it?'

'I had the feeling she'd known the person she was meeting for a long time. She hadn't recently met him or her.'

'Why?'

'Just a feeling. It was like she'd met them before.'

Emily leant forward. 'Him or her?'

'Yeah, Jane never talked about it being a he or a she. It was always they.' She stared off into mid-air for a long time. 'Jane was always in charge. I must admit I was a bit of a follower too, probably why I resented Andrea. I think she planned to go away at the festival. I can't be sure, of course, you never knew what Jane was thinking.'

'Thanks, Rose. Call me if there's anything else you remember, no matter how small.' Ridpath slid his card across the table.

'I've just thought of a question, Rose.' Emily paused for a moment. 'Did Jane ever tell you which care home she lived in?'

'It was Daisy House, the one in Northenden, not far from where we live now. I pass it walking the dog most days.' She paused for a moment, her eyes glassing over. 'I always think of Jane.'

Chapter 59

Ridpath sat in his car outside the Coroner's Court. Instead of getting out, he stayed there for a moment gathering his thoughts.

This case was becoming more and more complicated. Before briefing Mrs Challinor, he had to get it straight in his own head.

After Rose Anstey had returned to work, he had a quick chat with Emily. 'What do you think?'

'We need to follow up on the social worker, Patricia Patterson, as soon as possible. Why was she so closely involved with Jane Ryder? When did she meet her at Daisy House? What crime did the Operation Pharaoh investigating team think she committed? If they passed a case file to CPS, the officers must have found some evidence of wrongdoing. I'll have chat with a mate of mine who worked on the case. Perhaps he'll be able to tell me stuff not in the files.'

'Get on it, Emily. Let's meet tomorrow morning in Stretford nick to see where we are. I'll message the others.'

He'd driven from Media City to the Coroner's Court, half his mind on the road and the rest on the case. As he parked up, he looked out of the window of his car. The old Victorian building sheltering the Coroner's Court had the look of a schoolhouse. But not a building out of Dickens, operated by Wackford Squeers. Rather it was something far more enlightened, like the old workmen's institutes offering lifelong learning to anybody and everybody.

A good place. A just place.

Ridpath glanced down at his fingers resting on the steering wheel. The nails were bitten and the cuticles red. It was always like this. His nails suffering for every case he worked.

He took three deep breaths and went to his safe place: on top of the hill overlooking Ladybower Reservoir, the wind blowing in his hair and the world at his feet.

Afterwards, he felt calm and collected, ready to face the coroner. The children's home at Daisy House was key to this case. What had happened there to Jane Ryder?

He got out of the car and stood in front of the court. As he walked up the steps, a group of people were coming out. One of the women was crying, being consoled by her husband and daughter. 'It was an accident, Hilary, a stupid accident.'

Ridpath caught the words as he stepped to one side, allowing them to pass. The people must have been coming from an inquest.

'But it shouldn't have happened to him, he had so much to live for. He was special…'

'I know, love, I know.'

The man put his arms round his wife and led her past Ridpath, her face and eyes scarlet with tears.

The woman stopped for a moment. 'My brother was only thirty-two, he wouldn't hurt a fly.'

Another woman, dressed in black, passed them on the stairs. Suddenly Hilary pushed past her husband and flew at the woman. 'You did this. You and your stupid cult killed him.'

The woman in black's eyes flared in anger. She raised her fists and moved backwards away from her attacker.

'It's your fault. I know all about you. My brother told me what you're up to.'

Ridpath readied himself in case the grieving woman attacked again. But all her strength seemed to leave her and she began to sob uncontrollably.

The woman in black didn't answer but kept her eyes on her attacker as the husband and daughter ushered her away.

Ridpath stood there as they passed. He mustn't forget, every case was always about people. The hands in the backpack weren't objects but people who'd lived and loved and lost and learned. Jane Ryder wasn't only a victim who'd vanished one summer's day in 2009, she was also a young girl with her whole future in front of her.

He glanced across at the woman in black. She looked familiar. Was she a lawyer who'd worked on inquests before? Probably.

She ignored him and walked down the steps, checking the family were going in a different direction before walking off towards town.

It was always about people. Brothers, sisters, aunts, uncles, mothers and fathers.

Perhaps this was the lesson he'd learnt most from the death of Polly and the time he spent grieving for her.

Life was always about people. And so was death.

Nothing else mattered.

Chapter 60

'Hi, Sophia, is the coroner in?'

'She's preparing her notes for an inquest, Ridpath.'

'I saw some relatives outside.'

'Helen Moore's inquest. Accidental death was the verdict. I think Helen is writing a prevention of future deaths report for the chief coroner.'

'Mrs Challinor won't mind if I interrupt.'

'Before you go in, I have something to tell you.'

'Let me see the coroner first, we'll talk afterwards.'

Ridpath knocked on the door.

'Come,' came a voice from the inside.

He entered to see Mrs Challinor sitting at the desk; her face was drawn and white, weariness etched into the creases around her eyes.

'Is this a bad time?'

'It's always a bad time at the moment.'

'I thought I'd let you know how the Jane Ryder investigation is progressing.'

'Good, come in, there's something I have to tell you too. You first.'

'There have been some interesting developments since we last talked. First, either deliberately or innocently, it seems the Ryders didn't tell us everything about their relationship with their adopted daughter.'

'Adopted?'

'Jane wasn't their natural daughter. She was fostered first and then adopted by the Ryders when she was nine.'

'That's news to me.'

'As it was to me. But there's more. She spent her early years in Daisy House Children's Home—'

'The same place you are investigating for MIT?'

'Correct. We've now confirmed the backpack in which we found the hands was owned by Jane Ryder. It was the one she took to the music festival on the day she disappeared.'

'The two cases are definitely connected?'

'It would seem so. We're trying to find out more about the social worker, Patricia Patterson, who was involved with Jane Ryder.'

'Involved? How?'

'We don't know yet, but we'll find out.'

'Good, thank you for the update. I've made a decision regarding the inquest on her presumption of death. Mrs Ryder is now receiving terminal care at the hospice. You know what that means?'

'She could die at any time.'

Mrs Challinor took a deep breath. 'So I've decided to hold the inquest on Monday.'

'What? You can't. I haven't finished my investigation yet, and didn't you hear what I said? There are links between Jane Ryder and the hands we found at Daisy House. She may have been one of the victims. I need more time.'

'But who will give Mrs Ryder more time, Ridpath?'

'I understand, Coroner, but I also know there should be enough evidence to presume death. I haven't had the time yet to give you certainty. And I must be certain.'

Mrs Challinor's jaw clenched. 'I hear you, Ridpath, but my mind is made up. I have contacted Claire Trent. She will arrange for a police legal representative to ask for an adjournment of the inquest after we have heard from the witnesses. That way I can issue a provisional certificate pending the police inquiry into Jane Ryder's death. It should be enough for the Ryders to sort out their financial affairs.'

'But you can't. We haven't arranged for the witnesses to attend.'

'It's already in progress. Jenny is sending out the requests as we speak.'

'To whom?'

'The Ryders have already been informed.' She checked her notes. 'The invitations have been sent to a Police Sergeant Colin Dowell, Doreen Hawkins, Rose Anstey and the social worker, Patricia Patterson.'

'What? But you don't even know their addresses.' Understanding spread across Ridpath's face. 'Sophia knew. It's what she wanted to tell me.'

'Correct. The inquest is going to happen on Monday. As we agreed earlier, I will call the witnesses and hear their testimony, then the inquest will be adjourned pending the result of MIT's inquiries. Claire Trent and I have agreed to give you till the end of the week to complete them. Afterwards, I will issue the presumption of death certificate.'

'But you can't do it.'

'I think you forget your position, Ridpath. I have made my decision.'

'Even though Jane Ryder's death may be linked with at least two others?'

The coroner's voice softened. 'We have to give closure to the Ryders. Mrs Ryder is dying, we don't know how long she will live. Can you tell me realistically when you will finish your investigation and I can hold the inquest without an adjournment?'

'You know it's impossible to predict when an investigation can be concluded at this stage, Coroner.'

'I understand, and therefore we will hold it on Monday. I have made my decision.'

Ridpath stood up. 'But there is a killer out there who has taken the lives of at least three people in the last ten years, all of whom were linked to Daisy House Children's Home. We need to find out who he is.'

'That is a police investigation, Ridpath, not one conducted by this coroner's office. Our sole focus is Jane Ryder. Can we presume she is dead?'

Ridpath stayed silent.

'Is there any documentary evidence she is alive? Has she been seen in the last eleven years? Was there a robust attempt to find her eleven years ago?'

'Not robust, no.'

'The police followed the correct procedures in a missing person investigation?'

'Yes, but—'

'All these questions tell me I can conduct an inquest on the girl on behalf of her parents. Remember, our job is to represent the dead in the world of the living, Ridpath.'

'There is one element you have forgotten, Coroner.'

'And what is that, Ridpath?'

'We have DNA from one of the hands that we can compare with DNA taken from Jane Ryder's toothbrush. If we get a match, it will confirm she is dead.'

Mrs Challinor exhaled loudly. 'When will you get the results?'

'I don't know.'

She took up her pen and began writing in her file. 'I suggest we have them before the inquest on Monday, and then it will be no longer necessary to request an adjournment.'

Ridpath stood up to leave.

'One more thing. Please do not confuse your work for me with your work for MIT. We are not looking for convictions, or even to find out who committed any crime. Our sole responsibly is to represent those who died.'

'Understood, Coroner. But can we truly represent Jane Ryder and the others unless we know who amputated their hands and why they did it? What happens if the killer strikes again?'

'I've made my decision, Ridpath.'

'I must ask that you minute my objections, Mrs Challinor.'

'Noted, Ridpath.'

Chapter 61

He saw Sophia as he came out of Mrs Challinor's room.

'Sorry, Ridpath, I had to give them the notes. I tried to tell you but—'

'No worries, Sophia, you were just doing your job.' He walked over to his desk and began packing his bag.

'Where are you going?'

'Home to see my daughter. It's obvious I can do no more here at the moment. It's time I spent some time with Eve.'

'They grow up so quickly, too quickly. That's what my mum always says. I think she wishes I was three years old all over again.'

'Call me if you need anything.' He made the universal sign by holding his thumb and little finger close to his ear.

'Before you go, here are some new photos sent by the photographer. These were his outtakes from the Mad Ferret Festival. He's happy for us to use them in any way.'

Ridpath picked up the one on top. It was a full frontal shot of the man. Jane Ryder was dancing next to him with her body facing away from the camera. The man seemed angry to be caught on film. Or was it Ridpath imagining something that wasn't there?

'I've already sent them to Chrissy and Oliver.'

'Thanks, Sophia, good work.'

She blinked once and nodded. 'Sorry.'

'Don't be, in your place I would have done exactly the same. In the coroner's place, I too would be ordering an inquest for Monday, I understand. It's just...'

'Just what?'

'There's a killer out there who has murdered at least three people, amputated their hands and kept them as trophies in formaldehyde. We don't know why they are doing it or if they will strike again. Perhaps it's this man.' He prodded the photograph forcefully and took a deep breath. 'The worst is nobody seems to care. Not the coroner. Not Claire Trent, not anybody else. My team have been working our bollocks off trying to solve this without being given the time or the resources necessary to complete the job.'

He looked at Sophia; she was staring back at him. He realised at that moment how young she was, and how inexperienced.

He picked up his bag from his desk. 'Sorry, venting at you when it's not your business.'

'Everything we do is my business.'

'Call me if you need anything. I'll email through my notes from today's meetings when I'm back at home.'

'Goodnight, Ridpath.'

He didn't turn to reply.

Chapter 62

At Mrs Dunwoody's house, Eve was pleased to see him. 'Dad, you're early for once.' She ran and hugged him round the waist. He looked down at her head and realised she was already up to his shoulders. How had she grown so quickly?

'Shall we go home now? What do you want for tea?'

Mrs Dunwoody stood to one side. 'You're welcome to stay here. I'm cooking shepherd's pie,' she said hopefully.

'Thank you so much, Angela, but I get so little time off and I'd like to use the little I have to cook for Eve tonight. I have one favour to ask.'

'Ask away.'

'Could you pick her up on Monday too? I have an inquest and I fear it will run late.'

'No problem. Perhaps you'd like to stay for dinner?'

Ridpath smiled. 'That would be lovely, I'll probably need some good home cooking that night.'

'Right, it's a date… I mean… I mean…'

Ridpath called to Eve to cover Mrs Dunwoody's embarrassment. 'Come on, Eve, let's go, time for me to cook.'

'Great, Dad can we have your lasagne?' She turned to her friend Jessica. 'Dad makes a mint lasagne with all the crispy burnt cheesy bits around the edges.'

She glanced at her mum. 'Sounds magic, better than shepherd's pie.'

'We'll finish the maths homework sometime over the weekend. I'll come round, OK?'

'Great, I haven't a clue what it all means.'

'Don't worry, it's a piece of cake. Bye, Jessica, bye, Mrs Dunwoody.'

They both exited the Dunwoodys' house, walking down the street to their new place. 'Jessica's great, but she doesn't have a clue about maths.'

'I thought you said she was one of the mean girls, the plastic people.'

Eve shrugged her shoulders. 'I was wrong. On her own, she's nice, a bit blur sometimes.'

'See, what did I tell you about judging people too quickly.'

'Put these words in order, Dad. Pot. Kettle. Black.'

He put the key in the door. 'You go upstairs and wash the grime of school off your face, not forgetting to sanitise your hands, while I get started on the lasagne.'

'Can I watch you cook?'

'So long as you promise not to help. Remember what happened last time.'

'The white cheese sauce ended up black.'

'How did that happen?'

'I haven't a clue. Tasted good though, if a little black.'

She ran upstairs while he walked to the kitchen.

After they had nearly finished a whole tray of lasagne, both lay back in their chairs with bellies extended.

'Can't eat any more, I'm stuffed,' said Ridpath.

'Save the rest for tomorrow, not that there's much left. It was good, Dad.'

'Yeah, not as good as Mum's though.'

Eve smiled, changing the subject quickly. 'We OK for Sunday?'

'Sunday?'

'Visiting Mum's grave, remember.'

He thought for a moment of the investigation and all the work still had to be done. So much to do and so little time to do it all. Sod it. It was time he gave more consideration to his daughter and less to the bloody job. 'Should be OK,' he finally said. 'You still need to visit your grandparents though.'

'Do I have to? Granny will nag me, saying my Chinese isn't good enough and my skirts are too short.'

'She's right on both counts.' He remembered the briefing at Stretford nick tomorrow morning. 'Are you OK if I go to work tomorrow?'

'No problem. I have Chinese classes until one and I'll take the tram home. I have enough homework to last till next Christmas.'

'Take care, won't you?'

'Nah, I'll take the tram, it's quicker.'

'You've used that joke before, smart arse.'

'The good ones never go out of style.'

After both of them had washed up and Eve had gone to bed, Ridpath sat alone in the living room nursing a glass of Macallan and going over the events of the last few days in his mind.

He didn't blame Mrs Challinor, in her place he would have done exactly the same. But by holding the inquest they would probably spook the killer. Whoever they were, they would go to ground and never be seen again. The case would remain unsolved and then quietly transferred over to the Cold Case Unit. If no new DNA evidence surfaced, it would just sit there on a shelf, as cold as a wet Tuesday in Accrington.

At exactly 11.01, his phone rang.

'Ridpath.'

'Hiya, it's Emily.'

Ridpath instantly felt guilty. While he had been sitting here sipping whisky and feeling sorry for himself, his team had been working late on a Friday night when they should have been out enjoying themselves.

'Hi, Emily,' he finally answered.

'I followed up on Patricia Patterson, the social worker, and guess what?'

'I don't know.' His voice sounded tired and lost.

'She went missing last Wednesday. The day after the hands were discovered.'

He sat up straight in his chair. 'What?'

'Patricia Patterson went missing last Wednesday.'

'Are you sure?'

'I'm with her partner at the moment. The woman's distraught, saying she didn't come back from work on Wednesday night and she's not answering her phone.'

Chapter 63

Patricia Patterson sat up straighter as the door opened. 'I wondered when you would come. Is it time?'

'Not yet, Pat.'

'But it will be soon?'

There was no answer. They both knew none was needed.

'I would never say anything. I'd always keep my mouth shut. I have so far, haven't I? Cherie doesn't even know.'

'They found the backpack.'

'I told you not to put it there. Somebody was always going to find it. Some druggie or some nosey kids.'

'You broke the rules, Pat.'

'What rule did I break?'

'You left us. It's not allowed.'

'But I spoke with Matthew, he said I could go.'

'He changed his mind. Or should I say Leviticus guided him. "Lay his hand on the head of his offering, and kill it in front of the tent of meeting; and Aaron's sons shall throw its blood against the sides of the altar."'

The words sent a chill through Patricia Patterson. She knew this was going to happen, but to hear it stated so bluntly terrified her.

'But… but I kept my word. I didn't tell anybody.'

'It's too late, it has been decided. The Sons of Aaron have decided.'

The door slammed shut, leaving Patricia alone.

What had she done to deserve this?

Unfortunately, she knew.

SATURDAY

Chapter 64

Ridpath was standing outside Stretford nick again. It seemed he spent his life going in and out of this place. Normally, it would be heaving on a Saturday, but today it was strangely quiet and peaceful. Stretford Police Station was less than half a mile from Manchester United's ground and served as a holding centre for all the cops on duty for a home game. Except the Covid restrictions were still in place and United were playing behind closed doors, watched by an army of red plastic seats.

He'd dropped off Eve to her Chinese teacher that morning. She shared a class with five other kids, all of whose parents were worried their children wouldn't be able to speak Chinese or understand the culture. Polly had insisted Eve attend the Manchester Chinese Centre opposite Ardwick Green and Ridpath continued to send her when classes had resumed in February.

She moaned about attending, but Ridpath felt she secretly enjoyed the time and meeting the other kids.

'But I have homework to do.'

'You have homework?'

'When don't I have homework?'

'When you've finished it.'

'Clever, Dad. Some History stuff and Geography.'

He was driving along the A56 into the centre of Manchester.

'Good, something to keep you busy this afternoon.'

'You have to work again?'

'Yeah, the case is heating up and we only have till Monday to solve it.'

She suddenly perked up. 'Can I help you? I helped with the backpack, didn't I?'

'*Noooooo*, a police station is not a suitable place for a young girl.'

'So it would be OK if I were a boy?'

'I didn't mean that. It's not a suitable place for a young person full stop.'

He'd dropped her off, arranging to pick her up again after noon, before heading back the way he'd come to Stretford.

'I can take the tram, you know. I'm old enough now.'

'It's not a problem, I'll pick you up. I don't want you walking around town on your own.'

'But I like window shopping, and you don't like to go with me.'

There it was again. The unspoken accusation. Mum did like to go window shopping with her. 'I'll take you when this case is finished.'

'There's always another case, Dad. The bad people in Manchester don't stop what they're doing just because you want to take me shopping.'

With that final admonition, she opened the car door, fixed her mask across her face, slung her backpack over her shoulder and sloped off to her Chinese class.

The others were already waiting for him in the situation room.

'Sorry I'm late again. Let's get down to it. Anything more on Patricia Patterson, Emily?'

The detective shook her head. 'I have a description of her car and the clothes she was wearing on the day she disappeared. Her boss said she didn't turn up for work that day.'

'But she left to go there?'

'According to her partner.'

'Was she meeting somebody? Not going straight in to work?'

'Not according to her partner.'

'Right, let's circulate a description of the car…'

'A red Ford Fiesta, registration GW05 PB1.'

'Oliver, you need to check ANPR for last Wednesday. See if you can find out what happened to the car.'

'Right, Ridpath.'

'Dave, how did you get on with Gerald Duffy?'

'An interesting character, a bit of a loner. He was thirty-four when he disappeared—'

'Disappeared?'

'Another one. This time in 2017. Vanished one day, nobody has seen him since.'

'Who reported him missing?'

'That's it. Nobody did. I went to his old flat in Fallowfield and a neighbour said he just vanished without trace one day. Didn't take any of his stuff either. Just disappeared.'

'Can we get a CSI team down to the flat?'

'No point, Ridpath. According to the landlord, it's been let to multiple tenants since 2017.'

'What about the stuff he left behind?'

'Sold by the landlord in lieu of rent. Nothing left.'

'There must be something we can do? What about his job? Where did he work?'

Dave consulted his notes. 'He had a variety of jobs, the last one with a bakery in Wythenshawe.'

'What jobs?'

'Taxi driver, shelf stacker at Waitrose, and then at the bakery as a labourer. He also volunteered with the scouts in the evenings, but stopped doing it in 2013.'

'Any link to Daisy House?'

'None I can see so far. There's not a lot on him, Ridpath. I can keep digging, if you want.'

'Yeah, keep going, Dave, you might find something. Chrissy, anything from your side?'

Despite the proximity to United's ground, the civilian researcher was wearing a full light blue and white City outfit.

'The Etihad isn't open, why are you decked out in the gear?'

'Habit, isn't it, on a Saturday.'

'You mean you've been wearing this stuff every weekend throughout lockdown?'

'Yeah, me and the lads sit in front of the box watching the games. Life and football doesn't stop because of some poxy virus. Wouldn't know what to do with myself otherwise. You should see my husband.'

'No, thanks. Anyway, what do you have for us?'

Oliver was poised with his pen next to one of the whiteboards.

'You asked me to pass the toothbrush to Hannah, which I did. She texted me this morning, she'll be joining us as soon as she can on Zoom.'

'Good, hopefully she has something.'

'I checked out the three names not charged by CPS.' She pointed to the whiteboard, where 'Robert Dunphy – Social Worker, Patricia Patterson – Social Worker, Peter Clarke – Odd Job Man' were all printed. 'None of them were on the Sexual Offenders Register.'

'What charges did the investigating team want to press?'

'Aiding and abetting an offence against a child under the Accessories and Abettors Act 1861 section eight. In addition, Robert Dunphy was questioned under the Sexual Offences Act 2003 section seventeen for abuse of position of trust: causing or inciting a child to engage in sexual activity. But like I said, nobody was charged by CPS for lack of evidence—'

Emily interrupted. 'I talked to my mate on Operation Pharaoh. He told me they thought these three were involved but couldn't prove it, and CPS felt none of the witnesses would stand up in court. So CPS went with the four they were certain would be convicted.' She shook her head and her voice became more agitated. 'We let these people back into the community so they could offend again because the CPS didn't want to spoil their conviction record.'

'I checked their records. There is no evidence of them ever offending again, Emily,' said Chrissy.

The detective sergeant shook her head.

'Anything else, Chrissy?'

'That's me done.'

'Right, we asked ourselves some questions yesterday. What links Joseph Rowlands, Jane Ryder, Gerald Duffy and now Patricia Patterson?'

'The one consistent factor is Daisy House Children's Home.' Emily had her voice and her emotions back under control.

'But that's not true, is it? The first two have links, but Gerald Duffy and Patricia Patterson don't seem connected to it.'

'Or we don't know what the connection is yet.'

'Right, Dave, can you check if Gerald Duffy had any links to the children's home? And Emily, follow up with Patricia Patterson's partner. Did she ever work at Daisy House?'

'She's not on the list, but she may have volunteered there.'

'Find out.'

'Will do.'

'There's one other thing.' Ridpath walked over to the pictures Sophia had discovered on the internet of the Mad Ferret Festival. 'Who is this man, and what was his link to Jane Ryder?'

'She obviously knows him,' said Emily, 'knows him quite well. Look at her body language, leaning in towards him.'

'We could see if we could match him through facial recognition?' said Chrissy. 'Probably a blind alley, but worth a check.'

'Can you arrange it with the digital team on the fifth floor? And we need it right now, not sometime in the next millennia.'

'Will do, they owe me more favours than United has last-minute penalties.'

Ridpath thought for a moment before walking back to the front of the room. 'All the people involved with Daisy House have either died or gone missing. Now the same has happened to Patricia Patterson. We need to find her as soon as possible.'

'I've had a text from Hannah. She has something for us.'

They quickly set up the laptop. Hannah's face beamed out to them from her lab.

'Hiya, I have some good news and some bad news.'

'The good news first, Hannah, I've had enough bad news to last me a lifetime,' said Ridpath.

'We expedited the testing, managing to obtain enough usable DNA from the female hand in the backpack to compare it with DNA taken from the toothbrush…'

'And?'

'Here's the bad news. It's not Jane Ryder. We'll run the tests again to check, though. Do you have any other DNA samples for her?'

Ridpath thought of the hairbrush lying on the dresser at the Ryders.

'I'll ask Sophia to get a hairbrush, if it will help.'

'Perfect, but honestly, the two samples were different on all the SNPs we took. Unless the toothbrush didn't belong to Jane Ryder, I'm not hopeful of a match.'

'The chain of custody was unbroken,' said Chrissy.

'We'll get you the hairbrush today, Hannah. Thanks for all your work.'

'Sorry I couldn't be more helpful.'

Ridpath cut the connection. 'Right, Oliver, we have two new questions for the board.'

The young detective was ready with his marker pen.

'Whose hand was in the backpack? And secondly, what happened to Jane Ryder?'

None of the assembled detectives tried to answer. The only sound was the squeak of pen on whiteboard.

Finally, Emily spoke. 'You know, Ridpath, it strikes me if all these people were connected to Daisy House, what we have here is a giant conspiracy. It also makes me ask a third question. Were people being murdered to cover up something that happened long ago in the children's home? And, if that's true, what the hell happened?'

'Write it down, Oliver,' Ridpath ordered.

As DC Davis wrote the question on the whiteboard, Ridpath's phone rang. He answered it, saying, 'Yes, yes, at once and yes,' before ending the call.

He looked up at all the detectives in front of him. 'I've just been summoned to Police HQ. Claire Trent and Turnbull want an update.'

Chapter 65

They were both waiting for him when he arrived.

'Come in, sit down,' ordered Turnbull.

When he had settled himself in front of them, Turnbull simply barked, 'Update, and make it brief. I don't want to be here on a Saturday when I could be on the golf course.'

Ridpath took a deep breath and counted silently to three. This man was deliberately goading him, trying to provoke a reaction. The team was working twenty-four seven trying to crack the case and all his erstwhile boss cared about was a round of golf. He could feel his face becoming redder and redder.

'Have you made any progress, Ridpath?' Claire Trent's voice was softer, more emollient.

'We have made a lot in the last couple of days. Firstly, we know the names of two of the people who had their hands amputated. They were Joseph Rowlands and Gerald Duffy. We are still testing the third hand.'

'So what links Rowlands and Duffy?' asked Claire Trent.

'A great question. We're not certain at the moment. We think it could be Daisy House.'

'The children's home where the backpack was found by the film crew?'

Ridpath nodded. 'Joseph Rowlands worked there as a gardener, and Duffy may have been connected to the place, perhaps as a volunteer. We have information Jane Ryder was a resident at Daisy House, too.'

'Hold on, who is Jane Ryder?' asked Turnbull.

'She's the missing person case Ridpath has been working on for the coroner,' Claire Trent answered for him. 'What has she got to do with the case?'

'The backpack in which the hands were found. We think it belonged to her.'

'Think?'

'Yes.'

'But you don't know?'

'We're pretty certain. It's limited edition, and Mr Ryder bought exactly the same one for his daughter. We have pictures of her with it on the day she disappeared in 2009.'

'You have pictures of her with it at the children's home?' asked Claire Trent.

'No.'

Turnbull smiled. 'It's circumstantial. Do you have proof it's the same backpack?'

'No, but we're pretty sure.'

'But you don't know.' Turnbull was pushing hard.

Ridpath sighed. 'Correct.'

'What happened to the backpack between 2009 and when it was found last Tuesday morning?' demanded Turnbull.

'We don't know.'

'More stuff you don't know.' A triumphant glance from Turnbull to his boss. 'Anything you *do* know?'

'We are convinced the hands in the backpack and the disappearance of Jane Ryder are linked.'

'How?'

'We don't know... yet.'

Another smirk from Turnbull. 'Where are the bodies of the victims?'

'We don't know.'

'Why were the hands removed?'

Ridpath stayed silent.

'I presume you don't know.' A dramatic pause. 'Do you have any suspects?'

Ridpath shook his head.

'Persons of interest?'

Ridpath stared at him.

'Or even any witnesses you haven't interviewed yet?'

'We have only been working on it for a few days, give us a break,' snapped Ridpath, instantly regretting that he had lost his temper.

Turnbull sat back in his chair and crossed his arms over his large chest.

'Do you have any leads?' Claire Trent asked.

'Two possibles. One is Patricia Patterson, the social worker involved with Jane Ryder.'

'I presume you will be interviewing her.'

Ridpath waited before quietly saying, 'She's disappeared.'

'What?'

'She vanished last Wednesday, the day after the hands were found.'

'Isn't that suspicious?' Claire Trent sat upright in her chair.

'We think so. We're looking for her at the moment.'

'You said there were two possibles.'

'The other is a man in the picture with Jane Ryder the day she disappeared.' He dug out a copy from the file. 'This man. We want to know who he is and how he is linked to Jane.'

'A long shot. The picture was taken in 2009.'

'We can hope. Chrissy is getting the facial recognition people on it today.'

'More resource and time.'

'I can't investigate this case, DCI Turnbull, without using them,' snapped Ridpath.

Another smile. 'Remember you have until Monday.'

'Speaking of Monday,' interrupted Claire Trent, 'Mrs Challinor and I have agreed she will go ahead with her inquest calling her preliminary witnesses. I have already briefed the Police Legal Service to be there and to request a postponement of the inquest pending our further enquiries.'

'Mrs Challinor told me last night.'

'Afterwards, MIT's involvement will gradually be phased out and the inquiry will be passed to the Cold Case Unit.'

'What?'

'We can't waste any more time or resources on it.' Turnbull was smiling.

'But we're actually getting somewhere. We need more time. There may be other victims and other deaths.'

'It will be for Chief Inspector Holburt and his team at the Cold Case Unit to decide. Not us. You have until Monday, Ridpath.'

'But that's unfair, I need more time. We could be dealing with a serial killer here.'

The two senior detectives stared at him, before Turnbull asked, 'What is your evidence there is a serial killer operating in Manchester? Three hands that may or may not have been linked to a children's home?'

Ridpath wished he'd stayed quiet. 'There seems to be a pattern in the deaths. Perhaps the hands were trophies kept by the killer.'

'What's his reason for killing?' asked Claire Trent.

'We don't know yet.'

'Have you confirmed a link between all three hands?'

'Not yet. It could be Daisy House. There could be a conspiracy to cover up something that happened in the past there.' Ridpath realised how vague his words sounded.

'Listen to yourself. So many weasel words and not a shred of hard evidence. If you're so convinced these hands in a backpack are linked to Daisy House, have you interviewed any of the former residents?'

Ridpath looked down.

'Spoken to any of the staff?'

Ridpath didn't answer.

'Have you even compiled a list of residents? People you could ask if anything criminal occurred that might lead to a conspiracy or a cover-up?'

Ridpath finally shook his head.

Turnbull turned to Claire Trent. 'I warned you about Ridpath's imagination, his reliance on "hunches" rather than the hard graft of evidence gathering. Now what do we have? A lot of questions and not a lot of answers. Conspiracy theories rather than concrete facts.'

'Listen, don't you get it? There is a serial killer or killers out there. People keep disappearing; Jane Ryder, Joseph Rowlands, Gerald Duffy and now Patricia Patterson. And somehow, they are all linked to Daisy House.'

Claire Trent spoke slowly. 'The disappearance of people is not proof there is a serial killer in Manchester. Nor is it proof of a conspiracy to cover up something that may or may not have happened in the past. Without evidence linking these people to Daisy House Children's Home, you have nothing, Ridpath.'

'People disappear all the time. You haven't thought this through, lad.'

'That's not fair, I—'

'Life is unfair, Ridpath,' smirked Turnbull, 'you'd better get used to it.'

Ridpath ignored him, appealing directly to Claire Trent. 'I just need another week, boss, I'm sure we could find the link, work out why these people have disappeared and how it relates to the children's home.'

'I've made up my mind.'

'Just a couple of extra days.'

'I have made my decision. You have till Monday. Now if you don't mind, I have a mountain of paperwork to get through.'

Chapter 66

After the Ridpath left, Turnbull stayed in Claire Trent's office.

'I don't think he's handling this investigation well, boss. He's out of his depth, can't hack it.'

'I don't agree, Paul, he's done quite well with limited resources.'

'You heard him. I asked a few basic questions and his answers were always the same. "I don't know." He's moving too slowly. Plus he's trying to do two jobs; working for the coroner and working on our case. He even has the gall to try to bundle them together with some spurious talk about matching backpacks, cover-ups and conspiracy theories.'

Claire Trent stared at the figures on her spreadsheet, trying desperately to make them add up to something more than a reduction in her manpower. 'As I said—'

'But there's one thing he said worried me, boss,' Turnbull interrupted before she finished her sentence.

She lifted her head for the first time. 'What was it?'

'What if he's right?'

'Right about what?'

'What if there is a serial killer out there?'

Claire Trent scratched her head. 'It's the last thing I need now. A major investigation with major costs.'

'I totally agree, boss. That's why I think I should take over.'

'What?'

'Take over this investigation. We need a big win right now, and Ridpath is too preoccupied with his hunches and theories, he's not doing the basics of an investigation. If there is a serial killer out there, the last thing we need is another Shipman or Yorkshire Ripper, with the press latching on to it and crucifying us.'

Claire Trent's eyes narrowed. 'You've changed your tune. I thought you said this was a no hope case.'

Turnbull coughed. 'I still think it is, but if there is even the slightest hint that a serial killer is operating in Manchester, we need to investigate.' A long pause, followed by a dramatic sigh. 'There is a small chance, an extremely small chance, I could turn it around, make it work for us. Turn it into a win for the department, boss. At the very least, if it does blow up, you can say you put senior personnel on the case.'

Claire Trent shook her head. 'No, Paul, you have too many other investigations happening at the moment. You'll spread yourself too thin.'

Turnbull grabbed a chunk of fat around his waist. 'Hardly any chance of that. I'd like to take over. Ridpath isn't going to solve it. He's the one spread too thin.'

'No, Paul, I need you to work the other cases. South Yorkshire looks good, and you know how keen the acting chief constable is on inter-force cooperation.'

'Peter can handle it. Our intel is the buy isn't going to happen for a couple of weeks. Mrs Docherty and Marcus Hayden are still doing the drug-dealers dance, haggling about delivery and cost.'

'The answer is still no, Paul. We've given Ridpath until Monday to solve it, let's leave him alone to do his work.' She sat back in her chair. 'I think you underestimate the resourcefulness of our DI Ridpath.'

'And I think you overestimate him, boss. He's not that good.'

'I've made my decision, Paul. I thought you had a golf course to go to?'

'Not today.'

'Well, I have a few rounds still to go with these figures before Monday.'

He stood up. 'I think you're making the wrong decision, boss. I have a feeling this case is about to blow up in our faces.'

'I'll take the risk, Paul.' She tapped the printout of her spreadsheet. 'You can help me with these, if you're so keen to get involved.'

'Numbers ain't my strength.'

'It's not mine either, but somebody has to do it.'

'Rather you than me.'

'Rather anybody else but me.'

Claire Trent bent her head down close to the paper, following a column with her pencil.

Turnbull decided to go; he wasn't going to convince her today. A wee birdie had told him this case was coming together. Ridpath was barking up the wrong tree with his conspiracy theories, but he'd read the files. All it needed was a little shove to take it over the line. That shove had to come from him, not from Mr Arsehole Ridpath. And he knew exactly what to do to give it an extra push.

Chapter 67

Both Emily and Chrissy were waiting for him in the situation room.

'We have until Monday, no longer.'

Their shoulders fell. 'There's too much to do, Ridpath.'

'Right, let's focus. Dave is concentrating on finding more about Duffy, Oliver is on the ANPR. Chrissy, have you arranged a time with the facial recognition people?'

'I've persuaded Tom Gorman to give me a couple of hours in—' she checked her watch '—five minutes.'

'Good, let's cross our fingers you get a result. Em, can you follow up on Patricia Patterson? Find out everything you can about her. See if you can get permission to look through her documents. Where has she gone? Has she done a runner because the hands were found, or—'

'Has she become a victim.'

'Exactly.'

'What are you doing, Ridpath?'

'If I'm honest, I'm picking up my daughter first and taking her home, and afterwards I'm off to the coroner's office to work with Sophia.'

'What's going on there?'

'I think there's one angle we may have missed. One lead we haven't followed up. It may be a long shot but I think I need to check it out.'

'Want me to come?' asked Emily.

'No, you stay on Patricia Patterson, she could be key.'

'When are we meeting next?'

'Tomorrow morning at nine a.m. I know it's Sunday, but I can't think of a way around it.'

'No worries,' they both said at the same time, before Emily carried on, 'I think we're both happy to be doing something not involving stats, looking at a laptop or being stuck in here all day long. Dave Connor won't be happy though.'

'Neither will my daughter. I'll take her to her grandparents.'

'I'd better be off before Tom Gorman decides he has better things to do on a Saturday and starts throwing his toys out of the pram.'

The civilian researcher ran off towards the door.

'Call me if you find anything?'

'OK.'

Emily Parkinson and Ridpath were left alone.

'What are the chances of solving this before Monday? Be straight with me.'

'Not great, Em. We need more time and more bodies to check the leads. Two things we don't have a lot of at the moment. But we'll just keep our heads down and keep plugging away. It's never over till the fat lady sings.'

'Or the jury says not guilty.'

'Aye, that as well.' He ran his fingers through his hair. 'I can't help feeling we're missing one piece of the puzzle. If we had it, everything would fall neatly into place.'

'I know what you mean, Ridpath, but we're not going to find it standing here. Isn't your daughter waiting for you to pick her up?'

'Shit, a grumpy Eve is not worth living with.'

'You probably deserve everything you get.'

'And more.' He picked up his bag, 'Call me if you get anything.'

'I'll call you even if I don't get anything.'

'Right.'

'Say hello to Eve,' were the last words he heard as he rushed out of the door.

Chapter 68

His daughter was sitting on the steps outside the Chinese Centre on her own.

'You're late, Dad.'

'Sorry, traffic was bad.'

She got into the car, slinging her things onto the back seat roughly.

'How was your class?'

'OK, same old.'

'You learnt some new vocab?'

'No, we went over the old stuff again and again and again. Apparently, my tones are incorrect and I sound too English.'

'Not surprising.'

'Luckily, the others are just as bad, some even worse than me. They sound too Cantonese.'

'What's wrong with sounding Cantonese?'

'When your teacher is from Beijing, apparently it's a sin worse than murder.'

Ridpath laughed. 'That's bad.'

He headed back down the A56 to their home – a journey he seemed to make all the time these days. 'I have to go back to work this afternoon. You don't mind, do you? I can ask Mrs Dunwoody if you can go round to her house if you want.'

'Nah, I'll be OK. I've got lots of homework to keep me occupied.'

'Sorry.' He paused for a moment, before deciding to take the plunge. 'About tomorrow. I don't think we can go to the cemetery.'

Her mouth opened wide. 'But you promised. It's Mum's time, we need to go, Dad.'

'I'll see if I can make it, but there's so much to do and the inquest opens on Monday morning.'

'You promised.'

He stared out of the windscreen. A few spots of rain began to fall, splattering the glass.

'Mum was right.'

She turned her body away from him.

'What?'

'She always said you cared more about the job than any of us.'

'Your mum said nothing of the sort.'

She answered without turning around. 'I used to listen to your arguments. She was always telling you to care less about the job and care more about us, to spend more time with us.'

'I do care about you and your mum.'

No answer.

'You know I do, it's just I have to work, cases need time and sometimes I can't decide not to get involved.'

'Doesn't your family need time too?'

She sounded exactly the same as Polly, even down to the intonation.

'Of course they do. Of course you do. I'll make it up to you. We'll go to London together when we can, now the lockdown's over.'

He saw her shoulders relax and stiffen again.

'Another promise?' she sneered.

He turned into their road and pulled up outside the house. 'I'll call you before I come home.'

'Don't bother,' she said without looking round. 'I'll manage without you.' Without saying another word, she took her back-pack from the back seat and strode up the driveway.

'Eve...' he shouted.

She didn't turn round, opening the front door and slamming it behind her.

He sat in the car, thinking about whether or not to go in and talk with her, try to calm her down. The dashboard clock clicked over to 1.12.

Shit. He had told Sophia he would be in at one p.m.

Shit.

He closed his eyes and shook his head.

Shit.

Putting the car in gear, he headed off to the Coroner's Court. He would have to make it up to Eve later.

Chapter 69

Detective Chief Inspector Turnbull spotted Molly Wright in the beer garden of Sinclair's Oyster Bar.

Not that there was any grass in the garden, rather it was a concrete picnic table area, set between three old pubs; Sinclair's, the Old Wellington and The Mitre. Two of the pubs were half-timbered and had been transported to this location when Market Street had been developed in the mid-seventies. Turnbull thought it was funny the only buildings Manchester had bothered to save were a couple of pubs.

Molly Wright offered him her cheek to kiss. 'I ordered a bottle of Rioja to keep us going.'

Turnbull glanced down; the bottle was already half empty. She poured him a glass of a deep, dark red and topped up her own. 'Bottoms up, pants down,' she said, raising her glass.

'Cheers. Long time no see, Molly.'

'Not since last year, I think it was.'

'How's things?'

'Great, I'm still on the crime beat, but I now have a regular column. You'd be surprised how many crimes of passion were committed during lockdown. Locking people together who don't get on is always a recipe for trouble.'

'Like me and my missus. Luckily, I kept working.'

'Ah, the stories of true love, how I miss them.'

'You've done well for yourself. I read the book. You weren't very kind.'

She mimed shock. 'I went easy on you. The Carsley case has become well known since I wrote the book about it. The new Moors Murders, according to the reviews.'

'Yeah, didn't help my career prospects.'

'I could have been tougher. You should have seen what I took out. Arresting the father was not a smart move, Paul.'

'Had to be done. Anyway, water under the bridge now.'

The both drank large swallows of Rioja, Molly Wright nearly finishing hers.

'As much as a love seeing your bald head, Paul, I know you didn't ring me because you were missing my wit and charm.'

He put down his glass. 'No, Molly, I have something for you.'

She took out her notebook. 'Something juicy, I hope.'

'Off the record?'

'Of course, but attributable to a source?'

'Yeah, but no mention of Police HQ or MIT.'

'Agreed. Fire away.'

'It's about the hands found in the backpack in Northenden.'

'I read about it. A juicy little discovery. Probably some medical students playing a prank.'

'It wasn't. It seems to be linked to the children's home, Daisy House.'

'I'm all ears, child abuse makes good copy.'

'Nothing much yet, but a little bird tells me the chief suspect, Patricia Patterson, disappeared the day after the hands were discovered.'

'Really? Haven't your colleagues found her yet?'

'They only found out she was missing yesterday.'

'That seems remiss of them. Who's the officer in charge?'

'DI Thomas Ridpath.'

'Ridpath?' She chewed the end of her pen. 'He was the copper I saved from Matthew Oram. The one who did a parallel investigation to yours during the Carsley case. Mauling Molly, they started calling me in the newsroom.' She paused for a moment, eyeing him up and down. 'You trying to stick the knife in, get your own back?'

It was his turn to mime innocence. 'What, me? I was wondering if you were interested in the case. If you don't want the scoop, I'll talk to another reporter.'

He stood up to go, but she clamped her hand on his arm.

'Don't be so touchy, Paul. I'm all for stabbing people in the back, but I usually prefer to use words, not a knife – much more hurtful. Now sit down and tell Auntie Molly all about it.'

Chapter 70

Sophia was already at her desk when Ridpath arrived at the coroner's office. 'How was your morning?'

'Busy, too much work and too little time. Dealing with Turnbull always sets my teeth on edge.'

'He's the bald-headed one, right?'

'The one and only.'

'Struck me as a bit of a wanker the one time I met him.'

'I love it when you are rude, Sophia, so unlike you.'

'Wash my mouth out with soap.'

'Did you check Andrea Briggs again, like I asked?'

'Yep, still nothing. She stayed at school for a while until she was sixteen and after that, I can't find anything on her. Nothing on the electoral register, no driving licence applications. Nada.'

Ridpath took off his jacket, setting it across the back of his chair, before sitting down opposite her. 'Do you have an address for her?'

She checked through her notes. 'Here it is, the school had it so it's at least ten years out of date. She was living with her parents, Tom and Elizabeth, at 245 Havistock Road, Sale. I guess it's not far from the Ryders.' She continued reading her notes. 'That's strange, I've just noticed their surname. It's Brooks, not Briggs. Why did they have a different surname?'

'Did you call them?'

'Yes, but there was no answer.'

Ridpath put his jacket back on.

'Where are you going?'

'Time to check out the address.'

'But they were living there nearly ten years ago. They've probably moved, or passed away.'

'They might still be there, and I have to check it out. I thought about it last night and it's the piece of the case that's been worrying me like a head full of nits. What happened to the other friend, Andrea Briggs?'

'Do you ever sleep?'

'Not on a case. I'm off to the house in Sale.'

'Can I come?'

'It would be good to have you there, Sophia.'

'Your car or mine?'

Chapter 71

'Is this the best you have?'

''Fraid so.'

Tom Gorman, the lead technician in the Digital Services Division of GMP, raised his eyebrows. 'Well, we may get a hit or we may not. But first I have to check whether we have permission to use this photograph.'

'The photographer sent it to us allowing all uses.'

'Great, make sure you send me the paperwork.'

'Covering your arse?'

'Always. First thing they teach you in GMP. Now, let me scan it in and we'll log on to the PND to do a search comparison.'

He loaded the photograph into a machine, which immediately began producing a startling array of clicks and whirrs.

'Thank God it isn't video footage.'

'Why? Does it take too long to load?'

Tom laughed. 'Nah, it's easier. Just it's a bit of a grey area for us.'

'Grey area?'

'We were caught in 2018 using live facial recognition technology to look at all the people who visited the Trafford Centre over a period of six months.'

'What? How many people?'

'Well, a rough guess is about thirty million people visit the centre each year...'

'So we will have captured fifteen million people?'

'Yeah, roughly.'

'And they hadn't committed any crime?'

'Not that we know of. Then again, we don't know if this guy has, until we run him through the database.' He pointed to the man's face slowly appearing on a screen as it was scanned in.

'It's been stopped now, hasn't it? Live facial recognition screening, I mean.'

'Well, officially GMP doesn't use it, but we do have access to the national database, which includes images from other times when it was used. Twenty-five million pictures on it now,' he said proudly, 'even though the High Court declared it unlawful to retain images of people arrested or questioned but who were never charged. Theresa May, remember her? When she was home secretary she required us to delete images from the database, but only on application from unconvicted persons.'

'But how do I know I'm on the database?'

'You don't. You can only apply to have your image deleted if you are on the database, but nobody knows whether their face has been captured or not. It's such a great catch-22, only Theresa May could have come up with it. You're probably on it.'

'Me? What about you?'

'Of course I am. Where do you think they store our staff photos?'

'Some of these people have not committed any crime?'

'Most of them.'

'It's a bit like the Tom Cruise movie. What was it called?'

'You mean *Minority Report*?'

'A great sci-fi movie.'

'Not so sci-fi any more. The Met introduced live video facial recognition in early 2020. And where the Met leads, the rest of us follow. It's only a matter of time.'

'Amazing.'

'You don't know the half of it. The technology was developed by the Japanese and can compare about three hundred images a second, eighteen thousand faces a minute.'

'Jesus.'

'Facial images are only the first in the new wave of biometrics. You know, the police are already experimenting with voice-recognition technology and others such as iris, gait and vein analysis are commercially available.'

'You mean we could identify somebody by the way he walks?'

Tom Gorman stopped pressing the keys on his computer for a second. His arm shot straight up in the air and he began singing *Stayin' Alive*.

'The Bee Gees will be turning over in their graves. I'd stick to the day job if I were you.'

He returned to the keyboard and tapped on a few keys. 'Right, we're set, connected to the PND. Now we just let the algorithms go to work and see if we get a match.'

'How long will it take?'

'How long's a piece of string? Fancy a coffee while this is working? I could murder a cheese toastie.'

Chapter 72

Emily knocked on the door of Patricia Patterson's house. Her partner answered the door almost immediately, her expression visibly saddening when she saw it was Emily.

'It's me again. Can I come in?'

'Sorry, thought it was her and she'd forgotten her key.'

The partner left the door open and walked away. Emily took it as a hint she should enter, closing the door behind her.

'Still no news, Cherie?' It was an attempt at breaking the ice with this woman. As soon as the words left Emily's mouth, she realised how weak they were.

The partner didn't bother to answer.

Emily followed her into the kitchen. A pot of coffee was in the machine. 'Would you like a cup?'

Emily shook her head. 'Too much makes my head go all woozy.'

'What can I do for you?'

'I'm following up on the visit yesterday. You've still had no contact with Patricia?'

'Pat. She preferred to be called Pat. And the answer is no.'

'Forgive me for asking, but she couldn't have found another partner?'

'And go away without saying anything? Not Pat's style. We've been together for eight years. If she wanted to leave, she would have made a dramatic exit, telling me exactly what was wrong. She wasn't afraid of a bit of confrontation.' A pause as she stared off into mid-air. 'It's one of the things I love about her. She takes no bullshit from anybody.'

'Does she have any enemies? People who don't like her?'

Cherie laughed. 'Half the bloody council and most of her colleagues hate her guts. But not enough to kidnap her.'

'Any strange letters or phone calls in the last month or so? Anything standing out as different?'

Cherie thought for a long time. 'We had been receiving some phone calls recently. You know the type, silence on the end of the phone. We thought it was just some kid playing around or a neighbour who didn't like the idea of two women living together happily.'

'Did you report the calls to the police?'

'No. They weren't that sort of call. And what would your lot do?'

Emily scratched her head. 'Probably put at number two hundred and fifty-one on the list of things to action for the local station.'

'Yeah, thanks for the honesty.'

'There's enough other stuff for us to get involved in, minor levels of harassment inevitably get ignored until they escalate.'

'You think this one has escalated?'

'Honestly?'

Cherie nodded her head.

'We don't know. In fact, we're still trying to work out why she vanished. Have you called her mobile again?'

'It goes to voicemail. No response since the morning she left.'

'Right.' Emily stood tall; it was time to get to the real reason she had returned to the house. 'It would help us in our search for Patricia if we knew more about her. Does she have any files or personal documents we could check?'

'There's her desk. It's what she uses when she's working from home.'

'Could I have a look through it?'

Cherie shrugged her shoulders. 'If it helps.'

'It might do.'

Cherie led Emily Parkinson upstairs to a small bedroom converted into an office. 'She liked working in here. Anything to avoid going into the office.'

Emily checked the drawers. Three were full of official files on cases she was working. Most seemed to deal with disability and care packages.

'She worked a lot on care packages for old people for the council. You wouldn't believe some of the stories she told me. Old women with severe rheumatoid arthritis being passed as fit for work by the bastards at the DWP. I often heard her shouting down the phone at them. As I say, she took no bullshit, especially not from those corpses.'

Emily tried the final drawer. It was locked

Cherie stepped forward and lifted up the lamp. Underneath was a small key. 'She never knew I'd twigged where she hid it.'

Emily opened the drawer. Inside was more personal stuff. Pictures of Patricia Patterson as a young woman, a copy of driving licence with her photo on it, a 2021 diary with short notes, mainly work related. Emily read the diary quickly. On the day she disappeared, there was just a single word in block capitals: MEET. 11 a.m.

Meet who? Meet where?

'Do you know anything about this?'

Cherie shook her head. 'She never said anything about meeting anybody. When she left on Wednesday morning, she just said she was going to the office.'

Emily had a thought. 'Were there any phone calls on Tuesday night, quite late?'

Cherie shook her head again. 'But there was one on Wednesday morning as I made breakfast. At first she said she wasn't going to bother going to the office. After the phone call, she said she was going in. I thought it must have been something urgent.'

Emily made a note to check with Patricia Patterson's workplace. Had they called her that morning?

She carried on searching through the drawer. Beneath the usual biros, paperclips, old Post-its and erasers she found a yellowing CV folded in two.

She glanced through it and immediately the hackles on her neck rose. Keeping her voice in control, she asked, 'Is this Patricia's CV?'

Cherie looked at it. 'Her name's at the top and that's the university where she did her CQSW, so I think so. See the last job, it's where she worked before.'

'Right,' said Emily, 'would you mind if I took it?'

'No, I'm sure there's lots printed out somewhere.'

Emily checked out the room. 'I don't see any computer?'

'Patricia took her laptop with her when she left on Wednesday morning.'

'And you're sure she took her phone with her?'

'Couldn't do without it. Pat without her phone was like a car without an engine. Pretty damn useless. Her whole life was contained inside. For God's sake, she used to sleep with it.'

Chapter 73

At the same time as Emily was knocking on Patricia Patterson's door in Bury, Ridpath and Sophia were standing outside 245 Havistock Road in Sale.

The house looked exactly the same as the Ryders', except a new extension had been added to the side, expanding the kitchen and creating a larger bedroom above.

'What do you think?' asked Sophia.

'Not overly confident. People usually add extensions when they buy a house, not after they've lived there a long time.'

They knocked on the door. A young voice shouted from the inside, 'I'll get it.'

An eleven-year-old opened the door. Ridpath showed him his warrant card. 'Can I speak with your dad?'

'Dad, it's the police… again.'

He walked away from door, leaving Ridpath and Sophia standing there. Eventually, a man in his thirties wearing a brown cardigan and slacks ran down the stairs. 'It's about time you lot came, he's been playing his music at three a.m. again.'

'Sorry?'

'Him next door. Woke the bloody kids and the wife. I'm not having it any more, either you lot sort it out or I will.'

'Sorry, Mr…?'

'Trevor. Keith Trevor. I called the station this morning. Spoke to a Sergeant Kerrigan.'

'Mr Trevor, we haven't come about the noise next door. My name is Detective Inspector Ridpath, and this Sophia Rahman.' He showed his warrant card. 'We're here about a family with the surname Brooks or Briggs who lived here in 2009.'

'You haven't come about the noise?'

'Sorry, not our department. We're looking for this family because they may be able to help us find a girl who went missing in 2009.' Ridpath didn't want to mention the hands at the moment.

'Dorothy, do you remember the Brooks or the Briggs, used to live here?' he shouted over his shoulder.

A woman came to the door wiping her hands on a tea towel. 'I thought they were here about the noise.'

'Not their department, apparently.'

'Well, he's the police, isn't he? Can't he do something about it?'

'I'll call Sergeant Kerrigan if you want? Make sure he sends somebody this afternoon. You rang Sale Police Station?'

'Yeah, they've been here before. Doesn't have much effect though.'

Sophia stepped forward. 'If I were you I'd apply for a noise abatement order through the local council. My mum had the same problem with her neighbours. It's a statutory nuisance and if someone breaks an abatement order about noise from their home they can be fined up to £5,000. Far more effective than some poor copper knocking on their door.'

'Through the local council?'

'Yeah, I'd record him the next time he does it. The local council has to act.'

'OK,' said the woman. 'You were asking about the Brooks?'

Ridpath nodded.

'I think they were the owners of the house before. Some letters still come here with their name on. But I'm not sure when they lived here. There's been two owners in the last three years.'

Ridpath sighed. 'OK, thanks for your help.' He turned to go.

The boy's voice came from the hall. 'You're looking for Mr Brooks? He helps out in the local food bank where I volunteer. He said he used to live in our house.'

Ridpath stopped and turned back, asking tentatively, 'Do you know where he lives?'

'Yeah, they didn't move far, just to the bungalows at the end of the street. Number 387.'

Chapter 74

Ridpath and Sophia walked down the road, finding the bungalow tucked into a small enclave at the end. The front garden was neatly manicured with a parked Hyundai SUV in the driveway.

Ridpath put his hand on the bonnet. 'Still warm, somebody has recently come back.'

They rang the bell and stepped away. Inside the yapping of a small dog could be heard, followed by, 'Shut up, Percy, it's only somebody at the door.'

A figure appeared, distorted by the frosted glass. 'Who is it?'

'Is this Mr Brooks?'

'It is, who is it?'

'It's the police, Mr Brooks. Could you open the door so we can have a chat?'

'How do I know it's the police? I've heard about these scams. Old folk open the door and suddenly they are being sold conservatories, or worse.'

'I'll post my warrant card through the letterbox. You take a look at it.'

Ridpath opened the flap and dropped his warrant card in, receiving an answer almost immediately. 'Looks right enough.'

The door opened. A man stood in the hallway, his hand clutched to the collar of a small dog of indeterminate breed that was desperately lunging forward, its teeth bared.

'Don't worry about her, she's just being friendly.'

'Looks like it.'

'How can I help you?'

'If we could come in for a minute and have a chat...'

'Can't let you in. The dog, she's—'

'Too friendly?'

'Summat like that.'

'My name is Detective Inspector Ridpath, and this is my assistant, Sophia Rahman. We're investigating the disappearance of Jane Ryder in 2009.'

'You're still checking on her after so long? Perhaps I should have reported the disappearance of Andrea.'

'What?'

'Andrea Briggs, our foster child.'

'Sorry, Mr Brooks, Andrea has disappeared?'

The little dog lunged again and the man struggled to hold her back by the collar. 'Just a minute, I'll put her in with the wife.'

He dragged the dog reluctantly down the hallway, opened a door and popped it into a room. Instantly, Ridpath could hear scratching and yelping as the dog desperately tried to get out.

'She'll give up soon enough. The wife'll calm her down.'

'You were saying your foster daughter disappeared, Mr Brooks?' Sophia asked the question gently.

'Haven't heard from her since 2012. Said she was leaving one day and never came back.'

Ridpath glanced back at Sophia, who was taking notes. 'No letters, phone calls or emails?'

'Nothing. Vanished into thin air. We were expecting it though.'

'Why?'

'Well, she'd been acting strangely for a long time, ever since Jane disappeared three years earlier. If I'm honest, Mr Ridpath, we were glad to see her go. We had other kids to look after and she was being disruptive.'

'Did you report it to the police?'

'No, what was the point? She was seventeen and could do what she wanted.'

'And you haven't heard from her since?'

'No.' The dog's noises subsided and they heard a woman's voice gently chastising it. 'By the end, well, she didn't like us, and the missus and I didn't like her much either. You don't have much choice with the foster kids. Some you take to, others you don't. Bit like people.'

'How long did she live with you?' Sophia asked.

'She was already quite old, eleven, I think, when she came to us after the home she was in closed.'

Ridpath knew the answer to his next question but asked it anyway. 'Which home was that?'

'Daisy House, the one in Northenden.'

Everything leads back to the same place, thought Ridpath, like a homing beacon.

Sophia asked another question while he was thinking about the last answer. 'Did you report her disappearance to anybody?'

'Of course, we had to, didn't we?'

'Who?'

'Her social worker. She had to know, didn't she?'

Again, Ridpath knew the answer to the next question before he asked it. 'What was the name of the social worker?'

'Patricia Patterson. She looked after all the kids from the home.'

Chapter 75

When Chrissy and Tom Gorman returned from the canteen, the machine was still connected to the Police National Database.

'It's still going?'

'What do you expect? I press a button and, hey presto, a perp pops out of the computer with his hands up saying "It's a fair cop, guvnor, you got me bang to rights"?'

'Nah, but I didn't think it would take so long.'

'It wouldn't if your shot followed the corporate data model standards.'

'What the hell are they?'

'Basically the same as your passport photo. The old days of some poor sergeant taking a mugshot with whatever he had handy have gone. Because of the PND, all shots have to conform to the CorDM standards, or else.'

'But perps don't always sit still against a white background.'

'That's why your search is taking a bit longer. It's checking facial characteristics, scars, tattoos and all the other stuff, looking for match. Your shot was taken on an analogue camera in the middle of a music festival. Granted, the pixel count is good, but there's still a lot of noise in the picture.'

'When's it going to be finished?'

A message appeared on the screen.

'You're in luck, about now.' His hands danced across the keyboard. 'You have a hit.'

A mugshot slowly appeared on the screen. 'According to the PND, this man has an eighty-nine per cent chance of being the same as the one in the shot. It won't stand up in court, though.'

'We have to go and interview him, don't we? What's his last known address?'

Tom Gorman leant forward. 'He's in Strangeways. Has been since 2016. Adam Jones was charged with two counts of kidnap, two of attempted kidnap, four counts of assault, possession of an offensive weapon, namely a hammer, dangerous driving and drink driving.'

'They threw everything at him.'

'And the kitchen sink. Sentenced to a minimum of ten years with little chance of early release.'

'Are you sure it's him, Tom?'

'Well, the machine says eighty-nine per cent and machines, unlike humans, don't lie… yet.'

'Right, thanks for your help, I owe you big time.'

'That's what they all say.'

But Chrissy was already walking out the door, talking on her phone.

Chapter 76

Ridpath answered his mobile straight away. He was sitting in the car with Sophia near the Brooks' house, about to go back to the coroner's office.

'I have a lead to the man in the photo. His name is Adam Jones.'

'Great news, Chrissy, hang on a minute while I patch Emily and Dave in on the call.' He passed the phone to Sophia. 'Can I get other people to listen to Chrissy?'

'Of course, just make it a conference call.'

'How do I do that?'

'Simples.' She spoke to Chrissy. 'Hang on, I'm putting you on hold while I patch in the others.' She showed the phone to Ridpath. 'Put Chrissy on hold, tap "add call" to make another call and then merge calls to bring everybody together.'

Ridpath's eyes glazed over. 'Could you do it for me?'

She shook her head, tapping the keys of his mobile. 'You're gonna have to get used to technology one day.'

'I'd rather it got used to me.'

'In your dreams.' A few more taps on the keys. 'There, done. Dave and Emily added.'

'Hi, guys, can everybody hear me?'

'What's up?' said Dave.

'Loud and clear,' answered Emily.

'Chrissy, can you go ahead.'

'Hi there, Tom Gorman has had a hit on the PND for the man in the photo. It's an Adam Jones. He's in Strangeways charged with, get this, kidnap and assault. But there's a problem – he's been inside since 2016.'

'So he couldn't have kidnapped Gerald Duffy in 2017 or Joseph Rowlands in 2018. Dave, did you find out anything more on Duffy?'

'Nothing so far. He doesn't seem to have any links I can find to Daisy House. Oliver is still checking ANPR for Patricia Patterson's car.'

'Em, can you call Strangeways and arrange for both of us to visit Adam Jones tomorrow?' He stopped for a moment, realising he was supposed to be taking Eve to visit her mum's grave. He'd already floated the possibility he couldn't go and it had gone down like a cup of cold sick.

'What time, Ridpath?'

'What time, what?'

'What time shall I arrange the visit to Adam Jones?'

'Any time you can, but after ten a.m. We should meet up to review progress at nine again. Everybody OK with the time?'

There was a chorus of OKs from the other people on the conference call.

Emily continued speaking. 'Apparently, Patricia Patterson took her mobile and laptop with her when she left for work. I'm going to go back to HQ and see if we can track her phone. I have the number so we should be able to track her movements on the day she disappeared.'

'Great work, Em. Chrissy, can you do one more task for me?'

'No problem, Ridpath.'

'It's another missing person. Andrea Briggs, possibly using the name Andrea Brooks, disappeared in 2012.'

'Was it reported, Ridpath?'

'Not to the police, but to her social worker, who just happened to be Patricia Patterson.'

'Shit,' whispered Emily.

'I'll follow up, Ridpath, there must be a record somewhere.'

'Right, good work, everyone. See you tomorrow at nine. If anything comes up, call me straightaway. Clear?'

'Clear,' echoed three voices.

Ridpath ended the call.

'Where to now, Ridpath?'

'I'm going to take you back to the Coroner's Court, and afterwards I have to break the bad news to my daughter.'

'Bad news?'

'We won't be going to my wife's grave tomorrow. Instead, I'll be going to Strangeways Prison.'

'I'm sorry, Ridpath. I'm sure she'll understand.'

'You don't know, Eve.'

'I think you underestimate us girls. We have far more strength and backbone than you think. It's in our genes.'

Ridpath stared at her. 'What did you say?'

'She has far more strength and backbone—'

He opened the car door and jumped out.

'Where are you going?'

'There's something I forgot to ask Mr Brooks,' he said over his shoulder, running down the street.

Chapter 77

He dropped Sophia off at the Coroner's Court. He'd offered to take her home but she had refused.

'I still have to finished the coroner's notes for Mrs Challinor, plus I'd rather avoid home at the moment.'

'The mum?'

'Nah, it's the sister, she's visiting with her new baby, born during lockdown. I can't stand the little asides. "When's it going to be your turn, Sophia?" or, "She has Sophia's eyes. It would be lovely to have another baby in the family".'

'I didn't know I was working with Auntie Sophia.'

'If you want to get home alive, don't go there, Ridpath.'

He took the not-so-subtle hint.

Afterwards, he stopped off to see Hannah, checking if there had been any more progress.

There hadn't.

'I've virtually given up on the fingerprints, Ridpath. We can't get a good enough impression from the female hand to offer any sort of image for IDENT 1.'

'Did you check the hairbrush from the Ryders against the female hand's DNA?'

'We did. Definitely not a match.'

'Are you sure?'

'Ninety-nine point nine nine per cent sure. DNA doesn't leave much to chance.'

Ridpath's heart sank. He'd been certain the female hand belonged to Jane Ryder, but he couldn't argue with science. There was one last throw of the dice.

'I took this from another family.' He showed Hannah a picture of Andrea Briggs, taken when she was fourteen. Inside was a lock of her hair.

Hannah examined it closely. 'It looks good, we should be able to get DNA, but I won't know until I try.'

'Great, please rush it, Hannah.'

'Will do. I presume you want a comparison to the female hand.'

Ridpath nodded. 'And if she came up on any database, that would be a bonus.'

'OK, leave it with me.'

He went back to the car and sat behind the wheel. This case had been one long rush to catch up with what was happening. Had he been so busy running around, he'd missed something important?

He hoped not.

He put the car in gear. The final stop of the day was Stretford nick. He wanted to have a chat with Dave and Oliver, chivvy them along. Both seemed to be taking years over simple tasks.

Neither was around when he arrived at the station. According to the duty sergeant, Dave Connor was out chasing some old perv while Oliver Davis was with Traffic working on an ANPR search.

He could have called them, but instead went into the situation room. All the investigation was still on the whiteboards: the pictures of the CLAK backpack; the shots of Jane Ryder at the Mad Ferrets Festival; the hands lying on a sterile table at the morgue; mugshots of Joseph Rowlands and two new shots of Gerald Duffy and Patricia Patterson.

Duffy was bleary-eyed and his hair bedraggled after a night in the cells. The shot must have been taken as he was charged for his DUI. Patricia Patterson was completely the opposite; neat and tidy, wearing a corporate power suit, short hair carefully cut and shaped.

What tied them all together?

Was it just Daisy House Children's Home, or was there something else, something they had all missed?

He checked his watch.

Shit. 5.40. He needed to go home to check on Eve.

He hated having to leave her alone, but there were some times when he had to work. He was just another single parent, trying to manage work and life and his child on his own. How did the others do it? There must have been so many in the same boat. Luckily, Eve was old enough to be left alone for short periods, and she was mature for her age, Polly had seen to that.

Now he had to make it up to her for the disappointment of not going to the cemetery tomorrow.

It wasn't going to be so easy, she didn't forgive mistakes so quickly.

Exactly like her mum.

So like her mum.

Chapter 78

Patricia tugged and tugged at the handle of the door but it was bolted top and bottom as well as being locked. She knew the exercise was futile, but she had to try, hoping against hope one of them had made a mistake.

After all, hadn't Sian Carter escaped?

But they had tightened security since then. She knew somebody would be sitting outside the door, always silent, forbidden to speak to detainees, but there nonetheless.

Patricia collapsed in a heap on the floor and curled up into a foetal ball.

What could she do?

Images of Cherie flashed though her mind. On the promenade at Blackpool, a kiss-me-quick hat on her head and a stick of rock clamped between her teeth. Bent over a hot stove stirring away, drinking a gallon of white wine. Getting ready for bed in the middle of winter, wearing knee-high purple socks and clutching a plastic hot water bottle across her chest.

Would she ever see her again?

'Let me out!' she screamed. 'LET ME OUT!!'

There was no response.

She began to sob, her chest heaving.

She would never see Cherie again, she knew that now.

Chapter 79

He opened the door and stepped across the threshold. 'Hi, Eve, I'm home.'

No answer.

Was she still sulking? Still not ready to speak to him?

He hung his jacket on the bannister. 'Hi, Eve, I'm back. What would you like for tea?'

Still no answer.

He walked into the living room. The place had a stillness, an emptiness. The television was off and the fire was cold.

Perhaps she was in the kitchen, or upstairs?

The kitchen was empty too, the table still showing the detritus of their breakfast that morning; a coffee mug for him and poached eggs on toast for Eve.

He found himself thinking it would take ages for him to scrub the egg yolk off her breakfast plate. He should have put it in water before he left, it's what Polly would have done.

She was always so organised, in a disorganised way.

Perhaps Eve was upstairs in her bedroom, or in the bathroom? Like many teenage girls, she had started to spend hours in there, combing and re-combing her hair and checking for zits. Not that she had any, of course. Her skin was like alabaster.

He went back into the hall and shouted up the stairs. 'Eve, I'm home, what do you want for tea?'

Still nothing.

He charged up the stairs, taking them two at a time. The bathroom door was closed. He knocked on it gently. 'Hi, Eve, can we talk?'

Nothing.

He knocked again.

No answer.

He tried the doorknob and it turned easily in his hand. He slowly pushed the door open, expecting to hear her voice, 'Don't come in, Dad.' But he didn't hear anything, the bathroom was empty.

He ran to her bedroom. It was as untidy as ever; clothes on the floor, school books scattered on the dressing table, posters of Korean boy bands dancing on the walls.

But no Eve.

Where was she?

A wave of fear rose in him like a tsunami. Had she been taken? Kidnapped?

He ran back downstairs, hunting in his jacket for his mobile and calling her number.

It rang and rang and rang.

Ridpath could hear it coming from the kitchen. Her mobile phone was sitting beneath the morning newspaper on the table next to his coffee mug.

In his ear, he heard her voice. 'Hi, this is Eve, you've reached my message. You know the drill, so chill, take a pill and don't leave nil.' A giggle, followed by, 'I can't believe I said that.'

He walked back into the living room and slumped down on the couch. Where had she gone? To her grandparents? He wouldn't ring them yet, any call would just scare them. Where else would she go?

He glanced up at the mantlepiece, half-expecting to see a note propped up against the clock. Not so long ago, Polly had left one there, telling him she was leaving. It had taken a lot of time and hard work to get her to come back.

But there was no note.

Where could she have gone?

Mrs Dunwoody's? Perhaps she had become bored of doing her homework on her own and wanted to spend time with Jessica.

He scrolled down his contacts, looking for Mrs Dunwoody's name. Had he saved it under Angela?

As he was about to call, he heard a key turn in the lock.

He rushed into the hallway; Eve was closing the door. 'Oh, you're back,' she said.

'Where did you go? Why did you go out?'

She frowned and held up a paper bag. 'I just wanted some crisps, chocolate and a Vimto.' Like all Mancunians, she pronounced the last word with a 'p' in the middle. 'Something for my tea.'

'But I thought I told you to stay home, not to go out.'

'I'm not a prisoner, Dad, and we're not in lockdown any more. Next you'll be wanting me to wear a tag around my leg.'

'But you should have let me know you were going out.'

'I didn't know what time you were coming back, and you didn't ring or text me.'

She had him, and he knew it. He should have messaged her sometime during the day, but it had totally slipped his mind. He had become so involved with the case, he had forgotten to let her know when he was coming back. 'Sorry, I should have let you know.'

'It's OK, I'm used to it.'

From the tone in her voice, it wasn't OK and she wasn't used to it.

She brushed past him to go to the kitchen.

'Look, I'm sorry.'

'I said it's OK. You have a case and I know it comes first. It always came first, Dad, even when Mum was alive.'

That was unfair. 'I have a job to do, Eve, I'm a detective with GMP and there is a case I need to work until Monday. Afterwards, things should return to normal.'

'There's always a case, Dad, isn't there? And tell me, what's normal? What does that look and feel like, because I sure as hell don't know.'

With those last words, she turned her back and walked into the kitchen.

She was so like Polly.

Chapter 80

After Eve had gone to bed, Ridpath was left alone with his thoughts.

He'd cooked her dinner, which they had eaten in silence. Or rather, he had spoken and she had refused to answer with all the obstinacy of the teenager she was.

'Did you chat with Jessica?'

No answer.

'Did you finish your homework?'

No answer.

'Did you play Roblox?'

No answer.

He'd tried every interview technique he'd ever learnt but still the same lack of response.

Eventually, he'd given up. It would have been easier to get answers from a Moss Side gangster than Eve. At least they had the courtesy to say 'No comment' once in a while.

She'd eventually gone upstairs without saying a word, leaving him alone in a silent kitchen.

Inevitably, he turned back to the case in an attempt to avoid thinking about his problem with Eve. How did other single fathers cope with doing a job and bringing up a daughter?

In the case, there was always evidence, something to work with to help solve the puzzle. This case had almost too much evidence. So much, it was clouding the truth.

Turnbull was right. There were so many things he didn't know.

Why had so many people disappeared over the last eleven years?

Was Jane Ryder the first, or were there others before her?

What had happened to the bodies?

How was Daisy House Children's Home involved?

As ever, when he didn't understand something, it helped to write it down.

Disappearances:

Jane Ryder June 2009

Andrea Briggs June 2012

Gerald Duffy June 2017

Joe Rowlands June 2018

Patricia Patterson April 2021

One thing immediately shouted out at him. All the disappearances, except the most recent, had happened in June. Was it an anniversary of some sort? Or worse, a celebration?

He then wrote everything to link all the disappearances.

Daisy House

Children's homes

Social Services

He paused for a moment before adding one more.

The police

But no police report had been made when Andrea Briggs vanished. Had there been earlier reports when she ran away as a teenager? He wrote a note for himself to check.

His phone rang: Emily Parkinson.

'Hiya, I've arranged an interview for eleven a.m. tomorrow with Adam Jones. He's agreed to see us.'

'Any reports on his behaviour?'

'The assistant governor says he's quiet, keeps himself to himself, hardly communicates with anybody except to respond to orders from prison security.'

Ridpath thought quickly. He could take Eve to her grandparents in the morning. She wouldn't be too happy, but they'd love to see her. It would probably lead to another round of sulking, but he would have to deal with it somehow. Tomorrow was the last day of the investigation before the inquest – he had to keep pushing, keep moving it forward.

'Ridpath, earth to Ridpath.'

He shook his head. 'Sorry, Em, I was miles away.'

'I was asking if you wanted me to pick you up tomorrow?'

'Nah, I'll see you in Strangeways car park at ten thirty.'

'What about the debrief with the others?'

He'd forgotten about the meeting. 'We'll do it afterwards. Say at one p.m.'

'OK, I'll let them know. And, Ridpath...'

'Yeah?'

'It's coming together, I can feel it.'

'I wish I could too, Em. I feel we're missing something. The big part of the picture that brings it all together. It's like there's a big hole in the middle of our investigation. Anything from Oliver, Dave or Chrissy?'

'Not a lot. Oliver is still checking ANPR. You know it's like looking for a single blade of grass in the middle of a ten-acre field? Chrissy tracked the phone records. The last call Patricia Patterson received was from an unregistered phone on Wednesday morning. She followed Patricia Patterson's route through the contacts with the mobile towers to an area near junction ten of the M60 in Urmston, before it was switched off.'

'Did she follow up?'

'She's doing that tomorrow morning. Going to see if anybody remembers seeing the car. But the chances are minimal, Ridpath. It'll be Sunday morning, not a lot of people around.'

'Worth doing though. And can you ask Oliver to check ANPR cameras in Urmston?'

'Will do. Dave followed up on Gerald Duffy. Definitely no links to Daisy House. Or at least none he can find.'

Would he have to check the older detective's work? So far, Daisy House was the only possibility linking all the disappearances. If Gerald Duffy had no connection, was there something else, something they had missed?

'But why did his hand turn up in a backpack in 2021? We still haven't answered the most basic question of the inquiry, Emily. And what happened to his body?'

'I know, I know, but give us a break, Ridpath, we've had less than a week.'

A long pause. 'The inquest starts on Monday morning, and yourself and Chrissy go back to checking stats again.'

'Surely Claire Trent will give us more time. We've come so far.'

'Maybe, maybe not. She might wash her hands of it and pass the investigation to the Cold Case Unit—'

'Where it will sit until new DNA or evidence comes in.'

'Right. So we need to work the case hard. Tomorrow is our last day, let's make it count.'

'See you tomorrow, Ridpath. Let's keep our fingers crossed we can make a breakthrough.'

'We must be missing something, Emily. I just don't know what it is... yet.'

SUNDAY

Chapter 81

They were waiting in the interview room at Strangeways Prison, sitting at a Formica desk that had seen better days ten years ago. They had already passed through the security checks, accompanied by a mob of relatives, women and children, all visiting the people in jail.

It was Sunday, the day of rest for most but a day of activity and bustle at the prison.

Luckily, Ridpath and Emily Parkinson had been separated from the crowd and placed in a relatively quiet room. The noise of children crying, adults shouting and prisoners coughing could still be heard from outside, but it wasn't too loud. At least Ridpath could hear himself think.

A fly buzzed around his head, searching for somewhere to land that wasn't too grubby.

A door opened and in stepped a tall, gaunt man. Ridpath vaguely recognised him from the photo, but he had aged remarkably in the last eleven years, going from being young and agile to middle-aged and haggard.

'Adam Jones?' Ridpath asked.

'Prisoner 75689, reporting,' the guard responded.

'Take a seat,' Ridpath gestured to the chair in front of him.

The guard nodded and the man slid into the seat opposite the two detectives. He gave off a sour, rancid smell which made Ridpath gag. Washing obviously wasn't on his list of things to do in the morning.

Emily placed her cigarettes and a lighter on the table in front of her. 'Help yourself.'

He shook his head. 'I don't smoke.'

'A man inside who doesn't smoke? You must be making a fortune selling your snout.'

The man looked down his nose at Emily. 'I don't sell it, I give it away.'

'More fool you.'

'Nor do I smoke weed, spice or any of the myriad other narcotics that serve to keep men subdued and in their place.'

'What do you do with your time? You still have six years to go.'

'I read and I study and I prepare.'

'For what?'

The man laughed ironically. 'For the day I get out, what else? Now I'm sure you detectives haven't come all the way here to enquire after my health or my reading habits?'

Ridpath decided to come straight to the point. He placed the picture taken at the Mad Ferret Festival in front of Adam Jones. 'Is this you?'

The squinted at it. 'Could be.'

'Could be, or is?'

'Could be. When was this taken?'

'In 2009, the same day this girl disappeared.' He pointed to Jane Ryder. 'Do you recognise her?'

The man shook his head.

'She's standing right next to you.'

'A lot of girls stood right next to me. It's not a crime… yet.'

'What about these photos?' He placed the other shots on the desk. 'Here, she seems to be talking with you. Here, she's dancing in front of you. You two seem to know each other.'

'I meet a lot of girls at festivals.'

'You don't remember this one? Her name was Jane Ryder, and she was sixteen years old.'

'The perfect age.'

'What do you mean?'

'Young enough to have the energy to enjoy the world. Not old enough to have been tainted by it.'

'For God's sake, she was sixteen years old and after this picture she was never seen again. You were the last person to see her alive,' shouted Emily.

The man sat back in his seat. 'You don't know that. This picture shows me probably talking to her, but I don't remember meeting her. Sorry.'

It was obvious Jones wasn't sorry in the slightest.

'Do you remember this backpack?' Ridpath tapped the bottom of the picture.

The man stared at it. 'No. There were thousands of backpacks strewn over Platt Fields that day. I can't even remember what my own looked like, never mind Jane's.'

'I didn't tell you it was Jane's backpack.'

The man looked at the picture again and without missing a beat answered, 'I presumed it was Jane's backpack. It is right next to her legs, after all.'

Silence descended on the room. The fly continued buzzing until the sound suddenly stopped and a small black body thudded down into the centre of the table. Its legs kicked twice and it was still.

'Remind me again, why are you in prison?'

'I was sentenced to ten years for the abduction and detention of a woman.'

'How old was she?'

'Seventeen.'

'More of a girl, wouldn't you say?'

'No, she was a woman who broke the rules.'

'What rules?'

The man stayed silent.

'What rules?' repeated Ridpath.

'Our rules. God's rules.'

'We read through your file. You were part of a commune on a farm in Carrington, south-east of Manchester.'

'It isn't a commune.'

'What is it?'

'A group of like-minded people who lived together and shared everything in common.'

'A communc.'

He laughed again. 'You have some strangely old-fashioned ideas, Detective. We aren't some hippies, turning on and dropping out. We run a business, we are part of the world.'

'What business?'

'We are a farm; pigs, sheep, chickens. We breed them and sell them on to be fattened up by other farms. We are a registered business.'

'But you have rules?'

'All societies have rules.'

'But they don't kidnap people and hold them against their will.'

'Don't they?' He looked all around him at the prison walls. 'Where the hell are we, detectives? Disneyland?'

'Did you kidnap other girls and hold them against their will?'

'No.'

'Just this girl.'

'Just this girl.'

'Did you kidnap Jane Ryder?'

Another knowing smile. 'No.'

'You think it's funny, a sixteen-year-old going missing?' Emily Parkinson slammed her fist down on the table.

The man cocked his head and narrowed his eyes. 'Such a strong reaction, Detective. Have you ever been in care? I think you have. Were you abused?' He sat forward, focusing on Emily. 'Did they take advantage of you? I think they would, your feistiness would have appealed to them. A spirit to break, to destroy, to devour.'

Emily stayed quiet, a red flush rising from her neck and covering her face.

'We ask the questions, not you, Mr Jones.'

'Is this how you get your own back? Being a policewoman? Righting wrongs, standing up for those who are weak and unprivileged?'

'We don't have to listen to this psychological mumbo-jumbo, Ridpath. Do you have anything else you'd like to ask him?'

Before Ridpath could answer, the man looked down at the photographs. 'I do remember her now. Jane, was that her name? I think she called herself something else when I met her. Now what was it?'

He mimed thinking by tapping his forehead with a long, elegant index finger.

'It'll come to me soon, I'm sure.' He snapped his fingers. 'She called herself Barbara, that was it. A nice name, Barbara, don't you think? It comes from the Greek originally, I think, the feminine form of the Greek word *barbaros*, meaning "strange" or "foreign".'

'You saw her at the festival?' asked Ridpath.

'It's what I said.'

'The surname she used?'

Again he mimed thinking. 'Sorry, can't remember. Perhaps it will come to me.'

'When did you last see her?'

'Abbott, that was her surname. Barbara Abbott.' He picked up the photo of the two of them. 'When I spoke to her at the festival, she was so full of life and joy, said she was going to London to make her name. But they all say that, don't they? Some of them actually believe it. Anyway, detectives, you've taken up far too much of my time. I have my service at eleven p.m. and I don't want to miss it.'

'We still have lots of questions to ask, Mr Jones.'

'But I have no more answers to give, DI Ridpath.' He stood up and gestured to be taken back to his cell.

'We can help you, put in a good word for you, if you help us.'

He turned back. 'You disappoint me, Detective. Here was I thinking you were smarter than to use such an obvious tactic with me. I think we have spoken enough.' Another little smile. 'My lips are sealed.'

'If we investigate and find you were involved in the disappearance and possible murder of Jane Ryder, you will never get out of this prison alive, Jones, I'll make sure of it.'

A long sigh. 'I assure you, DI Ridpath, Barbara was very much alive and kicking when I saw her.'

'Can you prove it?'

He nodded his head. 'I can.'

'How?'

He waved his fingers in front of his face. 'It's for me to know and you to find out, DI Ridpath. Goodbye. But I will leave you with one parting thought from the Gospel of Matthew. "If your right hand causes you to sin, cut it off and throw it away. For it is better that you lose one of your members than that your whole body go into hell".'

With those last words, he stepped through the door and vanished down the corridor, followed closely by the burly guard.

Chapter 82

'That arsehole was playing with us, Ridpath.'

They were in his car, driving to Stretford nick. Emily had taken the tram into Strangeways that morning rather than drive.

'He knows far more than he's telling us.'

'What did he say just before we left? "If your right hand causes you to sin, cut it off and throw it away. For it is better you lose one of your members than your whole body go into hell". Was he telling us he committed the killings and put the hands in the backpack?'

'But both Joseph Rowlands and Gerald Duffy were killed after he was jailed.' Ridpath tapped the steering wheel. 'Can you find out more about his arrest? Who was the female victim, and how was he caught?'

'Already did it. Her name was Sian Carter, she ran away from home six months earlier. She'd been imprisoned on the farm but escaped one day, begging for help from a passer-by who called the police. Jones admitted doing it, pleading guilty to all charges.'

'None of the other residents were involved?'

'According to Jones, they knew nothing about it, but get this…'

'What?'

'Sian Carter withdrew her complaint, didn't want to press charges.'

'But CPS went ahead to charge him anyway?'

'It was felt the offence was so serious they had to charge him. Plus, they had a full confession witnessed by the man's solicitor.'

'He could have retracted, claiming undue pressure.'

'That's the weird bit. He didn't retract. He pled guilty and was sentenced.'

'Strange. Scc if you can find out more.' Ridpath stopped at a red light. 'Why do I keep feeling we're missing something? Every time we make an advance in this case, it seems to reveal more things we don't know, like one of those bloody Russian dolls.'

'Matryoshkas.'

'What?'

'Matryoshkas. It's what the dolls are called. My foster mum used to collect them. For her, they represented the idea of a long line of women, each one giving birth to the next generation.'

'Whatever. For me, it's a long line of secrets, each one helping to hide the truth from us.'

'Eventually we'll get to the first doll.'

'Eventually may be too late.'

They pulled up outside Stretford station. 'How are you going to handle this?'

The newspaper with its article written by Molly Wright was lying between them, its headline shouting like a drunk on a Saturday night. THE HANDS CASE. MORE MISTAKES BY GMP? Ridpath had noticed a copy on the guard's table as they were leaving Strangeways. The guard had been happy to get rid of it.

'Like I always do. With a six-foot pole, wearing a hazmat suit and three pairs of gloves.'

'It might not be enough.' She picked up the paper. 'You realise we are being thrown under the bus. What does it say here… "A source within Greater Manchester Police has revealed that due to the inefficiencies in the initial investigation by some officers, GMP will need more senior involvement in the case moving forward. The discovery of the hands in the backpack may indicate a much larger and more detailed investigation is needed than had previously been planned. There may even be the possible involvement of an unknown serial killer in Manchester. It is believed the recent disappearance of a social worker, Ms Patricia Patterson, could also be linked to the case. 'We may have a serial killer on the loose,' said the source, 'one that is preying on vulnerable woman linked to the Daisy House Children's Home'."'

Ridpath frowned. 'Holloway will be furious. He was hoping this would go away quietly. Looks like somebody planted this story.'

'Who? Claire Trent, Turnbull, or was it Holloway himself? A great way to get more resource if it was him.'

'Listen, Em, we'll let the higher-ups play their games. We need to concentrate on solving this case. Nothing else matters. Clear?'

'As mud, Ridpath.'

'Come on. Let's go and find out what the others have dug up. We're close, Em, I know we're close.'

Chapter 83

'I thought I'd say a few words before we start.'

Ridpath and Emily Parkinson had walked in two minutes earlier, surprised to see the incident room full of detectives, many called in from their weekend off to attend the briefing at one p.m. Dave Connor and Oliver Davis were off to one side, sitting next to their boss, Chief Inspector Holloway.

DCI Turnbull was standing at the front of the room, brushing away a non-existent hair from the shoulder of his jacket.

'I've been asked to get involved with this investigation as it seems to have spiralled out of control.'

Dave Connor was about to speak, but Turnbull silenced him by raising his hand.

'Now, I'm not blaming any of you, nor am I blaming the detectives from Stretford.' A quick nod to Holloway, who was sitting at the back of the room. 'They have performed in an exemplary manner throughout this investigation. However, it has now been decided this case requires the involvement of more senior minds.' Once again, the hand stroked the shoulder. 'It is now apparent to me there are strong links between the hands discovered in the backpack in Daisy House Children's Home, the disappearance of a number of people and last week's disappearance of a social worker in Manchester.'

'You only know because of our work,' said Emily under her breath.

'What was that, DS Parkinson? If you have anything to say to this meeting, please make sure we all hear it?'

'Nothing, sir, clearing my throat.'

He carried on speaking. 'This morning's newspaper report has created a – I think the technical term is shitstorm – amongst the top brass. They have realised there may have been a serial killer hiding in plain sight for at least the last eleven years. Now, I read the case files this morning.'

Emily leant into Ridpath, whispering, 'He can't have read them all so quickly.'

'It seems to me there is a direct link between Daisy House Children's Home and these disappearances. Alan, get on to Manchester Children's Services, I want a complete list of everybody who went to Daisy House or who worked there since 1980.'

Ridpath put his hand up. 'You'll need a warrant, sir. I don't think Manchester Social Services will give the list to us without one, data protection laws. Chrissy did get a list of people who worked there from Operation Pharaoh.'

Turnbull ignored him. 'Alan, if you have a problem, get the director to call me, I've met him socially. I'm sure we can sort it out.'

'Yes, sir.'

'Now, Ridpath and Parkinson, you went to Strangeways this morning. Anything from Jones?'

'Not a lot, but—'

'I could have told you, Ridpath,' Turnbull interrupted, 'a bit of a wild goose chase if you ask me.'

'I think he knows more than he's telling us, sir,' said Emily Parkinson.

'Possibly, DS Parkinson, but we have far too many other leads to follow without us obsessing about one man. DC Davis, anything from ANPR on Patricia Patterson's car?'

'Nothing so far, sir. We had one sighting on the M60 exiting on junction ten. We're checking footage from cameras in Urmston as we speak. There aren't many cameras in that neck of the woods.'

'And her phone, Chrissy?'

'Last call was at her home early in the morning. Then we lose the signal, also near junction ten in Urmston. The phone may have been switched off.'

'Right, are we sure she hasn't done a runner? Had enough of her relationship and taken off?'

'She left without any clothes, passport still at home and her partner says they had a great, loving relationship,' said Emily.

'Well, she would, wouldn't she?' Before Emily could respond, Turnbull had turned towards Oliver Davis. 'Right, lad, write these on the board. I've heard you have the best handwriting around here. At least you can do joined-up words, not like most of this lot.'

Oliver Davis jumped up.

'Four priorities. One: checking Daisy House Children's Home. Alan, you're in charge, the rest of the MIT team can assist. There's going to be a lot of names to go through. Be prepared for long nights. Have any other people gone missing from the home? Two: check HOLMES. Chrissy, you're on this. I want to know if there have been any other crimes like this anywhere in the UK.'

'I already did it, gaffer. HOLMES didn't come up with anything.'

'Check again. There must have been something we missed.'

Chrissy sighed. 'Will do, boss.'

'Three: searching the area around Daisy House. We must have missed something. I want the place gone through with a fine-tooth comb. Tony, you're leading. Emily, you can help. Finally, what happened to the bodies? Why haven't they been found? Dave, I want you to lead this.'

'But I—'

'Check all sources, Dave, leave no stone unturned.'

'Yes, gaffer.'

'That's all. This investigation has been given priority one by the acting chief constable, so we have to get a result. Understood?'

A mumbled chorus of 'Yes, boss,' from the detectives.

'What about me?'

'You, Ridpath? I thought you worked for the coroner. Don't you have an inquest tomorrow?'

'On Jane Ryder, one of our victims in this case. She's also linked to the case.'

'How do you know?'

'The backpack. She was seen carrying it in a photo taken in 2009. It's the same one that contained the hands.'

'That's it? That's your link?'

'And the connection to Daisy House. She was one of the residents, and the backpack was found there.'

Turnbull shook his head. 'Listen, people, let's not get side-tracked by young girls who disappeared in 2009. We have one focus and one focus only in this investigation: the hands in the backpack discovered last Tuesday morning. Everything else is a waste of time.'

'What about Patricia Patterson?'

Turnbull bit his bottom lip. 'Her disappearance may or may not be linked to the other people vanishing and the mystery of the hands. But we're not sure yet. Alan, you keep looking for her, but make sure she hasn't just done a runner from her relationship.'

'Right, boss,' said Alan Butcher loudly.

'You still haven't told me what you want me to do.'

The other detectives stopped what they were doing and raised their heads to stare at this challenge to Turnbull's authority.

'I thought I made it clear, Ridpath. I want you to do your job with the coroner. You have an inquest tomorrow, concentrate on it. I will be there to represent the police.'

'What?'

'You heard. I will be there. We need to get to work.' He looked all around him, forcing the other detectives to look away, finally stopping at Ridpath. 'Do you understand?'

'Yes, sir,' chorused the detectives.

Chapter 84

There was nothing left for Ridpath to do. Turnbull had made it clear his presence was no longer required. He picked up his papers and notebooks and drove to the coroner's office in Stockfield. At least there he was wanted.

'Hiya, Ridpath, good to see you.'

'At least somebody thinks so.'

'One of those days?'

'One of those millennia, Sophia.'

'Good job I bought you a latte.'

'Does it have a double shot of arsenic?'

'Not today, they'd run out. I asked for the special beans instead. And the coroner wants to see you.'

'Is that good or bad? I don't think I can handle another disappointment.'

She shrugged her shoulders. 'Sorry, don't know.'

He knocked on the coroner's door.

'Come.'

'You wanted to see me?'

'Come in and sit down. I'd like to go over tomorrow's inquest with you.' She held up a pink file. 'Sophia has passed me the case notes. They seem to be comprehensive.'

Ridpath had read them last night. 'They are, Mrs Challinor. They summarise the main points of the investigation and the evidence each witness will give.'

'There are no indications Jane Ryder is still alive?'

'None so far. On the contrary, everything points to her being killed sometime on or around June 12, 2009. But...'

'That sounds ominous, Ridpath.'

'But, I'm not sure. We have found no indications of death. The female hand in the backpack tested negative for her DNA.'

'So there is still no evidence she is alive?'

'If you mean there is no documentary evidence, like driving licences, sightings, entries on electoral registers, you are correct. But I don't need to point out that the absence of evidence is not the evidence of absence. We have no positive proof Jane Ryder is dead.'

'That's where I come in, Ridpath. Recently, the Supreme Court ruled that coroners' inquests could conclude an individual had been unlawfully killed by applying the civil standard of proof. That is the balance of probabilities, rather than the traditional criminal standard of proof: beyond a reasonable doubt. As ever the law is an ass, but in Jane Ryder's case, it allows me to conclude, on the balance of probabilities, that she is no longer alive. I will then be able to issue a presumption of death certificate to the Ryders.'

'But the police enquiries aren't finished yet.'

'I received a phone call from Detective Chief Inspector Turnbull this morning. Apparently the police investigation into the death of Jane Ryder has been closed.'

'What?'

'He didn't tell you?'

'He said he didn't believe it was linked to the hands case, but—'

'Well, now he has closed it completely, allowing me to issue a narrative verdict on her death.'

'But he can't do that.'

'He just did.' Mrs Challinor closed her eyes briefly and began speaking again. 'Look, Ridpath, on the balance of probabilities, I believe she is dead. And in the absence of evidence to the contrary from any witness, I will be issuing a presumption of death certificate tomorrow.'

'I haven't completed my investigation yet. I thought you were going to postpone the verdict until I had.'

'MIT has decided your investigation is over. I can't keep the Ryders waiting any longer.'

Ridpath stood up. 'I think you are wrong, Coroner.'

'Right or wrong, I have to make a decision, it's my job.'

He leant forward, pleading with the coroner. 'Please give me more time.'

'I'm sorry, I wish I could. Mr Ryder told me his wife was given the last rites by her priest last night. You know what that means?'

'I was brought up a Catholic, Mrs Challinor.'

'She could die at any time, Ridpath. We need to give her closure.'

'I still think you are wrong, Mrs Challinor. We can't presume death, we have to prove it.'

The coroner took her pen and began writing in the margins of her file. 'You've done enough, Ridpath. It's time for me to hold an inquest and make a decision.'

Chapter 85

The house was silent when Ridpath arrived home. There was no greeting from Polly or Eve. Nothing but the creak of the joists in the ceiling to welcome him.

He went into Eve's room. Homework was scattered across her desk, clothes strewn across the floor and her bed was still unmade.

Automatically, he smoothed down the sheets, tucking them beneath the mattress, fluffing up the duvet before laying it over the bed. A dent in the pillow revealed where she had laid her head last night, a stray black hair still lying there.

She was at the grandparents. Should he bring her home and cook for her? Or should he work on the case, picking her up later?

What was the point of going through his notes once more? Turnbull had already decided the disappearance of Jane Ryder wasn't linked to the discovery of the hands. Maybe he was right. There might be more versions of the backpack out there. Perhaps some backstreet entrepreneur in Cheetham Hill had produced thousands of knock-offs of the limited edition to make a quick buck. They were doing it for Nike, Adidas and Supreme, why not for CLAK?

And Mrs Challinor had come to the conclusion Jane was dead too. The absence of evidence she was alive wasn't proof she was dead, but it was circumstantial. How often had he gone to the CPS or a judge with circumstantial evidence a crime had been committed?

But something didn't feel right.

He'd had the feeling for the last couple of days. He kept trying to explain it to Emily but he couldn't put it into words. It was like having an itch you knew was there but didn't know where to scratch.

In his rushing around from meeting to meeting, had he missed something important in the mountain of clues and evidence? Something he should have spotted a long time ago?

Sod it.

He would have to scratch the itch by going through his notes one more time. Perhaps he would find out what was troubling him.

'Sorry, Eve, just one more day. I promise I'll be the sort of dad you want me to be.' He spoke out loud as if trying to convince himself, bear witness on his own behalf.

He glanced at the clock.

He would have to pick her up at eight p.m. from her grandparents.

Only three hours from now.

Three hours to scratch the itch.

Chapter 86

Death when it came for Patricia Patterson was unexpected.

She thought they would come in the middle of the night and kill her in the same way they had killed the others: stunned with a taser first and then strangled from behind.

She'd never taken part in any killing, but she had seen the bodies afterwards.

It wasn't a pretty sight.

But who would kill her now Adam was in jail?

She didn't know.

They gave her a special meal, as they had given the others. Roast pork, apple sauce and all the trimmings. It was part of the ritual; eating the bodies of those who were about to eat you.

As with the others, hunger made sure she ate the food. They hadn't fed her for a couple of days.

She didn't taste the rat poison stirred into the apple sauce, but its effects began about twenty minutes after she finished the meal. Her muscles began to spasm, she had seizures, her breathing became difficult and more laboured, and eventually her heart stopped.

They came in when she was dead.

'Poor Patricia, she was such an angry soul.'

'It was God's work. I will remove the hand later. We'll get rid of the body in the usual way.'

'I liked her.'

'We have nearly finished our work, only a few more left to go. Adam has told me what to do.'

'I'll be ready.'

Then they all went about their separate jobs, ignoring the body lying cold and dead in its small cell.

Patricia Patterson would not see or hug Cherie again.

Chapter 87

He'd been through everything: all the documents from Chrissy, all the interviews, all the case notes, files, memos, research, telephone tracking and the house-to-house reports.

Nothing stood out.

Nothing.

He took the only option left open to him. He took a break, going to pick up Eve.

She still wasn't talking to him.

'How were your grandad and grandma?'

Silence.

'If you're hungry, I'll heat up some lasagne from the freezer?'

Silence.

'Do you have PE at school tomorrow?'

Silence. Followed by a long sigh.

'I've booked us on a trip to Korea tomorrow to see Blackpink live.'

A slow turn, a stare and a roll of the eyes, but still silence.

There is nobody who can roll their eyes like a disappointed teenager. Ridpath decided he probably would have preferred to be interviewing a career criminal who had the words No Comment taped to his forehead rather than endure this any longer.

He tried honesty.

'Look, I'm sorry I let you down today, but I had to go to Strangeways to interview a prisoner and I couldn't take you to your mum's grave. We can go next Sunday if you like.'

Another slow turn. 'If you are going to apologise, don't justify your behaviour by using "but" as a qualification.'

At last she was talking. It was a start.

'I'm sorry,' he finally said.

'You have to decide which you put first, Dad, me or the job?'

God, she sounded like her mother. 'Can't I put both things first, but at different times?' As soon as he said it, he knew the words sounded idiotic. He tried a different tack. 'It's not a question of putting either first, Eve, it's a question of making a living. I need to work in order to earn the money for your upkeep, pay the mortgage, buy Blackpink posters.'

If you can't understand what's going on, reframe the question. Charlie Whittaker's words came back to him. *Option number five when you are stuck in any investigation.*

Also true when you are dealing with an angry teenage daughter. But as he drove down the A56, it struck him that perhaps he needed to do the same with the hands case. Had they been asking the wrong questions?

'It's a question of balance, Dad, you need to get it in your life. You can't keep throwing yourself into these investigations, forgetting me, your health and everything else.'

His daughter's voice brought him back. It was a great question, and even better reframing than his own. Why did he do that? Was it the job? Was it his own nature? Was it the nature of the job?

Just ten seconds ago he had been thinking about work rather than his daughter.

'You're right, Eve. Let's go home and I'll heat up some lasagne. Let's chat, you, me and some béchamel sauce.'

For the first time, she smiled. 'I'd like that, Dad.'

'Good, it's a deal.' He reached across and tried to form the promise handshake with his thumb and little finger, but changed it into Spock's live long and prosper sign at the last minute.

'You're such a dork, Dad.'

He thought that meant she'd forgiven him.

Chapter 88

Later, after Eve had gone to bed, he sat in his armchair, staring into mid-air, a glass of Macallan warming in his hand.

On the table, the case notes lay where he had left them three hours ago. Had he totally cocked up the investigation? Had he led everybody down the garden path?

He imagined Charlie Whittaker sitting opposite him, checking his work.

'What are your assumptions, Ridpath? Assumptions in a case like this are bastards, they always lead you astray. What have you assumed, which may or may not have been true?'

'We assumed—'

'No, no, no, get it right, take responsibility. What have *you* assumed?'

Charlie was right. What had he assumed? He checked the list he'd made last night and began writing.

He'd assumed the case was linked to Daisy House. Was it? Or was there another reason people were being killed? Why had he made that assumption?

The hands were found there, and the people who were missing were all connected to the children's home.

But were they?

Ridpath thought for a moment, imagining his answer. They were all connected, except Gerald Duffy. We never found a connection to him.

Right. There might be another reason.

What else had he assumed?

The backpack we found containing the hands belonged to Jane Ryder. What if didn't? What if it was a knock-off? He'd assumed it was the limited edition. But didn't the father say he had bought it for Jane, and he didn't he ID it? He checked the notes. He was sure the backpack belonged to Jane Ryder.

What was his biggest assumption?

He racked his brain for the answer, and then a tiny idea wheedled its way in like a sharp stiletto piercing thin skin.

He'd always assumed Jane Ryder was dead.

Why?

Because it was his frame of reference, his brief when he started the case. She was presumed to be dead. Nobody had seen or heard from her in over eleven years.

But what if she was still alive?

As the ramifications of the question swirled around his mind, his phone beeped. It was a text message from Emily Parkinson.

> Get me out of here.

He replied:

> That bad?

> Worse. We're going through every child who ever was a resident at Daisy House.

> He got the records?

> Needed a court order. I'm going to be here until the next millennium. How u?

OK. Been through the files, checking assumptions. What if Jane Ryder isn't dead?

WHAT???!!!???

How's the search for Patricia Patterson?

Found the car dumped in a garden centre in Irlam, of all places. Oliver checking their CCTV. His eyes are going square.

It's important to find her. Did you check on Adam Jones?

No time. Turnbull has me going thru the children's home residents.

Check him. Call prison. Did he call anybody after we left? Get the transcripts if he did. They record all outgoing calls.

Will try. Gotta go. Turnbull staring at me.

Ring me when you get the answer from the prison, Em. It's important.

Ridpath put down the phone and took another long swallow of the Macallan, savouring the taste of bitter honey as it slipped down his throat.

He picked up the picture of the Mad Ferret Festival in 2009. What had Adam Jones said? 'If your right hand causes you to sin, cut it off and throw it away. For it is better you lose one of your members than that your whole body go into hell'. Did it all start here?

The key was Jane Ryder and Adam Jones, he was sure of it now.

But was it too late?

Had he been too slow working it all out?

He ran his fingers through his hair. Patricia Patterson was in serious danger. Perhaps she was the person who knew the truth, and that's why she had vanished. Or she had been vanished.

He had to get Turnbull to focus on her. He had to try one more time.

He dialled the number.

'DCI Turnbull.'

It was typical of the man to answer with his rank.

'It's Ridpath.'

'I told you to go home and forget about the case.'

'I am at home, but I can't forget about the case. I think Patricia Patterson is in serious danger. Somehow she is linked to Adam Jones and Jane Ryder. The case isn't about the children's home, it's about Jones and Ryder.'

'Another one of your bloody hunches, Ridpath. You're at home nice and cosy, no doubt having a glass of whisky, while the rest of the team is working hard to clean up your mess.'

'That's not true.'

'Listen to this.' Ridpath could hear the sound of voices and printers. 'That's your colleagues still working on a Sunday night.'

'But you have to find Patricia Patterson, I think she's involved somehow.'

'Somehow? I'm supposed to drop everything because you guess she is *somehow* involved? Go back to your whisky, Ridpath.

Patricia Patterson is one of the leads we are following. I have work to do, so goodnight.'

The phone went dead.

MONDAY

THE INQUEST

Chapter 89

Ridpath stared out over the Coroner's Court. The witnesses were assembled and the legal representatives for Greater Manchester Police and the council were behind their desks.

He hadn't slept at all last night, tossing and turning through the night, haunted by images from the investigation.

Had he done everything right?

Had he missed something important?

Could he have done more?

Even worse, he had developed a headache from lack of sleep, the continuous pounding in his head an annoyance. Two aspirin had only seemed to make it worse.

He'd still heard nothing from Emily. Why didn't she call him?

As Jenny banged the gavel on her table, the door at the back of the court opened and Mrs Challinor entered.

Ridpath moved to take his place standing by the door. Still the feeling of disquiet lingered like a bad smell in a bouquet of fresh flowers. Would he have to take part in this drama after all? He hoped not.

The buzz around the court ceased and Mrs Challinor began speaking.

'This inquest is now open regarding the disappearance of Jane Ryder in 2009 and the application from the family for a presumption of death certificate by the Coronal Service. The inquest has been called by the terms of the Coroners Act 1988, section fifteen, and the Presumption of Death Act 2013, both of which allow for such a certificate to be issued if there is no possibility the person involved, in this case Jane Ryder, is still alive.' She paused for a moment, looking around the court. 'We will hear evidence from witnesses to help us decide if Jane Ryder can indeed be presumed dead.'

Mr Ryder, sitting in front of her, sighed audibly, his shoulders hunched, and he rocked back and forth.

'Throughout these proceedings, the Covid guidelines established by the chief coroner will apply, including the giving of evidence in person and on camera by witnesses. The family is represented by Mr James Ryder, parent of the missing girl. Greater Manchester Police is represented by Mr Jonathan Spielman, while Mrs Jennifer Harris represents Manchester City Council.'

On hearing their names, the legal representatives rose slightly and bowed the heads.

'A reminder for everyone. This is an inquest, not a court of law. Our job… my job… is to discover the truth, not to apportion blame or to discover who may, or may not, have abducted or murdered Jane Ryder.'

Another audible sigh from Mr Ryder.

Mrs Challinor carried on. 'We have one focus and one focus only. It is simply to ascertain to the best of our abilities whether this young girl, sixteen as she was in 2009, is still alive.'

At the back of the court in the public gallery, somebody had risen from their chair. From where he was standing, Ridpath couldn't see who it was.

Mrs Challinor raised her head and stared at the person. 'Can I help you?' she asked.

Ridpath craned his neck forward, looking for the person who had stood up.

'No, but I think I can help you.'

Ridpath recognised the woman from the inquest last Friday, the raven-haired woman who had been attacked on the stairs. What was she doing here? And why was she speaking?

'I'm sorry, but this is an inquest, we do not allow interventions from the floor or the public gallery.'

'But I can save you a lot of time. I am Jane Ryder…'

Chapter 90

The Coroner's Court descended into chaos in less than a second.

In the public gallery, chairs were scraped back as people stood up. The reporters were shouting, 'What did she say?' Mrs Challinor was banging her gavel and demanding silence. Jenny Oldfield was waving her arms in the air. The witnesses were asking each other what had happened. Even Mr Ryder had turned around, staring hard at the person who claimed to be his daughter.

The only person who stood still, quiet and self-possessed, was Jane Ryder, a slight smile perched on her lips.

Ridpath moved forward quickly. The woman's hair was a different colour and she was much older, but perhaps there was the same smile he had seen in the photo of Jane Ryder, the same mischievous glint in the eyes.

Gradually, Mrs Challinor regained control of her court. 'Jenny, can you please swear this woman in as a witness.'

'Now, Coroner?'

'Immediately, Jenny. Ridpath, please escort the witness.'

Ridpath gestured for the woman to step forward and take a seat in the witness box. She walked with her head held high, striding elegantly to the chair with her back straight. He stood next to her as Jenny came with the oath cards and a Bible.

Without any hesitation, the woman laid her hand on the Bible and said, 'I swear to tell the truth, the whole truth and nothing but the truth. As God is my witness.'

Mrs Challinor waited for the buzz around the court to subside again before asking, 'Could you tell the court your name?'

The answer when it came was clear and confident. 'My name is Jane Ryder, but for over eleven years, since 2009, I have been living under the assumed name of Barbara Abbott.'

Ridpath remembered this was the name Adam Jones had given him. Had the man been telling the truth the whole time?

'You are Jane Ryder?' Mrs Challinor asked, a note of doubt in her voice.

'Correct. The surname was given to me by my adopted parents, James and Maureen Ryder. I believe my birth name was Bennett, but I'm not certain.'

James Ryder stared at the woman in the dock, his mouth open slightly.

'Why should we believe you are Jane Ryder? Nothing has been heard from her since she disappeared in 2009.'

'What can I tell you to make you believe me? I went to the Mad Ferret Festival and decided on that day, June 12, I was never going back home.'

'Why?'

'I met somebody I loved and who loved me. I met my God.' A slight pause, and a glance up to the ceiling before she continued. 'I'd been unhappy for a long time. Meeting him was the turning point in my life. For the first time, I understood what I needed to do to serve God.'

'I'm sorry, could you explain?'

'I met Him. Adam explained to me that to truly serve God we had to throw off the shackles of the past in whatever way we could. We had to become his handmaidens, serving only Him and His wishes, not bound by earthly attachments to parents, friends, money or possessions.'

'Adam?'

'The leader of our group. Our guardian, our guide.'

'Adam Jones?' asked Ridpath.

The woman nodded. 'Through Adam we could see God, be part of His creation. Follow His path, obey his laws and His commands.'

'You know this man, Ridpath?'

'I do, Coroner. He's currently serving ten years in Strangeways for the abduction of a young girl.'

'She broke our law, she broke God's law.'

'Jane?'

James Ryder's voice was weak and uncertain.

For the first time, the woman turned to her adoptive father. 'I'm truly sorry for not contacting you, James, for not letting you know what I was doing or why I was doing it. But I had to cut off all my contacts, it was the only way I could be free to serve Him.'

The old man stood up slowly and staggered towards the witness box with his arms held out. 'Jane,' he whispered.

Chapter 91

As the old man hugged his daughter, the coroner pounded her gavel, announcing, 'This presumption of death inquest is now adjourned pending the results of the coroner's investigation into the identity of this young woman. Mr Ridpath, please escort her and Mr Ryder to my office.'

The coroner stood up and exited through her door at the back. Ridpath made his way to the witness box. As he passed Turnbull, the man sneered, 'See, I told you she was nothing to do with it. But you wouldn't listen. You never listen.'

Ridpath ignored him, approaching the old man. 'Mr Ryder and Miss…'

'You can call me Barbara, Barbara Abbott, it's the name I prefer now.'

'If you could both come this way.'

He checked over this shoulder. A press gang of reporters was jostling around the doorway, waiting for them to come out.

'Let's go the back way.'

He led them out past the coroner's desk and through the door she had previously exited, down the stairs to the administrative area.

Mrs Challinor was waiting for them with Sophia. 'Please put Mr Ryder and his daughter in my office, Ridpath, I'm sure you have lots to talk about.'

'We do, Mrs Challinor, and thank you for finding my daughter.'

'I didn't find her, Mr Ryder. I think my staff did.'

'Actually, I saw the article in the paper yesterday and decided to come this morning. The separation had gone on far too long.'

She put her arm around the old man's shoulder. 'Come on, James, we have lots to talk about. I have so much to tell you.'

'I need to interview you, Ms Abbott. There are questions about your disappearance and other matters we need to straighten out.'

Mrs Challinor stepped forward. 'I'm sure your questions can wait until tomorrow, Ridpath, a father and his daughter have more important matters to discuss.'

'But, Coroner—'

'I'm sure it can wait one day, can't it?'

Ridpath nodded. At least a day would give him time to work it all out in his head. Had he got it totally wrong? Did Jane Ryder have nothing to do with the hands found in the backpack? Perhaps it had been stolen from her? Hadn't she said she renounced all her possessions? Perhaps she had given it away?

He needed to find out the truth of what had happened in 2009.

As the father and daughter walked arm and arm into Mrs Challinor's office, his phone buzzed with a text message. It was Emily.

I have something. Can you talk?

Chapter 92

He ran down the stairs and out onto the main road, dialling Emily's number.

'Hi, Em, what do you have?'

'Turnbull hasn't been here this morning so I was finally able to get on to the governor of Strangeways.'

'And?'

'You were right, Adam Jones did make a call immediately after we left the prison. It was to a number in Manchester.'

'Did they send you a transcript of the conversation?'

'Yeah, but I don't understand it.'

'Read it to me.'

'OK, Here goes:

> Jones: I'll make this short. We need to get rid of the garbage from the farm. Understand?
>
> Woman: When, Matthew?
>
> Jones: As soon as possible. It could produce a bad smell.
>
> Woman. OK, I'll do it today.
>
> Jones: Good, follow the usual procedures. (long pause) And it's time to go to the new place.
>
> Woman: What?
>
> Jones: We must leave, time to hide.
>
> Woman: But we can't leave all we have built.

Jones: Moses did. We will follow his example.

Woman: But it means leaving everything behind.

Jones: Things have no meaning. Only the word of God matters.

Woman: But—

Jones: So be it. You will obey my direction.

Woman: (sighing) Of course.

Jones: Also, you need to go to there tomorrow.

Woman: Do I have to? I don't want to go. They mean nothing to me.

Jones: (shouting) Go! You must go! (pause) We need a sacrificial lamb, and you will be it. Understand?

Woman: I don't want to.

Jones: God spoke to me last night. He wants you to go. It is important, and you will follow his rules. It is their time and you will carry out his work.

Woman: (long silence)

Jones: Do you understand?

Woman: I do, and I will obey.

That's when the phone call ended. What does it mean?'

Everything had become clear to Ridpath. 'Get Chrissy to check the reverse telephone directory. Find out the address he called and message me immediately.'

'Right, what are you going to do?'

'I'm going to call Claire Trent, we have to move quickly.'

Chapter 93

He ran back upstairs, breathing heavily as he reached the top. As usual, Sophia was sitting behind her desk.

He glanced towards the door of the coroner's office. 'Are they still in there?'

Sophia nodded. 'Mrs Challinor has asked me to organise an Uber to take them to the hospice when they are ready.'

'I need you to check something for me. What was her address when Barbara Abbott appeared at the inquest last Friday?'

'It will be in the files. Jenny is out the moment.'

'Can you find it?'

'Sure.'

Sophia stood up and went to filing cabinet in the corner of the office marked Helen Moore. She opened it, pulling out a file tied with pink thread. 'The address should be in the list of witnesses.' She ran her finger down the page. 'Here it is. Holdern Farm, Carrington. It's somewhere near United's training ground, I think.'

As she spoke another text came in from Emily.

> Chrissy says the address Jones called is registered as Holdern Farm, Moor Lane, Carrington. Does it help?

Ridpath looked back towards the coroner's room again. He could hear the faint sound of a woman's voice coming from inside. 'Try to keep them here as long as you can, Sophia.'

'But the coroner asked me to take them to the hospice.'

'It's important they don't leave.'

She frowned. 'OK, but what will I say?'

'I don't know, just keep them here.'

He ran towards the door.

'Where are you going?'

'Carrington,' he shouted over his shoulder.

Chapter 94

In the car, Ridpath raced down to the M60, speed dialling Claire Trent's number. Luckily, she answered immediately.

'Boss, it's Ridpath.'

'I thought you were in Jane Ryder's inquest this morning?'

'It's a long story, and I don't have time. I want you to trust me. I need a team to go to Holdern Farm on Moor Lane in Carrington immediately.'

'Why?'

'I believe our abducted woman, Patricia Patterson, is being held there.'

There was a long silence on the end of the phone. 'Have you told DCI Turnbull?'

'Not yet, boss, I don't know where he is.'

'Call him.'

'Boss, he won't believe me. You have to trust me on this one. I'm sure she's being held there.'

'This is not the chain of command, Ridpath. I'm about to go into a meeting with the assistant chief constable.'

'Boss, it's the only chance we have of saving Patricia Patterson. Please, they could have killed her already.'

Another long silence. Ridpath heard voices in the background.

'Right, I'll call out a PTU team and go with them myself. If this goes wrong, it's on your head, Ridpath.'

'Understood, boss.'

'Where are you now?'

'On my way there. I'll message you the address.'

'Wait! Don't go in on your own, wait for backup. That is an ord—'

Ridpath switched off his phone. He accelerated down the motorway, past the Didsbury, Sale and Stretford turnoffs, the wide road blurring as he drove as fast as he could. Why had it taken him so long to work it out? Why had he missed it when it was obvious?

He exited off the M60 via the Carrington Spur, barely slowing down as the approached the roundabout. The road changed now, becoming narrow and winding, with a strange mixture of farms, equestrian centres, factories and electrical power stations on either side. At the first set of lights, he texted the address to Claire Trent.

The answer pinged on his phone as he accelerated past United's training centre.

Do not go in. That is an order.

The satnav took him right, left and right again, before he drove up to a large barred gate. Behind it a large sign proudly stated: *Hordern Farm. Home of heritage pigs and chickens.* To his left, he could see a large field dotted with small huts where black-spotted sows and their young rooted around with their snouts.

On the right, two large barns painted black, the sound of a cock crowing loudly coming from within. In front of him, an old decaying house and other outbuildings.

He checked the message again.

Sorry, boss.

Arming himself with a truncheon from the boot, he approached the barred gate.

The farm appeared empty and deserted, with no signs of life. Ridpath stopped and listened for any unusual sounds, but heard nothing except the wind rustling through the trees, the pigs grunting, a barn door banging, wood against wood, and the muffled call of a cock crowing.

He lifted the latch, the gate squeaking loudly as he went in.

Chapter 95

'Paul, I need you to get a team out to Hordern Farm in Carrington immediately.'

'What? Why?'

'Ridpath just phoned it in. He thinks Patricia Patterson is being detained there.'

'He's lost the plot. You should have seen him this morning. Jane Ryder turned up alive at the inquest.'

'What?'

'She's alive. His stories about the backpack and links to the killings were all bollocks.'

'He didn't tell me.'

'Why would he? His whole investigation fell to pieces this morning.'

Another long silence.

'Boss, it's a wild goose chase. Another one of Ridpath's fantasies.'

'If you're right, Paul, it'll be the end of him. But I still need you to send a team to Hordern Farm. I promised we would check it out.'

'Boss, it's a waste of time.'

'Have you found Patricia Patterson yet?'

'No, but I think she's had an argument with her girlfriend and has gone away for some breathing space. No doubt we'll hear she's been living it up in some spa in the Lake District for the last week.'

'You may be right, Paul, but I still need you to send a team there.'

'Boss, let me call the local nick and ask them to send a squad car to take a look. My team are sorting out Ridpath's mess, and we're finally making progress. If I take them off it now to chase one of Ridpath's stupid hunches then we're going to lose time and momentum.'

There was a long pause.

The voice when it came had a core of steel in it. 'DCI Turnbull, I am giving you a direct order. Send a team immediately to support DI Ridpath at Hordern Farm.'

'I want my objections to be noted in the log, boss.'

'Duly noted. I am going there myself with a tactical unit.'

'This is a waste of time and resources.'

'I will be the judge of that, DCI Turnbull. Just follow my orders.'

'Yes, ma'am,' he finally grunted.

Chapter 96

Ridpath stood in front of the house, checking all the windows for signs of movement.

Nothing.

Should he go and wait for backup? He glanced over his shoulder; the road was empty save for his car. What about Patricia Patterson? What if she were in trouble?

He strode towards the door, banging on it with his fist. 'Police, open up.'

No answer.

He banged again, longer and louder this time.

Still no response.

He tried the door, feeling the handle turn in his hand. The door swung open.

'Hello. Police, anybody here?'

He stepped forward and stopped to listen.

The ticking of a clock on a mantelpiece. A slow drip of water into a sink in the kitchen. The sound of silence everywhere else.

'This is the police. Is anybody here?'

He glanced down at the stone floor. At his feet were a few splashes of something wet. He knelt down to look at it more closely. Was it blood?

Outside, the sound of sirens approaching rapidly cut through the silence. He stood up, took one last look around and strode out of the farmhouse.

Two tactical unit vans were arriving at speed, sirens blaring, followed by a unmarked car with a single flashing blue light on the roof.

The vans slid to a halt on the wet road surface. Armed coppers poured out of the rear of the vehicles and immediately began to form up. The door of the unmarked car opened and Claire Trent came running out towards the barred gate.

'I told you not to go inside,' she shouted.

'I thought I heard a shout. Preservation of life, ma'am.'

She looked at him dubiously but shouted at the lead Tactical Unit officer. 'Clear the place. We're looking for a woman. Be careful, possible armed presence.'

'Yes, ma'am.'

He went back to his men and briefed them. They formed into two groups. One went to the house and the second to the outbuildings and barns.

More cars arrived as the Police Tactical Unit stood outside the house, Heckler and Koch rifles at their shoulders, ready to enter.

Emily Parkinson and Dave Connor exited from one vehicle, followed by DCI Turnbull from another. They ran towards where Claire Trent and Ridpath were standing beside the gate.

'Anything?' asked Turnbull.

'Nothing so far,' answered Claire Trent.

As she spoke, one tactical team rushed into the house while the other began going through each of the outbuildings. Through their radios, Ridpath could hear the words:

'Living Room. Clear.'

'Kitchen. Clear.'

'Bedroom. Clear.'

'Cellar. Clear.'

On another radio, team two was declaring the outbuildings cleared one by one.

The lead sergeant ran back from the house. 'The place is empty, ma'am. Signs of recent occupation, but nobody here at the moment.'

'Nobody?'

'Definitely empty, ma'am.'

The second group leader ran back from the outbuildings. 'All clear, ma'am.'

'Empty?'

'Some chickens and pigs, but that's it. Nothing else.'

Turnbull smiled. 'What did I tell you, Claire?'

The detective superintendent began to turn towards Ridpath when a shout came from the furthest outbuilding. 'Got something.' Followed ten seconds later by, 'Jesus Christ.'

Chapter 97

'Have you ordered the taxi yet, Sophia?'

'Not yet, Mrs Challinor.'

'Why not? Jane and her father are waiting to go to see Mrs Ryder at the hospice.'

Sophia scratched her head. 'Ridpath asked me to keep them here.'

'Why?'

The young assistant shrugged her shoulders. 'He didn't say.'

'And where is he?'

'I don't know. He left here in a hurry. He was on the phone to Claire Trent when he ran down the stairs.'

Mr Ryder popped his head out of the door. 'Are we ready to leave yet?'

'Not yet, Sophia is contacting a driver.'

'If we don't get there before one thirty I'm afraid my wife will be out cold. They usually give her the afternoon pills at that time and she falls asleep straight afterwards. Jane, I mean Barbara, so wants to talk to her.'

'Make the call, Sophia,' Mrs Challinor ordered.

'But, Coroner—'

'No buts, Sophia, just do it.'

She turned back to Mr Ryder. 'While we're waiting for the car, let me explain the procedures we will follow from now. The most important thing is for Jane to get a DNA test…'

Her voice faded as she entered her office and closed the door behind her. Though not before staring at Sophia pointedly and indicating the phone on the desk.

'Sorry, Ridpath,' Sophia whispered as she picked up the phone and dialled the number. 'I'd like a car to go to St Jude's Hospice, please.'

Chapter 98

Ridpath ran towards the policeman's voice. He was followed by Claire Trent, Dave Connor and Emily, with Turnbull taking his time behind.

Another shout. 'In here.'

The voice seemed to be muffled, as if coming from below ground. Ridpath ran into the outbuilding furthest away from the farmhouse. A large wooden box had been pushed to one side to reveal steps leading down into an underground cellar.

A man's voice from below. 'Down here.'

Ridpath stumbled down the steps and was met at the bottom by one of the tactical officers.

'It's in there, weirdest bloody thing I've ever seen.'

They were in a large underground cellar with three doors leading from it. The constable was pointing to the door on the left.

Claire Trent came down the steps. 'What's going on? What have you found?'

Ridpath pushed open the door. Inside, against one wall, was an altar with a depiction of a crucified Jesus above it. This Jesus was haggard and drawn, the ribs clearly defined and the marks of torture on his body, blood seeping from open wounds.

On the altar itself, a human hand lay palm upwards on a single square of white linen, next to two silver chalices. The walls were painted bright white except for six streaks of vivid red where blood had been splashed like arterial spray.

'Oh my God,' said Claire Trent, 'what kind of hell is this?'

'You need to come and see this, boss.' Emily Parkinson was at the doorway.

She led them to the room across the cellar. Inside, a naked female body lay on a low table, the stump of its right arm missing a hand.

'It's Patricia Patterson, boss, I recognise her from her photo. And there's also these.' She pointed to a shelf on the left-hand side.

Four large clear-glass jars sat on the shelf. Inside each one, a human hand floated in embalming fluid.

Chapter 99

Jane Ryder took a seat next to her adopted mother's bed. She took out what looked like a pencil case and laid it on the side table.

'Is it really you, Jane? After all these years. You've come back.'

'It's me, Maureen. I promise, it's me.'

'Your hair looks so different. I used to love your blonde hair.'

The voice was weak and faltering, each word struggling to escape from her throat.

'I dyed it black, Mum. It's more fitting that way. Yellow hair is a sign of evil, of bewitchment.' She took her mother's hand, seeing its translucency, feeling the paper thinness stretched over the bones. 'But it is me, the person you called Jane. I've changed my name. I'm Barbara now, it's how I'm known to God.'

'Barbara? I prefer Jane, it suits you more.'

Mr Ryder hurried to his wife's side. 'Don't tax yourself too much, dear. It's great to have our Jane back, isn't it?'

The old woman nodded slowly. 'It is so good to see you. We thought you had died long ago, taken from us.'

Jane tilted her head to the left and stared at her mother. 'I think you're right, I did die, and I was taken from you in 2009, but I was reborn straightaway. I became me, the person you see in front of you.'

'Tell Maureen what you did in all those years, Jane, tell her like you told me.'

'I'm sure she doesn't want to hear my story.'

The old woman lifted her head a few inches off the pillow. 'I want to hear. All those nights lying in bed listening to the wind howling outside, I wondered what had become of you, hoping against hope you would return to us.'

'I met Matthew, the man they called Adam Jones, at the festival, and he opened my eyes to the world, to all its lies, corruption, stealing, dishonesty and cruelty. I'd seen it before at the children's home, of course, and with you, but I didn't understand it, nor did I understand what I was supposed to do.'

'What do you mean, Jane?' asked Mr Ryder.

The answer was cold and unfeeling. 'Please call me Barbara, that is my name now.' She turned back to stare into Maureen Ryder's eyes. 'I mean, this woman who called herself my mother, the one lying in bed. She was part of the cruel system which oppressed me, and all the other children who suffered the terrible torture of being in her care.'

'But it was at Daisy House she first saw you, Jane, I mean Barbara, when she was volunteering there at the weekends. It was when she fell in love with you.'

Jane's face changed in an instant. 'It was where she grew to hate me, not love me. Oh, you pretended not to notice the marks on my arms when you came home from work, believing the lies I had another fall.'

'But… but it's what you told me.'

'It's what you wanted to believe, what everybody wanted to believe. But this woman, the one you call your dear wife, inflicted them on me every day of my life.' She prodded her chest twice with her right hand and then fought to regain control of herself and her emotions, taking three deep breaths. 'But Matthew, the prophet, showed me the light, showed me how to exorcise the demons inside; to take an eye for an eye.' She held up the old woman's right hand. 'Mark 9.23. "And if your hand causes you to sin, cut it off. It is better for you to enter life crippled than with two hands to go to hell, to the unquenchable fire." All those who hurt us, we helped them avoid hell. That was our mission in life, what our prophet Matthew revealed to us when God spoke to him.'

Chapter 100

'Right, clear the area, I want a full forensic team down here as soon as possible. This is a crime scene.' Claire Trent instantly took control. 'Sergeant, get your men to search the rest of the farm. Check if any other surprises are waiting for us out there.'

'Roger that, ma'am.' He ran up the stairs and Ridpath heard shouting as he gave orders to his men.

'Dave, I want you to canvas the local area. Find out what people knew about this farm. See if they know when everybody left.'

'Right, boss.'

'Emily, I need you to discover all you can about this place. Who owns it? When was it bought? Names of people who lived here. Anything and everything you can find out. Got it?'

'On it, boss.'

'Paul, you need to stay here and take control of the crime scene. Make sure the technicians go over it with a fine-tooth comb. I want so much forensic evidence we'll be processing it for the next six months. And get Dr Schofield down here right away. We need him to certify this woman is dead.'

As she was speaking, the Tactical Unit sergeant returned and ran down the stairs.

'In the pig field, one of my men, well…'

'Out with it, man.'

'He thinks he's found a human skull.'

Ridpath's phone pinged with a message.

Sorry, Ridpath. Couldn't hold them any longer. The Ryders have left for the hospice already.

'Shit.'

'What is it, Ridpath?'

'I think we have another problem, boss.'

Chapter 101

'What are you saying, Barbara? I don't understand.'

'I'll try to explain it to you the same way Matthew explained it to me.' She laid her hands in her lap and sat up straight. 'We are all the products of our early lives. The Jesuits, those evil men, understood it best, when they said, "Give me the child until he is seven and I will give you the man." But who were we, the children Matthew had been given by God? We had been taken from our families, or they had given us away, and we were put into a place, definitely not a home, where we were abused, mistreated, misused and assaulted. Every day of our young lives.'

She took another deep breath and stared off into mid-air. Mrs Ryder had closed her eyes now, her head resting back on the pillow, too exhausted to understand her daughter's words.

'When I was in the place, the home as they called it, I was punished for speaking out of turn by being put in a small cell behind the kitchen. There I sat, my head on my knees, and cried and cried and cried. There were no blankets, nowhere to sleep, nowhere to lay my head. And I was cold, so cold. Even now, the thought of it sends an ache deep into my bones.'

She shivered visibly before continuing on.

'Once a day, I was fed. The door would open and a hand would place a tray with water and bread on it down on the ground. I never saw who it was, never heard them speak to me, never saw their face. Just a hand holding a tray. After three days, they let me out, telling me, "You must not be disobedient again, or else worse will happen to you." I remained good for the rest of the time I was there, because I knew what they meant. The others were not so lucky, they were given to Davidson, or Dunphy or the gardener.'

For a second, Mrs Ryder lifted her head from the pillow and tried to speak, but the effort was too much for her and her head drooped back down again.

'Matthew had been there too. It was where we first met. He had been treated badly by those men, used and sold to others like a slave. But he had come to understand why it happened. Even better, he understood how the sins could be expiated.'

'What are you saying, Jane? What sins? Whose sins?' Mr Ryder was leaning forward, trying to understand every word his daughter was saying.

Her eyes moved to his face. 'Not ours, we were innocents and still are. The sins of the trespassers. You see, Matthew taught us we had to forgive them and help them find forgiveness from God.'

'Forgiveness from God? I don't understand, Jane.' Mr Ryder tried to reach out to touch his daughter.

She pulled her arm away. 'I have told you, my name is Barbara.' The voice was icy cold. She closed her eyes for a second before continuing on. 'It became our mission, the purpose of our group, to expiate the sins of the trespassers. "And if your hand causes you to sin, cut it off. It is better for you to enter life crippled than with two hands to go to hell, to the unquenchable fire." We helped the people who sinned against us, saving them from the fires of eternal damnation.'

'How do you help them? I don't understand.'

She opened up the pencil case and took out a hypodermic, removing the cover and pushing the needle into a small glass bottle filled with a colourless liquid.

'What are you doing, Jane?'

'Helping the sinner who is your wife, James. And afterwards, I will help you. Because yours was the sin of omission. You did nothing to stop her when she was abusing me.'

'I didn't know.'

'You didn't want to know. You were as bad as she was. Everybody knew Jimmy Savile was abusing young girls and boys, but nobody did anything about it. Everybody knew children were being abused in Manchester, but nobody did anything. You are all sinners. You must be saved from the eternal flames of hell.'

Chapter 102

They raced down the M60, Claire Trent on the phone to Cheadle station asking them to send a squad car to the hospice urgently.

She put the phone down. 'What's our ETA, Henry?'

'At this speed, about eight minutes, boss,' the driver answered.

'The squad car will arrive at roughly the same time. You think she is going to kill them, Ridpath?'

'Yes, boss. As far as I can work out, she and Adam Jones have been planning this for years, killing the workers and volunteers at the children's home.'

'Why?'

'I'm not certain, boss. Revenge? A warped sense of justice? Religious fanaticism? You saw the altar at the farm, it reminded me of something Adam Jones said when we met him in prison. A verse from the Gospel of Matthew: "If your right hand causes you to sin, cut it off and throw it away. For it is better you lose one of your members than that your whole body go into hell."'

'What? They're cutting off people's hands because of some verse in the Bible?'

'I think so, boss.'

'How come we didn't know? How have they been killing people for all this time without us knowing?'

'It was a cult, presided over by a charismatic man, Adam Jones. Think of Manson and his followers. I think its members were made up of former residents of children's homes. People who had suffered abuse in their life.'

The exited the M60 at Cheadle, the houses on either side of the road blurring as the car accelerated in the outside lane, forcing its way through a red light. A sharp left threw Ridpath against the car door.

'But wasn't this Adam Jones in prison?'

'I think he carried on running the group from there and they continued killing people, kidnapping those who had abused them in the past.'

The police car swung sharply left into the driveway of the large house that served as the hospice, sliding to a stop outside the entrance portico.

Ridpath and Claire Trent jumped out and ran through the front door. A nurse on reception stood in front of them, trying to stop them going further.

Ridpath flashed his warrant card. 'Mrs Ryder, which room?'

The nurse ran behind her desk and checked the list. 'Room twenty-three.'

'Which way?'

She pointed down a long corridor. 'At the bottom on the left, but you can't—'

He ran down the corridor, hearing Claire Trent's high heels clacking behind him, the sound echoing off the green walls.

Room 18.

Room 19.

Room 20.

Room 21.

Room 22.

Room 23.

He burst through the door. Mr Ryder was slumped on the floor in the corner, his body at a strange angle. Jane Ryder was holding a hacksaw dripping with blood. She lifted up the wizened right hand of her mother proudly, her blue eyes as cold as ice. 'You're too late. I've already released her.' A used hypodermic lay on the bedside table.

Claire Trent brushed pat Ridpath, pulling handcuffs from her jacket. 'Jane Ryder, I am arresting you for the murder of Patricia Patterson and Maureen Ryder. You do not have to say anything.

But it may harm your defence if you do not mention when questioned something which you later rely on in court. Anything you do say will be taken down and may be used as evidence in court against you.'

She grabbed the woman's hands, twisted them behind her back and snapped the handcuffs around her wrists.

'Do you wish to say anything?'

'My name is Barbara Abbott, and I set her free.'

TWO WEEKS LATER

Chapter 103

'Good morning, Ridpath, I thought you'd like to know Helen will be reconvening her inquest into the death of Jordan Harrison at Hordern Farm. After the confession of Jane Ryder, or Barbara Abbott, as she keeps calling herself, we were left with no choice. It appears he was killed when he wanted to leave the farm, it wasn't an accident.'

'I heard as much, Mrs Challinor, thank you for letting me know.'

'How are you?'

'Not bad, still a bit tired. The doctor at Christies says I need to look after myself better.'

'That's obvious. Do you want to take a few days off?'

'Maybe later, we have so much to do at the moment.'

'Your call, but personally I would take the time away.' She paused for a moment, biting the end of her pencil. 'I'm sorry I put you under so much stress. I didn't mean to, the problem with Mrs Ryder meant the inquest had to be resolved as soon as possible. I should have listened to you and postponed it.'

Ridpath didn't answer. Part of him was still unhappy at Mrs Challinor. Her obsession with serving the families had created unnecessary pressure on the investigation.

'I knew you were unhappy with my decision—'

Ridpath now tried to speak, but she halted him with a raised hand.

'But given similar circumstances, I probably would make the same call again. It makes me wonder if I haven't reached my sell-by date in this job.'

Ridpath tried to interrupt, but again she stopped him.

'I've been asking myself over the last couple of weeks whether I have become so obsessed with serving the families that I've lost focus on my judicial role. We are part of the system of justice, whether we like it or not, and justice takes time, it can't be rushed.'

'I appreciate your honesty, Mrs Challinor, but isn't there a balance? We must serve justice *and* the families we represent equally. It often seems to me that one or the other suffers. Just look at the Hillsborough trials. Where was the justice for the families there?'

'Of course, you're right. It only makes me question my role even more.' She ran her fingers through her hair. 'You know I'm due to retire next year.'

'I didn't know, Coroner.'

'I had thought of continuing on, but now I'm not so sure. Perhaps a younger person, one less involved, would do a better job.'

'May I speak frankly, Mrs Challinor?'

'Please go ahead, I think you've earned that right.'

'I'll put it as bluntly as I can. I think the world of justice and the families we serve would be poorer if you left the profession.'

The coroner looked down at her desk. 'Thank you, Ridpath, you don't know how much that means.'

An awkward silence lay between them for a second before Ridpath continued, 'In one way your decision to hold the inquest broke the case. It brought Jane Ryder out of hiding, into the light.'

'I never really understood why she did that.'

'Loyalty. Obedience. Sheer devotion. I don't know what it was, but she was ordered by Adam Jones to attend the inquest and she did. She was a sacrificial lamb to enable the others to get away.'

'Have they been found yet?'

'DCI Turnbull is leading the search, but they seem to have vanished into thin air. He thinks at least six people lived at the farm at any one time; however, there may be other cells in different parts of the country.'

'It was shocking they could remain hidden for so long.'

'They held the lease on the farm for seven years. Barbara Abbott won't tell us where they were before then. I don't know if we'll ever find out.'

'If Adam Jones hadn't lost his nerve, they could have stayed there forever.'

Ridpath shook his head. 'I think he worked out the secrets of the farm would have been discovered eventually. After my visit to him in prison, he wanted to clear up the loose ends.'

'The Ryders were a loose end?'

'Mrs Ryder was. We checked with other former residents of Daisy House. She used to volunteer there before it closed. Apparently she had a vicious temper, used to enjoy beating the kids with her belt and restricting their food, locking them away in the room off the kitchen where we found the backpack.'

'Yet Jane was placed in her care?'

Ridpath shrugged his shoulders. 'The same people who advised on the decision were the ones abusing the children. It was a vicious little cabal.'

'How many people were killed?'

'We're not certain. Forensics has revealed at least nine different bodies in the field where the pigs were. The cult used the pigs to help them dispose of the bodies. Eight hands have been found, including the three in the backpack. Forensics now have the laborious job of matching the DNA to the workers and children who went to Daisy House. It will take a while.'

'Why weren't the deaths discovered earlier?'

'Good question. I think it was because there were no bodies, so the people who vanished just stayed on the missing persons list.'

Mrs Challinor stared out of her large window.

'I failed them, didn't I?'

Ridpath shook his head. 'This wasn't another Shipman case. The deaths were never reported to the Coroner's Service. They were missing people who would have stayed missing if the film crew hadn't discovered the backpack. The strange thing is we still haven't found out the identity of the third female hand.'

'Who do you think it is?'

'Because she was so young, I think it was a resident who somehow aided and abetted the abusers to save herself. But Jane Ryder isn't saying a word.'

He gestured towards the door.

'I'll get back to work now, we have the family waiting outside. After we've finished, I need to head over to MIT.'

'Another case?'

He shook his head. 'Not now. Just ploughing through the submission to the CPS on Jane Ryder.'

'What's going to happen to her?'

'I hope she gets locked away for the rest of her life, but it's all in the lap of the gods.'

Mrs Challinor smiled. 'Otherwise known as a judge and twelve jurors.' The smile vanished and she stared straight at him. 'I am sorry, Ridpath.'

He nodded once and closed the door behind him.

Mrs Challinor was left alone in her office. Still the feeling lurked inside her that she could have done more to help those who had died. How was it that no coroner was aware that any of them had been killed?

A wave of despair flowed through her. She had spent all her career dealing with death, perhaps it was time to care for the living.

She glanced at the picture on her desk of her daughter and her grandsons. Was it time to enjoy long days with them rather spending any more hours in this office?

She sighed and picked up another file, her latest case. Two young children had died in a house fire after an inflammable substance had been poured into their letterbox and set alight.

She realised it wasn't yet time for her to go. There was still so much she and Ridpath could still do.

The guilty needed to cry, not the innocent.